McKenna was the last one through the door. As he shut it behind him the President said, 'Maybe you'd all better sit down.'

Clayson, Fraser, Samuels, and Wedderkind each took the nearest chair. McKenna chose one end of the wide ledge of the window facing the sea. Connors took the other corner. As he settled back against the glass, he caught Fraser looking at him warily.

'The talk I've had with my friend in Moscow,' said the President, 'and the unequivocal nature of the reassurances I have received make it quite clear that our preliminary conclusions about this spacecraft are based on a fundamental error.'

'You mean it's not a weapons system?' Fraser sounded disappointed.

'I mean it's not Russian.'

The reaction, predictably, was one of stunned disbelief.

'Or anyone else we know.'

'You mean,' said Clayson, 'it's – ?'

Extraterrestrial. The thought exploded like a star-shell inside Wedderkind's brain. Sentient life, perhaps. Some kind of artefact, at least. From another planet. Another solar system. Maybe even from another galaxy. Here. Overhead. Within his own lifetime. It was . . .

Also by Patrick Tilley

PATRICK TILLEY
FADE-OUT

WARNER BOOKS

A WARNER BOOK

First published in Great Britain by Hodder & Stoughton Ltd 1975
Published by Sphere Books 1977
Revised edition published by Grafton Books 1987
This edition published by Warner Books 1992

A CIP catalogue record for this book
is available from the British Library.

ISBN 0 7515 0085 2

Printed in England by Clays Ltd, St Ives plc

Warner Books
A Division of
Little, Brown and Company (UK) Limited
165 Great Dover Street
London SE1 4YA

To my wife Janine who, as always, helped me
in every possible way
but didn't want her contribution acknowledged.
This one is for you. With love.

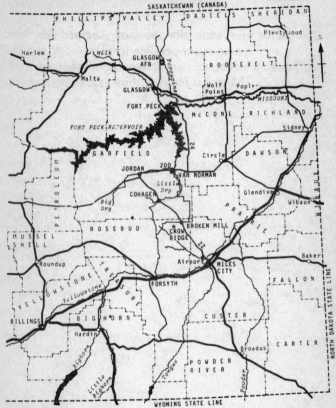

EASTERN MONTANA

SCALE:Miles 0 10 20 30

SASKATCHEWAN (CANADA)

PHILLIPS | VALLEY | DANIELS | SHERIDAN

Plentywood

Harlem | Milk

GLASGOW AFB

ROOSEVELT

Malta

GLASGOW

Wolf Point | Poplar

FORT PECK

MISSOURI

FORT PECK RESERVOIR

McCONE | RICHLAND

Sidney

GARFIELD

JORDAN | 200 | VAN NORMAN | Circle | DAWSON

24

COHAGEN | Little Dry

Big Dry

Glendive | Wibaux

PETROLEUM

ROSEBUD

BROKEN MILL

PRAIRIE

MUSSEL SHELL

CROW RIDGE

22

Roundup

Airport | MILES CITY

Baker

TREASURE

FORSYTH

FALLON

YELLOWSTONE

Yellowstone

CUSTER

BILLINGS

BIGHORN

Hardin

CARTER

Bighorn

Broadus

POWDER RIVER

Little Bighorn

Tongue

Powder

WYOMING STATE LINE

NORTH DAKOTA STATE LINE

Principal locations (real and fictitious) mentioned in story shown thus - ●JORDAN
Other centres of population shown thus - OHardin. Size of circle is not indicative
of number of inhabitants. County names shown thus - YELLOWSTONE

KEY TO MAP

━━━━━ = Interstate Highway

= US Highway

22 = State or County Highway

──── = Other roads (Not all shown for sake of clarity)

– – – – = County line

◉ = USAF Base

The date was Friday, the third of August. For some people, depending on where they lived, the day was just beginning. For others, it was the end of another, perfectly normal, day. Suddenly, all around the world, every ground and airborne radar screen went haywire . . .

Friday/August 3

For the Headquarters Staff of the Strategic Air Command, it was the tensest situation they'd faced since the Cuban missile crisis of 1962.

Created in 1946 as the backbone of America's nuclear deterrent policy, SAC had been, and still was, the best equipped, most highly trained and motivated force in the world. Its organization was superb, its planning faultless – a brilliant fusion of American money, skill, and dedication. That dedication had been needed. For over forty years, SAC's bombers had stayed alert and ready behind an increasingly sophisticated screen of electronic devices that monitored every move the Russians made. Suddenly, at 11:13 A.M. Central Standard Time, every radar screen SAC owned turned into a plate of luminous spaghetti.

Momentarily off balance, SAC started burning the wires between Omaha and the North American Air Defense Headquarters at Ent AFB, in neighbouring Colorado. Roughly translated, the high-speed teleprinter message asked just what in hell was happening. NORAD couldn't tell them. The worldwide network of American-owned radar stations, designed to give early warning of a sneak Russian missile attack, was feeding back nothing but confused static to NORAD's Operations Center deep inside the Cheyenne Mountains.

Instead of tracking Russian planes and missiles, setting

9

up interception courses and simultaneously relaying the appropriate instructions to all Air Defense Command bases, the serried ranks of computers at the heart of the complex system clicked and whirred like distraught fruit machines. It was a totally unforeseen and frightening breakdown of the most foolproof system ever devised by man.

For years, both the Americans and Russians had spent billions of dollars trying to find a way to jam each other's radar defences. Was this sudden snafu proof of a Russian breakthrough? And if it was, would they follow it up with a Sunday punch?

General William Mitchell Allbright, Commander in Chief, Strategic Air Command, pondered these questions as he took the elevator down from the daylight to his underground headquarters at Offutt AFB. To Allbright, it looked like the moment he and the rest of the SAC staff had spent the better part of their lives preparing for.

Allbright had already set things in motion from his upstairs office in the yellow brick headquarters building. As he settled into his basement seat, he got a quick rundown from his senior staff. The around-the-clock airborne patrols were already on their way to failsafe points around the globe. The remaining aircraft, streaming off runways scattered across the USA, would fly to similar holding points, their radios tuned in on SAC's special side-band communications network over which would come the crucially important Presidential Go-Code that would, if necessary, transform this defensive alert into an all-out attack on Russia.

But something had gone badly wrong. Contact had been lost with the orbiting Air Force communications and navigation satellites, and the static that was fouling the radar screens was also causing severe fade-out on the vital UHF frequencies that would carry the President's order. And without radar responses, there was nothing coming down the line from NORAD in Colorado. Nothing for the millions of dollars' worth of machinery to translate into coloured position markers on the huge situation maps. Nothing to show what might – or might not – be on its way in from Russia.

Their birds may already be up, thought Allbright – and we are flying blind. His wife and daughter were on vacation in Santa Barbara, California. His son was in his fourth and final year at the Air Force Academy in Colorado Springs. From the intelligence reports he had read on Soviet targeting, Allbright knew that both places lay within designated first-strike zones. If the Russians *had* launched their nuclear missiles, it meant that his family would be obliterated within the next seven to ten minutes.

Allbright lifted his gold telephone and conferred with the Joint Chiefs of Staff in Washington. They had an open line to the Secretary of Defense who, in turn, was briefing the President on the situation. Washington was desperately trying to establish the degree and nature of the crisis that seemed to have engulfed them – and whether or not it had been engineered by the Russians.

Five minutes and forty-two seconds after Allbright had called the alert, the last of SAC's big B-52s lifted off the runway at Loring AFB, Maine. It wasn't the best reaction time the crew had turned in, but they had blown a tyre on the main undercarriage and had had to stop to change a wheel. Allbright reported to Washington that his entire force was airborne.

At 11:23, after ten minutes of total fade-out, the White House authorized Allbright to bring his ICBMs to Condition Red. Instantaneously, via armoured underground telephone lines, the signal went out to alert the crews of the concrete missile silos sunk deep into the

11

wheatfields and the Rocky Mountain spine of the Midwest. Keys turned in sealed locks to start complex preignition sequences. Target data fed automatically into inertial guidance systems. The great countdown began.

At 11:24, while General Allbright was still on the line to the Joint Chiefs of Staff, a call came through from an Air Force base in Turkey. An airborne electronic surveillance unit patrolling the borders of Soviet Armenia had reported that the Russian radar network was fouled up too. Allbright asked for independent verification of the report. While he was waiting, the Russian Premier came through on the hot line to the White House.

At 11:33, while the two leaders were still reassuring each other of their peaceful intentions, the radar screens blipped back into life and the sitation maps in SAC's underground headquarters lit up like overloaded Christmas trees. There were plenty of Russian planes in the air, but their missiles were still on the ground. General Allbright sat back and watched the screens for the next hour as the US and Soviet Air Forces pulled off their collision courses and headed for home.

It was all over.

Somewhere around 15:30, Allbright handed over control to his senior duty officer and drove from Offutt Air Force Base to his nearby home. He dismissed his aide, poured himself a large drink and took a long, thoughtful shower. As he dried himself, he saw in the mirror that the stress of the sudden alert plus the gut-wrenching breakdown in the radar defences had turned his face into a taut, deeply-lined mask.

Allbright poured himself another drink and put in a person-to-person call to his wife in Santa Barbara. He asked her about the weather on the West Coast and his daughter Lynn. His wife told him, adding that she'd heard on the car radio that there had been a sudden breakdown in the Air Traffic Control system covering the major California airports. It had happened around 9:15 local time. Airlines had been diverted to avoid midair collisions and flight schedules had been disrupted throughout the day. The people next door were anxiously awaiting news of a relative who had, so far, failed to signal his safe arrival in Los Angeles.

Allbright told her he'd heard most of the states had been briefly affected but that he didn't know what had caused the breakdown. He checked the date of her return to Nebraska and hung up without telling her about the alert.

Saturday/August 4

THE WHITE HOUSE/WASHINGTON DC

The urgent inquest on the twenty-minute radar breakdown instituted by the Joint Chiefs of Staff did not produce any satisfactory answers in time for their breakfast meeting with President John "Jake" Lorenzo at the White House.

When the three of them arrived, they found Mel Fraser, Arnold Wedderkind and Bob Connors already sitting around the table with the President. Fraser was Secretary of Defense, Wedderkind was the Administration's chief scientific advisor. Connors' title was Special Assistant to the President.

There were plenty of rolls, bacon, and coffee on a side table, but no one seemed to want any.

The President raised a hand to acknowledge the arrival of Admiral Edward Garrison, Air Force General Chuck Clayson and Army General Vernon Wills. Admiral Kirk, the chairman of the Joint Chiefs of Staff, was cruising somewhere north of Diego Garcia aboard the US Navy carrier *Lexington,* getting a firsthand impression of the growing Russian naval presence in the Indian Ocean.

As the three Chiefs of Staff sat down, Arnold Wedderkind recapped briefly what he'd been saying about solar flares. 'The interference that hit us on Friday is known to radio buffs as "fade-out". It's a familiar problem and, in varying degrees, one that is with us most of the time – '

'Except nothing on this scale has ever happened before,' interjected Clayson.

'Not in the last ninety years,' admitted Wedderkind. 'But until Marconi invented the radio, the problem didn't exist.'

The President, Fraser and the others nodded in sombre agreement but General Chuck Clayson found little comfort in Wedderkind's reply. Of the three armed services, the Air Force had been the hardest hit by the paralysing effects of the radar breakdown and he was probably the most worried man in the room.

Wedderkind directed his explanation at the President and kept it as simple as he could. 'Fade-out is caused by magnetic storms in the upper layers of the Earth's atmosphere. They, in turn, are usually caused by bursts of short-wave radiation coming from the sun and they're emitted by volcanic eruptions of incandescent matter known as solar flares. Flares are associated with sunspots – which I'm sure you've heard of.

'By our scale of measurement, they're all huge but some are absolutely gigantic – exploding with the force of a billion H-bombs and flinging great arching plumes of molten lava tens, sometimes hundreds, of thousands of miles into space. These eruptions – which are even brighter than the sun itself – are accompanied by an equally massive blast of radiation which travels outwards like a shock wave. Twenty-six hours later, it hits the

14

Earth – BAM!' Wedderkind thudded his fist into an open palm.

'I'll spare you the details of what happens in the ionosphere. Let's just say it starts quivering like a bowl of Jello. And instead of going where they should, our radar and radio waves start bouncing around all over the place. After a while it settles down – just like the Jello – and we're back in business.'

'That's all very neat, Arnold,' said Fraser. 'But don't we have people watching out for these things?' As Secretary of Defense, Fraser had been over at the Pentagon harrying his own experts for most of the night.

Bob Connors, a friend and ally of Wedderkind, saw him blink rapidly and adjust his glasses. A purely defensive reflex.

'Yes. I have to admit that is one of the things that is puzzling me.'

The President waited for a few seconds then asked, 'Do we have to guess what it is or are you going to let us in on the secret?'

'Yeah, go ahead,' said Fraser. 'This should be interesting.'

Wedderkind adjusted his glasses again. 'What Mel is referring to is the fact that Mount Wilson – which constantly monitors sun-spot activity – recorded unusually large solar flares over a six-hour period last Thursday morning. As I was explaining, the resulting short-wave radiation could be expected to cause a partial fade-out in the high-frequency radar and radio wave-bands – rising to a maximum intensity some forty-five hours after the initial eruption.'

'And did it?' Another Presidential question.

Wedderkind threw a sideways glance at Mel Fraser before answering. 'As expected, the magnetic storm peaked around seven this morning. The problem is, the interference, although severe, didn't even begin to compare with the level of disruption we experienced on Friday.'

'Let me play that back to you to make sure I've understood,' said the President. 'If whatever hit us on Friday came from the sun then it would have been picked up by the people at Mount Wilson earlier in the week. In fact, from what you're saying, the explosion, or eruption, or whatever it is, would have to have been so big it would be impossible to miss.'

'Right . . .'

'But there wasn't one . . .'

'No.'

The President threw up his hands. 'Then why are we wasting time talking about this!?'

Wedderkind leaped to his own defence. 'Because the disruption had all the hallmarks of what happens when the Earth is hit by a heavy burst of cosmic radiation.'

'Hold on, Arnold,' said Connors. 'You just moved the goal posts. Don't you mean "solar" radiation?'

'Solar, cosmic . . . it's the same thing.'

'Except it wasn't a solar flare that screwed things up for us yesterday,' said Fraser, appearing to relish the fact that Wedderkind had painted himself into a corner. 'My science is a little hazy but, as I understand it, solar radiation comes from the sun while cosmic radiation comes from some other point in the cosmos.'

'If you want to split hairs, yes.' Wedderkind fingered the bridge of his glasses. 'The people at Mount Wilson and some other colleagues of mine are looking into it. Until I hear from them we can't dismiss the possibility that some, as yet undetected, solar activity is the cause of the problem. What I can state, quite categorically, is that the source of the interference lies somewhere in outer space.'

16

'A meteorite, perhaps . . . ?'

Wedderkind aimed a beady eye at Fraser. His staff over at the Pentagon had certainly been doing their homework. He turned back to the President. 'Several stations around the world have been tracking a large incoming meteorite. It was expected to enter the Earth's atmosphere and burn up harmlessly at about 11:15 on Friday morning.'

'About the same time we got hit by the fade-out,' said Connors. 'Could this – ?'

Wedderkind shook his head. 'It's possible that it might have had some temporary effect on the ionosphere – and thus the propagation of radio waves – but what we're discussing is of a different order of magnitude altogether.'

All this may have been clear to Wedderkind, but it was hard going for General Wills. He pulled out a large stogy, lit up and chewed on it aggressively to combat a sudden feeling of inadequacy.

The President picked absently at the corners of his scratch-pad. 'What d'you think, Mel?'

Fraser weighed up Connors and Wedderkind then exchanged a covert glance with the Chiefs of Staff before replying. 'Well, we all know Arnold has stars in his eyes but – based on what my people have told me, I think we'll find the cause of the fade-out is a little nearer to home.'

'You mean the Russians . . .'

'Who else?'

Wedderkind snorted dismissively. 'You can't be serious! Have you any idea just how – '

Fraser cut him off. 'Why not, Arnold? They've got themselves a nice new shiny space-station up there now. I'd say that was in "outer space" – wouldn't you?'

Fraser was referring to the growing collection of space modules that had been locked on to the orbiting Russian spacelab *Mir*, launched in 1986 to reinforce the ageing *Salyut 7*. Skylab – America's answer to the Salyut program and long since abandoned – had plunged earthwards in the early eighties, burning up on re-entry. It had not been replaced and, following the disastrous loss of Challenger in February '86, NASA's space-shuttle program had slowly foundered as interest switched to the development of an orbital vehicle that could take off and land like a conventional Jumbo jet. Since the first flight was years away, the net result had been to leave the Soviet cosmonauts in sole possession of outer space. *Mir* was the Russian word for "peace" but everyone around the table knew that ever since Marx had dreamed up dialectical materialism on a wet afternoon in the British Museum, communists the world over have tended to say one thing and mean another.

President Lorenzo turned to the Navy Chief of Staff. 'Any thoughts on this, Ed?'

Admiral Garrison tapped the file of intelligence reports into line with his notepad. 'We don't have any data that would indicate they have developed or deployed this type of capability.'

It's in moments like this, thought the President, when I long for people who can say 'yes' or 'no'.

'However – ' Garrison paused.

'They must have a few things we don't know about.'

'True, but – '

The President bypassed Garrison and glanced at the others around the table. 'Is it possible for them to knock out our radar like this?'

'You mean theoretically possible?'

'I mean in any way possible, Arnold.' Then as Wedderkind opened his mouth, the President added, 'Within the known limits of science.'

'Possible, yes, but in this instance not probable.' It was

18

Air Force General Clayson, halfway down the table. 'The reports from our border surveillance units all indicate total disruption of Russian radar frequencies during the same period.'

'I know that, Chuck. They also know we're listening in. Supposing they put this whole show on for our benefit?'

'You mean – ?' Admiral Garrison was still trying to get it together.

'This could be a dry run – just to test our response. If it *is* them, then the next time they black us out, we could be in real trouble. Right, Bob?'

Bob Connors was the President's closest aide. Some people thought he was too close. Like Mel Fraser, who faced him across the table. Connors advised the President on a wide variety of subjects that ranged from defence and foreign affairs down to what tie to wear. The State Department hated him, and so did certain people in the Defense Department. Like Mel Fraser.

Connors remained relaxed, with one arm over the back of his chair. 'We could be, but there's no reason why we should. We have a whole raft of trade agreements, our people at Geneva say they're only a whisker away from a deal on nuclear weapons, you went to Moscow this April and only last week the Russian Ambassador confirmed that Leonovich would come to Washington next year.'

'That's right,' said the President.

'Hell, don't you remember – when we were over there – he said he wanted to bring his grandson and his daughter-in-law over with him so that they could visit Disneyland. I'm not saying they don't need watching but since you came into office they've responded to our approaches in a reasonably positive manner. I really don't see why they would want to pull a stunt like this.'

'Well, it sure as hell shook me up. I know what these

19

bastards can do.' General Wills had helped put the original backbone into NATO. He'd been trying to keep ahead of the Russians ever since he'd faced up to them as a twenty-year-old lieutenant during the Berlin blockade back in 1948.

Clayson came back in. 'No one could dummy up an operation this big. They couldn't risk it blowing back in their faces.'

I'm right, thought Clayson. I have to be. The Civil Aeronautics Board had reported twenty minutes of almost total confusion as civilian air traffic control centres lost radar contact with the midmorning domestic airline flights. All the European air traffic control centres had had their radarscopes wiped out too. But by some freak-weather miracle, there was almost perfect visibility right where the densest traffic happened to be. By switching to emergency procedural control on the unaffected lower-frequency radio wavelengths, the Air Traffic Control Centers had managed to keep the ball in the air. All the same, there had been some hair-raising near-misses, and although there had still been plenty of daylight over Eastern Europe, the weather had been bad.

The President sucked in his breath as Clayson described how a Moscow-bound Tupolev had sheared through an ageing Polish Airlines jet stacked up in ten-tenths cloud over Warsaw. 'Nasty . . .'

'Fortunately, they were only half full,' added Clayson.

Yeah, but they don't have to make a profit, thought Connors irreverently.

Clayson continued. 'And Malev – the Hungarian line – lost one of their Ilyushins on a mountain top in Moldavia. Total – one hundred and ninety-five dead.'

Admiral Garrison voiced what the President was thinking. 'Is this what *they* say? Or have we had this checked

20

out?' Iron Curtain countries rarely, if ever, publicized airline crashes within their borders.

'We had an air attaché on board the Tupolev,' said Clayson.

'Anyone I know?' asked the President. Not that it really mattered. He was thinking about the people in those three airliners. Could the Russians have knowingly sent them to their deaths? Would they? Would any government? Still, look what the Russians had lost fighting the Germans in World War Two. What was it, ten, twelve – plus the civilians – twenty million?

Set against this scale of sacrifice, what was another one hundred and ninety-five people? It would depend, he supposed, on what was at stake. The Russians had proved they were prepared to bite the bullet with the shoot-down of KAL 007. Faced with the violation of a highly sensitive segment of Russian air space they had not baulked at blowing the off-course South Korean Jumbo jet out of the sky, killing all 269 passengers and crew. With luck, he would never find himself in a similar situation. If he did, he hoped like hell that somewhere down the line was a hatchet man who would make that kind of decision for him.

Bob Connors' voice cut through further speculation. 'I think we can reasonably take the Soviet Premier's message at face value. From what he said over the hot line, it seems pretty clear they thought we had pulled out the plug on *them*.'

'Did you all read the transcript?'

Everyone nodded at the President.

'As I remember it,' said Connors. 'You ended up reassuring *him*.'

'True.'

'Then it backs up General Clayson's theory.'

'Which is?'

Clayson leaned back on to the table again. 'A temporary, total disruption of radar and ultra high-frequency radio waves on a worldwide basis caused by some as yet unknown solar-generated phenomenon.'

'Arnold?'

'Yes, I'll go along with that.'

'Mel?'

'Chuck could have the right answer,' said Fraser. 'But I don't think we should preclude the possibility of some technological breakthrough by the Russians.' He eyed Connors briefly. 'Even though they are making the right diplomatic noises.'

Connors stared back at him. 'How come they had the same kind of foul-up?'

Fraser shrugged. 'It could have been a test transmission from a secret research unit – that even the armed forces don't know about.'

That's all we need, thought Admiral Garrison. Ordinary Russian secrets are bad enough.

The President beat him to the punch line. 'How do you propose to check this out?' asked the President.

'The whole of Eastern Europe and Asia is covered photographically by Air Force satellites,' said Fraser. 'We'll just have to go over every inch of the ground and re-evaluate each installation.'

'That's a big chunk of the map. How long is that going to take?'

'I'm gonna have to come back to you on that.'

'Okay, but let's keep it on a short line.' The President turned to Wedderkind. 'Do you have any ideas how we can follow up this geophysical angle?'

Wedderkind replaced his thick-framed spectacles. 'General Clayson and I have already got a study group together on this. The top Air Force physicists are talking it over with people from Cal Tech, MIT and NASA right now.'

'Pull in the best men, Arnold. Get whoever you need.'

'And let's hope they come up with something,' growled Wills. 'We don't want to get caught in this kind of mess again.'

Wedderkind felt honour bound to defend the cause of science. 'If we are, the one thing you *can* be sure of is that the Russians will be in big trouble too.'

'Arnold,' said Wills, 'don't ever confuse Russian scientists with Russian soldiers. They can still fight without all this electronic shit. And if they ever run out of guns and ammunition, they'll try to beat us to death with their mess tins. Take it from me, Arnold, *we're* the ones who need the radar.'

'Point taken,' said the President, perversely pleased to see his trusty friend put down. 'Looks like the ball's in your court, Arnold.'

It was indeed. Wedderkind didn't say anything, but a sharp increase in his blink rate signalled a direct hit.

After the others had gone, Connors poured out two cups of coffee. Both he and the President were on artificial sweeteners. Connors had gone off sugar after reading somewhere that it was destroying his brain cells.

The President was back behind his heavy blue leather-topped desk. He had swung his chair around to gaze out of the window.

'Would you like a roll with it?'

'No.'

Connors put the coffee down on the desk. 'I like Wills. He knows where it's at.'

'Yes, he's a good man. It's Garrison that gets me. The Navy ought to ship him out.'

'He's okay. You just didn't have time for him today.'

23

Connors' support for Garrison stemmed from the fact that he too had briefly been a sailor. He had interrupted his college education to join the Navy as a trainee carrier pilot during the Vietnam War. The day he'd soloed at San Diego, they had begun air-lifting people off the roof of the US Embassy in Saigon.

In the long term, it had been a good career move but in the short term it had proved a social disaster. Resuming his studies at UCLA, Connors discovered that vets from 'Nam and would-be heroes like himself were as welcome as dog-turds on the living-room carpet. Patriotism was a dirty word, draftcard burners were the new elite. It had taken a good ten years for the scars to heal, for the dead to be honoured, for the survivors to walk tall again and for the flag to be carried aloft with pride.

The President, who had seen action as a pilot in the Pacific, had ended up as a full colonel in the California Air National Guard. On bad days in the State Department, Connors and the President were referred to as Snoopy and the Red Baron. The practice had spread to Mel Fraser and his cronies in the Department of Defense. Oddly enough, although flying was about the only thing the two men had in common, it was something they had never discussed.

'Bob – '

'Yes?'

'Do you think the Russians could be putting something over on us?'

'No.' They can't be, thought Connors. Not after all the hard work we've put in.

The President swung his chair away from the window. 'I hope Arnold and Chuck are right about where this interference is coming from. But what the hell do we do if it happens again? The next time, the radar may be knocked out for hours, not minutes.' The President shook

24

his head. 'And how do we know this isn't the beginning of some major change in the earth's environment?'

We don't, thought Connors.

The President stood up. 'It's incredible. The whole of our defence system depends on radar. If that doesn't work, nothing works. We have no early warning, we can't track hostile aeroplanes or missiles or compute interception courses. Our own ground-to-air and air-to-air missiles can't lock on to their targets, our ships and planes can't find their way around – '

'Oh, hold on. We have plenty of planes and missiles fitted with inertial guidance systems. And there's always astronavigation.'

'Yes, and in daytime, they can always fly along the railroad tracks. Come on, Bob. You know what I mean. What are we going to do if it *is* the Russians?'

The Russians. Always the Russians . . . 'The first thing we have to do is stay loose,' said Connors.

The President waved his hand impatiently. 'Just give it to me without the bullshit.'

'It's not the Russians. Don't ask me why. I don't have any proof. I just know it isn't them. Call it a gut reaction if you like.'

'Okay. What happens if Fraser – '

'If Fraser finds something, ask me again.'

'If he does, I may not bother.'

Connors shrugged. 'Everybody's allowed one mistake.'

'Not about something like this.'

'You're the boss.' As he said it, Connors thought, If the Russians have cracked us wide open then we'll all be out of a job . . .

The President sank back deep in his chair and pressed his lips together. 'Do you think I still ought to go to Houston?'

'Yes. Everybody's expecting you. If you don't turn up, people will start to worry.'

'I think we were right to keep the alert secret, don't you?'

'Hell, yes,' said Connors. 'With what happened to the airlines yesterday, the papers have got enough to chew on for one weekend. The press statements we're putting out will all play up the solar-flare angle until we can come up with something better. The vital thing is to keep the Russians out of it.'

'Yeah . . .' The President closed his eyes, massaged the bridge of his nose for a few seconds, then looked up at Connors. 'Okay, we'll go to Houston.'

'Good.' Connors checked his watch. 'If we leave in – let's say half an hour, we can still make Houston in time for your lunch date. Then we can go on to Dallas for dinner. Sunday as planned, the Western White House. We can have some of the boys take pictures of you hooking a sailfish out of the Pacific. Monday morning, back here. Check with Clayson and Arnold to find out how far their boys got over the weekend. How does it sound?'

'Fine. Call Marion and have her tell my wife that the trip is on.'

Marion Wilson was the President's private secretary.

'She knows,' said Connors. 'She's all packed and ready to go.' He tried hard not to smile but his mouth gave way at the edges. 'We, ah . . . both kind of guessed what your decision would be.'

'In that case,' said the President, 'we'd better not keep her waiting.'

Connors ignored the deadpan look. It was one of several they had rehearsed to help the President deal with difficult interviewers on face-to-face TV shows.

26

Despite the fact that the big Sikorsky helicopter was as safe as human ingenuity could make it, Anne, the President's wife, hated every minute of the short trip to Andrews Air Force Base. She preferred, as she put it, 'things with wings on'.

Connors watched the brief moment of almost fussy attentiveness the President accorded his wife. One could almost believe they were still in love with each other. It was an idea that hadn't really occurred to Connors before.

Safe aboard Air Force One and climbing skyward, the First Lady relaxed while her husband went back to work. The Secretary of the Treasury and the Congressional Party Leader had joined the Presidential party at Andrews Field and most of the inflight time was spent putting the finishing touches to a fiscal aid package designed to rescue the newly impoverished Texas oil barons, many of whom were down to their last Learjet.

At his lunch with Houston businessmen and industrialists, the President vigorously outlined his plans for a renewed effort to insulate America from the destabilizing effects of the latest round in the price/production war between the member states of the crumbling OPEC oil cartel. Judging by the applause, it seemed to be what everyone wanted to hear.

The dinner in Dallas was a fund-raising affair. Texas was a state the President wanted to win over. Connors watched him at work among the Party faithful, cheerful, smiling, attentive, handshaking, backslapping, shoulder-gripping. The man was great on body contact. An ear and a word for everyone, and great on names too. There was nothing more wonderful than to feel insignificant and then find your presence acknowledged, your face recognized, your name remembered.

At 22:30, the Presidential jet lifted off the runway at Love Field and headed westward for the seventeen-hundred-mile run to Hamilton AFB just north of San Francisco. Up front, over the Rockies, the sky was a deep purple. The setting sun had got a head start, but with an air speed of over six hundred miles an hour, they would be chasing it all the way to the coast.

In the staterooms, most of the staff were dozing. Jerry Silvermann, the White House Press Secretary, had a small card game going at one of the tables. The President's wife was lying down in their private suite. Connors went through to see the President. He found him slumped back in a window seat, his chin cupped in one hand. He had taken off his shoes and dimmed the cabin lights. A wad of briefing papers lay pushed aside on the table in front of him.

'Everything okay?'

'Yes, fine . . .' The President turned his attention back to the darkness outside the window. Connors carefully chose an armchair that was not too close and sat down. He yawned silently, stretched a little and loosened his tie. Beyond and below the starboard wingtip, Las Vegas glittered diamond-bright against the black sand.

In the three years he had spent working his way upstream to his present position, Connors had become finely attuned to the President's abrupt shifts of mood. Connors was devious enough to appreciate the intricate structure and infinite variability of their relationship. He knew just when to be dominant, subservient, reassuring, knowledgeable, or blandly innocent. Now was a time for being near and saying nothing. Connors found himself wondering yet again if he had really finagled himself into the job or whether, in fact, the President had masterminded him into accepting it.

We all have a death wish, he thought. If we hadn't, I

wouldn't be where I am, and you wouldn't be thinking of running for a second term.

Situated some twenty miles south of Manchester, Jodrell Bank is the home of what was, at one time, the world's largest fully-steerable radio telescope. Operated by a research team that had pioneered many of the present techniques in radio astronomy, the 250-foot-diameter Mark One 'Big Dish' stands surrounded by rich farmland, studded with oak trees and grazing cattle.

Jodrell Bank began operations in 1957, contributing valuable research data to the first co-ordinated global research program – the first Geophysical Year. Soon afterward, the original installation was augmented with a 125-foot-long oval Mark Two dish. Mark Three, a smaller, circular dish, took over the job of tracking satellites.

Following the Friday fade-out, which had hit England in the early evening, the team on the big Mark One dish decided to run a quick calibration test to check out the installation on Saturday morning.

The test consisted of bouncing pulsed radar signals off the surface of the moon and checking the measurements obtained against previously recorded data. To the team's surprise, in the middle of the test transmission, one of the pulses bounced off something much nearer.

As one of the contributing sensor stations to the United States Air Force's SPACETRACK program, Jodrell Bank had a current catalogue of all manmade objects in space. The SPACETRACK centre in Colorado also supplied them with a constantly updated Look Angle List, which gave each station the exact position of all known objects in space in relation to their own ground location.

The Mark One team fed the co-ordinates of the mystery object into the computer for comparison with all currently listed items. The co-ordinates didn't match up with anything on the list. That meant it was new – and worth watching. The movement of the radio telescope was also controlled by the computer. New instructions were hurriedly keyed in and, as the Earth rotated, it kept the big dish pointed towards the same spot in the sky.

Four hours after the first unexpected blip, another radar pulse bounced back. The signal was as fuzzy as the first, but to Jodrell Bank it was a clear indication that something was orbiting the Earth once every four hours. From the two observations they were able to arrive at an approximation of its size and its height above the Earth.

Alerted by Jodrell Bank, a satellite tracking station in Carnarvon, Western Australia, pointed its radar antennae skyward. In Australia, it was already Sunday. After several hours' search, they picked up Jodrell Bank's target and were able to establish its speed, height, and plane of orbit.

Carnarvon transmitted its data by teleprinter to England where it was processed by Jodrell Bank's computer. By five o'clock on Sunday afternoon, the Mark Three dish was skin-tracking the spacecraft. A new print-out from the computer showed that it had been launched into a perfect circular orbit.

The acquisition of the spacecraft coincided with the arrival of Jodrell Bank's director, Dr Geoffrey Cargill, at his home in the nearby village of Twemlow Green. Cargill had been in Russia attending a scientific symposium at the Moscow Academy of Sciences. One of the unscheduled items on the agenda had been some lively theorizing about Friday's twenty-minute radar fade-out. Cargill had got his luggage as far as the hall when his deputy director phoned and told him the news. Cargill abandoned the cucumber sandwiches and tea his housekeeper had prepared and took three minutes off his previous best door-to-door time.

While he had been in Moscow, Cargill had pumped his Russian colleagues for details of their forthcoming space program. As usual, the Russians had sidestepped his questions. All he'd managed to cull were vague generalizations about some of their long-range research objectives. It was infuriating. There was absolutely no need for the blighters to be so damned cagey. Admittedly Jodrell Bank had close links with the American space program, but the place was still British, thank God. The chaps in Moscow obviously thought he was working for the CIA.

Cargill scanned the computer printout analysing the orbital characteristics of the spacecraft and remembered his conversations in Moscow. One of the things he had been trying to substantiate was a particularly strong rumour that the Russians were almost ready to launch a large automated spacelab destined to go into orbit around Jupiter.

His hosts had smiled at his questions but had declined to comment. Seeing his frustration, Vasily Grigorienko, an astrophysicist from Star City, had patted him on the shoulder and said, 'I'm sure you understand that in this country there are times when it's advisable not to be too specific. There are so many things that can go wrong. Let us just say that we still hope to give you a few surprises.'

To which the other Russians in the group had raised their glasses.

The cheeky buggers, thought Cargill. While he'd been ferreting around in Moscow, they had already put the damn thing into orbit. But there had been none of the usual data transmissions from the spacecraft, nor any interrogation signals from Russian ground stations – or any announcement. Cargill suddenly realized what Grigorienko had been trying to tell him. There had been a major balls-up. The Jupiter probe was up but in trouble.

Cargill told his deputy controller to relay all the data to America. He looked at his watch. It was 5:55 P.M. He was bang on time to get a front-page story in tomorrow's morning papers – in London *and* New York. With luck, he'd beat the rest of the world to it. It would be another major scoop for Jodrell Bank and a much-needed boost for British scientific skills and technology. And it wouldn't do Geoffrey Cargill any harm either.

Sunday/August 5

Following the fashion of his predecessors, the President had set up his own weekend White House. It was situated on a rocky strip of the West Coast up towards Arena Point. The climate wasn't to everyone's taste, but the President didn't like dry heat or sterile air conditioning. He needed mist-lined mountain country, steep-rising stands of towering redwoods, a fresh wind off the sea in his face.

His wife Anne liked things that way too. He counted himself fortunate in having made a politically-advantageous marriage to someone he genuinely loved. Anne had not only returned that love, she had used her family's vast wealth to help bring him to power.

It had been a long haul. As the first American President of Italian descent, Lorenzo had had to fight the inevitable campaign of smear and innuendo that if elected he would turn out to be the Mafia's man in the White House. The same tactics had been used to cripple Geraldine Ferraro's ambitions to high office but, after a string of investigations and open hearings which had examined his private life, his professional career, tax returns and business connections, he had emerged as the squeaky clean candidate. Having won the nomination he had gone on to win the election. But it had not been a landslide and, like many of his predecessors, he had problems with Congress and the Senate. Compromise had become the name of the game – and that was why Mel Fraser had been appointed Secretary of Defense.

The Californian estate which his wife had inherited and which was now the West Coast White House had been big enough to accommodate the necessary staff and secure enough to shelter a President without extensive alterations and additions. The communications facility and the helicopter pad had been the only problems but as soon as he had decided to set up shop there, everything had been organized swiftly and efficiently. The homely touches he had left to Anne and her gaggle of gay decorators who had already left their mark on 1600 Pennsylvania Avenue.

Connors didn't go out in the big cabin cruiser with the President. He watched from the small stone jetty as Silvermann shepherded his five favourite newsmen aboard and waved briefly as *Sant'Anna I* pulled away. The waiting Navy patrol boat took up station on the starboard rear quarter, then throttled back its big engines to match the *Sant'Anna's* thirty-five knots. The freshening wind whipped up spray from the wavetops and the sunlight, bouncing through the breakers, turned them a clear blue-green. Connors took a few deep breaths of sea air, then went back up the steps to the house.

Just about the time the President hooked into his first

sailfish, Jodrell Bank's data about the Jupiter probe began to clatter out of the high-speed teleprinter at NORAD's SPACETRACK centre, Ent AFB, Colorado. It was 11:05 Mountain Standard Time. The man who got the first buzz stateside was a NORAD civilian employee, Willard D. (for Duane) Charles, from Ridgewood, New Jersey. Charles had been running a routine check on the multitudinous collection of orbiting satellites and space junk that ranged in size from a Hasselblad camera to the new Russian heavy-weight *Mir*. Jodrell Bank's item was even bigger.

Charles alerted SPACETRACK's duty officer and routed the orbital data into the computer. Within minutes, it had calculated Look Angle co-ordinates for every sensor station in the SPACETRACK network and was relaying the information to them. All they had to do to pick up the Jupiter probe was to point their radar or radio telescope in the given direction. There was only one small problem. The probe was orbiting beyond the range of most of the SPACETRACK radar stations.

NORAD called General Clayson in Washington and finally located him with Wedderkind and his scientific conglomerate at the Air Force Research Laboratories in Cambridge, Massachusetts. Clayson pulled Wedderkind out of a meeting in mid-theory and told him about Jodrell Bank's discovery.

Wedderkind knew that Cargill had a well-earned scientific reputation, but he also knew more about the Jupiter probe than Cargill did. He put in a fast call to Arkhip Karamatov at Houston. Karamatov was head of the Russian group liaising with NASA on plans for a new series of joint space ventures. Karamatov confirmed Wedderkind's 80 per cent hunch. The Jupiter probe was still grounded. So what had the Russians put up there? It was a question that Karamatov wasn't able to answer. On the

34

East Coast, the sudden wave of speculation put a lot of people off their Sunday dinner. Clayson ordered a total security clampdown on the sighting, and called the Western White House.

The President got the news from Connors over the ship-to-shore scrambler phone. The skipper of the *Sant'Anna I* called the Navy patrol boat alongside; the President and Silvermann stepped over the rail and headed back to shore at sixty-five knots.

Luckily, the White House newsman had already got pictures of him smiling alongside a seven-foot sailfish.

Connors was waiting on the jetty as the patrol boat pulled alongside. Way out on the horizon was the white blob of *Sant'Anna I*'s hull. As the patrol boat nudged the jetty, the President jumped down without grabbing Connors' outstretched hand. Silvermann waited for the gangplank.

The first thing the President said was, 'How big is it?'

'We don't have any firm data yet. First estimates put it somewhere around two hundred and fifty tons – '

'Jee-zuss.'

' – polar orbit, about four thousand miles out.'

The President turned to Silvermann. 'Listen, keep your boys out of the way for the rest of the afternoon. And give me a good cover story.'

Silvermann nodded. Connors followed the President up to the house.

From the upstairs study on the north side of the house, you could look towards the tree-lined range that shielded the head of the Sacramento Valley, northward to Mount Linn, and out across the Pacific. Two of the Secret Service men who patrolled the grounds walked briefly into view. Through the trees, further down the slope, Connors caught a glimpse of the moored patrol boat. The

35

Sant'Anna I, now way out, was heading north past the point on an impromptu sight-seeing trip.

'Who's coming besides Clayson and Wedderkind?'

Connors pivoted around from the west window. 'Fraser's bringing Gene Samuels, and McKenna's on his way too.'

Samuels was head of the DIA, the Defense Intelligence Agency, and McKenna, the director of the CIA. Another keen Sunday fisherman, he had been dug out of the Canadian woods near the Minnesota border.

The chair the President sat in matched the one behind his desk in Washington. He liked chairs that rocked *and* swivelled. 'Who else do you think we should call in on this?'

'Nobody.' There are too many of us in on this already, thought Connors. Was it possible that he could have totally misjudged the Russians' intentions? Obviously. The few simple facts spoke for themselves. He sensed that the President had already linked the radar breakdown with whatever it was that the Russians had put into orbit.

Silvermann came in. 'Anything I can do?'

'Yes,' said the President. 'See if you can rustle me up a chicken sandwich or something. How about you, Bob?'

'No, thanks. I already had lunch.'

'One chicken sandwich – ?'

'Two.'

'Coming up,' said Silvermann. The door closed behind him.

'Do you think we should go back to Washington?'

'No. I think we should sit tight.' Connors sat down facing the President. 'Let them come to you. If we're going to get into a hassle, at least we can do it in private.'

The President thought it over and nodded his agreement. He leaned on the desk, cupped his nose and mouth between the palms of his hands and closed his eyes. 'Tell it to me over again.'

'It's in a circular parking orbit, north to south over the poles, once every four hours. Speed, thirteen thousand plus. Altitude four thousand miles. Two of NASA's tracking stations are on to it now. Plus Jodrell Bank.'

'Why is it orbiting so far out?'

'Nobody's come up with a good answer to that yet. It could be to avoid detection. Most of the skin-tracking radar stations – they're the ones that track satellites by bouncing a pulse off the satellite itself – only operate effectively up to a height of about a thousand miles. Most tracking in deep space depends on receiving a signal from the spacecraft itself.'

'And that's where the radio telescopes come in.'

'Right. They can pinpoint and amplify radio signals from more than a million miles away. We've bounced radar pulses off Mars, but to do it you need one hell of a lot of power.'

'Like they have at Jodrell Bank.'

'Right,' said Connors.

'Don't we have optical tracking equipment?'

'Yes, a whole stack. The Air Force has a setup down in New Mexico that can pick up satellites twenty thousand miles away. The problem with optical sensors is that they only work when their part of the world is in darkness and the satellite is illuminated by the sun.'

'I can wait till tonight,' said the President. 'If it's as big as you say – '

'Well, ah – those figures are provisional. There seems to be some difficulty in estimating its size accurately. The type of signal that is bouncing back indicates that the spacecraft has a surface that absorbs or distorts radar waves. Like the Air Force's new stealth bomber. And

37

none of our monitoring units have picked up any of the usual telemetric transmissions to Russian ground stations.'

A wild ray of hope brought a mild grin to the President's face. 'Maybe the English were right about that part of it. Maybe the Russians have lost contact. That really would be something, wouldn't it?' He stood up.

'Yes.' Connors hesitated. 'The only problem is that Jodrell Bank has recorded two slight changes in the angle of orbit since they first picked it up on their radar.'

The grin faded. 'So someone's steering it.'

'It's possible – except that we haven't picked up any signals from the ground either. That could mean one of two things. It's either automatic or – '

The President was ahead of him. 'Or it could be out of control.'

'It's just a thought I had.'

'It's the one I like best.' The President sat down again. Silvermann came back with two chicken on rye.

Melvin Fraser and Gene Samuels were the last to arrive at the big round table in the Pine Room, upstairs, next to the study.

Connors sat on the President's right. Clayson and Wedderkind were looking a bit grey around the edges. McKenna's rimless eyeglasses reflected ice-blue objectivity. Fraser and Samuels radiated happy malice. There were a few short sparring rounds. Then Clayson got right into it.

'Since the first sighting, we've recorded two adjustments to the angle of orbit. Each course change has been preceded by a ten-second breakdown in our radar navigation and surveillance systems – similar to the twenty-minute break on Friday.'

Connors sat back in his chair and exchanged glances with Wedderkind.

'This would appear to indicate that the source of the interference is the propulsion unit of the spacecraft.'

'You mean when the motor's working, our radar isn't,' said the President.

'It's one of the theories we're looking at,' admitted Clayson.

'So that could explain why we were unable to track it from the moment of lift-off until it went into orbit.'

Clayson nodded to Fraser, then turned to catch the President's next question.

'This is obviously a radically new kind of power plant. Any ideas on what it might be?'

Wedderkind got in first. 'There's only one that, in theory, could have some localized impact on radar and radio transmissions. A plasma-powered thrust device. I must admit to being a little disturbed by the idea that the Russians could have got one of those off the ground.'

'I'm even more disturbed by the thought of what it's pushing around up there,' said the President. 'How about some ideas on that?'

Connors watched Fraser exchange a look with Samuels. They'd obviously been rehearsing the answer to that one on the way over from Washington.

'There's only one thing that the Russians would want to put up there in secret,' said Fraser. 'And I'm sure we all know what that is.'

Connors saw three years of carefully constructed global diplomacy collapsing like a deck of cards. Three years in which the Russians, responding to the continued deployment of Cruise and Pershing missiles, had moved fleets of truck-mounted SS-20s and -22s into forward positions in Eastern Europe and, despite all the talk about disarmament, had maintained their overall numerical superiority in land- and sea-based nuclear weapon systems. Three years in which the numbers game continued to be played

39

by teams of smooth-suited career-diplomats across the table at Geneva and elsewhere. And now this . . .

The President said, 'Just in case we don't all know, Mel, why don't you spell it out?'

Fraser took a deep breath and shot a triumphant look at Connors. 'Gene and I think this could be their orbital nuclear-strike platform we talked about at the NSC meeting last January.'

'The idea of which we then discounted.' The President shot a sharp glance at Connors.

Code name SWAYBACK . . . Connors remembered the discussion, and the Defense Intelligence Agency file that Gene Samuels had presented at the routine monthly meeting of the National Security Council. The Russians had completed advanced studies of an orbital spacecraft from which nuclear missiles could be launched against the United States from outer space. It was an idea that both countries had played around with for a long time. Tacked on to the end of the DIA digest was an unconfirmed report that construction of a prototype was under way . . .

'Didn't we have some agreement banning this kind of thing?' asked the President.

'We still have,' said Connors. 'The snag is we've both bent the rules a little.'

'Who bent them first?'

'We did. Ah – by that, I mean a previous Administration. Don't you remember? We put up those test vehicles – the particle beam weapons that were going to be part of the SDI programme.'

'But we cancelled the whole Star Wars thing. That was part of the deal we made with Leonovich.'

Connors shrugged. 'Maybe they still don't trust us. Let's face it, a year from now they could find themselves with another cowboy in the White House.'

40

'Thanks for the vote of confidence.' The President turned to Fraser. 'What kind of a situation does this put us in? Mel?'

'Well – if this *is* SWAYBACK, all they have to do is fire those missiles under cover of a similar radar fade-out and we would never know what hit us.'

It was a sobering prospect but one that Connors found himself unable to accept. It just didn't fit in with what he had learned of the Russians in the last three years. It was true that despite all the talking, they hadn't given any ground in the futile battle for nuclear supremacy, but the latest escalation was a direct result of the last two big increases in the US defence budget. And the continuing financial and economic crises that threatened to rip the West apart didn't make them any less nervous.

The past political and military support of corrupt and greedy regimes on the grounds that they were a bulwark against communism had cost America dear. The dubious morality of such a policy had caused its long-time allies to despair and had earned it the hatred and enmity of all those who yearned to be free.

The Vietnam experience had vividly demonstrated the limitations of American firepower. Short of turning that ravaged country into a nuclear wasteland the war could not have been won by hardware alone. Wars were won by nations whose collective heart and mind was fully engaged and whose people were prepared to make the ultimate sacrifice.

One only had to compare the conduct of the US Marines on Tarawa in 1943 with their lack-lustre performance in Beirut some forty years later. The uncomfortable truth – which few cared to be reminded of – was that, since the victory over Nazi Germany and Japan in 1945, the only military action the United States had carried through to a successful conclusion had been the invasion

41

of the tiny Caribbean island of Grenada. If there was anything to be learned from the last four decades it was that thermo-nuclear war was unthinkable and any other kind was unwinnable. This sobering realization was one of the principal reasons why Connors believed that it was now the age of the diplomat, not of the Defense Department dinosaur.

'Mel, this whole proposition of yours is based on a series of assumptions. Just how do you propose to verify any of them? At the moment, I'm not aware of any proof that the spacecraft is the cause of this interference, or that it's full of H-bombs. We don't even know for sure that it's Russian.'

'Who else can it belong to?' asked the President with a touch of impatience. 'The Chinese?'

'Mr President?' It was CIA Director McKenna.

'Go ahead, Mack.'

'I think we can eliminate them. We've been running a close check on their whole program. They're preparing to put a communications satellite into orbit for the Japanese using one of their Long March rockets but apart from that they've had nothing on the pad for the last three months.'

'It's not the French. They're too busy making money out of Ariane. What do you think, Arnold? Who does that leave – the Israelis?' Fraser's anti-Semitic stare bounced harmlessly off Wedderkind's thick lenses.

Schnorrer . . .

'Okay, Mel,' said Connors. 'But just to make sure, why don't we call up Moscow and ask? The Russians have always kept details of their space program close to their chests. The fact that we didn't get prior notification of launching doesn't necessarily mean that this vehicle has any offensive capability.'

'That's true,' said Wedderkind. 'But – '

'It depends how you define offensive capability,' said Fraser. 'Okay, at this moment in time, I don't have any proof that this is SWAYBACK. I grant you that. But are you trying to tell us that this thing the Russians have put up isn't the source of the fade-out?'

'I admit that these latest ten-second bursts of interference seemed to be linked to changes in orbit,' said Connors.

'They don't *seem* to be, they are.'

'They could be linked in another way,' said Wedderkind. 'Chuck and I have been arguing about this on the way here. Instead of the bursts of radiation coming from the spacecraft's power plant, it could be coming from outer space. We already know that bursts of cosmic radiation can create drag on satellites, causing orbital decay. In which case these changes we've recorded may not be controlled. They may be due to the effect of some heavy cosmic radiation *on* the spacecraft.'

'That still leaves two hundred and fifty tons of Red hardware to be explained away.' said Fraser. 'And don't tell me it's going to Jupiter.'

'I wouldn't even try to guess what it is,' said Connors. 'It seems to me there's too much guessing going on already. I don't think you've really considered the colossal scale of this breakdown, Mel. I mean, this is big stuff. Arnold knows a hell of a lot more about this than I do, but I'm sure that a disturbance of this intensity could *only* be caused by some freak burst of radiation – either from the sun, or from some other source in outer space. Right, Arnold?'

Wedderkind puckered his lips. 'Well, for the moment, that's what Chuck and I have got our money on.'

Connors had been hoping to elicit a more constructive response. Wedderkind's reply left him still carrying the ball. He looked around the table. 'At least some answer on those lines is supported by our own intelligence reports about the Russians having the same kind of trouble as we had on Friday. We still don't have any precise information on the size of this thing. It could turn out to be another chunk of the space-station they're building. The way I see it, the launch just happened to coincide with the fade-out.' He shrugged. 'That would make more sense than some secret weapon.'

'Why?' asked Fraser.

'Because if they had found some way of blacking out our radar, they'd have told us by now – or the war would already be over.'

'Maybe they decided to give us a demonstration instead,' said Fraser. 'And maybe it's you who hasn't got the message.'

'Mel,' said Connors. 'You've forgotten I've had the advantage of meeting the people in Moscow. The Premier, the top half-dozen guys in the Praesidium, Marshal Rudenkov. Not just to split a bottle of vodka, but for serious, nose-to-nose discussions. I can assure you that an escalation of the arms race into outer space with the kind of weaponry you're proposing just doesn't fit into what we know of their long-term objectives.'

'I only know one thing about their objectives,' said Fraser. 'They dress them up differently every year, but they're the same as they've always been. Their war with us goes on.' He looked around the table. 'I know that's a very unfashionable view to hold around Washington these days, but that's what I believe. And every deal we make with them puts them one step nearer their *real* objective – the eventual overthrow of the United States of America and the enslavement of its people.'

Heady stuff, thought Connors, but out of date. It had become clear during the election campaign that Fraser's beliefs were directly opposed to his own and those of the

President, but his presence in their camp had been a vital part of the delicate balance of forces. Permanently withered by the Cold War, Fraser's view of the world had its roots in the isolationist policies of the thirties. Even so, it was unwise to ignore him. Fraser had a lot of powerful friends and there were a mass of people up and down the country who agreed with him.

'I think our response on Friday shows that this Administration is prepared to act against any real threat from Russia,' said the President quietly. 'At the moment, however, I believe the biggest danger facing the free world stems from our continued failure to mount a coherent response to the global threat from radical terrorist groups and their Middle Eastern paymasters.'

'We should deal with them the way we should deal with the Russians,' said Fraser. 'They may not be working hand in glove but it's no secret that every time a bomb explodes or an American hostage is murdered Moscow racks up another goal. And it's no coincidence that the public image of these sons of bitches is a masked gunman brandishing a Kalashnikov. But we're not here to discuss my views on that. Let me just give you some facts instead – about what I'm sure we all wish *was* a perfectly innocent Jupiter probe. We contacted all our radar installations in North America and overseas and got from them the exact time they were hit, and the duration of the fade-out. We also got the same information from every major airport and air traffic control centre and fed the figures into a computer.'

'Did they include Eastern Europe and Russia?' asked Connors.

'No,' said Fraser. 'They wouldn't play ball. It's up to you to guess why. What the figures did show was that we weren't all hit at the same time. The pattern thrown up by the computer showed a six-thousand-mile-wide shock wave of interference moving East to West around the globe at an angle of approximately sixty degrees to the equator. The speed of the shock wave matches that of the spacecraft, and its path coincides with the original plane of orbit.'

Connors looked at Wedderkind and got a nod that indicated he already knew about this. It explained why he hadn't backed him up earlier.

'It all adds up,' said Fraser. 'Our friend up there is the source of the fade-out. And that means that those bastards can lower the boom on us any time they choose.'

Connors felt the President's eyes upon him. He didn't look up. Arnold Wedderkind, who knew a friend in trouble when he saw one, came over the hill like the Fifth Cavalry.

'Mel, you and Gene may very well prove to be right, but there are still a few things bothering me. If I remember correctly, the report Gene showed us in January had SWAYBACK being put into orbit by a multiple cluster of solid-fuel rockets.'

'That's right,' said Samuels. 'But –'

Fraser cut him off. 'Listen. Let's not get bogged down discussing how many nuts and bolts SWAYBACK was supposed to have. Let's just wipe that out and start looking at this thing as a totally new piece of hardware.'

'It's certainly that all right,' said Wedderkind. 'And it raises three big question marks. In order to support this proposition of yours, we need more than that set of figures you've come up with. We have to postulate three hypothetical situations. First –'

The President raised a hand. 'Just hold it right there for a minute, Arnold. Let's keep our feet on the ground. Do you have any relevant data on this, Mack?'

McKenna already had his file open at the right page. 'We know they are carrying out theoretical research into a range of new propulsion systems. But everything we have to date indicates that all these projects are still in the experimental stage.'

'That was one of the points I was going to make,' said Wedderkind.

The President nodded and looked past him at General Clayson. 'Chuck, did any of your surveillance units intercept any of the usual pre-launch radio traffic?'

'No, sir, but if Mel is right – '

'And it's a big "if",' said Wedderkind.

' – SWAYBACK could, as you yourself suggested, have lifted off and gone into orbit under cover of the fade-out created by the propulsion unit.'

'Hold on,' said Connors. 'Science isn't my forte but, from what I've read, a space vehicle powered by a plasma reactor is unlikely to get off the ground until the second half of the next century. Right, Arnold?'

'Right . . .'

Fraser reached out and tapped the dossier that lay in front of Gene Samuels. 'The figures can't lie. How else can you explain the shock wave of interference that matched the speed and angle of orbit?'

'I can't, Mel,' conceded Wedderkind. 'At least not right now. I'm not disputing the figures but when you take all the other factors into account . . .' He shifted uneasily in his chair and poked at his glasses. 'Don't ask me why. It just . . . it just doesn't smell right.'

'I don't think we can base any worthwhile estimates of Russian military intentions on a sense of smell,' said Samuels. 'However acute that organ might be.' He looked round the table to see how well he'd done with that last bit.

Connors aimed a shaft of solidarity towards Wedderkind then turned a cold eye on Samuels. 'Whether those figures add up or not remains to be seen. Until then, I think we should cut out the speculation and the cheap shots and get back to basics.' He looked at General Chuck Clayson. 'When did we get the last set of Big Bird pictures of the launch sites?'

'Just under two weeks ago,' said Clayson. Big Bird was the Air Force's code name for a steerable photoreconnaissance satellite. There were several of them in orbit.

'In that case, you or the DIA must have a picture of this thing standing around somewhere on the ground,' said the President.

'There was a big rocket on the Number Two pad at Baikonur last week,' said Clayson.

'It was still there on Friday afternoon.'

The President accepted this information from Wedderkind without demur. They all knew that he was tuned into a shadowy scientific network that passed on scuttlebutt about the Russian space program. It was one of the reasons why he was with them around the table.

'How about the other launch sites?' asked Connors.

'Plesetsk was getting ready to put up two standard sows,' replied Clayson. 'All the other sites were clear.'

'Perhaps now you can understand why I found it hard to go along with Mel's proposition that the source of the fade-out is SWAYBACK,' said Wedderkind.

'Exactly,' said Connors. 'Where did the Russians launch this thing from, Gene? A hole in the ground?'

Everyone except Fraser turned their eyes on the head of the Defense Intelligence Agency. Samuels looked as if he'd been hit by a custard pie. 'It must have come from somewhere.'

Connors saw Fraser wince.

'Mel,' said the President. 'I'm not sure I know how, or why, or what it is that the Russians have put up there, but if you want to use it to bulldoze my foreign policy, your boys are going to have to do a lot better than this.'

As Samuels sank without trace, the phone behind Connors rang twice. He leaned back and lifted it off the hook '. . . Right. Put it through to the study.' Connors replaced the phone and put the front legs of his chair back on the floor. 'The Kremlin's on the line.' He smiled at the President. 'At least we don't have to pay for the call.'

The President leaned his elbows on the table, closed his eyes and massaged the bridge of his nose with both forefingers. Connors had noted that it was something he always did at moments like this. Two or three seconds of intense concentration . . . He stood up, waving the others back into their seats. All except Connors. 'Since it's your head, maybe you'd better be in on this.' His eyes took the edge off the words.

Fraser and the others watched the study door close behind the President and Connors. Wedderkind tore open a pack of cigarettes and passed them around. McKenna, like the President, didn't smoke. Clayson was trying to give it up.

Samuels lit Fraser's cigarette. 'I'm sorry,' he muttered. 'I really blew out on that. I just wasn't – '

'We'll survive,' said Fraser. He had already made up his mind that the *real* problem lay in the fact that both he and Samuels were almost three inches taller than the President, while Connors . . .

Jerry Silvermann came into the Pine Room. 'Some more dope has just come through on Lenin's Tomb.'

'Lenin's what?' asked Clayson.

'Lenin's Tomb.' Silvermann kept it deadpan. 'Isn't that what they've got flying around up there?'

'Save the jokes,' said Fraser. 'Just give us the message.'

'There's been thirty more seconds of spaghetti on the radar, and that Jupiter probe is now orbiting at just over a thousand miles up. It looks as if those British guys were right.' Silvermann adopted a heavy Slavic accent. 'Tzee Rooshee-anns hev probe-lemps.'

'Jerry, 'said Wedderkind patiently, 'go and put a new ribbon in your typewriter.'

'No sense of humour. That's what's wrong with this Administration,' said Silvermann. 'All the wire services have the story, by the way. NBC has already put it out as a news flash. Most of the dailies will probably give it a few lines tomorrow. Message ends.'

Wedderkind frowned as Silvermann left. 'Why is it coming down?'

'Maybe it *is* going to burn up,' said McKenna. He looked across at Fraser. 'If it does, you may end up with a real nonevent on your hands.'

'Not necessarily,' said Fraser.

Samuels puffed smoke. 'There is, at least, one bright spot. This bum steer the British have given everybody will take the heat away from us for a while. It'll give us a chance to find out what it is. Yeah . . .' He puffed out more smoke. 'It's a big break.'

'It's better than everyone knowing we were caught flat-footed,' said Fraser. He wasn't looking at Samuels but his voice trod all over him.

'Uh – yeh . . .' Samuels coughed. 'Ah – Chuck, how soon can you have one of your SAINTS look this thing over?'

The word SAINTS stood for *SA*tellite Surveillance and *INT*erception System. It was one of the United States' closely guarded secrets – armed reconnaissance satellites, controlled from the ground, and capable of altering their height and angle of orbit. Disguised as research satellites, and ostensibly part of America's continuing 'World Resources' survey program, each of the SAINTS was equipped with TV cameras and carried fifty tiny guided missiles with conventional explosive warheads.

Their task was to spy on the growing number of Russian satellites launched in secret, for purposes known only to the Kremlin. Twenty-four SAINTS were now in orbit at varying heights.

It was in June 1982 that one of the SAINTS recorded in secret a careful inspection by its first Russian counterpart. Since then, the Russians had put up a total of twenty 'killer' satellites. The Defense Department, in line with their usual policy of denigration, had christened them with the code name SOWS – for Soviet Orbital Weapons System.

The control and deployment of the SAINTS was the responsibility of the Air Force – which may have explained why Clayson had to clear his throat a couple of times before he could answer.

'I regret to say that at the present time we are unable to put this craft under surveillance.'

'Why?' asked Fraser.

'Because the latest operational status report indicates a total malfunction return from all SAINTS currently in orbit.' At moments like this, Clayson tended to lapse into Pentagonese.

Fraser stared at him. 'You mean to say *none* of them are working?'

'That's correct. We're getting zero response to all signals that normally trigger off the transmission of visual and telemetric data, and we've been unable to activate the backup circuits that are designed to take over in the event of a primary malfunction.'

'Fucking hell,' said Fraser. 'When did all this happen?'

'Over the last forty-eight hours,' said Clayson.

'And that's not all,' said Wedderkind. 'We're not getting transmissions from anything we've got up there. Research, navigation, weather, communications satellites – the whole civilian network's blown a fuse. Intelsats,

Comsats – everything.' He shook his head. 'I hate to think just how many millions of dollars' worth of investment that represents.'

'Yeah, well, thanks for telling me,' said Fraser. 'How come I didn't get any indication on the extent of these breakdowns before now?'

'I didn't start to get the whole picture myself until this morning,' said Clayson. 'This was a progressive failure. Before I got on to this, there had been several determined efforts at lower command levels to get on top of the situation. A lot of this satellite circuitry is very temperamental. Often what looks like a major breakdown clears after you sidetrack or shut down some of the circuits for a while. I tried to contact you before we left the East Coast but you were, uhh . . .'

'What about the Russian satellites?' asked Samuels.

'No one's heard a bleep from them since Friday,' said Wedderkind. 'It confirms what Chuck and I have been saying all along. Everything points to a colossal burst of X-ray or gamma radiation as the cause of the breakdown. It would affect their satellites too.'

'They've been shut down,' said Fraser.

'What about the cosmonauts aboard Salyut 7 and the Mir space-station?' asked McKenna.

'There's been no word from them since Friday morning,' said Wedderkind.

'Of course not,' said Fraser. 'They've been told to stay off the air too.'

McKenna frowned. 'Why?'

'To keep us in the dark,' said Fraser. 'While those sons of bitches in the Kremlin work out what to do next.'

Samuels closed his file of intelligence digests. 'Who's going to tell the Old Man about this?'

'I will,' said Fraser. It would be a moment he would relish.

* * *

52

In the study, Connors listened in on the line as the President talked to the Soviet Premier.

Apart from having, as Fraser firmly believed, the advantage of being a good half inch shorter than the President, one of the other things that had put Connors ahead was his ability to speak fluent Russian.

After a stint at UCLA, he had continued his Russian studies at Harvard where he'd collected As in everything except popularity. A year's postgraduate work at Oxford University had been followed by another living with a White Russian *émigré* family in Paris. His European stay had been followed by a five-month affair with a ballerina who had defected from Leningrad's Kirov Company during a tour of the USA. While this last stormy period of tuition had put the final gloss on his Russian, it had done absolutely nothing for his marriage.

Connors monitored the Moscow translation of what the Soviet Premier had to say and relayed the President's reply in Russian. All in all, Moscow was on the line for about twenty-five minutes. It wasn't the bad news Connors had half-expected to hear, but it wasn't good news either. It left him with a momentary feeling of helplessness.

Connors put down the extension as the President hung up. They looked at one another thoughtfully, then the President closed his eyes and again massaged the bridge of his nose. With his eyes still shut, he said, 'Who do you think we ought to bring in on this?'

Connors tried to collect his thoughts. 'Ah, hell, uh – right now, I'd say as few people as possible. Otherwise it could get out of control.'

'Yeah . . .'

It was an interesting situation, thought Connors. After all the arguments, he and Fraser had both been right – but in a way neither of them could possibly have expected.

'I think we'll have to tell all those guys in the other room.'

'Yes,' said Connors. 'I think you will.'

The President squared himself up in his chair. 'Okay, wheel them in.'

McKenna was the last one through the door. As he shut it behind him, the President said, 'Maybe you'd all better sit down.'

Clayson, Fraser, Samuels, and Wedderkind each took the nearest chair. McKenna chose one end of the wide ledge of the window facing the sea. Connors took the other corner. As he settled back against the glass, he caught Fraser looking at him warily.

'The talk I've had with my friend in Moscow,' said the President, 'and the unequivocal nature of the reassurances I have received make it quite clear that our preliminary conclusions about this spacecraft are based on a fundamental error.'

'You mean it's not a weapons system?' Fraser sounded disappointed.

'I mean it's not Russian.'

The reaction, predictably, was one of stunned disbelief.

'Or anyone else we know.'

'You mean,' said Clayson, 'it's – ?'

Extraterrestrial. The thought exploded like a star-shell inside Wedderkind's brain. Sentient life, perhaps. Some kind of artefact, at least. From another planet. Another solar system. Maybe even from another galaxy. Here. Overhead. Within his own lifetime. It was . . .

Fraser looked at the President. 'Do you think they're telling us the truth this time?'

'What would be the point of lying to us about a thing like this, Mel? They know we're going to check it out. I didn't call you in here to feed you some Russian fairy tale.'

'I'm sorry,' said Fraser. 'It's just that this is one hell of an idea to have to take on board.'

'You can say that again,' said Clayson.

'I know,' said the President. 'I'm still having trouble believing it myself. What do you think, Mack?'

McKenna raised his eyebrows. 'It had to happen sooner or later. But even so, it's – '

'Fantastic,' said Wedderkind. 'This could change our whole concept of Man, his origins, his place in the universe – everything.'

'Yes – well, that's something we'll have to think about.' The President looked at Samuels. 'Gene?'

'I'll feel a lot happier when we know more about it,' said Samuels.

'We all will,' said Connors. Having got over the first numbing shock of the Russian announcement, he felt apprehensive. He wasn't worried about little green men. It was the whole host of practical problems arising out of such a situation, affecting all kinds of things – including himself. But at the same time, he felt excited at the prospect of the imminent contact with something from up there.

Maybe it would only be an extraterrestrial version of a message in a bottle. It didn't matter. It would be proof that Man was not alone in the Universe. A sign, perhaps, that the nations of the world should join together. But would they? It was a nice idea, but Connors knew that anyone stepping off a spaceship would have both halves of the world giving him the hardsell on the merits of their own way of life.

On the other hand, if they were going to be hit by an H. G. Wells-type Martian invasion, there was the depressing prospect that the Russians might try to rip off a tactical advantage in the following confusion. And if they did, the US would have to get in on the action too . . .

'Bob . . .'

The President's voice brought Connors back to earth. 'Sorry, I was – '

'That's okay. Listen, this is one headache I can do without. I'm assigning you the responsibility for setting up a special task force to deal with this thing. Any objections?'

'No, none at all.'

The President looked at the others. 'I want to set this thing up so everything goes through Bob. He'll report directly to me. Anybody see any problems?'

Apparently nobody did.

'Good. Then I take it I can count on your unqualified co-operation and support.'

Connors watched them all say 'yes' – even those who didn't mean it.

'Great.' The President turned to Connors. 'Arnold will be able to help you on the scientific side, and I think you'd better tie in with the Air Force for logistic support. They're into the space business anyway. That okay, Mel?'

'Yes, I guess so,' said Fraser.

'Chuck?'

'Yes, fine. But what about NASA? Won't you want to bring them in on this?' Air Force General Clayson was great on protocol.

'Maybe later. I think we ought to hold back on this for a bit. Those boys have tied themselves in so tight with the media to hustle more money and enthusiasm for their space programs, they'd never be able to sit on this. It'd be banner headlines in tomorrow's press handouts.'

'They'd be selling grandstand seats,' said Connors.

'So until we know what we're getting into, let's keep this on an "Eyes Only" basis. Is that clear?'

It was. Nobody wanted to start a run on Wall Street.

'Good.' The President swung his chair round to face Connors. 'Bob, as from now, I want you to start active preparations for dealing with a possible landing.'

'In co-operation with the Russians?'

'I think we have to look into that area. Maybe you could have a talk with them about it. But starting tomorrow, I want a daily progress report. From here on in, your team will have first call on the scientific, technological and manpower resources of America. Don't worry about red tape. Just get the show on the road.'

Just get the show on the road . . . It must be marvellous to be the President of the United States. To be able to swivel round in a big blue high-backed chair and come out with lines like that. You just drew yourself one hell of an assignment, Connors. The big one . . .

'It's on the way,' said a voice.

Connors dimly recognized it as his own.

Apart from the seven of them in the President's study, only nine of the top men in the Kremlin knew that the world had a visitor from outer space. Both nations had agreed, for the moment at least, to maintain total secrecy on the whole affair. The American military and civilian organizations involved were to be encouraged to accept Jodrell Bank's statement that the orbiting craft was the ailing Jupiter probe. Conversely, the Russian personnel involved would be allowed to think that the craft was American. Because they were heavily insulated from the Western press and radio, there was a minimal chance of anyone over there catching the double play.

The Russians had agreed not to make any statements to the Western press. Since their past space-flight mishaps and, more recently, the catastrophic accident at the Chernobyl nuclear power plant had been characterized by the same tight-lipped approach, it would reinforce the conviction that they had another failure on their hands. In return, the President had promised to play down any reports linking the spacecraft with the fade-out. With the 'spacelab' satisfactorily identified and now predicted to descend and finally burn up as it entered the denser layers of the atmosphere, civilian observatories would turn their attentions elsewhere, and public interest would quickly wane. What happened after that would depend very much on what was up there.

'What are the chances of having one of our SAINTS look this thing over?' asked the President.

Fraser told him exactly what the chances were. Nil. There is always a risk to the bringer of bad news, but to Fraser it was worth it just to see Connors' face.

Considering the other shocks he'd had to absorb, the President took it rather well. He gave his nose a slow, sliding pinch but kept his eyes wide open. 'Arnold, how soon could we send up a manned space shot to look this thing over?'

'The short answer is "we can't",' replied Wedderkind. 'The whole shuttle programme was knocked for a loop when we lost Challenger. NASA's still trying to sort out the latest batch of design faults that have come to light.'

'So there's nothing on the pad at Cape Canaveral . . .'

'Nothing we can put a man in.'

'Okay, but there must be duplicate Apollo modules around that were used for tests and training.'

'There are. We could probably blow the cobwebs off one of them. The problem is we don't have any Saturn 5 rockets ready to lift it into orbit. We might be able to get something rolling but it'll take at least three months to get it off the ground.'

The President took a slow bite at his bottom lip and

considered Wedderkind's news. Connors caught his eye as his chair swivelled towards the window.

'In one sense, a manned flight is not a bad idea,' said Connors. 'But everybody in Houston Control and at the Cape is going to be in on this mission. They would have to be. It's the way the setup works.'

'Yes, you've got a point there,' said the President. 'Can you see a way round that, Arnold?'

'Well, I know you feel a little sensitive on this issue because they've been pressuring you for funds, but we have to face up to the fact that we can't lock NASA out of this much longer. We're going to need their know-how. A lot of good people have left, but they still have some of the best brains in the business. I admit they've been laying on some heavy PR, but let's also remember that for years they launched a lot of hardware for the Air Force and the CIA that a lot of people, including me, *still* know nothing about.'

McKenna looked at Connors and smiled.

'Security is not really the problem,' continued Wedderkind. 'The spacecraft is orbiting one thousand miles out – slap in the middle of the inner Van Allen belt. When we had Skylab up there, it was orbiting at a height of 270 miles – well below the bottom layer of radiation.'

'But the Apollo module has flown through the Van Allen belt on its way to the moon,' said Connors.

'And back, too,' said Wedderkind. 'Flying through it is a lot different than orbiting for an extended period inside it. Even under normal conditions there would be a definite radiation hazard to the Apollo module and the crew. At the moment, the energy levels in the Van Allen belts must be fantastically high. Since Telstar One and Two, all our satellites have been equipped with radiation shields. For all of them to be put temporarily out of action like that means they've taken a big shot of gamma rays. We could overcome the problem, but we'd have to measure the radiation levels with sounding rockets before we could modify the Apollo. And the shuttle would present an even bigger problem. We'd have to put in extra shielding to protect the crew and instrumentation, and if they're going to do any EVA to inspect our friend, we'll need to build some additional protection into their space suits. And that's going to take time.'

'Friend may be the wrong word,' said Connors. 'If he's knocked out all our satellites, and everything the Russians have put up there, he may knock out the Apollo mission too. This fade-out could be an uncontrollable side effect, or its use could be deliberate.'

'As a weapon.' It was Fraser. As warlike as ever.

Connors shrugged. 'The point is, if we do launch an Apollo, that thing up there isn't going to know there are men inside. Do we want to get into that kind of situation?'

'What are we suddenly talking about weapons for?' asked Wedderkind. 'Okay, we've got a few problems – '

'A few?' Fraser snorted. 'Jesus, Arnold, where have you been the last three days?'

Wedderkind blinked rapidly but didn't look at Fraser. 'That doesn't mean that the world is being circled by a malevolent intelligence. And why would anyone out there wish us any harm? For God's sake – even to reach us, they have to be more advanced than we are. In every way. To the point, perhaps, where communication – on our level – is impossible.'

'If that's the case, why bother to get in touch with us?' asked Fraser.

'The contact has to have some purpose.' said Wedderkind.

'What form do you think it will take?' asked Samuels.

Wedderkind hunched up his shoulders. 'If we're lucky, we may find someone has made us a gift of a harmless

60

piece of hardware. We have to look, to listen – and above all, try to understand.'

'Yeah, well, that all sounds great, Arnold. But meanwhile, what are we going to do back at the ranch?' Fraser was playing the Philistine, but it was a practical question – and one Connors would have asked, but less belligerently.

Wedderkind's lips pinched together. He looked towards Fraser but not at him. 'I think we should do all we can, without doing anything stupid.'

'So what's the final decision on the Apollo shot?' asked Connors.

'I think we'll hang fire on that for a while,' said the President. He stood up abruptly. 'I'm hungry. Do any of you fellas want to eat? All I've had since eight this morning is one lousy chicken sandwich.'

Silvermann had brought up two, as ordered, but the President had made the mistake of offering Connors the second one.

After dinner, the President called the Kremlin and discussed the situation for nearly thirty-five minutes. Connors handled the translation. The President began by commiserating with Premier Leonovich over the probable loss of the cosmonauts manning the two Russian spacestations. He then reviewed the various options available and told the Russians that an Apollo flight was under consideration. The Russians agreed not to take any action against the spacecraft without prior consultation with the United States.

After the call, Fraser and the others joined Connors in the President's study. The President told them that in exchange for the Russian agreement to hold their fire he had given an assurance that, if it was launched, any information gathered by the Apollo mission would be made immediately available to the Russians.

'I know I already said this over dinner,' said Fraser, 'but I'm going to say it again. I think this whole idea of wait-and-see is crazy. I think we and the Russians should blast off a couple of big ones and blow the damn thing – '

'No!' It came almost as a shout from Wedderkind. Then in a quieter voice he said, 'We have no right to do anything like that. An event like this might never happen again in the whole history of the human race.'

'Maybe the history of the human race is about to end right now,' said Fraser. 'Maybe that thing up there has been sent to wipe us all out.'

'One of our problems is that we've all seen too many bug-eyed B movies,' said Wedderkind. 'I think it would help a great deal if we remembered that every science fiction monster we ever read about was created right here – on earth.'

'Nevertheless,' said Clayson, 'I think we must be prepared for the worst and be ready to hit back.'

Wedderkind hunched up his shoulders and spread out the palms of his hands. 'Look. Be reasonable. Why all of a sudden does it have to be Armageddon? Maybe it will just take a look at us and go away. If I was up there and I could see what I see happening down here with my own eyes, that's what I would do. Believe me.'

'But what do we do if it decides to land?'

Another shrug. 'Let it land. Would that be so terrible?'

'And suppose it comes down in Times Square?'

Wedderkind turned to Fraser. 'If you were up there with the whole world to choose from, is that where you'd come down?'

Fraser didn't answer.

HAMILTON AFB/CALIFORNIA

Two USAF helicopters took Connors and the others back to Hamilton AFB where Air Force One stood gassed up and ready to go. It was nearly 11 P.M. As they climbed aboard, the US Navy Sea Queen chopper carrying the President and his wife settled into the nearby landing circle under the watchful eyes of the Secret Service. A small posse of station brass waited attentively in their best blues.

From his window, Connors watched the President and First Lady run the gauntlet of good-bye handshakes from the helicopter to the foot of the boarding ramp. He lost sight of them as the President followed his wife up the steps but he knew the scene by heart. They paused at the top. She turned. He turned, in front, but a step lower down. A brief straight-arm wave from her. A two-stroke, bent-elbow one from him plus a warm smile, with the lips just breaking clear of the teeth. They were both good on smiles. Then a light hand on her back, guiding her in through the door. Slight duck of the head. Curtain.

Connors stood up as they walked through. He smiled at the First Lady. 'You see, you made it.'

'Yes, I know – isn't it silly?' She gave a half laugh. 'I think it's because they look so much like insects that I – ' A shrug completed the rationale.

Lieutenant Jean Seagren, the cabin staff supervisor aboard Air Force One, opened the door to the private suite and ushered the President and his wife through. As the door closed behind them, Connors and the other passengers sat down and strapped themselves in.

The big Boeing rolled away smoothly into the darkness. Looking out through the window, Connors saw the blue lights that edged the perimeter track drift past under the wing like lazy tracer bullets. He settled back and tried to blot out the pictures of aeroplane crash sites that kept coming up like a slide show inside his head. It was always the same. On every takeoff and landing he was gripped by the same anxiety. He unclenched his hands and made a conscious effort to relax as Air Force One made another right turn and rolled straight out on to the runway.

Pressed back in to his seat by the sudden surge of acceleration, Connors found himself wishing once again he could be up front driving it. He closed his eyes and reminded himself he was on board the safest aeroplane in the world. There was nothing ahead of them for at least thirty minutes. The Air Traffic rules governing Presidential flights ensured that Air Force One would be safely wrapped in a large chunk of clear sky all the way to Washington.

Wedderkind had worked out that the spacecraft's flight path would cross theirs, more or less at right angles, somewhere east of the Rockies. 'But don't worry,' Arnold had said. 'He'll be nine hundred miles higher than we are.'

Air Force General Clayson and Mel Fraser had flown together to NORAD Headquarters near Colorado Springs to discuss how the air defence network might counter further radar fade-outs. From there, Clayson planned to go with representatives of the FAA – the Federal Aviation Administration – to discuss emergency flight procedures with the ICAO – the International Civil Aviation Organization in Montreal.

The Monday papers in the USA and Europe would probably contain some mention of Jodrell Bank's sighting of the 'Jupiter probe'. Before leaving California, Wedderkind had telephoned Chris Matson, NASA's director at Houston, to make sure that NASA didn't squelch the story in its own press releases. Cargill's passion for seeing his own name in print was well known in Houston. Matson agreed not to rock the boat in return for Wedderkind's promise to tell all – at a later date.

As far as the ICAO or anyone else was concerned, the fade-out was caused by freak solar radiation. There was to be no mention that the spacecraft lacked an identifiable owner, or that it appeared to be the source of the

64

interference. Delegates from Europe, Russia, and Japan were also expected in Montreal, and the meeting could result in a temporary ban on all bad-weather flying – and night flights such as this . . .

'Would you like me to get you a pillow?'

Connors opened his eyes and saw Jean Seagren.

'Pillow?'

'Yeah, good idea. Thanks.'

Connors eyed her mechanically as she reached up and pulled one off the rack. Not bad, Lieutenant J. Seagren. You have a very passable pair of knees. Pity I don't really care about that kind of thing any more. Not enough, anyway.

Seagren tucked the pillow down behind Connors' head.

Monday/August 6

ABOARD AIR FORCE ONE

Connors remembered nothing more till he woke to the faint smell of grilled bacon, fresh rolls, and coffee. Jean Seagren hovered over him.

'We'll be landing at Andrews in half an hour. Would you like some coffee?'

'I'll have some of everything.' What the hell, let's live a little. For most of the people on board and for almost everybody on the ground below, it was just another Monday. They had no idea that ever since Friday morning, while they had been living, loving, laughing, and lousing things up, the possible end of their world had been silently circling overhead. Today was Armageddon + 3. No time to worry about dieting. Maybe it would go

away, as Arnold had said. Maybe. After coming this far?
Like hell it would . . .

Jo Magill, another long-time member of Air Force
One's cabin staff, opened up the table flap in front of him
then Jean Seagren covered it with a breakfast tray.
Orange juice, toast, two helpings of crisp bacon just the
way he liked it, butter, cream – the works.

'That looks great.'

'My pleasure.'

Connors sat up, straightened his tie and unfolded his
napkin. Seagren started to move away. Be generous,
Connors. You can afford a little warm humanity on a day
like this.

'Miss Seagren.'

'Yes?'

'You have a beautiful pair of knees.'

'Why – thank you very much, sir.'

'My pleasure,' said Connors, master of the common
touch.

As they filed out through the door at Andrews Field,
Seagren was there in her smart little cap along with the
rest of the cabin crew. Good-bye. Good-bye. Good-bye.
Then it was Connors' turn.

'Good-bye, sir. Hope you enjoyed the flight.'

As Connors stepped over the doorsill he glanced back
over his shoulder half-expecting to catch Seagren's eye
but she was already giving Press Secretary Silvermann
the same smiling good-bye line.

THE WHITE HOUSE/WASHINGTON DC

In addition to his office down the hall from the President,
Connors had a small room with a fold-up bed and a
cupboard where he kept a change of clothes. The phone
rang as he was zipping up a fresh pair of pants.

It was Charlotte Annhauser. Her family was in the top third of the Washington social register and still rising. They had met about nine months ago. Not only had her parents approved, they had actually started the rumour that the two of them were going steady.

'Bob?'

'Hi, Charly. Just got back in.'

'I thought you were going to call me this weekend.' Her voice had a plaintive edge to it.

'That's what I thought too.'

'What happened?'

'Oh . . . it all got kind of busy.' Connors began to load up the pockets of his clean suit with the contents of his old one.

'I see.' A pause. 'Are we going to be able to get together this week?'

'Yeah, we might just about make it.'

'It would be nice if I could show you off at the Schumans' on Friday. Could you bear having supper with them?'

'I was hoping I might get to see you before that.'

'Well, you're the one with the key.'

Connors pulled his reading glasses out of the breast pocket of his old jacket and found a piece of folded paper. 'Charly, listen, whatever happens, I'll definitely call you tonight. Okay?'

'Okay.'

'And we'll fix up something.' Connors began to unfold the small piece of paper.

'Bob – '

'Yeah?'

'Do you know anything about this big Russian thing?'

'What big Russian thing?'

'Well, there's a rumour going around that they've put some kind of huge bomb up there in space.'

Where the hell could that idea have come from? thought Connors. And just how far had it spread?

'People have been talking about it all weekend.'

'Really? Oh . . .' He tried to sound bored. 'What does it say in the papers?'

'Hardly anything. The *Post* gave it about eight lines on an inside page. But they only say what someone in England thinks it is.'

'What have the Russians said?'

'Nothing.'

'Then there's your answer.'

'I know. That's what worries me. If it's nothing, why is everyone keeping so quiet about it?'

I can't fight logic like that, thought Connors. 'Charly – ' he began.

'I know, you have to go.'

'I'll call you this evening. I promise.'

'Okay, but listen – if the Russians have done something sneaky and we're all about to get blown to pieces, you'd tell *me*, wouldn't you?'

'Charly, don't worry about the Russians. It's all under control. Believe me.'

'I knew it,' said Charly. 'Something terrible's happened. Is it the Chinese?'

'Good-bye, Charly.'

Connors hung up and looked down at the piece of paper in his hand. On it, in firm feminine handwriting, was the name, address, and phone number of Lieutenant Jean Seagren. It must have got into his pocket while he was asleep. Neat. Connors folded the slip of paper in half, then slowly tore it into sixteen small pieces.

Connors walked back to his office and found McKenna waiting. He'd arrived a few minutes earlier. JoAnne, a smooth-looking brunette with matching shorthand, had just given him a cup of coffee.

'Make that two,' said Connors. 'Any news of Wedderkind?'

'Yes, he just called in from his car. Got a little snarled up in the traffic. He should be here any minute.'

'Okay.'

JoAnne brought Connors a coffee and left.

'Are any of your staff in on this?' asked McKenna.

'No – but I think I'll need to pull in Greg Mitchell. He runs the office for me. He's got a maximum security clearance.'

'This operation may require a new classification of its own.'

'I realize that.' Connors dropped two sweeteners into his coffee. 'The point is I'm going to need someone to run around for me, so it might as well be Greg. If you run him through your computer I think you'll find he checks out. But then, I imagine, the Agency already knows more about the two of us than we would care to remember.'

McKenna's lips remained sealed. His eyes gave nothing away either. Nature had clearly intended him to run the most powerful intelligence operation west of the Iron Curtain. And faced with that steely gaze, Connors was reminded that his most noted predecessor, Heinrich Himmler, had also favoured rimless glasses.

'And if they're not covered by you, then the FBI is bound to have files on all the scientists Arnold plans to recruit. The Air Force will process their people – and you can look after your own. Hell, we don't need to make a big deal of this thing. All we're looking for are people who aren't Russian agents, aren't psychotic – and who can keep their mouths shut.'

'Uh-huh . . . well, that gives us the broad guidelines,'

said McKenna. 'What kind of a deal are you planning to offer the people you recruit on to the project?'

'Mack, I haven't even had time to think about that yet. It'll have to cover things like compensation for dependants – all the usual junk. The CIA must already have contracts like this.'

'Do you want us to draft something for you to look at?'

'Listen, if it satisfies you, then I don't need to see it. It would be great if you could handle all that side of it.'

'Okay, I'll put one of our lawyers on that right away.' McKenna pulled out a slim black notebook and jotted down a reminder in small, neat handwriting. 'If you just let me have Arnold's shopping list, we'll go round and sign them up.'

'Great.' Connors' phone rang. He picked it up, listened, then covered the mouthpiece. 'It's Chuck Clayson. He's phoning from Colorado.'

Ent Air Force Base, Colorado. Headquarters of NORAD – the North American Air Defense Command – and also the control centre of the SPACETRACK network.

'Chuck, hi . . . yes, sure, go ahead. It's a very clear line . . . uh-huh . . . uh-huh . . . and there's absolutely no possibility of a mistake?'

McKenna watched Connors' eyes flicker nervously. 'Trouble?'

Connors held up his hand and frowned as he listened to what Air Force General Clayson had to say. 'Does Fraser – ? . . . Ah, he's with you . . . Yeah, fine, okay, Chuck, keep me posted if there are any developments . . . Okay, g'bye.' Connors put the receiver back and held it down with his hand – almost as if he wanted to stop it ever ringing again.

McKenna waited. Connors let go of the telephone, put his elbows on the desk and rubbed his face with both hands. He looked up at McKenna.

'The Air Force have had their tracking telescopes and cameras locked on to the spacecraft's orbit all night and . . . they haven't been able to make visual contact – in spite of the fact that they are still skin-tracking it with their radar.'

McKenna frowned. 'You mean it's up there, but they can't see it?'

'Exactly. The Air Force thinks it must have a matt-black, non-reflective type of surface – which makes it impossible for us to see it.' Connors stood up. 'I'd better break the news to the President. While I'm gone, why don't you phone your legal department?'

Connors met Arnold Wedderkind outside in the corridor. He told him about Clayson's call as they walked to the President's office. Marion told them to go straight in. Connors broke the news to the President, and Wedderkind followed it up with an explanation.

'All our satellites have an outer skin of highly-reflective material which insulates them from the heat of the sun – and enables us to see them as they circle the Earth. It looks as if this craft is absorbing the sun's light and heat – converting it to some other form of energy, the way our solar panels produce electricity.'

'But there is nothing wrong with our equipment?'

'No,' said Wedderkind. 'We've photographed a six-inch diameter Vanguard satellite at a range of twenty-four hundred miles. There's nothing wrong with the cameras. But there may be another reason why we can't see it.'

The President sat back warily and pressed the tips of his fingers together. 'What's that, Arnold?'

'Well, we may not be able to see it because it may be fluorescing on a different wavelength.'

'Keep it simple, Arnold.'

'It *is* simple. We see everything around us because the

71

light falling on objects is reflected back on wavelengths we can see. But there are certain molecular structures that possess a physical property known as fluorescence – '

'Give me a for-instance,' said the President.

'Fluorspar crystals, paraffin, essence of quinine. When a beam of light falls on them, it's reflected back – but on a slightly different wavelength. There's nothing magic about it, but if you extend this idea, it's possible to imagine an object that instead of reflecting light so we can see its shape and colour, absorbs the visible light waves, and sends back ultraviolet or, say, infrared rays. It would be fluorescing on a wavelength *outside* the spectrum of visible light. It would be there, but we wouldn't be able to *see* it.'

The President looked at Connors. 'Jesus, that's all we need. An invisible spaceship . . .'

Wedderkind hastened to reassure him. 'But if it was fluorescing on ultraviolet or infrared wavelengths, we could photograph it on film sensitive to those forms of radiation – X rays too.'

'So why can't the Air Force use this film?'

'They may not have thought of it yet,' said Connors. 'Not everyone has Arnold's imagination. But we can certainly recommend that they try.'

'They still may not get a picture,' said Wedderkind. 'The atmosphere only lets in a small amount of the longest ultraviolet waves – which gives the girls a nice suntan. We normally refer to them as near ultraviolet. The shorter wavelengths, or far ultraviolet, are pretty unhealthy. Fortunately, like a lot of other nasties, they're blocked off by the ionosphere. There's a larger infrared window, as we call it, but most of the infrared wavelengths are blocked off too. If the spacecraft is fluorescing on any of the blocked wavelengths, its photographic image won't reach us on the ground.'

'Unless it comes down lower – or lands,' said Connors.

'Right,' said Wedderkind. 'Until we get the readings from the sounding rocket, we can only guess at what has happened up there. You can jam radar and radio transmissions by transmitting a more powerful signal on the same wavelength. The spacecraft could be an immensely powerful source of radio waves – like a quasar – '

'A what?' asked the President.

'A quasar – quasi-stellar radio source.'

'Uh-huh . . .' The President decided to let it go.

'On the other hand, it *was* cosmic radiation that knocked out Telstar One in 1962. Either way it's quite a problem. If this thing is fluorescing on far ultraviolet, X rays, or anything shorter, and it decides to land, we'll need to carry geiger counters and dress up in lead suits.'

'Christ, Arnold, you're turning into a real doom merchant.'

Wedderkind turned to Connors. 'Not at all. It's a fascinating problem.' He waved to the corner of the President's desk. 'I'm just trying to work out what would happen if there was an object standing there, fluorescing on, let's say, an infrared wavelength. We would be able to sense it as a heat source. Basically, that's what infrared radiation is. But if it was invisible, would we be able to see the part of the desk it was standing on?' Wedderkind frowned thoughtfully at the imaginary object.

'Pick it up and take it with you, Arnold,' said the President. 'I've got work to do.'

Friday/August 10

It hadn't been a good week for the President. Ever since he had got back to Washington, he had been trying, without success, to concentrate on the day-to-day problems of government. Time after time as he pored over papers, or listened to briefings from his aides or members of his Cabinet, he had found himself morbidly distracted by that orbiting, two hundred and fifty ton question mark.

Even his wife had guessed he had some extra problem on his mind. As always, she had waited for him to share it with her. But this time, he had said nothing.

The President swung his chair round to face Connors. 'What the hell is it going to do, Bob? Even more to the point, what the hell are *we* going to do?'

It was a rhetorical question. The ball had already been set rolling.

Soon after his return to Washington at the beginning of the week, Connors had reached an agreement with McKenna on the setting up of a CIA cover company for the project if a landing took place within the United States, and if the location and circumstances of the landing permitted the project to proceed in secret.

Air Force General Clayson had been asked to assemble a mobile military component to provide a security screen for the landing site, the basic manpower for site operations, electronic specialists, technicians and engineers. The personnel chosen would be seconded to the CIA as 'civilians' for the duration of the project.

Via Clayson, Connors had established a hot line to the

Air Technical Intelligence Center at Wright-Patterson AFB, just north of Dayton, Ohio. Way back in March 1952, the Center had begun Project Blue Book, a compilation of all material evidence and eyewitness reports relating to sightings of unidentified flying objects within the USA and elsewhere.

The project had been officially terminated in 1969, but following a mysterious rash of airborne and undersea radar contacts and the unexplained disappearance of several military aircraft in the early seventies, the Blue Book had been quietly reopened. If there was any visual contact with the spacecraft within the United States, or via the worldwide network of US bases and communications facilities, ATI at Wright-Patterson would get the word.

Arnold Wedderkind, who was to head the research group, had already begun to contact the scientists he needed. As and when they were recruited, their assembly point would also be Wright-Patterson.

On Tuesday and Wednesday, Connors and Wedderkind had been in Russia. The trip had been made in secret, and without the knowledge of the US Embassy staff in Moscow. Hitching a ride on a routine supply flight from Andrews AFB, the C-5A Galaxy of Military Air Transport Command had set them down at Rhein-Main AFB outside Frankfurt. From there a car had whisked them straight on to the ramp at Frankfurt-am-Main where they had boarded a scheduled Polish Airlines flight via Warsaw to Moscow.

There they had talked with the Soviet Premier, Alekseii Leonovich, and Marshal Rudenkov, the Soviet Defence Minister. Leonovitch, a Georgian who had risen to power via the ranks of the KGB like his one-time boss Andropov, had also retained his post as First Secretary of the Communist Party. Since the presidency was largely a ceremonial position, it meant he was the man with the most clout in the Kremlin. Rudenkov was a tough, square man, with a ditchdigger's fists, who looked as if he could still be bad news with a mess tin. General Wills would have liked him.

At 9:05 A.M., the President and Connors were joined by Clayson, Fraser and Wedderkind. As they sat down around the desk, the President made minute positional adjustments of the framed portrait of his wife, his note-pad, blotter, and pen set. His eyes met Connors'. He clasped his hands together, then began.

'This is the deal we've fixed up with the Russians. Since they have complete control over their communications media, they've agreed to let us name them as owners of the spacecraft, just so long as it stays out of trouble. To be more precise, we can say it's theirs, they won't deny it.' He paused to let Connors come in.

'What we intend to do is to get Jerry Silvermann to refloat the Jodrell Bank story – this is the large robot spacelab that the Russians intended to put into orbit around Jupiter and which as a result of the unexplained twenty-minute burst of radiation has suffered a major power failure.'

'Which explains the total lack of radio transmissions,' said Wedderkind.

'And so they're saying nothing,' said the President. 'Which is fine, because that's what they usually do when things go wrong.'

Fraser gave a noncommittal grunt.

'We've also managed to steer Jodrell Bank off this thing,' said Connors. 'The only two stations tracking it now are under Air Force control.'

'With a small amount of encouragement from me, a group of my academic friends are continuing to push solar-flare radiation as the cause of the fade-out. That should keep the press happy.' Wedderkind smiled. 'Of course, none of them know what *we* know.'

'The important thing to remember,' said Connors, 'is now that this thing has been identified as another Russian loser, nobody out there is going to give a damn what happens to it. They're all going to be watching baseball.'

'What happens if it comes down?' asked Fraser.

The President replied for Wedderkind. 'If it comes down, that's another problem. As I understand it – correct me if I'm wrong, Arnold – to descend, it will have to switch on its propulsion system. That means we will get another radar breakdown, so until we make visual contact, no one will know where it is.'

'Correct,' said Wedderkind.

'Arnold,' said Fraser, 'how are we going to make visual contact? At the beginning of the week you were saying that this thing was invisible to the human eye.'

'I said that could be *one* of the reasons why the tracking cameras hadn't been able to pick it up. If I may remind you, I also agreed with the suggestion Chuck put forward – which was that the spacecraft must have a dark, non-reflective surface that absorbs light. It's as equally valid as the theory that the craft may be fluorescing on a wavelength beyond visible light.'

'And easier to understand,' said the President.

'But we're not going to announce we haven't made a visual sighting.' Connors looked at Fraser. 'Since the Air Force controls all the tracking cameras, all you have to do is think of a reason why the Defense Department is sitting on the pictures. Would you like us to draft a press release?'

'No, that's okay,' said Fraser. 'I think we might just be able to manage that.'

'I think – just to co-ordinate things – we ought maybe

to have a look at any statement you plan to put out, Mel.'

Fraser looked at the President. 'Of course.' His eyes switched briefly onto Connors.

The message was clear – and had been for a long time. Like a lot of his predecessors, Fraser tended to regard the Defense Department as his personal fief, a bastion of freedom whose role was to protect America from the passing folly of the temporary residents of the White House and their jumped-up con-men assistants. The Department knew how to stonewall unpopular directives, and if it didn't get the kind of Secretary it wanted, then the three armed services rendered him powerless with the subtlest kind of mutiny.

'The problem is this,' said Wedderkind. 'The spacecraft is orbiting at an angle of eighty degrees to the equator, virtually pole to pole, with the Earth rotating beneath it. If we *do* get another period of fade-out, it could mark the beginning of the spacecraft's entry into the atmosphere. As we know its flight path, we could make a guess at its trajectory – and where it would be likely to land. But *only* if it stays on the same course. I think in the case of this vehicle, we have to postulate an unlimited power capacity, which would give it total directional freedom. And there's something else – it may *not* begin its descent at the beginning of the fade-out. It may continue to orbit for a while and then come down, under cover, so to speak. If it does that, then the problem of locating it becomes very difficult.'

Fraser turned to the President. 'Do the Russians have any ideas on this?'

The President headed the question over to Connors.

'Well, first,' said Connors, 'they want to maintain a total news blackout on the whole operation. Second, we've made a tentative arrangement on setting up a joint search operation to locate the spacecraft in the event of a presumed landing, then a Joint Study Group to follow up the sighting and evaluate whatever they find. The problem is, when that motor starts working – and assuming that *is* the cause of the fade-out – we won't have any idea whether the spacecraft's gone up or come down.'

'Until someone trips over it,' said Fraser. 'Hell's teeth, how can we get organized on that kind of basis? The fucking thing could be anywhere!'

'Exactly,' said Wedderkind. 'But despite what I've said, I'm hoping that we may get *some* kind of sighting report if it does decide to land.'

'Me too,' said Connors. 'But before we all get excited, I think we ought to remember one thing. The proposed two-nation search and Joint Study Group is a great idea, but there's absolutely no guarantee that this thing is going to land in territory that we or the Soviet Union have jurisdiction over.'

'That's true,' said Wedderkind, 'but we both have access to a big area of the map – and we're the only ones who have any idea what we're looking for.'

'Granted, but we can't just put our wagon down and our tents up anywhere, Arnold. If it lands in Saudi Arabia, okay, we have access. There's a chance we can contain the situation. But if it were to land in France . . .' Connors shrugged. 'They could lock us and the Russians right out of the whole deal.'

'If it comes to that,' said Fraser, 'how do we know that the Russians will stick to their promise – all right, tentative agreement – should it come down inside the Soviet Union?'

'We don't,' said Connors. 'We'll just have to trust them.'

'And if it comes down inside America?'

'Then I guess they'll just have to trust us,' said the

President. He looked at Connors first, then the others. Everybody got the message.

Connors saw Wedderkind's raised eyebrows and replied with a slight shrug of his shoulders. *So much for détente* . . .

'Mr President, could I make one final comment?'

'Sure, go ahead, Mel.'

Fraser looked at Connors and Wedderkind. 'I've already stated this clearly before, but I'd like it to go on record one final time. I think we ought to go back to the Russians and tell them that we are going to blow up this craft before we get any deeper into this whole deal. They can either agree to join in the attack or stand back and watch. If they don't go along with us, it will be because they think they can make something out of it. We have to show them we're not going to fool around.'

The President looked at Connors. 'What do you say, Bob?'

Connors eyed Wedderkind and Fraser. Scientific curiosity apart, it didn't seem such a bad idea. As the old adage went, "What the eye doesn't see, the heart doesn't grieve for". Connors sensed Wedderkind's silent scream of anguish and felt like Cassius. Not Muhammad ex-Clay – the other one, in the play by Shakespeare.

Marion Wilson came in with a typewritten message for the President. It was only a half sheet of blue paper, but it was big enough to get Connors off the hook.

The President scanned the message with a frown, then passed the paper to Connors. Some of it was good news and some of it was bad. The good news was they didn't have to fire off any missiles. The bad news was they couldn't – even if they wanted to.

'Do you want me to read it out?' asked Connors.

The President nodded.

Connors exchanged a glance with Wedderkind. 'This

80

information is issued jointly by the Air Force Communications Service, the Federal Aviation Authority and the Federal Communications Commission – ' Connors saw Clayson lean forward expectantly. 'For the last twelve minutes there has been a steadily increasing disruption of all radar surveillance, navigation and air traffic control systems, and high-frequency radio transmissions.'

Fraser and General Clayson shot up in their chairs as if they had a bullet in their backsides.

'Not just us,' said the President. 'The Russians too – everyone.'

Connors read on. 'The breakdown is now complete, worldwide and continuing. Air Traffic Control Centers are diverting flights to the nearest airports. All civil airliners and private planes have been temporarily grounded. Military flights are continuing in areas of clear visibility.'

'Give them the capper, Bob.' The President's voice was flat and unemotional, but Connors, who could read the signs, knew just how worried he really was.

Connors tried to sound casual too. 'The same source of interference is already affecting TV transmissions and appears to be spreading through the commercial short-wave channels. Medium- and long-wave channels are at present unaffected.'

Fraser shot a loaded glance at Connors, then looked at Wedderkind. 'What in hell is going on up there, Arnold?'

Everyone else was looking at Wedderkind too.

Wedderkind gave a shrug like a sick owl and retreated behind his heavy-framed spectacles.

At least we still have the telephone, thought Connors. He made up his mind to call Charly. To tell her not to worry. To say that everything was going to be all right, but that he wouldn't be going with her to the Schumans' for dinner. Connors pushed the piece of paper towards the middle of the table. Nobody picked it up.

Highway 22 runs northwest from Miles City, in Custer County on the Yellowstone River, up through Cohagen to Jordan, in Garfield County. Between Miles City and Cohagen, the highway slices through the northeastern tip of Rosebud County. On the map, the land is coloured brown and the contour lines start at over two thousand feet and go up over three. On the ground, the overall colour is brown too.

North of Miles City, the land is known as 'The Big Open'. Bare, rolling, high plains country with as few trees as there are people. For mile after mile on either side of the two-lane hog-backed highway, there is nothing but endless stretches of buffalo grass and sage. Cattle country, scarred here and there by poisonous salt pans, and the intertwined, weathered clusters of gumbo and sandstone buttes that make up the eastern Montana badlands. Every so often, the buffalo grass gives way to alternating strips of spring or winter wheat and ploughed earth that ripple outward from the highway towards the horizon like the waves on some vast inland sea. What trees there are – cottonwoods, dwarf cedar, and pine – shelter in the creeks and draws, or hug the slopes of the rising buttes that break the smooth line between land and sky.

Hard up against the northern edge of the Rosebud County line, some four miles after a winding dirt road leaves the highway, is a place called Broken Mill – a handful of houses and trailers huddled around a post office, gas station, and general store. Of the twenty-two people listed as living there in the 1960 census, only twelve now remained. Most of these were under fifteen or over forty. Close to the gas station two graded roads, topped for part of the way with flakes of red scoria, run right and left off the highway in a straight line for as far as the eye can see. The only indication that there are people living beyond the emptiness are two hand-painted boards attached to the fences at the crossroad, bearing the names of the isolated ranchers and their distance in miles from the highway.

It was from Broken Mill, from Annie's Mercantile and General Store that Deputy Carl Volkert telephoned to the Rosebud County Sheriff's office in Forsyth details of what he thought was a plane crash. Normally, he would have used his car radio, but since early morning there had been some heavy fade-out on the normal police frequencies. It had been impossible to transmit or receive a coherent message. There was a lot of background noise on the phone line too. Volkert told his office that several of the people at Broken Mill claimed they had seen a bluish-white ball of fire cut through the overcast and curve down towards the southwest, going out of sight behind Crow Ridge. Volkert, who had been making a quick detour to visit his lady friend, had heard a long, distant rumble of thunder but had seen nothing from his car. Three kids were convinced they had seen a UFO. Volkert didn't take them too seriously.

The county sheriff's office told Volkert to take a look around Crow Ridge, then phoned the Air Force at Glasgow AFB, one hundred and thirty miles to the north. The base had been mothballed in the mid-seventies and was now host to a long line of cocooned B-52s but the tower was still operational. Air Traffic Control had no reports of any aircraft missing or in distress in Montana air space but agreed to arrange for a helicopter to check the area.

The county sheriff's office knew, of course, about the

temporary ban on civilian flying. What they didn't know was that ten-tenths cloud and heavy rain had socked in all the Air Force bases in the northern half of the United States. Blinded by the loss of radar navigation aids and the progressive disruption of radio transmissions, no military aircraft had left the ground. Apart from the birds, there was only one thing that could have been in the air over Montana that Friday morning, but nobody at Glasgow AFB, Broken Mill, or in the county sheriff's office in Forsyth had any idea what the people in the White House were expecting.

Volkert drove south on the highway and turned on to the ungraded dirt road that snaked up towards the top of Crow Ridge. The road had been cut by an oil company that had sniffed around the area at the tail end of World War Two and probably hadn't been used since.

Each spring, the rain and melting snow had softened the deep, scarring ruts in the fawn-coloured gumbo, but never enough. When the dry spells came, the ground hardened back into the weaving pattern cut by the last departing truck in those far-off days when Volkert had been glued anxiously to the family radio-set, wishing he was four years older so he could get himself some action and a few *fräuleins* before the shooting was all over.

The earlier, thunderous precipitation had turned the top half inch into mud. Volkert took a couple of the earlier turns too fast and almost slid off into the pines. He dropped his speed to about forty. He'd already taken several rocks against the underside of his car. One jolt had sounded as if his transmission box was coming through the floor. There was no point in piling it up this far from home . . .

As the edge of the rocky plateau came into sight, his car stalled. Volkert swore quickly to himself. He'd collected it that morning fresh out of Maintenance. He tried to restart the car. Nothing. The motor didn't even turn over. He got out, opened the hood and checked all the electrical leads. There was nothing loose. The battery was full. He slammed the hood shut and peeked under the car to see if he'd fractured an oil or fuel line on a rock. No leaks, nothing broken. He got in behind the wheel again, checked the wires under the dash for a loose connection, then tried to restart the car. No response. Volkert hit the wheel with his palm and pulled out the radio mike. That at least was independently powered. With the fade-out he might have trouble getting through, but it was worth trying.

'Car Four Seven to Rosebud One, over.'

The mike hissed a storm of static at him. The noise flared up and faded away several times. Volkert repeated his call sign, then suddenly the mike went dead. His radio batteries had failed too. He reached up and switched on the interior roof light. To Volkert's surprise it came on, then began to flare rhythmically. A few seconds later, the light went out. Volkert dropped the dead mike back on to the seat in disgust.

'Goddamn crap heap . . .' He got out of the car and took a long look around him, hands on his hips.

It was a good seven miles back down the dirt road to the highway, and it wasn't all downhill, so he couldn't freewheel back. Overhead, the low clouds looked ready to open up with another heavy squall of rain. Shee-yit . . . Still, now that he was up here, he might as well take a look around. He remembered that there was a couple living in a shack down over on the northern flank of the Ridge. Man by the name of Bodell. A World War Two Marine vet, and a hard-eyed sonofabitch. Looked mean enough to hunt bear with a razor strap. Volkert had seen him a couple of times down in Broken Mill, and had heard some more about him from Annie. Drove a beat-up old ex-US Army Dodge 4 by 4. Maybe he could talk him into giving him a tow.

Volkert followed the dirt road up to the point where it ended among the trees. From there on up, the route was marked by a series of deep, crisscrossing ruts imprinted with the tread of heavy-duty Goodyears. Probably from Bodell's old Dodge, thought Volkert. If so, it meant they'd be able to get the truck back up over the top to where he'd left the car. He aimed off left towards the rocky crest. From there he would be able to scan both flanks of the ridge.

Volkert clambered up on to the highest part of the ridge and took a good look around. The visibility was down to two or three miles. On a clear day in Montana, you could see more than fifty. Down below him on the plateau, he could see a big crater at the edge of the tree line. Behind it was a semicircle of blasted trees. They looked as if they had been flattened by a giant fist.

There was no sign of any wreckage of a plane.

Maybe it just blew to pieces, thought Volkert. There had been some talk of an explosion. He was just about to climb down when he heard the helicopter. It was about level with him, just below the overcast and coming in at an angle from the north. The black blob resolved itself into an olive drab Air Force Bell Iroquois. Volkert waved his stetson at it.

The helicopter altered course and lifted in a curve around the ridge to the left of him. Volkert could see the midships crewman leaning out of the hatch. Volkert waved again and pointed down towards the crater as the Iroquois flew a tight circle overhead. Volkert started down off the ridge. The helicopter banked sharply and came in low over the top of the ridge, almost running him down.

Crazy bastards . . .

The midships crewman gave him a thumbs-up sign. Volkert watched the helicopter float down across the plateau. With a bit of luck, he could maybe hitch a ride back to Rosebud. It would sure beat the hell out of Bodell's Dodge.

As the thought entered Volkert's head, the helicopter suddenly stood on its tail, then fell out of the sky.

Volkert broke into a run.

Blades windmilling, the helicopter spiralled down and clipped the side of the crater. Just before it thudded down on to the rim, the midships crewman jumped clear and went rolling down the slope of the crater. By a bizarre twist of fate he chose the wrong side. A flailing rotor blade sliced his head off as he was scrambling to his feet, then the helicopter keeled over and steam-rollered his body into the loose earth.

Volkert covered the half mile down to the crater as fast as he could. The pilot was wandering around the helicopter, his face drained of colour. He seemed pretty shaken up. Volkert checked him over, but the only thing broken was his wristwatch.

The pilot waved dazedly towards the broken body of his crewman. 'I can't find his head.'

'Keep looking,' said Volkert. He patted him on the shoulder then turned to take a look at the copilot. He was lying with the top half of his body inside the upturned cockpit. Volkert squatted down beside him.

'You okay?'

'Yeah, fine. Was just trying to raise somebody over this goddamn thing.' The copilot waved towards the radio. 'Was that you up on the ridge?'

'Yeah. They sent me over to check out reports of a crash. Looks like you're it. Volkert. Rosebud County Sheriff's Office.'

'Great. You got a radio?'

'No. Mine's out too. The whole car cut out on me a quarter of a mile back. Down towards the highway.

There's a man back over that way with a truck. Reckon he's our best bet.' Volkert cast an anxious eye over the helicopter. 'You sure you want to stay in there? I seen one of these things come down once. Fractured a gas tank – went up like the Fourth of July.'

'Yeah, that can happen,' said the copilot. He threw down the useless mike. 'Does this guy have a telephone?'

'No. But if he's home, we can maybe hitch a ride down to Broken Mill. We can phone from there. Okay?'

'Sure. Let's go.' The copilot wriggled out of the upturned cockpit.

The pilot, who still hadn't found the midships crewman's head, had to be dragged by the arms all the way to Bodell's house.

Three hours later, after the pilots had got back to the air base north of Glasgow, they felt a burning, prickling sensation on their hands and faces. The exposed areas of skin turned bright red, began to swell painfully, then started to erupt. The medical section diagnosed it as a massive dose of ultraviolet radiation and ordered immediate hospitalization.

Back at Forsyth, Volkert had also found himself similarly afflicted but to a lesser degree. The Sheriff sent him to the doctor. The doctor gave him a shot of pain-killer, put on a soothing lotion, told him he had sunburn, and sent him home.

There was just one problem – the sun hadn't been out all day.

THE WHITE HOUSE/WASHINGTON DC

It's an ill wind, as they say, that blows nobody no good. While the storm of static brought the networks to their knees, the newspapers boomed back into business nation-wide. Special lunchtime editions enlarged upon the solar-flare/magnetic-storm theory, and confidently underlined its temporary nature. Some confidence was needed. The uniformly bad weather had combined with the fade-out to cause a grim total of seventy-four airline crashes including several midair collisions. Nine aircraft had gone down in the Chicago area, seven around New York, five midairs over Boston, Washington, and Philadelphia. Most of the rest had been in Europe and Japan. Death toll, 4,128 and rising. Damage to property in millions of dollars. A shattering, global catastrophe, all within the first sixty minutes of the fade-out.

Soothing radio music and sugarcoated newscasts faded in and out through a rustling noise like a mouse inside a bag of potato chips, while on TV, the best that channel switchers could get was a woozy picture laced with an incoherent pattern of white lines.

During the morning, General Clayson urged the President to brief the other members of the Joint Chiefs of Staff and his Cabinet on the presence of the spacecraft, its extraterrestrial origin, and the current belief that it was the cause of the present fade-out. At that point in time, Washington didn't know about the crater on Crow Ridge, and Volkert, who had found it, didn't know about the spacecraft.

On the advice of Connors and Wedderkind, the President decided not to follow up Clayson's suggestion. Wedderkind had argued that the presence of the space-craft did not, in itself, constitute any immediate threat to the security of the United States. Fraser didn't agree, but his main concern centred on the more tangible dangers that might come from possible moves by Russia or China under cover of the fade-out. He felt that it was on this aspect of the situation that the Joint Chiefs of Staff and, if necessary, the Cabinet, should concentrate their attention.

The President decided to bring in the other Joint Chiefs of Staff, General Wills and Admiral Garrison, but not the members of his Cabinet. In spite of their differences, they all agreed that any unnecessary widening of the involvement at this highly speculative stage of the operation would increase the risk of a serious news leak. The country was already in an uneasy mood, jittery about layoffs, rising prices, the ripple effect of the new downturn in oil prices, and the rising tide of Far Eastern imports that had already caused several chinks of the American industrial landscape to sink without trace. Coming hard on the heels of the morning's air disasters, it didn't need much imagination to see that uncontrolled, uninformed, sensational publicity about the spacecraft's arrival could rip the country apart.

Called in by the President, Connors had laid it on with a trowel – the damage such news might cause to the stock market, banks and other financial institutions, how it would be a field day for every doom-laden end-of-the-world fanatic, rapist, arsonist, and mugger.

As the President sat listening he thought, Perhaps it is only us, who are in power, who fear this thing . . .

Clayson dropped his request and backed into line.

Connors knew that Clayson's concern for open government was not solely out of respect for the Constitution. It stemmed from his belief that the weakened post-Watergate powers of the Executive made it impossible to cover up this kind of collusion indefinitely. All he really wanted to do was keep the Air Force out of trouble until Congress had agreed to buy him another two hundred B-1s.

* * *

Connors dictated two telegraphic-style memos to JoAnne, told her to shut the door, then tuned back in to Wedderkind. 'You know, if we could get to this thing before the Russians and find out how it works, it could give us a real edge . . .'

'Bob – just for two milliseconds try and forget politics. What worries me is the potential power source this thing represents. To create this amount of static all around the world, well it's . . . I mean, the amount of energy you'd need is unbelievable.'

'But surely we already know something about the type of propulsion unit the craft might have. What are the alternatives – nuclear fission, plasma, ion, photon drive? We're already working on them ourselves.'

'On three of them. We've test-fired nuclear rocket reactors but we still haven't got 'em off the ground. The ion motor was tried out in 1964 – to adjust the spin of a satellite. Total thrust .006 pounds. Big deal. Even the giant ones we're planning now will only generate a few pounds' thrust. The photon drive is still on paper. Bob – have you any idea of the difficulties involved? Take the plasma propulsion unit. You fuse deuterium atoms together and you get a fantastic release of energy – plasma – which will push you along. But to generate that energy, those deuterium atoms have to be fused together at over two hundred and fifty million degrees centigrade. And the only way you can do that is to contain the molten mass inside a magnetic field – inside a total vacuum. The problems – ' Arnold waved them away. 'I can't tell you. Just the size of the Large Torus plant out at Princeton, New Jersey . . . and we are still having problems keeping a continuous reaction going for more than one or two *seconds*. But while we are still trying to get it together, it looks as if these *boychiks* have got one

91

working. And not only working – they've built a spacecraft around it and *schlepped* two hundred tons or more right across our galaxy. Maybe even further.'

'Is that really so fantastic?' asked Connors.

'Nearest star?'

'Alpha Centauri?'

'4.3 light years away. Procyon is 10.4, 61 Cygni, 10.7, Ophiuchi, 12. *Light* years. Have you any idea how *far* that is?'

'Yeah, okay – so they travel at the speed of light. Or ninety-nine per cent of it.'

'What about their life support systems?'

'It's unmanned. Nobody's going to send a manned probe first.'

'Who says it's the first?'

Connors didn't answer.

'Even if we discount every flying saucer story, how far would we have to go back to get beyond recorded history? Ten thousand years? On the cosmic time scale that's infinitesimal. It's not even one tick of the clock!'

'Arnold, all our lives we've been conditioned to expect that any contact from outer space is going to be with a civilization far in advance of our own. The chances are it will be. But it doesn't *have* to be so. That could be an unmanned probe up there. Like one of our Surveyor Craft. Now suppose instead of sending out probes to Mars and Venus, we sent one straight up – just aimed in the general direction of the Milky Way.'

'We did,' said Wedderkind. 'Pioneer 10. Launched in March 1972 to fly past Jupiter, then on out of our system.'

'Oh, yes, I forgot.'

'Never mind, go on.'

'Okay, but let's stick with the Surveyor, because it can land. It doesn't get hit by a meteor, it goes on functioning perfectly – '

92

'Powered by what?'

'Solar batteries.'

'But you just left our solar system.'

'Okay, it just coasts along till it reaches another star like our sun.'

'Ah . . .'

'The solar batteries charge up again, the instruments are reactivated. The star has a planetary system. The Surveyor gets pulled into orbit round a planet. It follows a preprogrammed flight pattern, softlands, then starts transmitting data. You know what Surveyor looked like. To an advanced civilization ten thousand years from now, it might seem as sophisticated as an iron bedstead is to us.'

'Bob, even reduced to its simplest form, the problems of controlling an unmanned interstellar flight are still pretty colossal. Even from the nearest star. Say you're four light years out from Alpha Centauri and heading for our sun. At this point you've still got another nine hundred and ninety-six thousand eight hundred *million* miles before you hit Pluto. We're another thirty-one hundred million miles further on. Your instruments confirm the presence of a planetary system. It will take eight years to transmit this news and receive a command signal back from Alpha Centauri.'

'If they're still in business.'

'All right, let's take your preprogrammed package on a random flight path – that just happens to be angled clear of the gravitational pull of Uranus, Jupiter, and Saturn – not to mention the Sun, and aimed right at Earth where we just *happen* to be. I suppose it is just conceivable.'

'Maybe it's programmed to home in on a specific gravitational mass which is emitting x amount of radio waves – in an intelligible pattern. Think of the number of radio signals that have been heading out into space over the last thirty years.'

It was Wedderkind's turn to look at Connors. Connors looked at his watch, then smiled. 'It's no more outrageous than any other theory.'

'True,' Wedderkind said. 'But – and God forgive me that as a scientist I should talk like this – ' Wedderkind tapped his navel. 'Something in here tells me we're in line for more than just an iron bedstead.'

Saturday/August 11

CROW RIDGE/MONTANA

Puzzled by the radiation burns and the inexplicable power failure in the helicopter, the Air Force decided to send a Crash and Rescue Unit and an Aircraft Recovery Team to Crow Ridge by road to pick up the body of the crewman and the downed helicopter.

When they drove up the winding track to the Ridge, they found a pickup truck sent by the Rosebud County sheriff's office stalled alongside Volkert's patrol car. As the Crash and Rescue truck drew alongside, their motor cut out too. The big recovery truck stopped a safe fifty yards behind and the crew hurried forward to help. They found that fuses had blown in all three vehicles.

After checking the area for ultraviolet radiation, the Air Force team walked up through the trees on to the plateau. They found the body of the crewman carefully wrapped in an old, patched canvas truck top. His feet were sticking out at one end. At the other end, someone had planted a rough cross made of branches and tied together with wire. On top of it was the crewman's bloodstained crash helmet.

The Recovery Team went over to the crashed helicopter, circled around it carefully, then exchanged surprised glances. When it had left Glasgow AFB, it had been a drab, regulation olive green. It was now a light pinkish-brown, and the blue around the white star insignia had turned a bright purple.

THE WHITE HOUSE/WASHINGTON DC

In the conference room, they all took the seats they had occupied the previous Saturday.

Army General Wills and Admiral Garrison had had the news about the spacecraft laid on them by the President over supper on Friday. They still looked a little punchy, but Fraser didn't waste any time coming out of his corner.

'All we've got out of this encounter so far is death, damage, and destruction. I say to hell with the possible advances to scientific knowledge. This fade-out constitutes a clear case of aggression. What we have to decide now is when and how to hit back.'

'With what?' asked Connors. 'A ground-to-air missile? With all our electronic guidance systems out of action we've got nothing more sophisticated than an artillery shell. The point I think Arnold is trying to make is that if it is not intentional, then it can't really be classified as aggression.'

'I don't buy that line of logic,' said Fraser. 'A dog doesn't *intend* to catch rabies, but when he does you kill him before he bites somebody.'

True enough, thought Connors. Your ball, Arnold.

Wedderkind tapped his glasses back up the bridge of his nose. 'If the basic assumptions we've made so far are

95

correct, this interference *could* be accidental. On the other hand, it could be part of a planned program.'

'To paralyse our defences.' Fraser looked pleased.

'Exactly,' said Garrison. 'The – '

Wedderkind upped the volume and drowned him out. 'The point I'm trying to make is that such a move need not necessarily be interpreted as aggressive. It could be defensive. It depends.'

'On what, Arnold?'

Wedderkind turned to the President. 'On what happens next.'

'That brings us right back to the mad dog.' said Wills.

Fraser smiled. 'I think Arnold wants us to wait until it bites somebody.'

'I don't think there's any need for us to get paranoid about this.' Wedderkind's blink rate had begun to edge up. 'We didn't land on the moon with the intention of blasting everything in sight. There's no reason to treat a similar landing on this planet as a hostile invasion.'

'The reason we didn't have any trouble on the moon and Mars,' said Fraser, 'was because there was nobody around to shoot back.'

'Exactly,' said Garrison.

'And is that what you want us to do?' asked Connors.

'I think we ought to be ready. Don't you, General?' Fraser turned to Wills.

General Wills pulled the cigar from his mouth and breathed out smoke. He had a soft spot for Wedderkind, but he and Fraser spoke the same language. 'Arnold, this flying crapheap of yours has knocked out our radar, grounded most of our aircraft, and screwed up our global communications. If the Russians or the Chinese had done the same kind of thing, I'd be inclined to say they were being hostile – wouldn't you?'

'Exactly.' Garrison was beginning to sound as if he was stuck in a groove.

'But it's not the Russians or the Chinese,' said Connors. 'They're as much in the dark as we are.'

'We've only got their word for that,' said Fraser.

'Oh, come on, Mel,' said Connors. 'Admittedly we're still hung up over disarmament but in general terms our relationship is on an upward curve, and we've got massive trade treaties with both Russia *and* China.'

'I'm not going to dispute that,' said Fraser. 'You've collected a lot of autographs.'

'It's more than just ink on paper. A lot of these are solid working agreements.' The President's voice had a sharp edge.

'And they'll go on working, Mr President – just as long as we're packing a big gun. But if we get thrown into a survival-type situation, those Red ant heaps will swarm right over us.'

'Mel, we already know how you feel about our foreign policy. Right now, I don't think that's the point at issue. However, in regard to what you have just said, I believe that the American people as a whole still possess the basic resilience, virtues, and vigour that made this country great. There is no doubt in my mind of our ability to survive pretty well in any kind of situation.'

'Mr President, could I – ?'

'Go ahead, Arnold.'

'Look – ' It was palm-spreading time. 'Suppose you were a blind man who had to meet five strange guys in a basement. You have no idea whether they are going to pat you on the back or beat you over the head. What's the safest thing to do?'

'Turn out the lights as you go in?' suggested Connors.

'Right,' said Wedderkind. 'The great equalizer. Might even put you ahead.' He turned to Fraser. 'And it's better than a gun, because if they turn out to be friendly, you can always switch the light back on. Our friend up there has been in orbit for more than a week. He's covered every part of the globe. He's flown past our satellites and all the other junk that NASA's left up there, so he knows he's dealing with an advanced technological society that has a global communications network – '

'Had,' said Fraser.

'And that we're into space flight,' continued Wedderkind. 'An organized society with a mixed economy inhabiting a world of irregularly-shaped land masses separated by water. He's now low enough to pick out cultivated areas and large urban centres. He also knows that *we* know he's up there checking us out. Reaction from us so far? None. No space flight to check him out. No nuclear rocket to blow him up. From the steady static we're getting now, I believe he could have jammed our radar from so far out, we would never have known he was on his way in. But he didn't. We got twenty minutes of fade-out as he slowed down prior to going into Earth orbit, then he let us get a fix on him, scrambling the scopes briefly as he dropped into a lower orbit. Perhaps to see what the reaction would be. Maybe even to warn us.'

'In that case,' said the President. 'I'm glad we decided to maintain a low profile.'

'All right, Arnold,' said Fraser. 'We've sat tight all this time. We didn't try to knock this thing out of the sky. We are now on our way to being totally fouled up. At what point in your theory of nonintervention do we start to feel some of the built-in benefits?'

'It's not down yet.'

'But it could be on its way,' said Garrison, finally getting it together. 'You think this communications fade-out will continue until it lands safely?'

98

'It's not too wild an assumption.'

'What would you like us to do then, Arnold? Put out flags?' Fraser found it hard to resist a smile.

'No, I agree with Chuck. I think we should be ready to defend ourselves if that proves necessary.' His glasses didn't need pushing back up his nose, but he pushed them back anyway. 'I also happen to think that Man's most powerful weapon is an open mind.'

'Arnold,' said Fraser, 'the Defense Department has always encouraged scientific and intellectual curiosity.'

Without which, thought Connors, we would never have had napalm . . .

'Chuck?' It was the President sounding out General Clayson.

'I think we should keep our options open at this point in time. Right now we don't have a great deal of choice. Tactically, we're at a temporary disadvantage, but – ' Clayson smiled. 'I'm trying to master my martial reflexes. Arnold's right. We ought not to consider this situation simply in terms of offence and defence. I go along with his openminded policy, but I'm not too happy about open arms.'

'Yes,' said Fraser. 'The Aztecs of Mexico welcomed Cortez with open arms. What happened? The Spaniards took them apart.'

'They were taken apart by men like you and me,' said Wedderkind. 'The mistake the Aztecs made was in thinking that the Spaniards were gods. The one thing we can be almost sure about is that we're not dealing with men. My guess is it's a machine.'

'That could be a helluva lot worse,' said Wills.

'The only thing worse than Man,' said Wedderkind, 'is a machine made by Man.'

'That's philosophy, not fact,' said Fraser. 'At this point, we don't know where it is, what it is, or *who* it is.'

'We've been calling it a lot of things,' said the President. 'From now on, I propose we use the code name "Crusoe".' The name had surfaced from his subconscious while the others had been speaking.

It was an appropriate parallel. Connors smiled. 'He was a fairly peaceful character.'

'And he didn't screw up the environment of the island he landed on,' added Wedderkind.

'Exactly.' The President allowed himself a brief smile of satisfaction. 'It may turn out to be wishful thinking, but right now, I'd like to think that the choice was intuitive.'

'Let's hope he's read the book,' said Fraser.

Sunday/August 12

OMAHA/NEBRASKA

At eight o'clock on Sunday morning, Fraser took off from Friendship Airport north of Washington and headed westward aboard a privately-owned Learjet. The aeroplane had been discreetly loaned to Fraser by an old friend and major stockholder in an industrial conglomerate to which a recently-awarded defence contract had given the kiss of life.

Fraser had got special clearance for his flight from the Air Force. As the Air Force was subordinate to the Department of Defense, it hadn't been too difficult, but for the less fortunate on the ground below him, the temporary ban on all civil flying had really begun to bite.

The airlines had been sweetened by a suggestion of financial support, but the owners of light planes, executive aircraft, and nonscheduled charter companies were already phoning their Congressmen and associations, and the luckless Federal Aeronautics Administration had been snowed under by a blizzard of protest wires. Not that the FAA needed any prompting. It had summoned representatives from the Civil Aeronautics Bureau, the Air Traffic Control Board, and the airlines to Washington to try and hammer out an emergency service that could be safely handled by the major airports and air crews using a medium-wave network. The meeting had got under way on Saturday morning and was still in progress. By the time Fraser took off, the fade-out had lasted for almost forty-eight hours. And it seemed to be getting worse.

Two and a half hours later, the sleek white aeroplane crossed the Missouri, dipped its starboard wing over the sprawling stockyards of Omaha, then throttled back for the approach run into the Municipal Airport.

The pilot turned off at the first taxiway and parked in front of the tower. As the fuselage door opened and the power steps unfolded, a lovingly-restored dark green Shelby Mustang, like Steve McQueen drove in 'Bullitt' a long, long time ago, pulled up by the port wing.

Fraser zipped up his blue windbreaker. It had the badge of the 'Big E' sewn on the left breast. The captain of the *Enterprise* had given it to him to mark his stay aboard the carrier during Pacific fleet manoeuvres. The pilot opened the cabin locker and pulled out Fraser's set of golf clubs. Fraser looked at his watch. It was 9:30 A.M. local time.

'I'll be back at three-thirty.' Fraser ducked out of the door and waved to the driver of the Mustang as he walked down the steps. General Allbright got out of the car and took Fraser's outstretched hand.

'Mitch – great to see you.'

'It's been a long time,' said Allbright. 'How's Joan?'

'Furious because I didn't bring her along. But she sends her love and says she's just redone the guest room. I think she's expecting you to use it.'

'We'd love to, but we won't be in Washington until November.'

'Could be sooner,' said Fraser. He ran his eye over the Mustang's immaculate showroom finish. It was more than twenty years old but it was still the kind of car a man could leave home for.

SPRING LAKE GOLF CLUB/OMAHA

Allbright and Fraser trundled their golf carts up to the first green and got the game underway.

As they progressed around the course, Fraser briefed Allbright on everything he knew about Crusoe and the crippling fade-out – whose effects had already caused Allbright so much trouble – and the course of action the White House had decided upon.

'I know it's a million-to-one outside chance, but if Crusoe *does* land in the USA in the circumstances I've described, the President is almost bound to let Connors go on masterminding the project. Wedderkind will be in on it too. Connors is working up some kind of cover with McKenna over at the CIA. You know what slippery bastards they are. I want to make sure there's a military element in this operation. Chuck Clayson played it down the middle as usual, but it's pretty clear that the Air Force is going to be involved. The plan is to get them to grab as much of the operation as possible. But in order to do that, Chuck is going to have to put up someone to organize the logistics of the operation, maintain security of the landing site, and who can, if necessary, take over if anything goes wrong. That means it has to be someone nobody is going to argue with. Someone like you, for instance.'

Allbright looked surprised. 'Why me?'

'First, because we both believe in the same things,' said Fraser. 'Second, because this seat is even hotter than the one you've been sitting in for the last three years. I know that, compared to running SAC, it will be a real pinball operation, but for the next few weeks – or months – this is where the action is going to be. And it could turn out to be a lot more dangerous than anything the Russians could throw at us.'

'I realize that,' said Allbright. He thought for a moment. 'How long are we going to stay at DefCon Status 3?'

'Until the end of this emergency. You have a good man as vice-commander. He can hold the fort till you get back. We can cover your appointment by co-opting you on to the National Security Council till this problem gets straightened out.' Fraser grinned. 'At least Fran will enjoy being in Washington. I can't guarantee where you'll be.'

'No . . .'

'Will you take the job?'

'Let me think about it while we finish the game,' said Allbright.

Fraser won by three strokes at eight over par for the course. For lunch, they worked through two charcoal-grilled T-bone steaks at the far table on the terrace.

'What do you see as the real problem with the present setup?' asked Allbright.

'There's a danger of Connors and, through him, the President, ending up in Wedderkind's pocket. We can't afford to let the scientists run away with this thing. Wedderkind is also buddies with the Old Man. He's a real flimflam artist. He can dress up Doomsday and make

103

it sound like as much fun as Halloween. You know what these guys are like, one minute they're happy as sandboys building an atom bomb to blow Japan out of the water, next thing you know, they're spilling their guts to the Russians so they can blow *us* out of the water.' Fraser shook his head and cut into some more red meat. 'That's why I want someone in on this who is aware of the real priorities.'

'But Connors will be in overall charge.'

'On paper, yes. But while he's out of town I plan to cut some of the ground from under him.'

'From what you've said he sounds quite an operator.'

'He's a pretty smooth son of a bitch,' admitted Fraser. 'They call him Snoopy, over at State.'

'What's he like physically?'

'Under medium height. A bit soft at the edges.' Fraser chewed on his steak and searched for an apt but uncharitable description. 'The kind of guy you find in a frilly shirt playing violin in a Hungarian restaurant.'

'Can he be ignored just as easily?' asked Allbright.

'No, but whatever it says on paper, *you'll* be the one in control on a day-to-day basis out there on the ground, backed up by your own people – and you'll have a direct line to me. Connors and Wedderkind may be close to the Old Man, but you and I know what's good for the country.'

'I like to think we do,' said Allbright.

'Will you take the job, Mitch?'

'Yes – if the President orders me to.'

'He will,' said Fraser. 'But just remember one thing – it wasn't *my* idea.'

Wednesday/August 15

It wasn't until thirty-six hours after the mysterious crash of the helicopter that the Air Force at Glasgow finally put together the pieces of the puzzle. Two Air Force medics sent to check up on Volkert found that his ultraviolet radiation burns were several degrees lighter than those sustained by the two pilots. They took a blood sample to check the increase in inorganic phosphorus and calcium, and the Air Force major who had accompanied them formally cautioned Volkert to say nothing about the incident – especially to any member of the press.

The most important piece of the jigsaw was acquired accidentally. On its way back to Glasgow AFB the aircraft recovery truck stopped at Broken Mill to let one of the crewmen buy some cigarettes at Annie's Mercantile. A couple of kids inside the store asked him if he'd come to dig up the 'flying saucer'. He told them that it had been a plane – and that he and the others had just come to recover the body of the pilot.

Glasgow AFB sent a routine UFO sighting report to the Air Technical Center at Wright-Patterson AFB, Ohio, and added the other information they had collected. The message, timed at 11:47 Central Standard Time, triggered off a covert chain reaction that didn't stop until it reached the Oval Room in the White House.

The President asked Connors to follow up the sighting report and find out just what had happened on Crow Ridge.

It took Connors a few days to get the information

105

together without blowing the whole thing wide open, but by Wednesday it looked as if they were in business.

The President studied the aerial photograph of Crow Ridge, then looked up at Connors, Clayson and Wedderkind.

'Is it this crater that is causing the trouble?'

'Yes,' said Wedderkind. 'There appears to be a strong alternating magnetic field around it with an estimated radius of about a quarter of a mile.'

'And was it this that caused the helicopter to crash?'

'We think so,' said Connors. 'The Air Force found that the helicopter's electrical system was completely burned out. Arnold thinks it was caused by a sudden, terrific surge in the current going through the wires. There must have been an instantaneous overload on the circuit. The fuses blew – wham! The pilot lost control.'

'And the patrolman's car?'

'The field cut the current to the spark plugs,' said Wedderkind.

'It also knocked out the tow truck that went to pick it up and the Crash and Rescue truck the Air Force sent to pick up the pieces,' said Connors. 'They all stalled more or less in the same place.'

'And an alternating magnetic field is what causes this?'

'It's one way of doing it,' said Wedderkind. 'During severe electrical storms you get an induction of current in overhead power lines which sometimes causes a breakdown.'

General Clayson pulled out a report. 'The CIA had one of their aircraft equipped for geophysical surveys overfly the area with a magnetometer. It registered a disturbance in the Earth's magnetic field in the area immediately around the crater.'

He placed a coloured photograph in front of the President. 'We also covered it on infrared film. The crater is that hot spot in the middle. It's about twenty degrees hotter than the rest of the plateau.'

'And you're sure this heat wasn't generated by the impact of something hitting the ground?'

'No, it's not an impact crater. The trees have been smashed down around it, but Arnold thinks the hole has been caused by something burrowing into the ground.'

'What about this ultraviolet radiation that burned the pilots?' asked the President.

'That's disappeared,' said Wedderkind. 'But it explains why the Air Force helicopter changed colour – the pigments in the paint reacted to the radiation. It also explains why we couldn't photograph it in orbit. The really interesting thing is this – the burns on the pilots were caused by far ultraviolet. The Deputy Sheriff's burns were less severe – and they were caused by *near* ultraviolet rays. The wavelengths were *longer* – nearer those of visible light. It looks as if Crusoe is changing from something we can't see into something we can.'

The President glanced at the others, then came back to Wedderkind. 'Why has he dug himself in?'

Wedderkind shrugged. 'I don't know. He went to a lot of trouble to get down under cover of the fade-out. Maybe he feels as nervous as we do.'

'What about this magnetic field, Arnold?' asked Connors. 'Radar and radio-wave static is one thing, but if he's going to pull the plug on all our electrical systems – I mean, that's big trouble, right?'

'Yes,' said the President. 'I wouldn't like to think that that was going to spread.'

Arnold's eyebrows shot up along with his blink rate. 'Could I just clarify one aspect of this discussion?'

'Go ahead, Arnold.' It was the President's turn to wave a palm.

'I'm getting the impression that everything seems to be *my* fault.'

'Nobody's blaming you, Arnold. I just want to convey my concern about what has happened, and the dangers that could be facing us. Just what they are and how you deal with them is your problem.'

The President's eyes took in the three of them. 'I want that area isolated with maximum security and minimum publicity. Arnold, your boys will be providing the brain-power and scientific know-how. Chuck, I'm counting on you to put in the manpower and the hardware.'

General Clayson nodded.

'These men will have to be hand picked, Chuck. We may get a situation where they need to be highly motiv-ated – above and beyond the call of duty.'

'We'll be able to handle that, sir.'

'Pick a good man, Chuck. I want someone strong in there on the ground.' The President waved at Connors. 'I want Bob to stay in charge of the whole operation. He will also have letters of authority giving him full powers to mobilize all local military and civilian personnel, estab-lishments, state organizations and resources to deal with any sudden field emergency arising out of this specific situation.'

The President smiled at Connors. 'That doesn't mean the three of you can go out and take over the whole country.'

'Okay,' said Connors. 'But if you decide not to run again, drop us a line.'

'You drop *me* a line,' said the President. 'From Mon-tana.' He got up from his desk. It was a signal that the meeting was at an end.

As Connors ushered the others out of the door, the President called him back.

'Do you think we ought to tell the Russians about Crow Ridge?'

'That option's still open to us,' said Connors. 'But right now, there's not a lot we can tell them.'

'No . . .'

'I think we all got the impression that you thought we ought to sit on the news for a while.'

'Yes – I know I implied that. It was a snap reaction. I just want to know how you feel about it. If the news leaked out, it could damage the relationship we've built up with them. We did, after all, agree on a joint response to Crusoe. You set it up yourself. There was to be no unilateral action.'

'There was to be no unilateral action to *destroy* Crusoe,' said Connors. 'As for the joint response, Arnold has asked Chris Matson to head the Joint Study Group.'

'Bob, we both know that group isn't going anywhere. Chris Matson's been hired to do a snow job.'

'Not entirely. When the group is fully constituted, they'll be working on the problem of the fade-out. It will do whatever we want it to do. The only thing they won't know about is Crow Ridge.'

'Does Chris – ?'

'Yes, he's been fully briefed. We have no security problem there.'

The President still looked troubled. 'There still remains the danger that if the Russians find out we have broken this agreement, it throws into question the integrity of the other agreements we've arrived at, and to which you've contributed. I'm not just thinking about the progress on nuclear weapons and the new trade deals, there's also the whole China thing. I don't want to risk destroying all that. We still have a long way to go before we achieve the goals I outlined in my inauguration speech. I know you wrote it for me but it wasn't just hot air.'

'I'm aware of that.' Connors took a deep breath. 'But I believe that if we told the Russians where we think Crusoe is now, we might put the lives of several millions of Americans at risk.'

The President looked at Connors for what seemed a long time. 'For someone not prone to exaggeration, that's a pretty dramatic statement. Would you like to qualify it?'

'Yes. I believe our original motivation in holding back news of a landing inside America was to try and give ourselves a head start on any alien technology – and especially the processes that caused the jamming on our radar, which we originally attributed to Crusoe's motor. There were other peripheral considerations, including the remote possibility of engaging in a dialogue as ambassadors of a free society, but the main thrust of our thinking was directed towards exploiting any technological advantage to be gained by Crusoe's presence in the USA.'

'I remember our conversations. Go on.'

'That decision was reached before last Friday's breakdown. None of us had anticipated a prolonged jamming of the radar frequencies – or the progressive fade-out of radio transmissions. We're now faced with an escalating open-ended communications problem, the only identifiable source of which is Crusoe. There may still be a command module in orbit, but without radar we have no way of knowing. Crusoe is our only point of reference, and unless we can find some way to switch him off, his presence, here in America, now constitutes a massive liability.'

'But the communications breakdown is worldwide,' said the President. 'The Russians have exactly the same problems.'

'That's true. But just suppose Crusoe *is* the cause of this problem, and we don't manage to find a way to

110

switch him off. If the Russians *knew* where he was, they might decide to try and switch him off without asking us.'

'You mean by a nuclear missile strike?'

'We know they still have contingency plans for a pre-emptive strike against the Chinese nuclear production and research installations. If they're prepared to risk war to remove the threat of a future Chinese nuclear-rocket attack, they might consider a strike on Crow Ridge. Indeed, if things got worse, if we became powerless, they might have no other option but to try.'

The President shook his head in stunned disbelief.

'Would we hesitate to do something similar if we thought we were doing the world a favour?' asked Connors.

'The logic is persuasive,' said the President. 'It's just that the prospect is – well, unthinkable. Surely with this breakdown in the radar . . .'

'You don't need radar to launch a missile strike. You only need it to defend yourself against one. It's a good enough reason for not telling the Russians where Crusoe is.'

'But if we invited a team of their scientists over here to join the project,' suggested the President, 'surely there would be no risk then. They wouldn't turn round and bomb their own people.'

'If we allow them to participate they will know Crusoe's location. Supposing neither the Russians nor ourselves find out how to switch Crusoe off. Suppose we start arguing about what to do next, and reach an impasse – '

'But, Bob, we'd have a negotiable situation. They might issue an ultimatum, but at least we could talk things over with them. People in the area would have a chance to move out. After all, we may be forced to take some drastic action against Crusoe ourselves. Bringing the Russians in on the project would at least eliminate the possibility of their attacking Crow Ridge.'

It was Connors' turn to shake his head. 'You have to remember that however good our relations have been, we're now in an entirely *new* situation – which may cause them to deteriorate rapidly. The fade-out has changed the whole balance of power. General Wills was right. We can't wage a conventional intercontinental land, sea, and air war under these conditions. But the Russians are still in the game. With their huge weight of military manpower they could still fight a non-electronic war. Those tank divisions lining the East German border would be in Bordeaux in under three days and they could roll up the Middle East while the Pentagon was still waiting for dispatches. The only chance we'd have of winning would be by a surprise, all-out nuclear missile attack. They can't defend themselves against that – '

'And neither can we,' said the President.

'Exactly,' said Connors. 'There are only three things that can eliminate the possibility of a surprise Russian attack. One, maintain a low profile and keep making the right noises. Two, radar – and, at the moment, none of our equipment is operational. Three, keep Crusoe's existence and location a secret. If the Russians don't suspect anything, they are no danger to us *or* the project.'

The President's eyes flickered towards Connors, then past on to other points in the room as he considered his proposition. They came back to rest squarely on him. 'Okay, Bob. We'll go it alone.'

Connors felt it was the right decision. Part of the deal he had brought back from Moscow was that in the event of a continuing fade-out, there were to be no infringements of each other's air space, no reconnaissance overflights, no extraterritorial troop movements or fleet reinforcements without prior notification. But since last

Friday, when the second fade-out had begun, the Russians had sealed off Eastern Europe. All borders were closed to traffic. All mail services had been suspended, all Western telephone links had been cut, all movements of embassy staff frozen. The sole remaining link was the 'hot line' between the Kremlin and the White House. Apart from that, nobody could get in or out of Russia and nobody in the West knew what they were up to.

And China had done the same.

Friday/August 17

CONNORS' HOUSE/ROCK CREEK PARK/WASHINGTON DC

There was a brief, exquisite moment of suspended time. Then Connors' mind filled up again with the million and one things he had to do. He closed his eyes and lay back, his head deep in the pillow.

Charlotte raised herself up on one elbow. 'Is it all right if I get dressed?'

'Sure go ahead.' Connors reached for his watch, checked the time, then strapped it round his wrist. 'I'm going to have to get moving anyway.'

Charlotte never liked being naked any longer than was necessary. Connors watched her get out of the bed and scurry self-consciously into the bathroom.

'I wish you wouldn't look at me like that,' Charlotte was now safe behind the half-open door.

'Why not? You're very beautiful.'

Although the statement was patently untrue, it didn't draw a rebuttal from the bathroom. Charlotte was a gifted, intelligent girl of twenty-nine. Or a woman of thirty. That remained to be discovered. But certainly too intelligent to worry about what she looked like. But worry she did – mainly about putting on weight. Her mother suffered from the same problem, a genetic defect that had endowed both of them with an insatiable desire for handmade chocolates and Viennese pastry.

'I'd begun to think I wasn't ever going to see you again.'

'Me too.' And after tonight, that could well happen . . .

'Mother sends her love, by the way.'

'Uh-huh . . .'

'She and Pops almost blew their minds about having the President – I mean you can imagine . . . to have both of them drop in for dinner like that.'

'The man has to eat.'

'You know what I mean, and I love you for it.'

Given Connors' present mood, that seemed a bleak perspective. 'I hope your mother didn't spend too much on the meal.'

Charlotte peeked around the bathroom door, a comb poised halfway through her rich, dark hair.

'Why'd you say that?'

'Because it's going to cost her another half million dollars at the next election.'

Charlotte had a well-developed sense of humour, but she'd been taught to ignore jokes about money.

'Do you have to lie there like that?'

'I'm waiting for the bathroom.'

Charlotte withdrew behind the door to avoid his nakedness.

'Are you going to be out of Washington for long?'

'It depends.'

'And you really can't tell me where you're going?'

'Not yet.'

'Well, I think it's ridiculous. I mean, it's not as if there is a war on or anything.'

114

'Would it make you feel better if I told you I was in Russia a couple of weeks ago?'

'What were you doing there?'

'Just talking.'

'I hear the food there is absolutely terrible. What were you talking about?'

Colonel Sanders. Pizza Hut and Macdonalds have done so well, they want Kentucky Fried Chicken from Moscow to Vladivostock.'

Charlotte finished buttoning up her dress as she came out of the bathroom. She sat on the edge of the bed and pulled a sheet up over Connors. 'Be serious. Do they expect this solar radiation, or whatever it is, to go on jamming the TV and radio much longer?'

'I don't know, Charly. I'm not holding out on you. We don't have the answers yet. The fade-out is like an earthquake or a tornado. We just have to hang tough till it blows over.'

'Is it the fade-out that's making that hissing noise every time I pick up my telephone?' asked Charly.

'Yes. It's something to do with the way the atmosphere is supercharged with static electricity. I don't know exactly how it works, but it's all related. That's why we've had such heavy summer lightning.'

'I read in the paper that in Canada and Europe they're getting the most fantastic displays of northern lights,' said Charly. 'People are staying up to watch instead of going to the movies . . . I'm glad it wasn't the Russians. It makes things a whole lot better to know they're in as big a mess as we are. That's if they're telling the truth, of course.'

'Things could be worse,' said Connors. 'We could have normal, uninterrupted service on all our tv channels.'

Charlotte gave him a look that reminded him of his mother. 'Bob, you're not fooling me. When I can't get a straight answer, it means you've got trouble. Is something bad about to happen?'

'Nothing's about to happen, Charly. Nothing bad, and nothing good either. Things are probably going to go on pretty much as they always have.'

'And this you call reassurance?'

'It's the best I can do.'

Charlotte knelt down by the side of the bed, took hold of his hand, kissed it, then cradled it against her face.

'Do you think you'd be able to talk to me more if I were your wife?'

'If you were my wife, I probably wouldn't be speaking to you at all.'

'Yes, but she wasn't interested in politics. I am.'

Connors got up and went into the bathroom.

When he was washed and dressed, he let her help him pack. Then they went out for supper. Connors would have preferred to stay at home, but he knew Charlotte got a lot of mileage out of being seen with him.

He went along with it because he had decided to be kind and understanding to at least one person in his life. That was what his good half said, and Charlotte had rewarded his attentions in so many ways. His bad half reminded him that her father was into real estate, hotels, and resort development in a big way. Charlotte was not only good company, she was Gucci-shod life insurance.

Saturday/August 18

SANTA BARBARA/CALIFORNIA

Sanford G. Woods was a fifteen-year-old aeroplane buff from Santa Barbara. Every Saturday he would prowl around the airport at Goleta Point, noting down the type, registration number, and owner of every aeroplane he could lay eyes on.

On the eighteenth, Sanford chained his bicycle to its regular spot on the airport fence, checked the lightplane park, then wandered down the depressingly familiar line of big twins to where an ageing B-26 Invader sat on the rim of its wheels, hanging together in the hope that some handsome Colonel of the Confederate Air Force would come and rescue her. It was then that Sanford hit pay dirt.

Two big, four-engined C-130 Hercules transports belonging to Thailand Air Freight had been parked over on the west side for weeks. They were still there, only now they bore the chrome yellow and olive-drab trim of the Mineral Research and Development Corporation, and they were being readied for flight.

With a surge of excitement that only another aeroplane nut could understand, Sanford duly logged the change of ownership and took a photograph of both aeroplanes with his Kodak Instamatic 300. What Sanford didn't know was that there had not, in fact, been any change in ownership. Thailand Air Freight, which had once been busy in Southeast Asia, and the Mineral Research and Development Corporation were both end links of complex corporate chains forged by the Central Intelligence Agency in Langley, Virginia.

Set up late in 1958, the 'front office' activities consisted of aerial and ground geological surveys, mining and drilling. Its overseas operations had provided bases and cover for several successful CIA assignments in the early sixties. They had also resulted in three useful strikes, two of ore and one of oil, which had been leased off for development.

For the last few years, MRDC had just been filing tax

returns from an address in Fort Worth, Texas, but now it was back in business.

Its revival was the result of the meeting between Connors and McKenna at the White House on the Monday of the previous week. Wedderkind had sat in on the meeting while they discussed ways and means of containing a landing site within the United States with a minimum of publicity. A lot depended on Crusoe's manner of arrival, but, unlike Mel Fraser, they had been hoping Crusoe wouldn't choose Times Square.

When he had been given his assignment two weeks before, at the Western White House, Connors had sounded out Air Force General Clayson. While he was happy to help, Clayson had baulked at the idea of a direct containment by uniformed units of the Air Force, and had hinted that the use of Army units might present an even greater risk to the secrecy of the project. The CIA, suggested Clayson, was better organized to mount this unorthodox type of operation – and keep it secret.

There was always the risk that their cover might be blown, Clayson had said, but if the CIA could survive the Bay of Pigs disaster, Chile, the unforeseen collapse of the Shah of Iran and all the other ugly bugs that had crawled out from under the carpet, it could certainly survive any disclosures about its role in the Crusoe Project.

McKenna, who had been with Connors, and had also survived the triple threat, decided Clayson had intended a backhanded compliment. It was in their subsequent discussions in Washington that he'd come up with the idea of using the Mineral Research and Development Corporation. Now that Crusoe was lying buried under a heap of Montana shale, it seemed like the best idea they had had all week.

While Connors and Wedderkind had been talking to the Soviet Premier, MRDC was reactivated and hurriedly restaffed with Texas-based CIA front men. Money was pumped into MRDC's bank account from the Director's Contingency Fund, and the newly-appointed purchasing officer began hiring drill rigs, equipment and basic transportation. By Saturday the eighteenth, just two weeks after Crusoe had been located in orbit, MRDC was in good enough shape to convince even a hard-nosed panhandler that they were the real thing.

Saturday the eighteenth was also a big day for some of the hardier weekend fliers. Following the 'Friday Morning Massacre' and the government ban on all civil flying, airports across the country had been reduced to expensive parking lots. Exactly a week later, following mounting protest from lightplane owners' associations and air charter firms, the Federal Aviation Authority rescinded its order. A brief moment of rejoicing by private fliers and nonscheduled operators was terminated on discovering Catch-22, an almost simultaneous announcement by the aviation insurance companies stating that, for the duration of the fade-out, the cover on their aeroplanes and passengers would become invalid the moment their wheels left the ground. The freeze also included cover on third-party claims.

Despite the sledgehammer caution of the insurance companies, by the week's end, a surprising number of people had taken to the air in what quickly became known as 'Suicide Specials'. Depending on one's point of view, it was either a unique demonstration of faith in the high standard of workmanship of American aeroplane manufacturers, or proof that the pioneer, frontier spirit was alive and well – and airborne.

GLASGOW AFB/MONTANA

Connors left Washington early on Saturday and flew to Glasgow Air Force Base in northeastern Montana. They touched down at 08:10 local time, a full two minutes ahead of their ETA. As the T-39 Sabreliner turned off the runway, a 'Follow Me' truck pulled out ahead of them and led the way to the base of the tower where a Dayglo-jacketed ground handler wheeled them into line with the other parked aircraft.

Connors looked out of his window and saw a blue Air Force Chevy pull up alongside. Greg Mitchell, his chief assistant, was up front with the driver. Another man, whom he didn't know, was in the back.

Connors had sent Greg on ahead the day before to smooth out any wrinkles. A born fixer, Greg earned every cent of his salary – and probably tripled it on the side.

Greg took charge of Connors' thick briefcase while the Air Force driver stowed the two bits of matching luggage in the trunk of the Chevy.

'Good trip?'

'Yes. Where's Arnold?'

'Over at the Base Commander's house waiting for you to have breakfast.'

'Do we have time?'

'For a courtesy call, yes. It's Colonel John Zwickert, by the way. Wife's name is Margaret.'

'Is he in on any of this?'

Greg shook his head. 'He's just pouring the coffee.'

'Who's the guy in the back of the car?'

'Lou Weissmann. He's the Corporation's lawyer.'

The Mineral Research and Development Corporation.

'Okay,' said Connors. 'Let's go.'

The Base Commander's house was a low-slung stone and weathered-timber duplex with deep overhanging eaves. It sat uncomfortably on a mound of lettuce-green crew-cut turf surrounded by flower beds.

Connors decided that it probably looked better after a

heavy fall of snow. He led the others up the curving stone path. Colonel Zwickert and his wife met them on the porch.

The living room was cool, clean, and comfortable, and the breakfast table was laid with the family silver and Mrs Zwickert's grandmother's table linen.

Wedderkind was over by the window, keying an eighteenth-century harpsichord back into tune. 'Isn't this a beauty? I'll be with you in a minute.'

It was long enough for Connors to learn that Mrs Zwickert's grandmother had brought it over from Leipzig along with the table linen, and that she, Mrs Zwickert, had braved the perils of East Germany to visit her grandmother's birthplace during her husband's last European tour of duty.

'There are hot pancakes, syrup, ham rolls, orange juice, coffee, cream for those who want it, and milk for those who don't. I guess you gentlemen will want to talk so I'll leave you to help yourselves.'

The Colonel and his wife withdrew, the Colonel to the base, his wife to a red alert in the kitchen.

Connors poured himself a glass of orange juice. He saw Greg poised with a plate. 'Just a roll and coffee. Black, no sugar.'

'Coming up. Lou?'

Lou Weissmann was already helping himself to two of everything. Wedderkind inspected the food on the table and settled for a cup of coffee. He sat down opposite Connors and stirred in four spoonfuls of sugar. Connors tried to keep a straight face.

'What's so funny?'

'Nothing, Arnold.'

'Listen,' said Wedderkind. 'If I want ham, I eat ham. Only ham I don't feel like. Right?'

121

'Right,' said Connors. 'You tuned her piano. Ask her for a chicken sandwich.'

Wedderkind gave him an owl-eyed look of reproach.

'Are you all set up on Crow Ridge?'

'No,' said Wedderkind. 'They're still at Wright-Patterson.'

'What the hell are they doing in Ohio?'

'Well,' said Wedderkind. 'Some of them are playing chess and the others are considering the cutout zone and what preliminary conclusions can be drawn, if any, from Crusoe's choice of landing site.'

'And what about Clayson's private army?'

Greg swallowed hurriedly. 'That's coming together. Clayson is expected in later today. I guess he'll tell us then who he's putting in charge of the fire engine.'

'Who have you got up on Crow Ridge?'

'Well, nobody right now, Bob. We've kind of run into a little problem on that.'

'What kind of a problem?'

'Well, primarily one of access.'

'You mean we can't get our equipment up there on the existing routes?'

'No . . .'

'Got it. You can't get anything to function in the magnetic field around the crater.'

'No, it's not that either,' said Greg. 'Crow Ridge is owned by a guy called Bodell and – '

'The son of a bitch won't sell,' said Weissmann. He jabbed a forkful of syrupy pancake at Connors.

Connors looked at Wedderkind. 'Hell, I never thought about that.'

'Well, think about it,' said Weissmann. 'He damn near killed one of the Air Force guys that went in to clear that wrecked helicopter. They had to call in a couple of deputy sheriffs to hold him off.'

'Now hold on, Lou,' said Greg. 'You're way over the top there. The only guy that got killed was the crewman from the chopper. The only point Bodell was trying to make was that people should ask him before they start swarming all over the place. The man knows his rights. After all, it is his land – '

'His land?' Weissmann stuffed his mouth full of pancake and waved the empty fork at Connors and Wedderkind. 'The goddamn state gave it to him in 1945!'

'For two hundred and fifty dollars.'

Weissman looked disdainfully at Greg Mitchell. 'Four sections, at ten cents an acre! They gave it to him. It's fronted by the ranch road on one side and Highway 22 on the other, and Crow Ridge is stuck right in the fucking middle!'

'He did win the Congressional Medal of Honor,' said Greg.

'Who didn't?' said Weissmann. His jaws seemed to be endowed with perpetual motion. He began to work through his two ham rolls. 'I checked the lease. It's watertight. Ain't no way to break it.'

'Did that cover mineral rights?' asked Connors.

'Everything. It's deeded land.'

'How about getting it under the law of Eminent Domain?' asked Connors.

'We can't – at least not without blowing our cover so far as everyone else is concerned. MRDC is a private company.'

'Hell, yes, of course . . . did you try for exploration rights?'

'No deal.'

'How much did you offer him?'

'Fifty thousand for a year's lease on the ridge plus twenty-five per cent, gross, off the top, of any subsequent exploitation.'

'Not that there's anything down there,' said Greg.

'Then why twenty-five per cent? Why not give him fifty?'

Weissmann pointed half a roll at Connors. 'I once made that mistake in Ecuador. When the ink was dry we found we were sitting on a lead mountain. That's when we started recruiting geologists. You have to structure these deals right. Give too much away and you blow it. This guy isn't interested in money.'

'Did you try just the one time?'

'Twice. I waited till he drove out, then went back to talk to his wife. She's dumber than he is, and the place – I can't tell you . . . a hovel. I'm thinking of having my clothes burned. Anyway, I'm listing all the good things in life she can buy with the money when Bodell walks back in through the door and pulls this shotgun on me.'

'You're still in one piece,' said Connors.

'Just,' said Weissmann. 'The raggedy-assed son of a bitch pumped five slugs into the trunk of my car. Twelve-gauge BB, clean through. Bastard. You can never match the fucking paint.'

'It's the pigments,' said Wedderkind. 'They're unstable.'

'Where did Bodell win his Medal of Honor?' asked Connors.

'Okinawa. Got a Purple Heart with cluster, too.' As usual, Greg had done his homework.

'The Japs should have killed him,' said Weissmann.

'I think I know how we might be able to get to him,' said Connors.

'So do I,' said Weissmann. 'Get them both on the southbound lane of the highway and have a northbound Mack truck cross over the centre line. It never fails.'

Connors' solution was just as effective, but not so messy.

One of Greg's assignments had been to set up a direct telephone link with the White House. Connors called the President, outlined the Bodell situation and his proposed solution, then got Greg to type a letter on his portable Smith-Corona. They used a sheet of the pale blue paper with the Presidential seal and the words 'From the office of the President'. Connors always carried a few sheets around in his briefcase.

'Who's this supposed to be from?' asked Greg.

'The President,' said Connors. 'Just type his name and I'll sign it.'

Greg eyed him for a second, then finished the letter. Connors added a passable forgery of the President's looping signature. Greg folded the letter and sealed it in the matching envelope.

'Let me take it up there,' he said.

'Not a chance,' said Connors. 'I'm going to enjoy this.'

CROW RIDGE/MONTANA

Officially, Volkert was still on sick leave that Saturday, but the sheriff's office in Forsyth pulled him in to drive Connors up to see Bodell. 'Seein' as how you two is almost kin,' the Sheriff had said. It was true that Volkert was one of the few people outside Broken Mill Bodell had spoken to during the last twenty-odd years.

When Volkert had called at his shack with the two pilots from the crashed helicopter, Bodell had surprised him by offering them a lift to Broken Mill without being asked. His conversation on the way there had consisted of no more than a dozen words, eked out one at a time, yet as he sat watching him gulp his Adam's apple up and down, Volkert had the feeling that Bodell's throat was stuffed full of words like fish in a pelican's beak – but that, like the pelican, Bodell preferred to swallow them

125

rather than open his mouth and risk giving something away.

Volkert met Connors' helicopter at Broken Mill. He offered Connors a back seat but Connors took the front. They set off down the dirt road west of the highway. It ran in a straight line for three long, empty miles before dipping out of sight. Fifty yards ahead of them, a hawk flapped prudently off a fencepost and skimmed away on curling, loose-fingered wings.

Beyond the rise, another stretch of straight road narrowed towards the next horizon. Volkert forked left on to an even rougher road that snaked up into some low buttes.

'This man Bodell,' said Connors. 'Does he give you a lot of trouble?'

'Hell, no,' said Volkert. 'It's them Air Force boys of yours that's doing that. What in hell'd they go and drop up there – some new-fangled kind of bomb?'

'I don't know,' said Connors. 'It's not really my department.'

'Well, whatever it was, it damn near burned the hide offa me.' Volkert grinned. 'If I'd gone any blacker, they'd've run me out of town on a rail.'

Connors glanced at Volkert's peeling face. 'Must've been pretty painful. Did anyone say what might have caused it?'

'No. But I've had at least eight people telling me the whole thing's classified, so you'd better forget I said that.'

'Don't worry,' said Connors. 'I will.'

Weissman's reaction to Bodell may have lacked a certain cool, legal objectivity, but his description of Bodell's place was right on the nose. The one-storey wood-frame house had been constructed from the weathered remnants of several abandoned claimshacks. The effect was messy, but it looked solid enough. It would

126

need to be. In the winter, the wind that swept across eastern Montana cut like a riptoothed buzz saw.

Volkert turned the car around so that it pointed downhill. This also put Connors between him and the house. No doubt it could prove useful if they had to drive away in a hurry. Connors didn't say anything.

'Better let me go up ahead of you,' said Volkert, then added with engaging candour, 'If he sees that suit he might think you're another of them Jewboy hustlers.'

Connors nodded towards the pines that acted as a windbreak for the house and covered the flanks of the ridge above. 'How come there are so many trees around here?'

'Bodell,' said Volkert. 'He planted them. Been doing it for years.'

'What does he do with them – cut them down for lumber?'

'Nope. He just keeps putting 'em in.'

'Why?' asked Connors.

Volkert shrugged. 'I guess he must like trees.'

Brown and white chickens scattered in front of them as they picked their way across the junk-littered yard. A pair of stained, patched long johns swung limply from a line. The line was tied to the cab of a gutted '52 Ford pickup that had weeds growing through the chassis.

As they ducked under the line, a voice said, 'That's far enough.'

Connors felt the skin quiver on his back. Volkert stopped, eased up the brim of his stetson and scanned the front of the lifeless house. 'Just turn around nice and slow,' he said quietly. He didn't look at Connors.

Bodell stepped out from behind the truck. He had an old Winchester pump shotgun cradled in his left arm. His right hand was on the trigger. His US Army-issue shirt and braces looked as if they had been around since Pearl

Harbor, his trousers even longer. Thick with grease and black as crankcase oil, they hung around his thin legs like crumpled stovepipes. A khaki-coloured baseball cap was pulled hard down over deepset eyes.

'Morning, Luke,' said Volkert. 'This gentleman here's from Washington and he's got some mighty important business that concerns you and Sarah.'

'I sure as hell hope he ain't come here to try and buy nothing.' Bodell's wind-whipped face was as friendly as a clenched fist.

'No, he's brung you a letter from the President of the United States of America. And that's a fact, Luke. I seen the envelope myself and your name and Sarah's is right there on the front of it.'

Connors pulled the envelope out of his inside pocket and held it out for Bodell to see. Bodell took a couple of steps forward and gingerly took the envelope. He read his name and address with a frown, then turned over the envelope to look at the Presidential seal on the flap. He considered it for a while, then looked at Connors.

'Why the hell would he sit down and write to me? I don't even know the man.'

'Well, he knows you, Mr Bodell. Your name's in the history books of World War Two.'

'What's he care about that? He weren't nowhere near bein' President then.'

'No,' said Connors. 'But he *was* on Okinawa.'

Bodell considered the letter again. He lowered his shotgun. 'Does he remember that?'

'Yes, he does.'

'I think maybe we should go inside,' said Bodell.

The one big barnlike room was partitioned off with old curtains hung on lines that doubled as wardrobes. What furniture there was had been salvaged from junk heaps. There were also books. Piles of them, everywhere. Some

128

on shelves made out of old planks and upended bricks, but most of them on the floor. All kinds of books, secondhand battered books, books with covers missing, books still tied together with string that looked as if they had been bought by weight, still covered with the dust from someone's attic.

Connors noticed a Mobil Calendar for 1947 on the wall. Whoever tore off the pages had stopped at the month of November. It wasn't as bad as Weissmann had said, but Connors felt a long way from home.

Bodell's wife Sarah had pale, wispy hair tied tight at the back with baling twine. She was wearing a washed-out, nine-dollar-fifty mail-order dress with an apron over it. Her elbow and wrist bones seemed to be two sizes too big for the rest of her body.

She hurriedly dusted a chair for Connors, then he sat down at the table with her and Bodell. In the middle of the table was a bunch of yellow wild flowers in a pickle jar. Volkert leaned against the porch door with his arms folded.

Bodell had the kind of hands that could skin a rabbit in under a minute, but it was painful to watch him trying to open the envelope.

He studied the letter line by line with the frowning concentration of a graduate reading an exam paper, his mouth half-forming the words. When he had finished, he passed the letter to his wife.

Despite the piles of books, Connors wasn't sure whether Bodell or his wife could read very well. Maybe they used them to feed the stove. He decided to explain things rather than risk causing them any embarrassment.

'You see, every year since the President has been in office, he has invited one or more holders of the Congressional Medal of Honor and their wives to be his guests at the White House.'

129

'What outfit was he with on Okinawa?' asked Bodell.

'The Air Force,' said Connors. 'He flew one of the first bombing missions to Japan after you Marines had secured the island.' It was a lie, of course, but only a small one. The President's squadron of B-29s didn't arrive on Okinawa until after the Enola Gay had dropped the big one on Hiroshima, August 6, 1945.

'That was quite a fight,' said Bodell.

His wife Sarah got up from the table, went behind one of the curtained partitions and brought back a bundle of red cloth.

Bodell carefully unwrapped it and it became a tattered, blood-stained Japanese flag. Connors found himself hoping that he wasn't in for a rerun of World War Two, then hated himself for thinking that, and thought of how to short-circuit the conversation. All he wanted was to get Bodell on the hook, and up and out of there. The President would do his snow job, and the way would be clear to get at Crusoe.

Inside the flag were two medal cases, a folded photograph and a string necklace of dog tags. Bodell opened the cases. One was the Medal of Honor, the other the Purple Heart with cluster. They gleamed on the velvet like newly-minted coins, the ribbon colours bright and clear, untouched by time.

'Harry Truman handed them to me,' said Bodell.

'He was a good man,' said Connors.

'Yes, he was. They had good men around then.'

Mrs Bodell had been looking at the photograph. She put it back on the table. It was a news syndicate picture of a young soldier and a girl on the grounds of the White House. A young marine holding an open medal case. The smiling girl, in a shoulder-padded dress and Andrews Sisters haircut, holding another. The medals were the only thing Connors could recognize.

Bodell fingered the necklace of dog tags like a rosary. 'They was all my buddies,' he said. 'Guadalcanal, Iwo Jima. Okinawa . . . I was the only one who made it.'

'I know it's short notice,' said Connors. 'But if you'd like to accept his invitation, I could arrange for a car to pick you up tomorrow. There'll be a plane standing by to fly you to Washington.'

He gave them both his look of statesmanlike concern. 'As you and your wife will no doubt appreciate, the President's schedule is pretty tight. But one thing I can promise you – ' Connors touched the folded photograph. 'The President will be in the picture with you this time.'

Bodell looked at his wife for a long moment, then closed the medal cases. 'Should I take these along with me?'

'Yes,' said Connors. 'I think you should.'

As Bodell rolled his souvenirs back into the folded flag, Connors knew he had it all wrapped up. Tomorrow, Bodell and his wife would be on their way to Washington, and on Monday, the Corporation would be up on Crow Ridge.

Volkert took Connors back from Bodell's house to Broken Mill with the speedometer needle wavering between fifty and sixty. Pebbles from the loose, gravelly surface spurted from under the tyres and whacked against the arches and subframe like machine-gun fire. Behind them, a trail of dust hung in the air. Volkert drove with his left elbow out of the window and his right hand resting on the bottom of the rocking steering wheel. Several times Connors thought they were going to bounce out of the ruts and into the ditch on his side of the car.

'Do you have to take it this close?'

Volkert looked across at him with a grin. 'If you're plannin' on drivin' round here, Rule One is to git yourself just as far over to the right as she'll go without cuttin' hay.'

'Why's that?' asked Connors.

''Cause the cowboys take their half out of the middle.'

Having conjured up the spectre of a head-on collision with a speeding car hidden in a dip in the road, Volkert put his foot on the floor and surged towards the next rise at over sixty.

Connors, who had made the mistake of watching all the slow-motion crash tests on TV, tightened his safety belt into a tourniquet across his stomach and tried not to think of himself curving through an exploding windscreen like those chamois-leather-faced dummies.

Volkert's twentieth-century trail lore was sound. As they crested yet another rise, Connors suddenly found himself looking down the throat of a red GMC pickup coming at them up the slope, right out of nowhere. Five seconds slower coming over the top and one foot over to the left and they'd have taken him right in the kisser.

'Whoo-eee . . .' said Volkert laconically. His left elbow was still hanging out of the window as they ploughed back on to the road. 'See what I mean?'

Connors did – and could have done without the demonstration. This was obviously a Montana version of Russian roulette – probably played for his benefit. It was only four more miles back to Broken Mill but it seemed like four hundred.

They found the waiting Air Force helicopter surrounded by a small crowd of young kids. The two pilots were doing a great recruiting job.

Volkert shepherded the kids back out of the way as Connors climbed gratefully into the cabin. Up front, the pilot wound up the rotors to takeoff speed, then lifted off, nose down over the patrol car and away in a steep climbing turn towards the north.

Connors saw the kids wave to him and waved back. When he'd been young, it was always something he'd wanted people in aeroplanes to do.

Greg Mitchell was waiting by the landing pad when the helicopter touched down at Glasgow AFB. He ducked in under the whirling blades and escorted Connors over to the same Air Force Chevy.

'General Clayson's over in the Base Commander's office with a couple of aides.'

'Have you talked to him?'

'No, but Arnold's over there.'

'Did that guy Volkert get through to you with my message about Bodell?'

'Yes. I've fixed up transportation. We'll have them out on schedule.'

They rode the rest of the way to the Base Commander's office in silence. The two-man KP detail sweeping the path stood aside to let them through. Connors shook his head. 'We've barely started and already there are more people involved than on de Mille's *Ten Commandments*. How are we going to keep them all from sounding off?'

'We could always recruit them on to the project.'

'That's not a bad idea,' said Connors. 'Maybe we could work on that. What about the Crash and Rescue Team?'

'They've been reassigned to Thule in Greenland. Flew out this morning. That still leaves another twenty or so up at Glasgow with some peripheral involvement – and that deputy who was up on Crow Ridge at the time of the crash. Volkert.'

'I don't think we need worry too much about him,' said Connors.

'You mean he's too dumb to realize what's going on?'

'No, I wouldn't call him dumb,' said Connors, 'but he's certainly not about to rush out and discover gravity. What about those other guys from the county sheriff's office who were up on Crow Ridge the day after the crash?'

'They're covered.'

'What about the local newspapers? If they're like the ones back home, you only have to sneeze and they print your name and address and where you bought the Kleenex. If they pick it up, the wire services may – '

'Don't worry,' said Greg. 'The Corporation is taking care of all that.'

The outer office was secured by a captain from the base and Clayson's two Air Force aides. The captain bore the look of someone who had expected to have the whole of the weekend off. One of Clayson's aides took them on through.

'Bob. Nice to see you.' Clayson got up from behind the Base Commander's desk. Wedderkind was sitting over on the sofa. 'Arnold's been telling me about the legal problem you ran into.'

'We should have the all clear on that by midday Monday. Right now, we've got a bigger problem. Has Arnold told you about the cutoff zone round the crater?'

'He's told me he thinks it's an alternating magnetic field, generated by whatever is buried down there.'

'Right.'

'And that it has a neutralizing effect on electrical current.'

'That's it. As soon as any electrical system enters the field, a surge starts to build up in the current. This overloads the circuit to the point where – depending on the system – it burns out, blows a fuse, or trips the circuit breaker that automatically shuts off the power when the circuit becomes overloaded. Which is great, because all you have to do is reset the cutout to switch everything back on. But as fast as you do that, the surge builds up and the circuit cuts out again.'

'We haven't tested the field exhaustively,' said Wedderkind. 'But the preliminary experiments carried out along the access road indicate that the effect of the surge is weakest on the extreme edge of the field – about a quarter of a mile from the crater. As you move inward, there's a rapid, and rather dramatic, buildup. The magnetometer we took with us wasn't calibrated far enough. The reading went right off the dial.'

'And we're also screwed for transportation,' said Connors. 'If we want to move any heavy equipment into the cutout zone, we'll have to use diesel-engine trucks. We'll have to pull out the electric starters, and fit cartridge starters like the Air Force uses on their jet engines. That's going to need some snappy conversion work. I don't quite know what we'll do for lighting.'

'Acetylene lamps,' said Greg. 'Beyond that quarter-mile radius, of course, you should be able to use all the normal equipment.'

'I hope you can.' Clayson looked worried. 'Communications are getting to be a big problem. The radar wavelengths are still jammed, the fade-out on the TV and radio wavelengths has got worse. And we're starting to get some bad line interference too.'

Connors looked at Wedderkind, then back at Clayson. 'How's the world taking that?'

Clayson shrugged. 'It's hard to get the whole picture from Washington, but we seem to be building towards a global-sized jam in the telecommunications network. If we don't get a break soon, the wires are going to burn out.'

'We're going to need some lines of communication ourselves,' said Connors. 'Can the Air Force get us hooked up to Washington?'

135

'The Air Force has troubles of its own,' said Clayson. 'Hell, have you forgotten? We've lost contact with all our military navigation, and communications satellites as well. We've got a major operational crisis on our hands.'

'You'll be able to handle it,' said Connors.

'Yes . . . I'll see what I can do.'

'Give it top priority, Chuck. We could find ourselves in a situation that needs a fast call to the White House. I want to be able to pick up a phone and get straight through.'

'Right now, I can only guarantee one thing,' said Clayson. 'If it's urgent, we'll fly you there.'

'Great,' said Connors. 'I'm going to end my life as a carrier pigeon.'

'There's one other thing worrying me. How is this solar radiation theory going to hold up? We've had over a week of intense fade-out and my people tell me that there's no observable flare activity on the sun at the moment. Everyone with a telescope is going to know that too. Aren't they going to start asking questions?'

'They already are,' said Wedderkind. 'But the marvellous thing is they're already coming up with answers. There's nothing scientists like more than proving that their colleagues have got hold of the wrong end of the theoretical stick. Right now, the freak-solar-flare school is standing around with egg on their faces. The current theory is that the fade-out is caused by a prolonged burst of deep-space radiation.'

'Where from?' asked Clayson.

'No one knows. All our radio telescopes are out. But there's some talk that a quasar might have gone supernova.'

Connors grinned. 'That's not a bad theory. Crusoe is the source of the interference and he is from deep space.'

'Yes, but there's one thing that worries me,' said

Wedderkind. 'Fraser used the times that the radar stations broke down to prove that Crusoe wrapped a residual band of interference clear around the globe while he was in orbit. If he's under Crow Ridge, and if he is the cause of the fade-out, then he must be doing it in a different way.'

'Do I gather you no longer think Crusoe's propulsion unit is the cause of the interference?' asked Clayson.

'That idea still holds, but only just. What's beating me is how the interference is spread so evenly through the whole atmosphere. I would have expected some falloff the further you got from Montana.'

'Maybe he's beaming it right through the Earth and out the other side,' said Greg.

'I'll go one better than that,' said Connors. 'Maybe there's still a mother ship in orbit.'

'Don't,' said Clayson. 'Don't make it any worse. Are we any nearer knowing what causes the fade-out, Arnold?'

'Well, advance reports indicated tremendous disturbances in the Earth's magnetic field. This data takes time to filter through so we don't have a complete picture yet. The Telluric currents – that's a measurable electric current flowing through the Earth itself – this week reached the highest level ever recorded. This rise indicates an intense – and continuing – magnetic storm. There have also been some extraordinary displays of northern lights. I don't need to tell you about the thunderstorms and lightning. Today we got the first data back from the small research rockets we sent into space. The measurements show that the ionosphere is saturated with negatively-charged particles, and there's been a fivefold increase in the amount of cosmic radiation in the two Van Allen belts. Any new satellite we put up would be knocked out immediately . . .'

'Well, at least that's one thing we have going for us', said Greg.

'A communications fade-out makes it a whole lot easier to keep this project under wraps.'

'What about this place called Broken Mill?' asked Clayson.

'There are only a dozen people down there,' said Connors. 'The Corporation is going to check their mail and outside calls.'

'And once you've set up shop, what happens if any of them come looking for a job?'

'The plan is to set up a "front office" operation at the junction of the dirt road with Highway 22. It will also act as base camp for the Ridge. There aren't going to be any vacancies but we plan to use local suppliers for minor services and part of our food. We want it to look as though there's only a handful of people involved.'

'The local people are pretty used to this kind of thing,' said Greg. 'Oil companies have had outfits prowling around eastern Montana for years.'

Clayson nodded. 'And your centre of operations?'

'I think we have to put everything up on Crow Ridge. We flew a wide circle around it before landing at Broken Mill today. There's enough space to set up the accommodation we need and the facilities that Arnold's team has asked for. But first we have to secure and fence off the whole ridge. Which is where your people come in. We can't really start moving until they get here.'

Clayson looked at his watch. 'They should be landing at Billings about now.'

Billings was about one hundred and fifty miles west of Crow Ridge. By road, it was nearer two hundred.

'They're coming in on MRDC aircraft. That's why they are using a civilian airport. You'll have a unit of fifty topgrade technicians. All master sergeants or above, and

138

all with good security classifications. Most of them are from Kirtland.'

Kirtland AFB was the Air Force's Special Weapons Center, situated deep in the desert of New Mexico. Only a very few people knew the full scope of its operations.

'There is a second unit of two hundred and fifty men,' continued Clayson. 'They will provide the manpower for your basic workforce, and will be available for any kind of duty.'

'Where do they come from?' asked Connors.

'They are all third- or fourth-year cadets from the Air Force Academy at Colorado Springs. All volunteers. You'll find them intelligent, tough, and highly motivated.'

Clayson was right. It would have been hard to imagine a more gung ho bunch than the senior classmen from Lowry. 'Who's holding the reins?' asked Connors.

'General Allbright.'

'Allbright? The head of SAC?' Connors stared in surprise at Clayson, then looked at Arnold Wedderkind. He got the feeling that Arnold already knew.

'You don't look too happy,' said Clayson.

'I should,' said Connors. 'He's one of the best men you've got.' He smiled. 'I guess the reason I looked surprised was because I wasn't expecting anyone so – high-powered.'

'I can't think of a better man to back you up in this situation.'

'Neither can I', said Connors. 'I've never met him but I've heard he's – '

'An extremely able and totally dedicated commander,' added Clayson.

Connors had the feeling he was being oversold. He heard a phone ring in the outer office. Someone answered it, then buzzed the call through to one of the phones on the Base Commander's desk. General Clayson picked it up, listened, then smiled.

'Good. Let me speak to him.' A pause. He looked at Connors and Wedderkind. 'Allbright . . . Hello, Mitch? . . . glad you could make it.' Clayson listened some more, then said, 'No, there's been no change in the situation . . . No, I'll be flying back straight to Washington.' And then, looking at Connors, 'Mitch, I'm going to hand you over to someone who's very anxious to meet you. I won't come back on the line, so I'll say good-bye – and good luck. Keep in touch. Oh, how's Frances? . . . Good. Bob Connors will speak to you now.'

Connors took the phone. 'Hello, General Allbright? General Clayson just gave me news about your assignment to this project. I'd just like to say, at this point, that we all feel very good about having you on the team, and that I'm looking forward to meeting you.'

'Why, thank you very much, Mr Connors. I'm also looking forward to meeting you.' Allbright's voice had a dry cutting edge – like Gregory Peck in *Twelve O'clock High*.

Connors explained the situation to Allbright, and between them they arranged that his party would stay overnight at Billings. The MRDC transport aircraft would then fly the Air Force technicians and their mobile workshops into Miles City during Sunday.

The CIA advance party that was to man the MRDC 'front office' operation had arrived the day before. Lodged on the outskirts of town at the Red Rock Motel, they had already begun to integrate themselves into the local scene. The process, reportedly, had not been a difficult one. The roadside billboards justly proclaimed Miles City 'The Friendliest Town in the West' and proof of Miles Citians' famous hospitality came within hours of their arrival when two of the more aggressive members of the party drank themselves into a warmhearted, welcoming fistfight with local ranch hands outside the Buffalo Bar.

The sober element of the Corporation would provide transportation for the Air Force Academy cadets to travel in varying-sized groups by road to Crow Ridge. Connors suggested that it might be a better idea than having two hundred and fifty straight-backed young men march out of Miles City's modest airport which, according to Greg Mitchell, only came alive twice a day when a twin-engined Otter of Frontier Airlines flew in.

Allbright took it rather well. Connors hung up with the thought that he might even have a sense of humour. Which was good – except that Allbright hadn't been injected into this situation because he was a laugh-a-minute man. There was more to it than that. Connors had the feeling that, while he was managing the road show out in Montana, Fraser was back in Washington rewriting the script.

Sunday/August 19

ROCK CREEK PARK/WASHINGTON DC

After his telephone conversation with Allbright, Connors left Greg to mind the store in Montana and flew back overnight to Washington with Wedderkind. Connors would have liked to talk to him about the Allbright-Fraser connection, but once they were airborne Wedderkind switched off and went to sleep. Connors closed his eyes but his brain kept ticking and didn't wind down until they reached Andrews Field. He dozed off in the back of the car on the way to his house in Rock Creek Park, and when he got home, he drew the curtains and went to bed.

At midday, he rang Charly.

'Weren't you supposed to be out of town?'

Connors yawned. 'Change of plan.'

'You sound as though you're still in bed.'

'I am.'

'Are you, ah – going to be in town for long?'

'Till tomorrow morning. I have to see the President.'

'He's at Camp David,' said Charly. 'They announced it on the radio.'

'Thank God something's still working.'

'One measly station,' said Charly. 'Just music and newscasts. The police and fire department and the airports have taken over the medium-wave bands. Most of the Sunday papers say that the fade-out may get worse. They say it may take out all the long-wave stations too.'

'Are you frightened?'

'I don't know. Not really. I only listen to the radio in the car, and I hardly ever watch TV. But why do you ask – is there anything to be frightened about?'

'No,' said Connors. 'But I guess a lot of people must be worried when things like the TV networks and airlines are hit.'

'That's it. People take them so much for granted. If only someone would tell us how long this thing is going to last. One could at least make plans. But with all this uncertainty – '

'Yes . . .'

Although the FAA had lifted the ban on private flying, the newspapers had carried ads from all the major airlines announcing the suspension of all scheduled services for the duration of the fade-out. After test flights with volunteer crews, the airlines had decided that they could not operate even a limited passenger service with what they regarded as an acceptable degree of safety.

Talks had started at the Treasury on a proposed Federal subsidy to cover the loss of revenue suffered by the airlines. The big question was, how much, and whom to help? The airline shutdown had had a domino effect on a surprising number of service industries, and there was the bizarre prospect of Jumbo-jet pilots joining the queue for food-stamps. Without prompt and effective aid, they would not be the only ones waiting in line.

'How are your mother and father taking it?' asked Connors.

'They're worried, what else? Dad's lost a lot of money. Okay, most of it is just on paper, but it was a bad week on Wall Street. The bottom fell out of the big electricals. The total losses are around twelve billion dollars – right across the board.'

'Sounds like a good time to buy.' Any money Connors had he kept in the bank, but if the fade-out continued, it might prove smarter to stuff it under his mattress.

'Wall Street's not the only problem,' said Charly. 'Now that fewer people are able to fly, the whole holiday scene is a real disaster area. Do you realize how much money we have tied up in hotels and resort development?'

'Yeah, it must be tough,' said Connors. 'I'd better get started for Camp David.'

'If you're coming back to town tonight, do you want to come over?'

'For supper?'

'Well, that depends on what time you get here.'

'Okay, listen, I'll give you a call from Camp David.'

'Marvellous.'

'Don't get too excited, I've got a big day tomorrow.'

There was a second's hesitation at the other end of the

line. 'I really don't know what my mother sees in you,' said Charly.

When Connors arrived, the President was just finishing a late lunch. Connors joined him and the First Lady for coffee, then set off with the President for a digestive walk through the woods. A few yards away, on either side of the path and behind them, were six of the President's Secret Service bodyguard. Up ahead, two more rode point.

Connors gave him the fine print on the Crow Ridge situation and some additional background material on Bodell. 'I won't be here tomorrow but you won't have any trouble with him.' Connors smiled. 'He's one of the few genuine silent heroes we have left.'

'Yes,' said the President. 'We could do with a few more. Where will you be?'

'Ohio. I'm flying out to Wright-Patterson to meet the people Arnold has pulled in for the project. He flew up to Boston today to round up the last of the stragglers.'

'Has he picked good men?'

'I'll have to call you tomorrow on that,' said Connors. 'Knowing Arnold, I imagine he's got the best available. Not all the people he contacted were willing to go into this thing blind – with no guarantee of coming out at the other end. But the last time I talked to him, he sounded fairly happy. I think his team will stay out in front.'

'You make it sound like some kind of contest.'

'Well, let's face it. Crusoe isn't the only one in this ball game.'

The President's face gave nothing away. 'That second helping of pie must have slowed me down. What is it you're trying to tell me?'

'I thought we had decided to set up the Crusoe Project as a civilian operation, using a CIA company as cover – with the Air Force supplying secondary personnel for the workforce and basic technical backup.'

'Isn't that what you've got?'

'No. What we've got is General Allbright, Commander in Chief of the Strategic Air Command, and the Air Force poised to make a takeover bid on behalf of the Defense Department.'

'That sounds like something written by one of your friends in Hollywood,' said the President.

'Who wired Allbright into the project?'

'I did. Chuck Clayson put him at the top of his short list. I saw no reason to reject his recommendation, and I certainly didn't expect you to object.'

'Chuck didn't put him on that list. He wanted to keep the Air Force's involvement to a minimum,' said Connors. 'We don't need a heavyweight like Allbright to run that site, we – '

'We need the best men we've got. Why do you think I put you in charge?'

Connors shrugged. 'You may have put me in charge of the project, but are we going to be able to keep control of it? I think we'll find that Fraser put Allbright on to Crow Ridge. And if he did, Allbright is there to do more than just count the C rations.'

'I take your point, but I don't see that we have a problem,' said the President. 'What you seem to have forgotten is that all three of you are working for *me*.'

There really was no answer to that.

Monday/August 20

Wedderkind was waiting for Connors when he stepped off the Jetstar at Wright-Patterson. Emerging from the cool filtered light of the aircraft's interior, Connors was momentarily dazzled by the huge expanse of sunbleached concrete. Overhead, the sky was a cloudless cobalt blue. He put on his mirrored sunglasses.

Wedderkind took his outstretched hand, and clapped him on the shoulder. 'Hi. Do you want something to eat?'

'No, thanks. I had breakfast just before I left.' He walked with Wedderkind towards a metallic-blue, top of the range, BMW. 'Is this yours?'

Wedderkind pulled the door open. 'No, it belongs to a friend of mine who works here. He's one of the top men at the Aerospace Research Lab.'

They got into the car. 'Not bad,' said Connors. 'At least whoring for the military has some compensations.'

'Don't give me that old radical crap,' said Wedderkind. 'If we hadn't helped make America strong, who in the world would be interested in what you people in the White House had to say?'

Touché . . . 'I was only joking, Arnold.'

Wedderkind put the car into gear. 'Let's go and meet the folks.'

Wedderkind had recruited a pair of physicists, biologists, and chemists from different university campuses. All six had been engaged in or had contributed to the space program at one time or another. He had also pulled in a geographer who doubled as a historian, and a language scientist who would have the well-nigh impossible task of trying to decipher any signs of communication that might emanate from Crusoe. The team was completed by four systems engineers from NASA and another two borrowed from the Air Force.

Connors had a hard time remembering all their names the first time around. One thing, however, was clear. They all knew Arnold very well, and they all seemed to have known each other for a long time. That in itself was hardly surprising. What intrigued Connors was their reaction to Crusoe's arrival. Somehow, he had imagined they would have been more excited, more surprised. Amazed, even. But, as they talked to him, he couldn't help feeling like an outsider who had blundered into a carefully prepared private reception for a long-awaited guest.

Once he'd met everybody, Connors took a private coffee break with Wedderkind.

'The Air Force shot some more infrared film early yesterday and early this morning,' said Wedderkind. 'The heat source is still directly under the crater but it's a lot cooler than it was on Saturday.' He showed Connors the prints.

'If there is something buried down there, why is there a hole instead of a heap of earth?'

'You're looking at it the wrong way,' said Wedderkind. 'The earth is heaped up around the point of entry. That's what makes it look like a hole. Look. I'll show you.'

Wedderkind picked up a polished steel ball. It was a little bit smaller than a table-tennis ball. 'The shape, of course, we can only guess at.' He took the sugar bowl from the coffee tray and shook it till the surface of the sugar was flat. He then pressed the steel ball into the sugar, twisting it left and right until it became completely

147

buried. The displaced sugar formed the rim of a shallow crater within the bowl.

Wedderkind handed the bowl to Connors. 'That's one explanation.'

'And the heat?'

'Probably generated through boring its way underground. It all ties in with the other moves it has made to protect its arrival into a possibly hostile environment.'

'And how do you propose to make contact?'

Wedderkind shrugged. 'The President told me to dig it out.'

At lunch, they were joined by two of Wedderkind's closest associates, Phil Brecetti, one of the physicists, from Berkeley, and Alan Wetherby, a geographer from the University of Chicago. When Wedderkind had made the first round of introductions, Connors questioned the usefulness of a geographer on the project. Wedderkind replied, 'He's fun to have around. If we're going to be cooped up for weeks on Crow Ridge, I want to be with people I enjoy talking to.'

Wetherby, who was from England, was an expert on the origins of the ancient Chinese village. His books on the subject, which he claimed nobody read, were as thick as New York City telephone directories. He also had an encyclopedic knowledge of almost every other subject Connors cared to mention – including flying.

Wedderkind pointed a fork at Brecetti. 'Phil was up on Crow Ridge with me last week.'

'When you checked the cutout zone?'

'Attempted to,' said Brecetti. 'Until that field is neutralized, I don't see how we can carry out any serious research.'

'You mean without electricity?'

'Yes,' said Brecetti. 'It's a real body blow.'

'You may already know this,' said Wedderkind. 'But

the fact is, despite the really fantastic advances in scientific knowledge over the past seventy years, the related phenomena of magnetism and electricity are still not fully understood. We can detect their presence, we know what properties they possess, and we can recreate them in the laboratory and in industry, but the *how* and *why* still elude us. The Earth, for instance, possesses a vast magnetic field, but it occurs without any of the complex mechanical systems we would need to reproduce a field just a fraction of that size. We've tracked down electricity and magnetism as far as the basic particle of matter – the atom. That is composed of electrically charged particles, and it also possesses what we call a magnetic moment. And we now know that smaller units exist beyond the electron and neutron of the atom. That's Phil's field – particle physics – and that takes us to the extreme edge of scientific knowledge.'

'To the point where science becomes philosophy,' said Brecetti.

Connors toyed with the potatoes on his plate, then weakened and ate some of them. 'Why do you think Crusoe chose to land in America?'

'It could be because of the theory you put forward,' said Wedderkind.

'Which one was that?'

'Homing in on radio and TV transmissions. After a week orbiting the entire world, he would be able to pinpoint North America as the biggest single source of radio and TV traffic. With the proper optical equipment he could also see the buildup of cities and roads, the cultivated areas. Western Europe would have some of the same characteristics, but lumped together as a single land mass with Asia it wouldn't look so active. Africa would have minimal radio traffic, and so would South America and Australia.'

'We've been listing the characteristics of the landing site,' said Wetherby. 'But at the moment, they don't enable us to draw any conclusions.' He ticked off the points on his fingers. 'One, it is situated midway between the Rocky Mountains and the plains of the Middle West. Two, this point is roughly in the middle of the North American continent. It depends on the criteria you use, but it's just about the visual centre of gravity. That at least points to a tidy mind. Three, it's a sparsely populated area, but four, it's an area that is rich in minerals, including uranium. Five, it's old. The surface rocks are from the Cretaceous period, that's the last third of the Mesozoic era, when pterodactyls, dinosaurs, and other large reptiles flourished.'

'And it's the period during which they were all mysteriously wiped out,' said Wedderkind.

'It's also near one of the oldest-known geological areas in the United States. The Black Hills of Dakota contain rocks over six hundred million years old.'

'What would be the point of landing in a spot like that?' asked Connors.

'Well – it depends on the purpose of your visit,' said Wetherby. 'Our exploration of similar areas on the moon was to find out more about its origins – and evolution. The results exploded the long-held theory that the moon once formed part of the Earth. It didn't. But they probably came into existence at about the same time. To anyone who's interested, this area contains a big chunk of geological time for them to study.' Wetherby smiled. 'On the other hand, they may have *been* here six hundred million years ago.'

'And they've come back for their umbrella,' said Connors.

'Yes – or to check up on what has happened since. Or maybe to meet somebody.' Wetherby paused to pour chocolate sauce over his ice cream. 'Don't forget that, historically, this is Kiowa-Apache country. With the recent backdating of Man's appearance in North America, their ancestors go back a long way.'

'We're lucky Crusoe didn't land in one of the Indian reservations,' said Wedderkind. 'A few more minutes in the air and he'd have ended up south of the Yellowstone, in the Crow reservation on the Little Bighorn.'

'That would have made a nice legal problem,' said Wetherby.

'Yeah . . .' Connors looked at Wedderkind. 'Weissmann would have probably ended up getting scalped.'

'Who's Weissmann?' asked Brecetti.

'Nobody,' said Connors. 'Forget it.'

THE WHITE HOUSE/WASHINGTON DC

Just after midday, Bodell and his wife were photographed on the lawn of the White House with the President standing between them. They then went inside to have lunch with the President and his wife Anne. Jerry Silvermann, the White House Press Secretary, and Marion Wilson, the President's private secretary, were on hand to lighten the occasion, but the Bodells were so overawed they could hardly lift a fork.

Mrs Bodell was then given the short tour around the residential rooms by the First Lady, while the President took Bodell into the Oval Office and, after a short preamble, asked him to serve, once again, 'the highest interest of the nation'. On the desk was a document prepared by Weissmann that assigned his land to the Mineral Research and Development Corporation. Bodell asked to be able to keep his shack and garden, and the President, who'd been a lawyer, amended the document

151

in longhand. Bodell signed on the dotted line. The whole thing from the hello to the good-bye handshake took just under an hour and a half.

Weissmann, who had kept well out of Bodell's way, phoned the news to Connors, who was still in Ohio. 'I'll file all the necessary papers, but as from now we're at go-status.'

'Where are they now?' asked Connors.

'Who?'

'The Bodells.'

'On their way to Disneyworld.'

'Did they get a good deal?'

'They did all right.' Weissmann obviously found it hard to part with money, even when it wasn't his own.

'Well, don't lose any sleep over it,' said Connors. 'Just send us the bill for a new car.'

Tuesday/August 21

GLASGOW AIR FORCE BASE/MONTANA

The 707 bringing Connors, Wedderkind, and the research group from Ohio landed at Glasgow just after midday. An aircrew bus took them over to the officer's mess for lunch. Greg Mitchell was there, packed and ready to ride the 707 back to Washington. He told Connors that Allbright's group was on the Ridge and that the CIA 'front office' operation was already in position on Highway 22.

'It couldn't be better,' Greg concluded. 'On a busy day, you get all of two cars an hour going past the front door. The only security problem you're likely to get is from the few light planes in the area. There's a dirt strip at Jordan, and an air-taxi outfit based at the Miles City airport. I think they do some control work for the State Fish and Game Department.'

'Well, you have a three and a half hour trip ahead of you,' said Connors. 'See if you can come up with some ideas before you get to Washington. Have you met Allbright?'

'Yes,' said Greg. 'Before he rose to be head of SAC, he commanded one of the B-52 wings that carpet-bombed Cambodia for Nixon and dear old Henry K.'

'While pretending to be elsewhere . . .'

'That's right. The Menu raids.'

Connors gave Greg a raised-eyebrow look as the details of this shabby, and ultimately futile, venture flashed through his mind.

The Viet Cong had been using the cross-border trails to bring supplies and reinforcements down from the north. They'd also set up bases on Cambodian territory from which attacks were launched against South Vietnam. It was a clear violation of Cambodia's neutrality but the government in Phnom Penh, lacking the political will and the military muscle to throw its unwelcome visitors out, turned a blind eye to what was going on.

Code-named Menu, the raids were designed to deny the VC sanctuary by destroying these bases and supply lines but Nixon knew that any extension of the war into Cambodia would trigger a new storm of protest from the domestic anti-war lobby and fellow-travellers the world over. To get around this, the Air Force was ordered to cover its tracks with an impenetrable layer of fake paperwork. The bombing, which began in February 1969, continued under a cloud of secrecy and a barrage of denials from the White House until April 1970 when units of the US and South Vietnamese army staged an abortive invasion.

153

Once again, American technology and firepower failed to halt the rice-bowl and bicycle battalions of Hanoi. South Vietnam collapsed in disarray as the US of A finally decided to cut its losses and sailed for home while next door, the blank-eyed teen-age killers of the Khmer Rouge came out of the jungle and took over the smoking ruins of Cambodia.

An unknown number of Cambodians had died in the raids; upwards of three million more perished when Pol Pot's regime turned back the clock to Year Zero and proceeded to impose their homicidally-insane brand of Marxism upon the luckless population. An entire country was transformed into one vast concentration camp as a direct result of a 'let's go bomb the hell out of them' cry from a frustrated US President.

And an embarrassed world had looked the other way.

Greg read Connors' mind and smiled, tongue in cheek. 'I know. Not exactly your kind of person. But his record shows he's a man who does what he's told and knows how to keep a secret. And as the head of SAC, he's obviously a man who can be relied on to keep a cool head when the chips are down. What more could you ask?'

'What more, indeed,' said Connors. 'Have a nice day.'

After lunch, Connors, Wedderkind, Wetherby, and Brecetti left the base in a rented car. Two miles down the road towards the town of Glasgow, a yellow MRDC helicopter was parked on an empty stretch of ground. They climbed aboard and headed south towards the Fort Peck reservoir.

As they crossed the huge expanse of water, Wetherby tapped Connors on the shoulder and pointed downward out of the window.

'Did you know this is still the largest earth-fill dam in the world?'

Connors nodded. Tremendous . . . He decided that next time he would ask the pilot to take the long way around.

About thirty minutes later, they landed on a bare patch of ground at the junction of Highway 22 and the dirt road that led up to Crow Ridge. It had been decided not to risk any landings nearer the Ridge until the full extent of the cutout zone had been carefully charted.

Behind a sign which read 'MRDC – AUTHORIZED PERSON-NEL ONLY' four of the base camp's prefabricated shacks had already been positioned on Bodell's land, a short distance from the road.

On the other side of the highway a lineman was busy at the top of a telephone pole.

One of Allbright's cadets from Colorado Springs was waiting with a yellow four-door jeep. He wore a blue hard hat and had the name LARSEN stencilled on the breast tag of his olive-drab fatigues. He handed out four yellow hard hats. Connors got into the front seat of the station wagon. The others got into the back.

'Has General Allbright arived?' asked Connors.

'I don't think I'm able to answer that, sir. To the best of my knowledge there are no military personnel associated with this project.' Larsen gave it an absolutely straight delivery.

Connors looked over his shouder at Wedderkind, then back at Larsen. 'You are right, of course. Perhaps I'd better rephrase the question.'

'I think the best thing is for you to talk to the site organizer, sir. He's up on the Ridge.'

Six miles from the highway, Connors caught sight of some more cadets through the trees. They were driving in a line of marker stakes around the Ridge. There was a temporary barrier of dirt-filled oil drums where the marker stakes hit the road. It was manned by four more

155

of the look-alike cadets. Two of them had shotguns. All of them had the peaks of their blue hard hats pulled down over their eyes in the best drill-sergeant fashion.

'Connors, Brecetti, Wedderkind, and Wetherby,' said Larsen.

A cadet checked the names against the list on his clipboard, and handed out four plastic name tags that included a mug shot. 'Please put these on and wear them at all times.' He stepped back and waved up the barrier.

They drove through, rounded a curve and parked in between the pines alongside several other vehicles.

'We have to walk from here,' said Larsen.

Ahead of them, across the dirt road, was a line of red stakes. Beyond them, Connors could see Volkert's patrol car, the tow truck and the Air Force Rescue truck, still parked where they had stalled over a week before.

Connors turned to Larsen. 'Do the stakes mark the edge of the cutout zone?'

'Only approximately, sir. We haven't driven up any further than our parking point back there. We put the stakes in halfway between there and the stalled vehicles to serve as a basic reference point.'

Connors felt a tingle of excitement as he followed Larsen through the line of red stakes. He looked back at Wedderkind and saw that his eyes had taken on a new shine. Brecetti was rubbing his hands together. Wetherby had stopped to take in the whole scene along with a few deep breaths of pine-laden air.

On the windshields of all three vehicles were taped notices: 'DO NOT TAMPER WITH OR ATTEMPT TO MOVE THIS VEHICLE.' The hood of Volkert's patrol car had been left open.

Connors took a peek at the engine, then turned to Wedderkind. 'Has anybody examined these?'

'Yes,' said Wedderkind. 'I went over them all when we were up here last week. Before you went to see Bodell.'

'You were taking a risk, weren't you?'

'He was too busy shooting at Weissmann,' said Wedderkind.

Connors turned to Larsen. 'Has there been any word on the converted diesel trucks?'

'Yes, sir. We anticipate receiving the first batch this evening. Would you like to move on to the plateau?'

'Sure, let's go.' Connors exchanged an amused look with Wedderkind, and fell into step beside Larsen. The others tagged along behind. Connors looked back over his shoulder at Wedderkind. 'Now that I think of it, how come you know so much about automobiles?'

'This may surprise you,' said Wedderkind, 'but twenty-five years ago I was still doing my own hot rod conversions.'

'That was before he became ambitious,' said Brecetti.

The dirt road degenerated into the dried mud tracks of Bodell's old Dodge. Above them, they could hear the sound of another helicopter bringing in more people from Glasgow.

Connors looked back at Wedderkind. 'We're going to have to get this road cut through to the plateau.'

'I think the plan is to get started on that tonight, sir.' It was Larsen being helpful again. He angled off to the right of the tyre tracks. A band of white paint on the tree trunks marked the way through.

'How old are you, Larsen?'

'Twenty-three, sir.'

'This must be a whole lot more fun than walking in right angles and eating at attention, right?'

'You only do that as a freshman, sir,' explained Larsen patiently. 'In addition to our military training, upperclass cadets are required to complete a Bachelor of Science degree course and a program of enrichment studies. We are also called upon to perform command and staff functions within the Cadet Wing.'

And we also learn how to put down wheeler-dealers from Washington without being insubordinate, thought Connors. Full marks, Larsen.

The ground became littered with broken branches. There were more hanging in the trees. Ahead of them, they could see shattered tree trunks and the open sky.

They stepped out into the semicircular area of devastation. The ground was covered with small splinters of wood – as if someone had emptied a million matchboxes. The rim of the crater was about a hundred yards away. The ground was heaped up around it just like the sugar in Wedderkind's demonstration bowl.

Connors looked at Larsen as they walked towards the crater. 'How big is this thing?'

'About thirty yards across, sir.'

Connors turned to the others. 'There were three hours between the time people reported seeing the fireball over Broken Mill and the time Volkert got up to the top of Crow Ridge and found this crater. How the hell could it have buried itself so fast?'

'I don't know,' said Wedderkind. He stooped down and picked up a handful of wood splinters. He looked around him. 'There's no sign of a fire.' He showed the splinters to Brecetti. 'They're not charred. You see? It looks as if they have been shredded. Look at how the wood fibres have disintegrated. The pressure from the blast must have been tremendous. One would have expected it to devastate the whole plateau, but as you can see, the rest of the trees are still standing.'

'The damage could have been caused by ultralow-frequency sound waves,' said Brecetti. 'The right wavelength could set up a resonance in the timber that would blow it apart. Remember the experiments the French carried out at Marseilles in 1964?'

'Was that the "Jericho Trumpet?"' asked Connors. 'They split concrete apart with a sound gun.'

'That's right,' said Brecetti. 'Lower frequencies are even more destructive. At 3.5 hertz the sound waves create subsonic vibrations that can literally shake humans apart.'

'Insane,' said Connors. 'I can never understand why you guys fool around with that kind of thing.'

'Ultrasonic high-frequency vibrations was another possibility we discussed back in Ohio. Crusoe could have buried himself by shaking the ground loose around him – rather like the way insects burrow into sand.'

'This fireball that people saw,' said Connors. 'Could that have been retro-rockets firing, to slow its rate of descent before landing?'

Wedderkind shook his head. 'Not possible. The heat would have burned or scorched this area. There's no sign of that.' He tossed the handful of wood splinters away.

'At least we now know Crusoe isn't invisible,' said Connors.

'Don't count on that.'

Connors stared at Wedderkind. 'What do you mean?'

'Bob, if Crusoe can alter the physical properties of his surface structure so that it fluoresces on a wavelength we can see, he must be able to reverse the process to get himself out of trouble.'

'Oh, tremendous . . .'

'Bob, all we're doing is tossing a few ideas around. You might as well get used to it because there're going to be a lot of sessions like this. We don't have one single reference point from which we can begin to work out what this thing is or what it does. And when we dig it up,

159

we *still* may not know. So if you're waiting for a set of blueprints and a service manual, forget it.'

'I know what the problems are,' said Connors. 'And I am not expecting any miracles.'

'Not expecting any? You've got a miracle.' Wedderkind waved towards the crater. 'Down there. Something conceived by intelligent life beyond Earth. Maybe even containing it. Something that's travelled across our galaxy past the billions of other stars to the one we circle every year. Why ours? As a star, our sun is way down the list. A *shmendrick*. And yet Crusoe's here – not only on our planet, but on our *part* of it! If you were to try and calculate the chances of something like this happening, they'd be – '

'Out of this world?' suggested Connors.

'Exactly,' said Wedderkind. 'Forget the problems. We can find a way around them. Just be grateful. A chance like this comes once in a million – no, what am I talking about? Not even that – once in a *billion* years!'

They walked up on to the rim of the crater and looked down into it. It was twelve to fifteen feet deep, with shallow sloping sides of loose earth and scattered stones.

'You'll probably notice a slight tingling inside the head after a few minutes,' said Larsen. 'It occurs in the immediate vicinity of the crater.'

'Yes, that makes senes,' said Wedderkind.

'Some people are more affected than others,' said Larsen.

'How?' asked Connors. He could already feel a faint prickling inside his head. Like tiny needles. Ice cool. It wasn't unpleasant.

'Mild dizziness. Disorientation. Temporary loss of balance,' said Larsen. 'It clears up once you leave the area of the crater.'

'What causes it, Arnold? Crusoe's magnetic field?'

'Yes. You have minute but measurable chemically-created electric currents flow through the brain, triggering off signals that are translated into thoughts, speech, body functions, or movement. Once you step inside Crusoe's cutout zone, a surge starts to build up in those currents – just like any other electrical circuit.'

'Does that mean my brain is going to blow a fuse?' asked Connors.

'No,' said Wedderkind. 'But it might stall.' He walked down the slope towards the centre of the crater with Brecetti.

Connors followed with Wetherby and Larsen. He still found it hard to believe that Crusoe was buried somewhere underneath them. 'What do you think he's going to do?'

Wedderkind looked at him. 'Do? The big question isn't what, but *when*. You have to remember that he could be operating on an entirely different time scale to us. He may have taken a thousand, ten thousand or ten *million* years to reach us. He may not be in a hurry to *do* anything.'

'You mean there might not be any activity in our lifetime?'

'It's possible. We can either wait and see, or we can let him know that *we* know he's down there.'

Connors felt as if he was about to float. 'I'm getting some real vibrations, Arnold. Do you feel anything?'

'A slight dizziness,' said Wedderkind. 'How about you, Phil?'

'I'm getting a sensation of imbalance,' said Brecetti.

Connors nodded. 'Yes, me too.'

They all looked at Wetherby.

'I feel as if I'm going to be sick.'

'Sir?'

Connors looked around. Beyond Larsen, on the rim of

161

the crater, was General Allbright. He was dressed in spotless olive-drab fatigues, with a bright blue scarf tucked in the open neck, and one of those curvy-brimmed stetsons that the Guam and Thailand-based B-52 crews had made fashionable during the Vietnam War. And he was sitting on a horse – a magnificent, long-maned palomino.

Behind him, wearing blue hard hats, were two young aides, also mounted, but on lesser breeds.

Allbright looked down at Connors and the others with deepset prairie farmer's eyes two shades lighter than his scarf.

'Gentlemen,' he said, in a way that somehow robbed the word of all respect.' Welcome to Crow Ridge.'

Given the fact that no motor vehicles could operate on the Ridge, Allbright's choice of personal transportation was immensely practical. Nevertheless, it still took Connors by surprise.

Connors decided it was the horse that had thrown him. The palomino was too good-looking, too photogenic. It wasn't a solid, US Fifth Cavalry type of horse, it was the type Gene Autry and Ronald Reagan used to ride. It threw an interesting sidelight on Allbright's character.

Allbright dropped easily out of the saddle as Connors led the others out of the crater to meet him. Although he topped six feet, once they were face to face, Connors found Allbright less overpowering than he had expected. Like so many heroic figures, he looked a lot taller in the saddle than he did on the ground.

Connors shook his firm right hand, then introduced the others. If he was expecting sparks to fly, he was disappointed. Allbright was attentive, courteous and briskly efficient. He also possessed the easy amiability of a bridge player with a handful of trump cards.

162

He led the way to a vantage point on the peak of the ridge and pointed out the proposed locations for the housing, workshop and research facilities. 'The boundaries of Bodell's land are being staked out now. They'll be patrolled day and night until the high wire and chain link fence go up. We have a civilian contractor starting in on that tomorrow. They'll be working three shifts from a base camp down by Highway 22.' As if reading Connors' mind, he added, 'Don't worry. None of them will get any further than the fence.'

'I'm counting on that,' said Connors. 'But while they're around, I think it would be a good idea if your people could keep the hardware out of sight. The two I saw riding shotgun on the gate looked as if they were guarding the Treasure of the Sierra Madre. I know we can't afford to take any chances on the security of this project, but we don't want to create a situation where people on the outside start asking the wrong kind of questions.'

Allbright nodded politely. 'I think I get the idea.' He signalled to his aide to bring up the palomino.

'If you gentlemen will excuse me, I'd like to check the progress of the work in hand. Some temporary tented accommodation has been set aside for your use over on the south flank of the ridge.' Allbright pointed over their heads. 'You'll find your luggage there.'

'Before you go, General, did you experience any reaction at the crater?' asked Wedderkind.

'Yes. A slight coolness – here.' Allbright put a thumb and forefinger to his temples.

'A tingling sensation?' asked Connors.

Allbright nodded. 'Yes. Not at all unpleasant.'

'Yes, rather like a mild high.'

Allbright took hold of the palomino's reins and put a foot in the stirrup. 'I'm familiar with the terminology of the drug culture, Mr Connors, but not the experience.'

He swung up into the saddle. 'Let's say a slight feeling of elation.'

Connors smiled. 'That would be about it.'

Allbright patted the neck of his restive horse. 'I've arranged a briefing session for the project leaders at 19:00 hours. There will be food and drink available. Mr Larsen will accompany you till then. You can also contact me through him if the need arises.' Allbright gave them a casual salute, then wheeled his horse around and cantered off down the slope followed by his two wingmen.

Connors exchanged a look with Wedderkind, then turned to Brecetti. 'These, er – vibrations that people are getting from the crater. Could they cause any permanent damage – I mean, to the brain?'

'I'm not really competent to answer that,' said Brecetti. 'I know the brain currents can vary between fifty and one hundred and fifty microvolts but I don't know the maximum level of tolerance.'

Wedderkind turned to Wetherby. 'Do you still feel sick?'

'No, I'm okay . . .'

'Would it be possible for us to generate a field as powerful as this?' asked Connors.

'It's theoretically possible,' replied Brecetti. 'We are already producing immensely powerful magnetic fields for our researches into plasma.'

'I've told him about Princeton's Large Torus,' said Wedderkind.

'Ah, yes, that's quite something. You've seen the way the light glows down the middle of a neon tube? Well, in the PLT, a line of plasma, pure molten energy, is held away from the sides of a circular tube by this magnetic field.' Brecetti shook his head. 'The problems – '

'He doesn't want to know about the problems,' said Wedderkind.

'Sorry, I got carried away.'

'Arnold said the operation was burning up a lot of electrical energy,' said Connors.

'Enough to heat and light a whole city,' said Brecetti.

'One thing that no one has mentioned so far is super conductivity,' said Wetherby. 'You can generate enormous field stengths with quite small units – and with very little electrical energy.'

'Hell, yes, of course.' Wedderkind turned to Connors. 'Do you know what we're talking about?'

'Vaguely. Is it a low temperature magnet?'

'Right. We've been opening up this whole field over the last ten years or so. The electrical resistance of a metal decreases as its temperature drops. When certain metals – like lead, tin, vanadium, and alloys such as niobium and tin – are cooled to a few degrees above absolute zero, their resistance suddenly vanishes. All you need is a ring of one of these metals cooled to the transition temperature – introduce an electrical current, and wham! It creates a fantastically strong magnetic field.'

'Got it,' said Connors. 'While you were talking, a thought occurred to me – could Crusoe harness the *Earth's* magnetic field to form a shield around itself?'

'Good question,' said Brecetti.

'It's possible, but he would have to find some way to intensify it.' Terrestrial magnetism fell within Wetherby's scope as a geographer. 'The Earth's field is normally rated as being about ten thousand times weaker than an ordinary horseshoe magnet.'

'That's right,' said Brecetti. 'My guess is that Crusoe's probably generating his own field. It will be interesting to find out how he does it.'

'And why it jams our radar,' said Connors. 'If we can crack that problem and find some way to use it ourselves . . .'

Wedderkind gave him a pitying look. 'You really do have a one-track mind.'

'Arnold, let's get one thing straight. Regardless of what my personal views may be, if all we're going to get out of this encounter is a blueprint for a brave new world, forget it. The people in Washington won't want to know – nor will the people in Akiak, Alaska, or Zanesville, Ohio.'

'You don't really believe that.'

'I wish I didn't. For anything that affects our national security, money is no problem. But you know the government's policy on pure research. There have to be spin-offs. The right kind of spin-offs – like the military got from the space program. The private foundations may take a more altruistic point of view, but the US Navy doesn't pay people to play around with dolphins just because they like fish – '

'The dolphin isn't a fish,' said Wetherby.

'It doesn't make any difference,' said Connors. 'They're laying down good government money because they think the dolphins are going to produce a sonar breakthrough that will be bad news for Russian submarines.'

'Bob, we know all that. But this is different.' Wedderkind pointed towards the crater. 'Somewhere under there could be the answers to the questions that Man has been asking for centuries. That some of the greatest minds have spent a lifetime trying to answer. Is there intelligent life elsewhere in the universe? Is Man unique – or has the seed of Man been sown throughout the universe? Are we a purposeless evolutionary accident, biological freaks? Or do we have a higher purpose?'

'Arnold, *we* all want to know the answers, but nobody else does. Look what a big yawn the space program has turned out to be. The television networks soon found that out. I don't think the world is ready yet – and the way things are going, it may never be.'

'But Man *has* to know,' said Brecetti. 'That's what distinguishes him from the rest of the animals. He searches for knowledge, for truth. It's a fundamental drive one cannot suppress.'

'You haven't been in government,' said Connors. 'Aren't we concealing this project?'

'Yes, but only temporarily – for practical reasons,' said Wedderkind.

'Don't count on that,' said Connors. 'We're in business just as long as we come up with the right answers. No one is going to let Crusoe upset the apple cart.'

'Bob, the process is irreversible. You can't stop technological progress. You can't hold back knowledge. The Luddites went around smashing mechanical looms but they didn't stop the Industrial Revolution.'

'Perhaps they should have tried harder,' said Wetherby.

'This is hardly the time to start opening *that* can of beans,' said Wedderkind.

'Just what kind of knowledge would you consider unwelcome?' asked Brecetti. 'I don't mean you, personally.'

'Well,' said Connors, 'it could be argued that it serves no useful purpose for us to know that there is intelligent life in a star system a thousand light years from here – or even one that's nearer. It's a totally irrelevant piece of information. To know he is not alone in the universe is not going to improve the quality of Man's existence. It doesn't help solve any of the problems that face us here on Earth. Maybe that's where all our energies should be directed. After all, 99.999 per cent of the population isn't going anywhere else.

'As for bad news, I'm sure we could all make out a list, but I'll throw in three ideas straight off the top of my head – supposing Crusoe was found to contain the secret of everlasting life, would we want that? Would the

Vatican want irrefutable proof that they'd been handing down the wrong message for the last two thousand years? Would we want to be told how to run things by a bunch of Soviet-type spaceniks fresh off a collective in Cassiopeia?'

As Connors asked the question, they all became aware of a deep-throated roar. They looked down the ridge and saw a heavy yellow truck come grinding up through the pines and on to the plateau. There were about a dozen people hanging on to the outside of the cab and the back of the truck, all waving orange hard hats. As the truck pulled up near the crater with its motor running, the men on it gave a ragged cheer of triumph.

Connors and the others walked down towards them. Wedderkind took hold of Connors' arm briefly.

'Robert, you and I need to have a talk,' he said. 'Just to make sure we're on the same side.'

'I thought we were,' said Connors.

Max Nilsson jumped down from the cab as they approached. Max was a big, broad-shouldered block-buster whose body seemed charged with the compressed energy of a Superball. He smoothed down his extravagant black moustache and swaggered forward with a broad grin.

'Bob Connors?'

'Yes.'

'Max Nilsson, CIA. I'm MRDC's Operations Manager on this Project.'

'Good to meet you. This is Arnold Wedderkind, head of the research group – Phil Brecetti – Al Wetherby.' Connors nodded towards the diesel. 'Is that the first of the converted trucks?'

Max shook his head. 'They're still being worked on. We decided not to wait. I thought you might want to get started with this.' He waved at the stack of girders and equipment on the long trailer.

'What is it?' asked Connors.

'A light drill rig. We've brought enough pipe to go down two thousand feet. Got a core sampler as well.'

'What do you plan to use for power?'

'Steam.'

'Steam?'

Max grinned. 'It was good enough to get this whole industry started back in 1859 – has to be better than a pick and shovel – right?'

'Right,' said Connors. 'Away you go, Max. Arnold here will tell you where he wants the rig spotted.'

'Okay. It shouldn't take us too long to get set up. We might even make contact before midnight.'

The heavy beat of the truck's motor faded as the driver took his foot off the pedal to ease the cramp out of his right leg.

Max spun around and shouted. 'Keep it running, keep it running!'

The motor roared back into life.

'Back it up to the edge of that hole and get that rig unloaded!' yelled Max through cupped hands. He turned back to Connors. 'I guess we were kind of reluctant about driving up here. Nobody wanted to stall halfway and be left standing around with egg on their face. Now I know how easy it is, I'll get some more trucks up with the trailer units.'

Max snapped his fingers and pointed to Wedderkind, 'Oh, yeah, one thing you may want to know. We had all our lights on as we drove up. They cut out just past that line of red stakes.'

'Where the other vehicles are.'

'Yeah. Otherwise no problem.'

HASKILL, one of Allbright's aides, cantered over to

see what was going on. 'Are you going to be bringing up more equipment on to the ridge?' he asked Max.

'Yeah, I'm going to start shipping in the trailer units first. I'd like a few of your boys to trim out some of those pines.'

'Okay, we'll get going on that.'

'Our tyre tracks'll show you the route,' said Max.

Haskill nodded and larruped his horse into a canter from a standing start.

'Hey, cowboy!' yelled Max.

The horse's back legs almost slid from under him as Haskill pulled up short.

'Give me a good ten feet on either side!'

'Wilco!' yelled Haskill. He rode off across the plateau like a Junior Rough Rider.

Max gave Wedderkind a friendly thump on the shoulder. 'Okay, Einstein. You wanna show me where you want this hole?'

Wedderkind rolled his eyes at Connors, then walked off with Max. Brecetti and Wetherby followed.

Connors turned to Larsen. 'If anybody wants me I'll be over on the south side. I've got some paperwork to do.'

'Very good, sir. You'll find one of the tents has your name posted outside.' Larsen signed off with a snappy salute.

By the time Max Nilsson's first truck had been unloaded, news of its safe arrival had been sent down to the base camp with instructions for more big diesels to load up and head for Crow Ridge.

The crew of roughnecks got the drilling platform levelled up in the centre of the crater and rapidly assembled the prefabricated sections of the rig. The first thirty-foot length of drill was locked into the rotary table just after six o'clock. Steam hissed out of the valves of the engine

170

and it thumped away smoothly as Max, with a show of ceremony, threw the lever to connect the drive. The rock drill began to bite into the loosely-packed topping of gravel.

Max patted the vibrating engine housing and grinned broadly at Connors. 'Hear that sweet sound? Who'd think this little lady's more'n eighty years old?'

'Where did you dig it up?'

'Borrowed it from a private museum. Belongs to an oil millionaire down in Texas who owes me a favour. He's got all kinds of junk there, and it all works. Does most of the repairs himself.'

Two more heavy trucks ground their way up through the trees. Ever since the late afternoon there had been a constant background roar from their heavy engines as the drivers obeyed Max's injunction not to cut the motors.

The trucks were bringing more accommodation units. Some were already in position on their jacks, and with the arrival of the fifty Air Force technicians from Kirtland AFB, and the rest of Wedderkind's people, Crow Ridge suddenly seemed to come to life.

Wedderkind came over to the rim of the crater where Connors now stood watching the drilling. 'I've just heard there's now a phone down by the red stakes. It's hooked up to the base camp. Allbright's going to get us wired into the SAC landline system to give us a direct link with Washington. How's it going here?'

'They're down to about eighty feet. Max had to pull one of his guys off the platform. Same trouble as Wetherby.'

'Nausea?'

'Yes.'

'How about the others?' asked Wedderkind.

'Varying degrees of dizziness. They're taking turns manning the rig.'

'How do you feel yourself?'

'Me? I feel fine. Although for all I know this field could be quietly dissolving my brain away. Maybe I'm about to discover that I'm only running on two microvolts instead of fifty. It could be embarrassing.'

'Well, I think you should back off for a while,' said Wedderkind. 'My guess is that it's harmless, but that's all it is – a guess. Like almost everything up to now.'

'Did the medical team from NASA get here?'

'Yes.' Wedderkind smiled. 'They're rolling bandages now. I've told them I want regular checks on everybody working on the site starting tomorrow morning. That includes you.'

'That's fine, as long as I'm first in line,' said Connors. 'I've got an early plane to catch.'

'I'm sure we can fix that. Oh, there is one piece of bad news.'

'What's that?'

'No pretty nurses.'

'That's okay,' said Connors. 'As a matter of fact, I'm glad there aren't any women around.' He broke into a laugh.

'What's so funny?'

'I was just thinking – have you ever noticed how, in all the old science fiction movies, there's always a girlfriend, wife, daughter, or a niece on holiday, who stumbles across the monster and starts screaming her head off. And when it's time to run, they're *always* wearing high-heeled shoes, and they *always* fall down and twist their ankle.'

Wedderkind gave him a look of mild reproof. 'I fear you're in the process of becoming what is called a male chauvinist pig.'

'From way back,' said Connors.

* * *

The seven o'clock meeting was held in one of the empty, forty-foot-long prefabricated units that had been brought up during the afternoon. All fourteen members of the research group were there along with the leaders of the Air Force specialists from Kirtland AFB and the cadet squad commanders. Allbright had had a folding table rigged at one end of the room with three chairs and a briefing board on an easel. Connors was invited to take the middle chair, with Allbright on his left and Wedderkind on the other side. Everybody else sat on the floor or leaned against the walls.

Even though they were all, nominally, civilians, and although Allbright wore no badges of rank, he was still a commanding figure. When he stood up, everybody went quiet. He welcomed them all to Crow Ridge, introduced Connors as head of the project, and Wedderkind as head of the research group, and then asked Connors to say his piece.

Connors kept it brief and to the point. 'Gentlemen, you all know why you are here. Each of you has been briefed on the reasons why we need to keep this project secret and secure. I hope you will all accept the restrictions on your personal liberty that are required to make our security measures effective. We will try to make your temporary imprisonment as comfortable as we can. We have an opportunity to participate in an historic event. Something which may never happen again during the total life span of Mankind and of Earth. It's almost impossible to overestimate its importance to us and future generations. At the same time, we should not underestimate the dangers. They may be complex – and considerable.' He smiled. 'In case I don't get another opportunity, I'd like to thank you on behalf of the President, for volunteering for this assignment, and he asked me to say, and I quote, "In serving this nation you serve all nations, and may God bless you and enable you to bring this enterprise to a successful conclusion." Thank you.'

Connors sat down. Allbright got up to explain the organization and layout of the site, the duties of the various groups of Air Force personnel, the backup they would provide for the scientists, and the services that were planned to be available. A lot would depend on how Crusoe behaved. He was still the big question mark that hung over everything.

After he'd finished, there was a brief session of questions and answers to clear up some points of procedure, then the session broke up into informal groups so that everyone could get to know each other and find out the really important things like which were the most comfortable trailers, how to get an extra blanket, where to get cigarettes and booze, and the chances of getting laid.

On outside work details, the Air Force cadets wore blue hard hats. Each group on the project had been given a different identification colour. The Air Force technicians were green, the research group yellow, and the CIA 'front-office' employees down at the Highway 22 base camp, orange.

'Have you decided whether you will stay here tonight?' asked Allbright.

'Yes, I've told Larsen,' said Connors. 'He's organizing something for me.'

'It may be a little rougher than you're used to.'

'I'm not too worried,' said Connors. 'As long as there's somewhere to sleep and a chance of some action, I prefer to hang on here and fly back to Washington tomorrow.' He smiled. 'I'd like to be able to give the President some hard information. Up to now we've been neck-deep in scientific theories and hypotheses, possibilities and probabilities. It will be a relief to know that something –

anything – is actually *down* there, and that this whole thing isn't just some electronic mirage.'

'The interference on our radar and communications networks is real enough.'

'Yes, I know,' said Connors. He was struck by Allbright's eyes. They didn't flicker about nervously, they fastened on to a face or object with the predatory stare of a falcon. 'How do you feel about all this?'

Allbright frowned. 'Do you mean my reactions to this particular mission?'

'To the whole situation.'

'I'm just a serving officer, Mr Connors. The whole of my service life has been directed towards the defence of this country and its institutions. I regard my involvement here as an extension of that commitment.'

'That's not really an answer to my question, General. We're all obeying orders.'

Allbright smiled and his eyes lost their hard edge. 'I'm not unaware of the philosophical implications generated by this encounter, and I am not unconcerned. Nevertheless I regard such abstractions as being outside the bounds of my professional competence. My primary function here is to provide and maintain total security on this project – from without *and* within.'

'I know what the job profile is,' said Connors. 'I helped write it. But apart from that – no curiosity? Surprise? Dismay?'

'Curiosity?' said Allbright. 'Yes, naturally. Surprise? Only that it's taken so long to obtain the first example of what I suppose people will call a flying saucer. When you think that the Air Force compiled literally thousands of sighting reports during Project Blue Book – '

'But failed to come up with one indisputable piece of photographic evidence,' said Connors. 'There were rumours that the Condon report was a whitewash. Did the Air Force suppress any of the evidence?'

'Not to my knowledge. Most of the sightings could be accounted for, but, if you dismiss the lunatic fringe and their little green men, there still remains a small hard core of detailed observations by trained aircrews that defy rational explanation.'

'Did *you* ever see a flying saucer?'

'Not once in the nine thousand seven hundred and eighty-three hours I've spent in the air.'

Faced with a tally like that, Connors saw little purpose in mentioning his own modest log of five hundred and thirty-two hours. Allbright had probably spent more time taxiing to dispersal.

'How about dismay?' he asked.

'Dismay?' The pale blue eyes fastened on him again as Allbright considered the question. 'Not really. Let me put it this way. This encounter, like any significant event, can either have a benign influence on our lives or an evil one. If we are to believe the computer forecasts, we are already heading towards food, energy, and pollution crises, any one of which could trigger a global catastrophe. But even if we survive those, that's not the end of our problems. It's only a matter of time.' Allbright smiled again. 'I don't know how familiar you are with the Bible, Mr Connors, but if we are to believe St John the Divine, most of us don't do too well on Judgement Day.'

Max came into the hut, edged his way through the groups of people, culled a drink off a passing tray, and tapped Wedderkind on the shoulder. 'We've got some core samples. Wanna take a look?'

'Yes, please,' said Wedderkind. 'Hang on.' He introduced Max to the group he was with and went over to Connors and Allbright.

'Excuse me, am I interrupting anything?'

'Only contemplation of the Apocalypse,' said Connors.

'That's what comes of reading the New Testament. We've got some core samples. Can you spare a minute?'

'Yes, sure.' Connors shook hands cordially with Allbright and left the others to finish the K-ration sandwiches.

The core samples were laid out in neat rows on a folding table, and labelled to show drilling depth and composition.

Max tapped the cores from eighty feet. 'We're well into the solid rock that underpins this whole area. I brought a sample along with me.' Max picked up a fist-sized chunk of rock and showed it to Connors. 'That's what it should look like. See the difference? The rock in this core sample has been liquefied and then fused together, like volcanic lava.'

'Could it be a natural feature of this area?' asked Connors.

'No,' said Max. 'I checked with the Duchess.'

The Duchess, it turned out, was Max's instant nickname for Alan Wetherby, the English geographer.

'What do you think, Arnold? Could Crusoe have melted his way through this rock?'

'It's feasible. That's assuming he made this hole in the first place.'

'But to melt that rock, wouldn't he have to become practically incandescent himself?'

'Not necessarily. It could cook the rock like you cook steak in a microwave oven.'

There was a shout for Max from one of the roughnecks on the platform as the needle on the drill loading gauge whipped around past the danger point. The crew on the

177

rig whacked the rotary table out of gear and raised the string of drill pipes ten feet clear of the hidden obstacle.

Max ran down the slope of the crater and went into a huddle with his men. Connors and Wedderkind waited on the rim of the crater till he returned.

'Trouble?' asked Connors.

'Maybe, but it looks like paydirt. We've got something really solid at just over one hundred and thirty feet. The pressure on the drill head was pretty fantastic – if we hadn't lifted it clear, it would have twisted the shaft into a corkscrew.'

'Has the drill burned out?'

'Could be. We're pulling it up to have a look,' said Max.

Behind him, the relief crew was already scrambling on to the platform to help raise the five lengths of drill pipe.

When the drill bit came up, they found that the complex array of tungsten-tipped teeth had been burned smooth. Max supervised the fitting of a diamond-tipped drill and the two crews started to sink the string back down the borehole on the double.

Allbright and one of his aides rode over to join Connors and Wedderkind as the fifth section of pipe was locked into the spinning rotary table. The drill sank down to – and past – the previous point of contact.

Max cupped his hands around his mouth and bellowed, 'Let it ride all the way down to one hundred and fifty!'

As he spoke, there was a deep rumbling roar. The drilling crew leaped off the platform as a tall plume of brown steam burst out of the borehole and enveloped the rig.

'Goddammit, you son of a bitch!' yelled Max. He yanked off his helmet and threw it down so hard it bounced twice.

The steam boiled out for a couple of minutes, then the

pressure faded away. The crew clambered back on to the platform and started to pull up the drill once more.

'What was it that boiled up?' asked Connors.

'It's what we call "mud,"' said Max. 'It's a mixture of clay, water, and chemicals that lubricate the drilling bit. Did you see how we went right through that point we stuck at before? That bastard must have moved sideways and left us to boil in a bath of molten rock. Lucky we didn't get any of that in our faces!'

Max retrieved his helmet, rammed it back on his head and ran down to join his men on the rig.

Wednesday/August 22

CROW RIDGE/MONTANA

It was after midnight when a sweat-stained Max and Wedderkind joined Connors and Allbright in the same prefab unit.

'We drilled down past that first contact point at one hundred and thirty feet,' said Max. 'The bedrock was still white hot when we brought up the core. We've drilled clear through the heated area. Down at two hundred and fifty feet the rock sample is normal. It's a little warm, but it hasn't been melted.'

Connors looked at Wedderkind. 'This all sounds like bad news to me.'

Wedderkind held up a calming hand. 'If he was able to bury himself, it's obvious he must be able to move around underground – if only to stay out of trouble. At least we know how he does it – he melts the rock and floats through it. It then cools and solidifies behind him.'

'Great. Which way has he gone – up, down, or sideways?'

'From what Max has said, it must be sideways.'

'North, south, east, or west?'

Wedderkind shook his head. 'We may need to drill several boreholes to check that, but if he stays near the surface, we can pick up his location by more aerial infrared pictures. If he decides to go deeper, the pattern given off by the heat will be too diffuse. And if he cools down, then we've got problems. This cutoff zone that is wrapped around him is also zapping the radio-wave detection equipment one would normally use for geological surveys.'

Connors tried again. 'Isn't there some kind of instrument that works off shock waves – in the way they trace earthquakes?'

'Yes – using seismographic techniques. We set up two units this afternoon on either side of the ridge. The waves are supposed to bounce back the way radar does. The readings are completely cluttered up with random echoes. Crusoe is beaming out varying-strength shock waves that are bouncing back and forth off every chunk of rock inside the ridge. We know he's in there, but that's about all.'

'So he's still ahead.'

'For the moment,' said Wedderkind. 'But at least we now know Crusoe is programmed to avoid unwelcome contacts.'

Connors glanced around the table. 'I would have thought the whole point of his arrival was to *make* contact.'

'We're proceeding on that assumption,' said Wedderkind. 'But that depends on what Crusoe is. If he's an automated package of instruments, he may be capable of nothing more than "on-off", "yes-no" responses that would enable him to survive in a hostile environment. His reactions up to now could fit into a framework of low-level instinctual responses – in this case, to avoid any contact which might threaten his functional integrity. If he is a very sophisticated package of machinery, we could expect a more complex range of responses to external stimuli. There is also the more remote possibility that Crusoe could contain some kind of alien life-form. I'm inclined to discount this idea myself.'

'The question may seem premature,' said Connors, 'but have any of your people come to any conclusions about Crusoe's mission? I know none of us has seen him, but there now seems a real risk that we may *never* see him at all.'

Wedderkind ticked off the possibilities on his fingers. 'It can be a one-way static reconnaissance probe like Russia's Venera, designed to land by parachute on Venus and then transmit back data about its immediate surroundings. It can be a one-trip mobile reconnaissance vehicle like the Lunakhod moon-bug controlled from its point of origin. If that was outside our solar system, it might take years before it received a signal to activate it. It would make more sense to send a preprogrammed vehicle able to monitor its environment and modify its mission accordingly.

'The third possibility is a two-way mobile version of LEM, the Lunar Module used in the Apollo missions, operating by itself, or in conjunction with a command module – or mother ship – orbiting within the solar system, but not necessarily around Earth, and to which it could return. This type of vehicle could be preprogrammed for its mission, or be remote-controlled from the command ship.'

'Or be manned,' said Connors.

'It could be,' replied Wedderkind, 'but we might not be able to verify that.'

'Could you explain why?' Up to this point, Allbright had been listening quietly to the exchanges between Connors and Wedderkind.

'I'll try, General. In preparing for an event like this, the fundamental problem has always been how the human mind can grasp the concepts of an alien intelligence, or even recognize its existence.

'There may be biological or physiological limitations that make it impossible. Take the computer – it can perform many of the functions of the human brain, it can calculate, store, recall, and analyse data, but it is incapable of any abstract conceptual processes. Yet can we really grasp the concept of, say – infinity? We now accept the idea of time as the fourth dimension – but how many of us can visualize the fifth, sixth, or even tenth dimension that is theoretically possible? Man lives in a finite world. He needs to know how far, how fast, how large, how heavy . . .'

'But nevertheless,' insisted Allbright, '*something is physically* down there.' He looked at Connors and then to Wedderkind for confirmation.

'Yes.'

'And if we don't find some way of getting to it,' said Connors, 'it could move away from under Crow Ridge.'

'That's possible.'

'What ideas have you got, Arnold?'

'There's something I've worked out with Max that I'd like to try.'

Max went to the blackboard in the corner of the room and picked up a piece of chalk. 'We've managed to locate a number of cartridge-fired diesel rigs . . .' He drew a small circle in the middle of the board, then put two large, shaky concentric circles around it.

'Around these two rings at one hundred and two hundred yards from the crater, we're going to drill a series of boreholes fifty yards apart.' Max spattered chalky dots around the edge of the inner circle. 'These holes'll be drilled down to a depth of five hundred feet . . .' He jabbed on some more chalk dots. '. . . These here in the outside ring we're going to sink down to one thousand feet.'

Max tapped one of the dots. 'Down each hole, we're going to put an insulated detonator wired to an explosive charge. One hundred pounds in the inner ring, five hundred pounds on the outer ring. The charges will detonate if Crusoe burns his way through the shaft.'

Connors frowned. 'Do you have to use explosives?'

Wedderkind fielded the question. 'It's a calculated risk. Crusoe's hull *must* be built to withstand sustained heat and pressure. The charge will be exploded by the molten rock, not Crusoe. But the shock wave will register on his hull, and should produce a reaction. He didn't like being hit with the drill.'

'Okay. What do you hope to achieve?'

Wedderkind tapped his glasses back into place. 'There's been a logical sequence to his actions up to now. I want to try to check his capability for logical analysis – and I also want to try to convey our intentions to him.

'If he breaks through the first ring, and then the second, he should register the fivefold increase in the explosive charge. If *we* were down there, we'd probably conclude there could be a series of rings with progressively stronger charges. I'm hoping he'll understand that this is a controlled reaction on our part.'

'To let him know we could blow him out of the ground if we wanted to,' said Connors.

Wedderkind nodded. 'And that the safest place is back inside the circle. The whole idea is to let him know *we* know he's down there – and that we are not trying to destroy him.'

'How long is it going to take to organize this operation?' asked Connors.

Max removed his cigar. 'If the General will let some of his boys man the rigs, five, maybe six days. Seven at the outside.'

'Do you have any comments, General?'

'The cadets have volunteered to carry out any duty assigned to them. However, I would like to ask Mr Wedderkind if he considers this containment operation might endanger the safety of the personnel on the site.'

'Arnold?'

'General, we are all risking our lives just being here. Insofar as *this* plan is concerned, I don't see any need to evacuate the Ridge.'

'Max?'

'No problem . . .'

'There's always the possibility of a reaction from Crusoe,' said Wedderkind. 'But no one can predict what that might be. So far, everything points towards the fact that Crusoe is *avoiding* a confrontation. If his intentions were hostile, they would have been manifestly apparent by now.'

A wintry smile flickered across Allbright's face. 'A little while back you advanced the idea that we might find it difficult to understand an alien intelligence. Alien hostility – if such a thing exists, may also take a form we might find difficult to recognize.'

'That's a good point,' said Connors.

Wedderkind spread out his palms. 'Which proves exactly what I was saying. General Allbright is quite correct. As a human being, I'm programmed to recognize as hostile only those actions which, by their nature, fall within the limits of meaning we have assigned to the overall concept. For example, we might define the ultimate hostile act as the taking of life. To us, life and death are quantifiable states. Life we revere, death we abhor, in varying degrees according to our religion or philosophy. But they are both essentially *human* states, and, as such, could be beyond the grasp of an alien intelligence.'

'But surely,' said Connors, 'the existence and definition of life must be something that we share with every other sentient being throughout the Cosmos.'

'Perhaps the same biological definition,' said Wedderkind, 'but we also define life as being the period between birth and death. Our attitude to life is related to the death which must inevitably follow. But what if there were no death – but merely a continuing cycle of existence? What if the makers of Crusoe were immortal?'

'I get the idea,' said Connors. 'I just don't see how it relates to our present situation.'

'It sprang out of General Allbright's question. I think what I'm trying to say is that an alien intelligence could profoundly change the circumstances and nature of our existence without being able to understand that the effect might be, in human terms, totally disastrous.'

'You mean in the way the loss of radar has fouled up the domestic airline situation,' said Connors.

'*And* seriously weakened our capacity to defend ourselves against a surprise nuclear rocket attack,' added Allbright.

'They are both limited examples of what I'm getting at,' said Wedderkind. 'I was really thinking about the serious long-range effects of more fundamental changes in the Earth's environment.'

'Such as?' asked Connors.

Wedderkind ticked off the possibilities starting with his thumb. 'De-ionization of the atmosphere – that would let through harmful, probably fatal radiation from the sun.

Diminution of the Earth's gravitational force, so that the atmosphere leaks off into space. This is what may have happened on Mars. Displacement of the Earth's axis of rotation so that the polar regions shift to the equator. We know it has happened before – millions of years ago, the North Pole was around Hawaii, and the equator ran up through North America at an angle of forty-five degrees a few miles north of Chicago.

'Disturbance of the Earth's crust causing the level of the seabed to rise. Think what would happen to the map if the water level rose two hundred feet – permanently.'

Connors stopped him before he got to his little finger. 'That's great. The President is going to love all that. I'm supposed to be taking back *good* news.'

'They are only ideas, Bob. Coffee talk. Pure speculation – that need go no further than this room. All we've got at the moment is a hole in the ground. The important thing is to get those boreholes sunk around Crusoe before he moves too far.'

'All the same, you could have mentioned some of these ideas before he came down.'

Wedderkind hunched his shoulders and spread out his palms. 'There was no point, but if I had, was there any way of stopping him?'

There wasn't much left of the night, but tired though he was, Connors hardly slept at all.

The first of the converted bulldozers came grinding up the dirt road as Allbright walked with Connors and Wedderkind down to the line of red stakes. It was 7 A.M. The sky was absolutely clear.

A yellow Corporation jeep was waiting on the other side of the stakes to take them down to the highway.

'I imagine you must be glad to get out of here and back to the White House,' said Allbright.

'Not entirely. I've rather enjoyed being up at the sharp end.' Connors smiled. 'Although I must confess I'll be relieved to get back to a water-based sanitary system.'

Allbright smiled too. 'There are plans to have that facility available for VIPs by the time you return.'

'I appreciate the gesture,' said Connors, 'but I think we ought to hold off on all the frills until Crusoe is boxed in. It's absolutely vital we maintain contact. If Crusoe moves out from under Crow Ridge, we'll be left sitting on top of nothing but the world's most expensive toilet.'

'I've got a clear picture of the priorities, Mr Connors. Have a safe trip.'

As they passed through the control point, Connors saw that the civilian contractors were already at work setting up the posts for the high chain link fence around Bodell's land. He also noticed that cadets guarding the gate had got rid of their shotguns.

Down at the base camp on Highway 22, Connors went through the medical checks under Wedderkind's watchful eye. They included the usual blood and urine samples, cardiogram, and encephalogram. Wedderkind wanted to carry out some research to see if there was any relation between individual brain-wave patterns and people's physical reactions to Crusoe's protective field.

'Are you sure you won't come back to Washington with me?' It was the second time Connors had put the question to Wedderkind.

'Not unless you make it an order.'

'Arnold, nothing is going to happen here until the end of the week.'

'Maybe.' Wedderkind smiled. 'But I'd never forgive myself if something did and I wasn't here to see it. In any case, there's still a lot to organize.'

'You've got competent people here who can handle that.'

187

'Bob, the future of the whole world is up there under the ridge, not back in Washington.'

'I'll try to remember that. However, for the moment, Washington is where the decisions are made that make or break this project.'

'I know. That's why it's important that you go back there and tell them that everything's under control.'

It was Connors' turn to smile. 'Whose control – ours or Crusoe's?'

'Say ours – whatever you may believe privately.'

'Is there anything special you'd like me to ask for?'

'Time,' said Wedderkind. 'Just as much time as you can get. Everyone back there has been weaned on Hollywood features where some goon solves the secret of the universe in a hundred and ten minutes with the aid of a screwdriver and the love of a good woman. In real life, it always takes a little longer. The answers – if we ever find them – may be incredibly simple, but it may take a long time to realize just how simple they are.'

'I'll be back at the weekend.' Connors laid a hand on Wedderkind's shoulder. 'Take care.'

'Give my love to Charly.'

'I will.'

'And promise me one thing.'

'What's that?'

'One day, be a *mensch* and marry the girl.'

'I'll think about it,' said Connors.

THE WHITE HOUSE/WASHINGTON DC

Marion buzzed to tell Connors that the President was ready to talk to him in his private office next to the Oval Room.

'Bob. It's good to see you.'

The President's handshake and voice were warm and

188

friendly, but his face had changed noticeably. Although it had been only a couple of days since Connors had seen the President, he seemed to have aged a couple of years.

Connors' eyes must have given him away, because the President said, 'Don't ask me how I feel. Anne's been asking me that for the last two weeks. I feel fine, and McVickers agrees with me.'

'I'm glad to hear it.' McVickers was the President's personal physician.

'A little tired, maybe, but then you look as if you could do with a good night's sleep yourself.'

'I'll get around to it eventually,' said Connors. 'What's it been like so far this week?'

'The pressures are beginning to build.' The President sat down and gestured to Connors to do the same. 'How is Allbright shaping up?'

'He seems to have everything under control,' said Connors.

The President nodded. 'You apparently gave Chuck Clayson the impression that you weren't entirely happy to have Allbright along on this thing.'

'In that case, I need to get my face fixed,' said Connors. 'Did he say anything else?'

'No. I suggested your reaction may have been coloured by the fact that you'd never met Allbright before. I didn't mention our conversation at Camp David.'

'Good.'

The President fingered the cover of the blue file that lay on the desk in front of him. 'I've read your latest situation report. Did one of your girls – ?'

'No, Greg Mitchell typed it. Was everything clear?'

'Yes – perfectly.' The President put on his reading glasses and flipped over several pages.

'The situation isn't quite as straightforward as we

expected,' said Connors. 'But it's nothing we can't deal with – given time.'

'Yes . . .' The President took off his glasses and rubbed the bridge of his nose. 'That may be the one item we're running out of.'

Wedderkind was right. They were starting to lean on the project less than two weeks after touchdown.

'We didn't get our first people on to the Ridge until four days ago,' said Connors.

'I appreciate that.' The President put his glasses back on and turned over another page of the file. 'Is there no way you can speed up this drilling operation?'

'They're planning to work twenty-four hours a day on that,' said Connors. 'But even if we complete ahead of schedule, there is no guarantee that we'll succeed in forcing Crusoe to the surface.'

'No . . .' The President closed the file, laid his glasses on top of it, and sat back in his chair. 'If this goes on, we're going to find ourselves in one hell of a bind.'

'Are you getting pressure from the Pentagon?'

'Some of the things they're saying make sense.'

'Such as?'

'Safeguarding our interests in Saudi Arabia – and the Persian Gulf.'

'Don't tell me you've sent in the Marines.'

'Not yet, but I have authorized the airlift of a Marine division to Diego Garcia and the transfer of more naval units to the Indian Ocean.'

It was provocative but it made sense. Connors had seen copies of the cables sent by Admiral Kirk, Chairman of the Joint Chiefs of Staff. The Russians had a big chunk of their blue-water navy in the area. Worried by the impact of the first twenty-minute fade-out on communications, Fraser had ordered Kirk to stay aboard the carrier *Lexington* and set up a forward command post.

Kirk had the authority to make vital tactical command decisions without referring them to Washington.

It was another wise move. Since early morning, it had been impossible to receive or transmit any coherent messages on the long wavelengths. There was now a total, worldwide radio blackout.

'We've talked a lot about setting up the Crusoe Project,' said Connors. 'But what we haven't really touched is your reaction to Crusoe itself. I got the impression on Sunday that we weren't quite connecting. Do you want to tell me where you stand on this?'

The President looked at Connors, then moved the bottom right-hand corner of his wife's picture by a fraction of an inch.

'You don't have to tell me the truth.'

'I don't have to tell you anything.' The President moved the picture back to its original position.

'That's right,' said Connors. 'That's what makes this job so exciting.'

The President got up from his chair and gazed out of the window for a moment, hands clasped behind his back. He turned around and waved Connors back into his seat. 'Okay, you've asked me where I stand on this. It's a fair question. Whatever the potential gains in terms of scientific and general knowledge, whatever long-term benefit to humanity this contact may represent, those gains are, and must remain, totally subordinate to the maintenance of our democratic system of government, our concept of a free society and a free-enterprise economy, and the continued well-being of the people of the United States as set forth in, and guaranteed by, the Constitution.'

Connors nodded his agreement. Whenever the President used words like 'democracy', 'free society', and 'the

Constitution', it meant he was making a speech, not holding a conversation.

'Our effectiveness as a world power and our defensive capacity are already threatened by this open-ended jamming of the radar and radio frequencies. It's already started to send bad vibrations through the economy, and if it goes on, it will create chaos on an international scale. Have you seen the reports from our embassies in Europe?'

'Yes, it's tough. But there's nothing we can do.'

'I know,' said the President. 'But we may not be able to conceal Crusoe's presence indefinitely. If word gets out, we're going to be held responsible for every hour this disruption is allowed to continue.'

'In that case, we have to make doubly sure no one finds out he's in Montana until we work out how to switch him off.'

'And before the Russians take advantage of the situation.'

'That sounds like one of Fraser's ideas.'

'You suggested something similar.'

'Yes, but that was specifically related to Crusoe. I don't think they will make any military moves, not yet anyway. That's not just because of the time we've spent working towards better relations. The risks are too great. The fade-out has left us with one option. Nuclear war. They won't push for that. Admittedly they're in better shape on the ground, but the overall effects of the fade-out must still be crippling. There are two things we must remember. First, they have the Chinese along their eastern frontier. In the present situation that's dynamite. Second, they don't need to risk a war with us over Europe. If the fade-out lasts several months, Europe might collapse and fall into their hands without a shot being fired. I think the Russians are more worried about what *we* might do to prevent that happening.'

'Yes . . . it's like getting your fingers caught in a meat grinder. Whichever way you turn the handle it hurts. And it's all due to your friend Crusoe.'

'Hang on,' said Connors. 'We haven't even got acquainted yet.'

'Okay, but now that we've started, let's get things quite clear. Your area of responsibility covers the containment and evaluation of the spacecraft. Containment, in this case, is defined as maintaining total security on this whole operation by the isolation of Crow Ridge and its contents from the rest of the United States. That includes any problems, whatever their nature, contamination or infection – and let's not underestimate the risks of that. Any side effects, harmful or otherwise. The whole circus is to be confined to that immediate geographical area until every part of Crusoe has been carefully examined. It also means the isolation of everyone physically involved in the project on Crow Ridge until they've been checked and rechecked.'

'Does that include me too?'

'It could. It depends on what happens when contact is made with whatever is down there.'

'I'll remember that.' Connors decided against mentioning the icecold tingling he'd felt near the crater. Perhaps, without their knowing, Crusoe had got to them already.

'Evaluation,' continued the President, 'is at least straightforward. We need to know what it is, how it works, what its mission is, and, if possible, where it is from.'

'We'll do our best.'

'Then let's hope that this encounter will turn out to be as peaceful and harmless as you and Arnold have forecast.'

193

'That's not quite accurate,' said Connors. 'I'm sympathetic to Arnold's views, but if you care to check the record, I've merely counselled caution. I've never opposed any attempt to destroy Crusoe.'

'Good.' The President sat down and pointed his forefinger at Connors. 'As soon as Crusoe was located in Montana, Mel Fraser urged me to set up a special defensive capability, to protect the rest of the United States from any threat from Crow Ridge.'

Connors grinned. 'What did he tell you to expect – an H. G. Wells-type Martian invasion?'

The President gave a wry smile. 'I haven't succumbed to Mel's Armageddon complex, but some of his arguments were quite persuasive. It would be foolish not to be prepared for every possibility.'

'I agree with you,' said Connors. 'But I disagree with Fraser. The dangers, if any exist, lie beyond those delineated in the dime novel. Arnold is worried that they may even be beyond our comprehension.'

'That's an even better reason for not taking any chances. Which is why, for the last seven days, we've been ready, at the first sign of trouble, to mount an immediate strike against Crow Ridge.'

'To take out Crusoe?'

'If it proved necessary, the strike would include everything and everybody on the Ridge.' The President's voice matched the grimness of the prospect. 'The code name for the operation is CAMPFIRE.'

Connors' eyes met the President's. The possibility that Arnold and the others – and himself too – might be risking their lives in such a dramatic fashion had not really occurred to him so forcibly before.

He'd been aware that there were risks, of course, but somehow he couldn't bring himself to believe that Crusoe was about to perform like a pulp sci-fi creation. As

Wedderkind had said over and over again, the real danger lay in their own ill-considered reactions. Connors knew that whatever the ultimate benefits to science and mankind, the fade-out couldn't be allowed to continue indefinitely. But they needed time. Time to coax Crusoe to the surface. Time to find out all they could. Time to make the right decisions. Now that Fraser had been given his head, it only needed one crackpot to sound the alarm, and the whole project would go up, literally, in smoke.

'Just how far can we go before we decide we're in trouble?' asked Connors.

'I've outlined what our priorities are,' said the President. 'It will be up to you to make that decision. You will notify me, then take whatever action is necessary to terminate the project.'

'And if, for some reason, I am unable to make that decision?'

The President swung his chair round to face Connors squarely. 'If by that you mean incapacitated in some way, then it will be Allbright's job. He's there to give you whatever backup you need.'

It was a shrewd move. Someone had assessed, quite correctly, that Connors might be swayed by reasoned, or even impassioned, scientific argument into keeping the project going beyond the fail-safe point. Then it would be Allbright's finger on the trigger.

That was why he'd been picked to help Connors run the Ridge. Allbright was there not only to seal off Crow Ridge from the outside world; he was there to make sure that, if necessary, the people *on* the Ridge stayed there. Permanently.

'Allbright also has another responsibility,' said the President. 'That is to get you and Arnold out fast if you happen to be there when it all goes wrong.'

Yes, maybe, thought Connors. But don't count on it.

195

Having looked into those hard blue eyes, Connors had the feeling that, if it came to the crunch, Allbright wouldn't hesitate to include himself and his big palomino on the casualty list.

It was MOODY, one of Allbright's fourth-year cadets, who, a few hours after Connors had left for Washington, suggested the airport lights. The idea consisted of covering the plateau with a twenty-five-yard-square grid of blue taxi-way lights. The lights, fixed to the tops of wooden stakes, were to be individually powered by car batteries and protected by cutouts.

Since the circular magnetic field around Crusoe would activate the cutouts – and disconnect the circuit – his position could be easily plotted on the grid by noting the blacked-out lights. Any further movement would be indicated visually by a change in the pattern.

Assuming the cutout zone was spherical and constant in size, a decrease in the area of blacked-out lights would indicate that Crusoe was going deeper, and an increase would mean he was surfacing.

The one snag in Moody's plan was that once the cutout had disconnected the circuit, the lights would stay out even if they were no longer affected by the cutout zone. The research group mulled over various mechanical devices and finally settled for a 'cutout patrol' that would periodically reset the cutouts of the blacked-out lights to check on any change in the size of the field.

Max was so happy he forced one of his cigars on the nonsmoking Moody and actually got as far as lighting it. The grid of blue lights would give them Crusoe's new position and thus enable them to avoid hitting him when they drilled the two encircling rings of boreholes. It would also show them that they weren't going to spend a week setting an elaborate trap in an empty chunk of rock.

It took a day and a half to get the lights and batteries, but by the time they arrived, the grid of stakes had been planted on a north-south axis.

Starting on the centrelines that ran through the crater, the four teams each took a quarter of the zone and began to work methodically outward. There were a lot of stakes and it was a long time before any of the lights worked. Then slowly, a neat pattern of blue dots started to surround a circle of darkness under which lay Crusoe.

While the grid was being wired up, the Air Force technicians produced a black, stylized contour model of the Ridge, complete with crater and miniature prefab huts. Small blue bulbs represented the lights on the grid, each of which had been numbered so that Crusoe's position could be given as a map reference.

Wedderkind and the other members of the research group clustered around the model and studied the pattern of blue lights. Crusoe's new position was about a hundred yards from the original crater. The diameter of the cutoff zone, which could now be measured by counting across the lines of blacked-out lights, was six hundred yards.

Max, who was standing behind the group, chewed up the end of another cigar. 'How far is he down now?'

Brecetti, the physicist, searched in his pockets for a pencil. 'Has anyone got something to write on?' Brecetti was renowned for having done most of his best work on the backs of envelopes and paper napkins. Wetherby found a clean page in his spiral-bound notebook and handed it over.

'Let's accept the idea of a spherical field, with a constant radius of – say five hundred yards,' said Brecetti. 'The patrol car broke down about a quarter of a mile from the crater not long after the first sighting, in which case it's reasonable to assume that the cutoff zone was at its maximum radius. So . . . if the field now has a surface radius of three hundred yards . . .' Brecetti scribbled a series of figures. '. . . That means Crusoe is now about twelve hundred feet down.'

'Jee-zuss,' growled Max. 'He's practically out of sight.'

'You're going to have to drill those holes a lot deeper,' said Wedderkind.

'And fast,' growled Max. He relit his stubby cigar, pulled his yellow hard hat down over his eyes, and left.

While the grid of lights was being set up, Max and his roughnecks had been showing the cadet group leaders how to operate a rig. Under the Texans' watchful eyes, the raw crews began work at midnight, sinking the first holes in the inner and outer rings ahead of Crusoe's new position.

They worked continuously until Sunday morning, then were replaced by the second eight-hour shift. To keep the rigs working around the clock twenty-four hours a day, Max's crew racked up a solid eighteen hours a day, working, overseeing, cursing, cajoling, and putting in an occasional boot whenever a cadet began dragging his ass.

Wednesday/August 29

Wedderkind telephoned Connors in Washington. Connors had stayed to help the President in his discussions with the Cabinet, Senate leaders and representatives of various business groups on the cumulative effects of the fade-out.

Wedderkind gave him a situation report. The drilling,

which had gone on for five days and nights, had been completed, and each borehole had been primed with an explosive charge. To provide some additional insurance, Max had sunk the inner ring of holes to a depth of two thousand feet and the outer ring down to three. There had been no further change in the pattern of blue lights, and a new overflight by an MRDC survey aircraft with infrared film showed no discernible 'hot spot' on Crow Ridge. Crusoe had apparently decided to cool it for a while at twelve hundred feet.

'Okay, now you've got him surrounded. What do you plan to do, hit him with the drill again?'

'Yes. With luck, that should get him moving into the first ring of charges. Keep your fingers crossed.'

'I will. How's Allbright?'

'He's okay. The latest rumour is he's offered a week's leave to the first man who finds a way to put a crease in his horse. There's only one snag.'

'What's that?' asked Connors obligingly.

'You have to spend it on the Rock.'

Since the completion of the high chain link and barbed wire fence around the site, Crow Ridge had been wryly christened 'The Rock' – once the nickname of the infamous prison island of Alcatraz.

Allbright's passion for impeccable dress had inspired a number of jokes. According to Milsom, his trailer had been sited the farthest away from the crater so that, if Crusoe moved, Allbright's electric iron would be the last thing to cut out.

After five days of around-the-clock work, the cadet drilling detail were on their knees and rig-happy. Max gathered up his original crew of Texas roughnecks and got them to sink a final shaft in the centre of the blacked-out circle of lights.

The drill overloaded and burned out at 1,180 feet. As

they hurriedly hauled up the string of drill pipes, Crusoe sent a column of boiling mud and steam rocketing up the shaft to confirm the hit.

Half an hour later, the cutout patrol reported a change in the pattern of lights on the grid. The changes were transferred to the model. It showed Crusoe was on the move.

Wedderkind went up to join the group of spectators crowded up on the rocky peak of the plateau.

A little under an hour after contact, smoke and earth funnelled into the air as one of the one-hundred-pound charges in the inner ring exploded ahead of Crusoe's original line of advance.

Shortly after the first blast, there was an almost simultaneous explosion as the two charges on either side of the first were detonated.

Wedderkind gave the bridge of his glasses several nervous taps. 'He's moving out, he's moving out,' he muttered, half to himself, and although it was not usually considered part of the reasoned, scientific method, he crossed both sets of fingers.

Crusoe's dark circle continued to move slowly across the carpet of blue lights, and began to contract as he headed down at a steep angle. One of the five-hundred-pound charges in the outer ring blew. The sound of the explosion came rumbling up from three thousand feet and erupted from the narrow shaft with a tremendous roar.

Crusoe's forward movement slowed, then stopped altogether. Wedderkind kept up his vigil on the Ridge until 1:30 A.M., then went to bed. No further movement was recorded that Wednesday night.

Thursday/August 30

There was still nothing to report when Wedderkind sat down for breakfast. He began to worry that they might have damaged Crusoe with the big charge. Maybe he was floundering down there like a wounded whale, surrounded by a ring of explosive harpoons. Maybe they had totally misjudged the strength of his construction. Maybe . . .

In the middle of the morning, Crusoe began to move – backward, at a thirty-degree angle to his original line of advance. Wedderkind clapped his hands together exultantly, bounced off his chair with relief and borrowed another cigarette from one of the Air Force technicians manning the hut.

Crusoe's new course took him straight back across the rim of the inner circle, and detonated five more of the hundred-pound charges of dynamite. Undeterred, Crusoe continued his steady progress beneath the plateau. The circle of blacked-out lights continued to diminish in size. Just after three o'clock in the afternoon, the cutout patrol rode through the grid to reset the lights. This time, none of them went out. It meant Crusoe was over fifteen hundred feet down. From now on, only the exploding charges in the two rings would tell them where Crusoe was.

Wedderkind turned away from the model and looked at Max. 'It's a good thing you drilled that outer ring down to three thousand.'

'We should have gone deeper.'

201

'There was no time,' said Wedderkind. 'Maybe if we'd cut horizontal shafts through from the sides of the ridge . . .'

Max shook his head. 'Ain't no way we could catch him. He's burning his way through that rock at the rate of two to three hundred feet an hour. No one can dig a shaft that fast. And even if we could, this son of a bitch cooks up a lot of rock. It would be like digging into the side of a volcano. If we'd got anywhere near him, we'd have ended up with barbecued knees.'

A little before 5 P.M. one of the five-hundred-pound charges in the deep outer ring exploded. Crusoe had now moved right across the circles they had set around him. It was now make or break. He had turned back once. The big question now was, would he turn back again – or keep on going?

The answer came within the hour as another of the big charges in the outer ring exploded. It was to the left of the previous blast. By nine o'clock, five more charges in the outer ring had exploded one after the other as Crusoe burned his way through the shafts.

In the research group's hut, Wedderkind went into a huddle with the systems engineers from NASA and the Air Force. They looked at a chart showing the two rings around the original crater and the charges that had already exploded.

Roger Neame, one of the ex-NASA engineers, pointed to the two pencil lines he'd drawn on the chart. 'I don't know whether this proves anything, but it's interesting. If you join up the centre of the crater to this point here – where the first charge exploded – then join that to the first explosion on the far side, the angle between those two lines is thirty degrees and . . .' Neame drew a third line which cut the outer circle between the last two

202

charges that had exploded. '. . . See where that puts him? Right in line with his original course.'

Neame joined up the last point with the centre of the crater to complete a classic thirty-sixty-ninety-degree triangle. He pointed to the two charges in the inner ring on either side of the line he'd just drawn. 'If those two blow, then we'll know he's coming back – right on target.'

It seemed too much to hope for. The next patrols reported that all the lights in the grid were still on, and unaffected by Crusoe's cutoff zone. It meant one of three things. Crusoe was stationary, off on a new course away from the Ridge to somewhere quieter, or heading straight down.

Friday/August 31

CROW RIDGE/MONTANA

Wedderkind hung around the research shack until after midnight, then retired, leaving instructions to waken him if anything broke.

He undressed and took a long shower.

The fibre-glass unit in his trailer was like a stand-up coffin. Wedderkind slumped round-shouldered against one of the walls and let the spray blast down over the back of his neck. He tried to marshal into some sort of order the myriad possibilities that were whirling around inside his head.

Crusoe had turned back twice. Would he turn back again? He had blocked their radio communications, stalled cars, downed a helicopter, cut their power . . . why did he need to go underground? To protect himself? Against what – Man?

Or had he gone underground for some other reason? While they thought they were getting the measure of his reactions, was he merely testing *theirs* – measuring *their* intelligence?

Wedderkind mulled over Neame's ideas on the geometry of Crusoe's course and tried to read some significance into it. If Crusoe made a sixty-degree course change he would come back to the crater.

If the two charges indicated by Neame exploded, that at least would be proved beyond doubt . . . Wedderkind got an idea. Supposing Crusoe changed course as they hoped and found that the charges he expected to find weren't there? Would he get the message that they had predicted his move and were prepared to accommodate him?

Wedderkind lurched out of the shower, towelled the more vital parts of himself dry, and pulled on his pyjama trousers and bathrobe. He went out leaving the water running.

Max, who could really have done with the sleep, was still up playing cards and drinking bourbon.

'Those two charges that we're expecting to blow,' said Wedderkind. 'Can you pull them up?'

Max looked at the five cards in his hand. 'You mean *now*?'

'Yes, right away. It's urgent.'

Max hissed out the word 'shit' between clenched teeth, threw his cards face down on the table, and scooped up his money.

The roughneck who was dealing began to gather up the cards.

'Leave that.' Max jerked his thumb at the door. 'Go wake up Cab and Lee.'

'Right.'

'Okay,' said Max to the other three cardplayers. 'The

sooner you get your asses out of here, the sooner we can get back to the game.'

Working under the glare of hissing acetylene gas lamps, the roughnecks hauled up the two one-hundred-pound charges of dynamite. The five-pound sticks, taped together in five sections of four each, were almost too hot to handle with bare hands.

Wedderkind was about to reach out to test the heat for himself when Max pushed him aside.

'If you've got warm hands I wouldn't touch them.' Max broke the charges up and had them dumped into buckets of water.

Wedderkind suddenly realized that in his excitement, he'd been standing between two potential explosions, either of which could have reduced him to hamburger meat.

'That was close,' he said, simultaneously aware of the bravery of Max's crew and his own incredible foolhardiness.

'Looks as if he's headed back this way,' said Max.

'That's why I wanted those two charges lifted,' said Wedderkind. 'If he's braced for more explosions and nothing happens, it might give him something to think about.'

Max gave him a mean look. 'If I thought he was guaranteed to come back through here, I'd put a couple of thousand pounds down either side of him and blow his brains out.'

'After all your hard work?' asked Wedderkind. 'Think of the loss to science.'

'Fuck science,' said Max.

Wedderkind walked back with Max towards the trailer site in gloomy silence. He felt cold and rather ridiculous.

They reached Max's trailer first.

'Thanks, Max. I'm sorry I had to interrupt your card game.'

'Yeah . . .'

'Still, who knows?' said Wedderkind. 'I probably saved you some money.'

Max turned around in the entrance to his trailer. 'On four kings and an ace?'

The door slammed shut in Wedderkind's face.

Breakfast, as well as bathtime, was another unsatisfactory experience for Wedderkind. He liked real, black, strong coffee. Everything to drink on the Ridge, apart from the liquor, came out of a machine. It was a sobering object lesson. The science and technology that had put men on the moon still couldn't reconstitute coffee that tasted like the real thing made fresh from the bean.

Neame came into the breakfast room and leaned on Wedderkind's table as he was spooning up cereal and wondering if he should send off for the slingshot jet glider advertised on the pack to give to his grandson.

'Crusoe's back on the grid,' said Neame.

Wedderkind tore the glider coupon from the cereal pack, and followed Neame to the research hut.

Inside, they found eight more of the research group crowded around the model of the Ridge. Neame and Gilligan disconnected the small blue bulbs as Spencer read out the numbers supplied by the cutoff patrol. Crusoe had blacked out a hundred-yard-wide circle of lights.

By ten o'clock, it had nearly doubled in size and was edging along Neame's projected course towards the crater.

Brecetti clapped Wedderkind jubilantly on the back. 'He's coming up!'

Everyone began to talk at once, speculating on what

206

might appear, and watching Crusoe's progress across the grid with a growing sense of excitement.

Wedderkind rode one of the diesels down to the gatehouse and got through to Connors in Washington. 'If you hurry, you might just get here in time to see it.'

'Will you be able to film it?' asked Connors.

'Yes, on a telephoto lens from outside the cutoff zone.'

'Great. I'll run and get my toothbrush and grab the first available plane.' Connors put the phone down, buzzed Greg, and told him to line up a westbound flight.

'Right away?'

'No, there's no panic.' Connors looked at his watch. 'The late afternoon will do.'

'That should put you on the Ridge at about eight this evening.'

'Fine . . .'

With the big event being recorded on film, Connors didn't mind missing the chance of a grandstand seat. He was still digesting the full implications of the President's plan to take out Crow Ridge at the first sign of trouble. Now that he was aware of its existence, it seemed more prudent to stand well back while Crusoe surfaced. It was true he would miss a moment of history, but he could always watch the recorded highlights.

On Crow Ridge, the surface area of the cutout zone continued to widen and its centre continued to edge towards that of the crater. There was now little room for doubt. Crusoe was climbing steadily towards his original point of entry.

Wedderkind's one fear was that after the underground bombardment Crusoe had undergone, he might surface and head for home without stopping to meet his tormentors.

Yesterday, Crusoe had been moving at about 250 feet

an hour. If he maintained a similar constant rate of ascent, they could expect him to surface some time between one and two o'clock that afternoon.

On the high part of the plateau, two Air Force photographers set up movie cameras well outside the expected cutoff zone.

By twelve-thirty, the air was charged with excitement. Nobody but Max's crew felt like having lunch. Max guessed that Crusoe would still be around when they were through and drove off on a borrowed bulldozer with his friends hanging on to the cab.

An hour later, the circle of blacked-out lights was firmly centred on the crater. It now measured one thousand yards across. Wisps of smoke began to curl up from the loose soil at the bottom of the crater.

At ten minutes to two, the floor of the research hut began to vibrate under Wedderkind's feet as a series of minor earth tremors ran through the Ridge. He rushed out of the hut and up the path on to the plateau, closely followed by Brecetti and Wetherby.

Almost all the population of Crow Ridge seemed to be lining the edge of the plateau – sheltering behind large rocks in case Crusoe turned out to be a Hollywood B-picture space monster.

Wedderkind found Spencer, Neame, and Gilligan at the top of the path.

'He's blacked out the whole grid,' said Spencer.

Wedderkind looked up towards the crest of the Ridge where the Air Force photographers had sited their movie cameras. Both film crews appeared to be grappling with a technical fault. One of the cadets broke away and came bounding down the slope. Wedderkind put out an arm as he drew level.

'What's the problem?'

208

'He just zapped both cameras,' gasped the cadet. 'They fused.'

'*Scheisse* – !'

'We left all the spares in the shack.' The cadet ran off.

The rhythmic ground tremors continued to shake the Ridge, and gradually they all became aware of a steady, oscillating wave of sound that was not so much heard as felt inside the head as vibrations, drilling first through the bone of the skull, then pulsating through the enclosed tissue with growing intensity. People began to edge back, crouch down, or seek cover.

Wedderkind thought that his brain was about to explode inside his skull. Even so, some impulse drove him forward. He pushed between Wetherby and Spencer and ran towards the crater.

One of the cadets began to move after him. 'Sir – !'

Brecetti grabbed his arm. 'Leave it – I'll catch him.' He ambled off after Wedderkind with one arm outstretched, beckoning him back.

Fifty yards from the crater, the ground rocked violently under Wedderkind causing him to almost lose his balance. The soil in the crater began to quiver. Loose chunks of earth and small stones rolled down the sloping sides. Smoke was now pouring out of the ground and Wedderkind could see small darting tongues of flame. The glowing top of a large dome-shaped object burst through the soil. It was white-hot, like a freshly cast ingot. Wedderkind felt a wave of heat strike his face as he was dragged back from the edge of the crater by Brecetti and the cadet who had followed him.

Crusoe continued his upward thrust for about five minutes. Then the pulsing vibrations faded away, and with it any further movement.

There was a moment's silence. Then, quite unexpectedly, all the remaining charges planted by Max in the two rings around the crater detonated in a single mass explosion.

Caught totally by surprise inside the rings, Wedderkind, Brecetti and the cadet fell to the ground and covered their heads. For a moment, they didn't know what had hit them. Then, as they looked at each other cowering on the ground, they realized what had happened and felt rather foolish.

The whole episode looked much more dramatic from the spectators' point of view. As the plumes of smoke drifted away from the boreholes, and the last of the dirt spattered down, a dozen more heroes ran in to rescue Crow Ridge's first three casualties, all of whom were on their feet and full of apologies by the time help arrived.

Wedderkind led the party back to the edge of the plateau. Allbright was waiting for him.

'Mr Wedderkind, perhaps you and I ought to get together to talk over a few basic safety rules.'

'Yes, that's a good idea,' said Wedderkind. He brushed some of the dirt off his crumpled suit and tugged disgustedly at the sleeves. 'Three hundred dollars from my wife's nephew. A horseblanket would fit me better.' Wedderkind produced a handkerchief, wiped some of the dust and sweat from his plump face, then waved the handkerchief towards Crusoe. 'That was like standing next to an open oven.'

Wedderkind slithered down to where Allbright was standing. This left only his head and shoulders above the general level of the plateau. After the two-ring explosion, everybody seemed to have taken up less exposed positions. Allbright passed over his field glasses.

'Thanks.' Wedderkind focused on Crusoe. Now cooling on contact with the air, the glowing orange hull was turning a reddish black.

Wedderkind turned to the cadet who had helped pull

210

him back from the crater. 'Could you run up and see if the two movie crews managed to get their cameras working?'

'Yes, sir.' The young man raced away.

Brecetti touched Wedderkind's arm. 'Can I, er – ?'

'Sure,' said Wedderkind. He handed Brecetti the field glasses.

'What do you make of it?' asked Allbright.

'Well, it's big, but it doesn't look too gruesome. In fact, I'm a little disappointed.'

'Why?'

'The shape looks so familiar. Curving hull like an upturned saucer – with a small dome on top. It reminds me of every fake flying saucer I've ever seen. Frankly I was hoping for something more – '

'More what?' Brecetti passed the field glasses back to Allbright.

'More exotic,' said Wedderkind. 'What do you think, General?'

'I think I'll reserve judgement until the whole thing has been dug out of the ground,' said Allbright. 'Am I correct in assuming that is what you intend to do?'

'When he's cooled down,' said Wedderkind. 'In the meantime, I think we ought to run another check for radioactivity before anyone goes out there.'

'Let me know the result,' said Allbright. 'There's no point in taking any needless risks – *is* there, Mr Wedderkind?'

'No. I'm sorry. I don't know what came over me.'

Allbright gave them a brief salute and walked away, followed by his two aides. The cadet returned from his errand on the crest. 'The cameras are both working. They started shooting film just after Crusoe broke through.'

'Great. Thank you.'

* * *

As an additional precaution, the research group exposed photographic plates that were sensitive to X rays as well as ultraviolet radiation. The results proved negative, and confirmed the measurements obtained by the MRDC survey plane based at Miles City. Allbright sent a cutout patrol riding across the Ridge resetting the cutouts on two lines of lights, one running north-south, the other east-west. The rocker-switch cutouts had been set near the top of the six-foot-high wooden stakes so that a rider could flick them back on with a glancing blow from his gloved hand as he rode past.

Wedderkind walked part way up the crest of the Ridge to watch the progress of the riders across the plateau. The two lines of blue lights blipped on one after another from edge to edge of the grid, crossing at right angles only ten yards from the crater.

The cutoff zone had disappeared.

Wedderkind turned happily to Brecetti. 'We're back in the electricity business! Heat, light, power, and no more transport problems. Marvellous!' They hurried down to break the news to the rest of the group.

At the same time as Crusoe surfaced, the total fade-out on the radio wavelengths began to recede, and by the time Connors landed at Glasgow AFB, reception on the long-wave bands was almost normal, and the medium-wave bands had begun to clear. The people in the Glasgow control tower were beginning to get excited at the prospect of a return to clear, uncluttered radio communications. After being cut off for almost three weeks, their excitement was understandable. Before leaving the base, Connors telephoned the Crow Ridge base camp to check on the state of play. He learned that Crusoe had surfaced, apparently without incident, and was cooling into a depressingly familiar shape. Reassured,

Connors boarded the helicopter and flew south, landing at the base camp at 8:10 P.M.

When Connors reached Rockville, he found Wedderkind and most of the research group having supper in the canteen. He told them about the noticeable improvement in radio communications and ended by apologizing to Wedderkind. 'Sorry, Arnold, I had a few last-minute problems.'

'That's okay, you didn't miss very much.'

'Only Arnold's *kamikaze* attack on the crater,' said Wetherby.

'Very funny,' said Wedderkind. 'When Bob's through eating, why don't you run the film for him?'

'With pleasure.'

'Did you see Crusoe as you came over the plateau?' asked Wedderkind.

'It would have been difficult to miss him,' said Connors.

'What do you think?'

'He looks like something dreamed up by RKO.'

'Yes, I know, that's how we feel.' Wedderkind got up and slid his chair back under the table. 'I'll see you later. Phil and I are just going for a walk.'

Brecetti followed Wedderkind out of the canteen. They walked along the northern flank of the Ridge, then angled up the slope when they were about level with Crusoe. The sun had dipped behind the crest of the Ridge, throwing the plateau into shadow.

Wedderkind looked at Crusoe, then turned towards Brecetti. 'No one else seems to have noticed, Phil, but do you see what I see?'

Brecetti took a long look at the exposed portion of Crusoe's domed hull. 'Do you mean – what happens if you project the hull lines down under the earth?'

'Yes.' Wedderkind moved up beside him. 'I may be

213

wrong but – ' He stuck out his hands, to describe Crusoe's shape. 'If you continue those curves logically. . . .'

'It means he's now larger than the hole he made when he buried himself.'

'Right,' said Wedderkind. 'But don't spread it around. This is one thing I'd like to be wrong about.'

Saturday/September 1–2

CROW RIDGE/MONTANA

Early in the morning they began to examine Crusoe in detail. The visible portion of the hull consisted of a smooth, circular dome about seventy-five feet across by about fifteen feet high. On top of this, exactly in the centre, was a small shallow dome about ten feet across. For those whose minds inclined that way, the overall shape suggested a female breast. Now that it had cooled to match the surrounding air temperature, the colour of the hull was an intense black. Its surface had the smooth polished lustre of a gemstone.

There were no hatches, joints or panel lines, no rivets or fastenings, no markings. Just a smooth, dark dome which, when more closely examined, proved to be made of a semitranslucent material.

Just visible, some two feet below and parallel to the surface of the hull, was a second layer moulded in a convoluted pattern similar to that of the human brain. The discovery of this second mysterious layer, which they christened 'the cortex', caused mixed feelings among the research group. Its form was disturbingly familiar – and all the more ominous for being so.

In fact, Crusoe's whole appearance roused the same

contradictory feelings. He was as sleek and precise as a Buckminster Fuller dome, yet at the same time he was as creepy as one of those Gothic piles in a Hammer horror movie.

Connors had breakfast with Allbright and Wedderkind in the command hut.

'What I want to get clear, Arnold,' said Connors, 'is the plan from here on in.'

'It's fairly straightforward. We have to test the soil and hull for contamination, make exhaustive tests for alien micro-organisms, and we also want to try to find out what Crusoe is made of. That will entail various chemical tests to reveal composition, spectrographic analysis, Rockwell hardness test – the standard procedure.'

'And how long will that take?'

Wedderkind shrugged. 'That's hard to say. The top priority task is to give the hull a clean bill of health. We'll be using the streamlined quarantine and decontamination techniques developed by NASA. So, if we're lucky, we should get a thumbs up–thumbs down signal by the end of the day. Or tomorrow at the latest. Detailed analysis of any micro-organisms we find will take longer, but my guess is you should be able to lay hands on him within forty-eight hours.'

'Yes – well, I'll watch you do it first,' said Connors.

'Now that our operations are no longer restricted by the cutout zone,' said Allbright, 'I would like to recommend the installation of TV cameras to give us total coverage of Crusoe.'

'Yes. Good idea.'

'I suggest five – one hung below a balloon moored at five hundred feet directly over the crater, and four mounted on thirty-foot masts north, south, east, and west of the crater. Remote-controlled, zoom lenses, three-hundred-and-sixty-degree traverse, ninety degrees of vertical sweep. The whole system controlled from a monitor hut.'

'That sounds fine,' said Connors. 'Any comments, Arnold?'

'Could we have a duplicate set of screens in the research hut?'

'I'll get that put in,' said Allbright. 'Now that we no longer have any electrical problems, we're planning to install a comprehensive video communications facility throughout Rockville.'

Connors smiled at Allbright's use of the research group's nickname for the Crow Ridge encampment. 'I see you finally got the word.'

Allbright smiled back. 'I always get the word, Mr Connors.'

Wedderkind looked at Connors. 'What are *you* planning to do?'

'I thought I'd take the film of Crusoe back to Washington,' said Connors.'

'Today?' asked Allbright.

'Yes. It doesn't look as if there's going to be much action here.'

'I don't think it is going to be possible for you to do that.' Allbright's voice was quiet but firm.

'Oh,' said Connors. 'Why not?'

'Because until Crusoe gets a clean bill of health, no one is allowed to leave Crow Ridge.'

Connors stared at Allbright.

'That order came straight from the President, Mr Connors.'

Connors looked at Wedderkind. 'Did you know about this?'

'No, but in a way it makes sense.'

216

'What way? Crusoe's been exposed to the air for nearly eighteen hours. If he was covered with alien spores, they'd all be airborne by now and halfway to Idaho. It's ludicrous. Look at the trouble we went to to sterilize the Lunar Module. You keep telling me Crusoe is the product of an advanced society – '

'True – '

'So it's hardly likely that he's come here to spread the Black Death.'

'No,' said Wedderkind. 'But if he had, I'm sure you wouldn't want to carry it to Washington.'

Connors sighed. 'No, I suppose not.' Suddenly finding himself trapped on the Ridge was a sharp reminder of the risk they were all running. The difference was that he and Allbright knew about CAMPFIRE. Arnold and the others didn't.

Dressed in protective clothing that masked them from head to foot, Page, Armenez, and Davis took scrapings of the dust and soil particles on Crusoe's hull and carried out exhaustive tests for alien micro-organisms in the sterile section of the field laboratory. They also made some direct tests on the hull. Since Crusoe had been intermittently baked in molten rock during the previous three weeks, they had little hope of improving on the negative results of the first soil tests from the crater. The work went on all day and through the night, and by breakfast time on Sunday morning, Page reported, with obvious disappointment, that Crusoe was clean – on the outside.

Working in groups, the scientists and engineers examined every square inch of the hull. They discovered that the small, shallow dome on top of the hull appeared to be part of a large black crystal sphere contained within the hull, and embedded in the underlying cortex. Neame, one of the engineers, and not easily overawed, was already referring to it as 'sliced cabbage'. It was an apt, if scornful, analogy. The discovery of the sphere focussed their attention on the area where the small dome – the exposed part of the sphere – entered the hull. There was no joint visible, even under microscopic examination. The two planes of black crystal appeared to be fused together, forming one continuous layer. There seemed to be no way for anything to come out – and no way for them to get in.

'Maybe the access points are on the underside of the hull,' suggested Spencer. He was another one of the ex-NASA systems engineers. 'If we dig away all this earth around it, and expose the whole gazoo, we'll have a better idea where we're at.'

It seemed a simple enough proposition.

The first part of the operation went smoothly. Bulldozers, driven by Max Nilsson's Texas roughnecks, cleared away the raised rim of the crater and levelled a ten-yard strip around Crusoe's hull, revealing a few more feet of it in the process. Wedderkind and Brecetti exchanged looks, but, amazingly, no one else commented on the disparity between Crusoe's present size and the original crater. Five twenty-man squads of cadets spread out around the edge of the hull and prepared to dig, under the supervision of the fourteen-man research group. As the cadet on Wetherby's left swung his shovel into the earth, it bounced back up over the surprised digger's shoulder and nearly brained the man next to him. Someone else took a firmer grip on his own shovel, but as he tried to dig, the shovel twisted sideways in his hand.

'Hey, look at this!' yelled another of the cadets. Connors, Wedderkind, and the other people on his side of the hull looked in his direction. The cadet stood holding the shovel loosely by the handle. The metal blade rested against an invisible surface about eighteen inches above the ground, at the rim of the hull.

Brecetti walked towards him. 'Let go of the handle!'

The cadet let go. The handle of the shovel fell to the ground, but the blade remained in the air, held up by a powerful magnetic field that ran around the edge of the exposed portion of the hull.

Wedderkind swore quietly under his breath, then looked around and spotted Max Nilsson. 'Max! Could you bring back one of the bulldozers?'

Max brought it back personally. Wedderkind climbed up to the door of the cab and explained what he wanted to do. Max lined up the bulldozer at a tangent to Crusoe, lowered its big blade, and rolled forward, scooping out a long trough of earth. It looked like the irresistible answer right up until the moment the blade hit the invisible barrier, and the ten-ton machine careened off to the right like a bumper-car at an amusement park.

Wedderkind asked Max to try again. Max backed off and lowered his blade on to a new line that would just shave the rim of the hull.

'Take it nice and slow!' yelled Spencer. 'As you start to get that deflection to the right, give it full throttle and steer hard over to the left.' Now that he'd stuck his neck out suggesting they dig Crusoe up, Spencer was anxious to see his idea work.

Max nodded, sat back in his cab, got a good grip on the track levers, and moved forward. The blade started to gouge out another strip of soil. When it got within six feet of the rim, the magnetic field began to force the bulldozer off to the right. Max whacked full power on to the right-hand track and slowed down on the left. The bulldozer bored back into line, but the force of the magnetic field held back the blade. Unable to move forward, but with full power on the right-hand track, the bulldozer pivoted slowly around on the blade leaving Max facing the way he came. Wedderkind waved to him to back off and kill the motor.

'How about trying wooden shovels?' said Milsom, another engineer and a friend of Spencer. It wasn't an unreasonable suggestion, but at the time everyone thought he was trying to be funny.

Max's suggestion to use a high-pressure hose got a better reception. They would need to cut lines for drainage. Then a controlled, continuous blast of water would wash away the loose soil and shale around Crusoe.

Everyone suddenly felt optimistic. Sluice mining, as it was called, had been used successfully in several commercial operations for a number of years, and during the Yom Kippur War the Egyptians had used it to punch a hole through the Israeli defences on the Suez Canal. There was no reason to think it wouldn't work on Crusoe.

The immediate problem was an adequate supply of water. Max's crew had begun sinking a trial borehole down by Bodell's shack, but until that was completed, every drop on Crow Ridge had to be brought in by tanker. Max suggested that one tanker load and a high-pressure pump would be enough to test out the technique. If the results looked promising, they could always pipe in a special supply.

By the end of the afternoon, after a lot of swearing down the base camp telephone, Max had fifty thousand gallons of water up on the plateau. He helped manhandle the high-pressure pump into place, supervised the linkup of the heavy metal hose, and pressed the button on the electric-starter motor. The disappearance of the cutout zone had put an end to their electromechanical problems, but Crusoe had perversely created others. The high-pressure jet blasted the earth away from a five-yard section of Crusoe's hull for all of eighteen seconds, then

220

suddenly exploded into steam. This time Max not only threw his hard hat down, he drop-kicked it over Crusoe. The earth around Crusoe continued to smoulder for two or three hours after Max finally ran out of water or, as Connors put it more uncharitably, steam.

Although the motive remained a mystery, the message was clear. Crusoe was trying to tell them that he wasn't ready to expose himself. They talked about it over supper that night.

'I just don't get it,' said Milsom, the wooden-shovel man. 'He reads the circle we put around him, analyses the differential in the charges down the boreholes, comes back to the centre, and partially surfaces at his original entry point. He's shown himself. Why doesn't he want to be dug up?'

'Perhaps he likes it here,' said Wetherby jocularly. 'He may have decided to put down roots.'

Wedderkind banged his hand on the table, his eyes glowing behind his thick-lensed glasses like lights on a pinball machine. 'That's it! Of course! Why not . . . ? Alan, what a marvellous idea!'

'What marvellous idea?' asked Wetherby. He seemed unable to grasp the fact that he might have inadvertently uttered a remark of cosmic significance with a mouth half full of food.

'That's why we can't see any doors or joints yet,' said Wedderkind excitedly. 'He's *growing*!'

The significance of this idea and its possible consequences took a few seconds to digest. Some of the group found it hard to swallow.

'Are you seriously trying to tell us that Crusoe is some kind of mechanized turnip?' asked Spencer.

'Listen,' said Wedderkind. 'I don't know whether any of you have noticed, but Phil and I are pretty sure that

221

the maximum diameter of his hull is bigger than the diameter of the original crater.'

'Maybe, but until you dig him up, you don't know what his dimensions are.' It was Roger Neame, one of the engineers, being practical again.

'And in that demonstration you gave me with the sugar bowl, you got a creep-back as the steel ball went under,' said Connors. 'If Crusoe vibrated himself into the ground, the soil could also have vibrated back round him.'

'I know that,' said Wedderkind. 'That's why I didn't mention it before. But now that we've had this show of resistance from Crusoe, something like this might *just* be possible. After all, we're already at work ourselves on biochemical relays that will enable us to create computers with the input-output potential of the human brain. If you link that to the new breakthroughs in the field of organic metals, it's possible to envisage the creation of a machine-consciousness – self-awareness in an object we previously classified as inanimate. It's equally conceivable that Crusoe could be the seed state of – well, some *thing*. But hardly a mechanized turnip.' He pointed at Neame. 'Roger, here, is already labelling Crusoe's second layer "sliced-cabbage". Personally, I think that that kind of descriptive downgrading tends to lull us into a false sense of complacency. I think we have to consider the possibility that Crusoe could be the embryo of a machine that grows.'

'Into what?' asked Connors.

They all looked at each other, but nobody rushed in with an answer to his question.

Monday/September 3

At 4:25 A.M. Eastern Standard Time, the last interference cleared from the radar microwavelengths. At 6 A.M., the first radio newscasts made it official. The fade-out was over. The second, more prolonged burst of interference had lasted just over three weeks. The networks served up a 7 A.M. breakfast special of news, views, boffo fun, and music that gave viewers a chance to break in their eyeballs before they went to work.

From then on, throughout the day, local TV and radio stations came back on the air with taped material that had been frozen in the pipeline. TV actors went back thankfully into rehearsal, and agents blew the dust off their contracts and started reserving tables in expensive restaurants.

Domestic and international airline traffic had been the hardest-hit sector of the economy, but plans had already been drawn up for a phased resumption of normal services, and the airlines' bankers had begun to breathe again.

It was also business as usual for the worldwide US radar network and the planes, guns, and ships of the Air Force, Army, and Navy. A huge backlog of coded radio messages from embassies and overseas bases began flooding into the State Department and Pentagon, and reactivated bugs began broadcasting the nation's indiscretions.

Connors and Wedderkind had flown back to Washington overnight with a videotape version of Crusoe's film

223

debut. They screened it for the President after his morning session with the White House Domestic Chief of Staff, then ran it through again an hour later when they were joined by Fraser, Samuels, the three Joint Chiefs of Staff, and McKenna.

Curiously, the reaction to the tapes was muted, and most of the questions were unanswerable. Apparently, it was the effect of the fade-out that had preoccupied the President, Fraser, and the others. Now that it had disappeared, everyone seemed quite content to let Wedderkind's team get on with the job of taking Crusoe apart. They were certainly curious about what it was, but they were more concerned about what it might do next.

For Wedderkind, the meeting was a total anticlimax. After attending the live show, he found that watching Crusoe repeat his performance on a twenty-one-inch TV screen somehow reduced the event to the scale and importance of a daytime soap opera. Worse still, his own impromptu foray had become an embarrassing diversion. He left Connors to replay the tapes and answer any further questions.

As Wedderkind made his exit, the President said, 'Try and stay out of the front line, Arnold.'

At 10:30 A.M. the President led the way into the Cabinet Room where they were joined by the Secretary of State for a meeting of the National Security Council. The Secretary of State didn't know about Crusoe, and no mention of him or the project was made at the meeting. Various departmental reports on the impact of the fade-out were reviewed and it was decided that a new set of national contingency plans was needed to cover any repeat of the recent emergency. A memorandum was addressed to the Hudson Institute think tank asking it to produce a series of economic, defence, and political scenarios based on the possible effects of a prolonged period of radar and radio fade-out. The request was marked 'URGENT'.

Everyone at the meeting was painfully conscious of the fact that, if the fade-out could be switched off, it could also be switched on again. Next time, it might not last three weeks, but three *months*. Any further time projections did not bear thinking about.

FORD GEOPHYSICAL INSTITUTE/BALTIMORE/MARYLAND

Since the beginning of the Crusoe Project, Professor George York, one of the senior geophysicists at the Institute, had been secretly processing data for Wedderkind. As a result of some careful programming over the previous five years, York, a close friend of Wedderkind since their college days, had managed to gain almost sole control of the Institute's largest computer.

By a stroke of good fortune, one of Wedderkind's sisters-in-law was married to a professor at the adjacent Johns Hopkins University. In case there were any prying eyes, Wedderkind drove up with his wife Lillian, parked outside her sister's house, walked through the yard, out of the back gate, and into York's car.

From the major airports of the world, York had collected the times that the fade-out ended and radar contact was restored. The 'switch-on' times for airports inside the North American continent showed a ripple effect spreading out from Montana. Thus Chicago's radar had come back on a few fractions of a second before Washington's, Seattle's before San Francisco's.

York had got no information from Russia or Eastern Europe, but even so, the figures didn't fit into the expected pattern. Hawaii had its radar restored before Washington and so did Karachi and Beirut. At Capetown the times almost coincided. Yet there was no doubt that

225

within the US a wave effect had rippled outward at a speed of nearly one hundred thousand miles an hour.

'There's only one way these timings would make sense,' said York. 'This ripple effect would have to be spreading out simultaneously from more than one point.'

More than one point . . . Wedderkind considered the implications. That must mean that Crusoe was only *part* of the orbiting spacecraft. It must have split up like the multiple warheads of an intercontinental ballistic missile. But why had there been no reports from the rest of the world of incandescent fireballs?

'Take the times for Teheran, Karachi, and Calcutta. The times are almost the same. If we stick to this wave theory it would have to be spreading outwards from somewhere inside Russia.'

'That's an interesting thought,' said Wedderkind. Could this be the reason why the Russians had suddenly clammed up?

'The trouble is these times are not accurate enough to provide a basis for any meaningful calculations,' said York. 'I haven't really got global cover.'

'Still it's given us a lead, George, you've been storing up data on the Earth's magnetic field – '

'Yes, for the last two years.' York's computer was being used to prepare maps of the Earth's field.

'Al Wetherby came up with an idea. Could you contact the stations and get their latest readings?'

York's eyebrows shot up. 'What, from all two hundred and fifty?'

'If we wait till the data filters through the IGY network it could take a year. I told you that we picked up strong directional variations in the Earth's field around Crow Ridge. I'd like to see what shifts there have been on a worldwide basis. Can you do it?'

'I'll try, ' said York. 'But only because you've got a kind face.'

'How soon can you get the information?'

'All I can say is that it's going to take some time. Our work has really been slowed since we lost contact with our research satellites. It's put us back to the Stone Age days of the fifties.'

'I know it will be difficult, George. Just do the best you can.'

Wedderkind went back to Washington with his brain in overdrive. He decided not to say anything to anyone until he had more information. Especially Bob. He tended to get frustrated when confronted by anything other than hard facts.

About thirty minutes after Wedderkind arrived home, NASA Director Chris Matson telephoned with some new information.

Cargill and his Jodrell Bank team had been busy checking the orbits of some of the American satellites. All the orbits had begun to decay – a sure sign that the satellites had been hit by a heavy burst of radiation. The second bit of news was that Arkhip Karamatov and his Russian space team at NASA had been abruptly summoned back to Russia. Before leaving, Karamatov had told Matson that the Russians had launched two sows on Saturday the fourth of August and a large solar observatory satellite on the fifth. Both had failed to transmit or respond to ground signals. The time of entry into orbit coincided exactly with the two ten-second and one thirty-second bursts of fade-out experienced that weekend. It was a clear indication that Crusoe had not been in a mood to welcome curious visitors. Karamatov also confirmed what NASA had suspected: there had been no contact with the cosmonauts aboard *Salyut*-7 and

227

the *Mir* space-station since the initial twenty-minute fade-out on August 3rd and they were now presumed to be dead or in the process of dying from a lethal shot of cosmic radiation.

Finally, Matson passed on the news that the Air Force's NORAD/SPACETRACK centre had organized a rapid radar scan of outer space and had found no trace of any other unexpected objects in Earth orbit. If Crusoe *was* linked to a command module, then the craft, as Wedderkind had suggested, must be in orbit around one of the other planets – or even around the sun itself. If nothing was found, it *could* mean the Earth was Crusoe's final destination.

Thursday/September 6

CROW RIDGE/MONTANA

During the early part of the week, more tests were carried out on Crusoe's hull to find out what he was made of. There were no reactions to acid tests, the hardest cutting tool melted within seconds without even scratching the surface, and the searing flame of a thermic lance left the hull unscorched. The black crystal absorbed the intense heat like desert sand devouring rain.

An attempt to scan Crusoe's internal structure by means of sound waves, X-rays and a laser beam also ended in failure. The black crystal hull absorbed all three without producing even the ghost of an echo. The results set off some lively argument between members of the research group. They could see and feel Crusoe; yet, if they were to believe their instruments, there was nothing there – just a mysterious hole in the facade of the physical universe. The group took the instruments apart and checked every component.

Another puzzling discovery was that the spectrographs of Crusoe's superhard hull revealed several diamondlike characteristics.

'Have you any idea how much that adds up to?' asked Milsom. He was having coffee in the canteen with Spencer and Tomkin, the zoologist. 'A rare black diamond one hundred feet across and maybe fifty feet deep? That must be about twenty-two zillion carats. You know, if we just sat here and quietly cut him up, everybody on Crow Ridge could be a millionaire. MRDC could even end up with a quotation on Wall Street.'

'Forget it,' said Spencer. 'It's probably a synthetic silicate, but about a thousand times tougher than our best.'

'No romance. That's your trouble. No imagination . . .' Milsom sipped his coffee. A thought struck him. 'Jeez – I wonder if you *can* buy shares in this outfit?'

Spencer shook his head resignedly and turned to Tomkin. 'This ding-a-ling didn't really work for NASA, he's a survivor from *Laugh-In*.'

Having attempted to analyse the composition of the hull, the scientists turned it over to the systems engineers for a second, microscopic inspection. Milsom, who had moments of lucidity between laughs, was convinced that the ten-foot-wide dome was the thing to watch, despite the fact that an earlier examination had revealed no separation between the dome and the hull. Now, there was an incredibly fine joint. So fine, in fact, that it was only visible under a powerful lens.

Milsom called Neame and Gilligan over to check his findings.

'That's a good fit.' Gilligan handed the jeweller's eye-piece back to Milsom.

'Even so, I don't know how we missed it before. We didn't go over the whole hull, but I did check around the dome. It was the obvious place to look.'

Spencer squatted down beside them and ran his palm over the dome.

'What do you think, Chris?'

'I think we ought to put some sighting marks on it,' said Milsom. 'A cross on the dome, and matching register marks on the hull.'

Neame drove away and came back with several reels of masking tape, newspaper, and white cellulose spray paint.

'What do you want me to do?' asked Milsom.

'Nothing,' said Neame. He had a mania for neatness.

Milsom sat back and watched as Neame stuck down arrow-straight strips of masking tape and newspaper and sprayed matching white bars on to the dome and hull. When the paint was dry, Neame let Milsom help him strip off the paper and masking tape.

Spencer got the monitor hut to make a videotape record of the sighting marks using the overhead camera in the balloon. The tape was looped, so they could run it continuously and intercut later recordings for instant comparison on the same screen. If the markings appeared to 'jump' it would mean that the dome had moved in relation to the hull.

The three of them went over to the canteen for a cup of coffee.

'Which way do you think it's going to go?' asked Neame.

'I can see only two possibilities,' said Milsom. 'The dome could be the top of a cylinder that rises vertically out of the hull, or it's part of a sphere – in which case it will have to rotate like the ball turret on those old B-17s. My money is on the sphere.'

230

'What do you think that is, the accommodation section?' asked Spencer.

'It's either that or just the way in,' said Milsom. 'Let's sketch it out.' He reached for a paper napkin and clicked up the point of his ball pen. He drew two lemon shapes which he labelled 'A' and 'B', then added a circle to each and arrows to show direction of rotation.

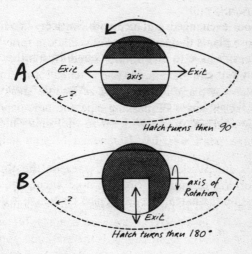

'Since Crusoe won't let us dig him up, we have to assume that Arnold's guess at his shape is correct. It doesn't actually affect our problem with the hatch. Take A – the dot in the middle is the axis of rotation. There could be a hole right through the sphere giving you access to both sides of the craft. To open, the sphere rotates through ninety degrees.

'In B, there is only one way into the sphere – and it rotates through one hundred and eighty degrees to open. The sphere could also rotate on more than one axis,

231

which would give you access to and from several points within the hull.'

'Yes, that's good,' said Spencer.

'Except that I don't know what we're all getting excited about,' said Milsom. 'If that dome does move, it can only be because something inside is going to come out.'

'Or someone,' added Spencer.

'Not necessarily,' said Neame. 'Crusoe might open up to let us *in*.'

Milsom exchanged a glance with Spencer. 'You mean like those plants that catch flies?'

'It doesn't have to be a trap. It could be a self-opening birthday present.'

'That's a pretty wild idea, Rog. When did you dream that up?' asked Spencer.

Neame shrugged. 'I don't know. It just occurred to me.'

Connors and Wedderkind arrived back on the Ridge in time for a late supper. Spencer told them about the progress on the hatch, but didn't pass on Neame's theory.

Friday/September 7

Neame popped into the monitor hut on his way to breakfast and ran the looped master against the first reel of the morning. The dome *was* rotating, on an axis roughly 30 degrees to their horizontal sighting marks.

Neame called up the canteen, got Milsom on the phone, told him the news and ruined everybody's breakfast. Within about three minutes, practically the whole research group, both scientists and engineers, were crowded into the monitor hut. Wedderkind still had some shaving cream on his face.

'We'd better get some more marks on that dome,' said Spencer.

Milsom turned to Neame. 'What did you do with the paint?'

'Everything's still in the back of the jeep.'

'Right.'

'I'll come with you.'

Wedderkind wiped some more of his Old Spice foam away. 'I'll go and tell Bob. We'll be in the operations room.'

'That's in the command hut . . . ?'

'Yes. We'll be with Allbright. But first I'm going to have some breakfast. It looks like it could be quite a day.'

Within thirty minutes, the second set of sighting marks had moved towards the top right-hand corner of the TV screen and had been swallowed up as the dome continued to rotate into the hull. There was now no doubt that the dome formed part of a large sphere turning on an axis deep within Crusoe's hull.

Milsom toyed with the idea of asking if anyone was good at reading crystal balls, then decided it might not go down too well.

A circle started to appear in the left-hand bottom corner of their screens. As it rose clear of the hull they saw that it was a shallow circular well cut into the surface of the sphere, rather like a screw countersunk below the surface of a piece of wood. It was the first sign of anything remotely resembling a hatch. When the circle reached the centre of the screen, it stopped moving.

Spencer telephoned Wedderkind, who was now sitting

233

in front of the bank of TV monitors in the command hut's operations room.

'This is looking good. Is it okay to go and check it out?'

'Yes,' said Wedderkind. 'But not all at once.'

Spencer drove out with Milsom, Neame, and Gilligan and padded up on to the hull. They'd taken to wearing rubber-soled basketball shoes when walking about on Crusoe in case he had another bout of magnetism.

To avoid confusion, it was agreed to retain the word 'dome' to describe the exposed portion of the black crystal sphere above the line of the hull. The circular well, which had come to rest in the top dead centre of the dome, had an external diameter of six feet, a depth of twelve inches, and an internal diameter of five feet. Like most of Crusoe's quoted measurements, these were only close approximations. The sides of the well tapered inward, and the bottom of the well had a convex surface like a magnifying glass.

Spencer and the others each checked the bottom rim of the well to see if it was part of, or fitted to, the sloping sides. If there was a joint, it was too fine to see, even with the hefty magnification of a jeweller's eyepiece.

They sprayed a new set of sighting marks on the dome and the bottom of the circular well, so that any movement would show up on the monitor screens. As they were gathering up their gear, something at the rim of the dome caught Gilligan's eye.

'Hey, look at this.' He knelt down to examine it and beckoned to the others.

Spencer, Neame, and Milsom bent over to take a look at what he had found. Gilligan carefully picked up several thin, shredded, white fragments and sniffed them.

'It's that white cellulose paint.'

The fragments were curled into tiny rolls.

'Do you think the surface rejected it?' asked Neame.

'No,' said Spencer. 'I think I know what happened. The tolerance between the dome and the hull is so fine, the paint was scraped off as the dome turned over.'

'Now that's what I call microtolerance,' said Milsom. 'That was a *thin* coat of spray.'

'We could work to that,' said Neame.

'On a sphere nearly fifteen feet across?'

'Let's get out of here,' said Spencer. 'We're spoiling everybody's view.'

Connors sat watching the bank of TV screens in the operations room of the command hut. Allbright was on his right, Wedderkind on his left. On the big centre screen they saw the four engineers get back into the jeep and drive away from Crusoe.

Wedderkind hit the mike button. 'Neal, can you give us an overhead close-up on the dome, please?'

Neal Zabrodski was the Air Force Master Sergeant in charge of the monitor team.

'Coming up on main screen,' said Zabrodski.

The dome expanded rapidly to fill the twenty-one-inch screen. Connors sat up in his chair. The bottom of the circular well had already begun to move – at right angles to the axis of rotation of the dome. There was a second sphere fitting snugly inside the first, just like those sets of intricately-carved hollow ivory balls the Chinese delight in producing.

'Arnold, it *is* a hatch. We're in business.'

Wedderkind kept his finger on the mike button. 'Neal, is Dan there?'

'Yes, he's sitting on my shoulder.'

Spencer's voice came over the loudspeaker. 'What is it, Arnold?'

'Dan, I know you've just got back, but we're going to need some more sighting marks on that hatch.'

235

'No problem. We're on our way.'

'Okay, but be careful.'

The curved surface continued to move towards the upper left-hand corner of the screen. Milsom and Neame added as many marks as they could, then as a darker shape appeared at the edge of the circle, they scuttled off the hull.

The dark curved shape continued to move across the circular hole in the dome like the moon eclipsing the sun. The second inner sphere was hollow. The dark shape was another circular hatch exactly the same size as that in the dome. When both hatches were in line, the inner sphere stopped rotating.

'Gentlemen,' said Wedderkind. 'As you can all see, we have two hollow spheres fitting one inside the other, and rotating at right angles to one another. This is a real Swiss-watch job. We'll call the circular aperture in the dome the outer hatch, and its matchmate in the second sphere the inner hatch. Okay, Neal – can you take us in closer?'

The overhead camera zoomed in for a tight close-up. Connors and the others found themselves looking into a dark well, containing an eight-sided box with sloping sides. It appeared to be attached to the sides of the well by a series of angular struts. The box appeared to be made of the same translucent black crystalline material as the rest of Crusoe, but without the underlying brain-coral pattern. The top of the box was faceted like a gemstone with eight sloping panels butted together round another octagon containing four, insect-like, compound eyes.

Spencer's voice came through again. 'I think there's some upward movement on that box.'

Wedderkind leaned forward and spoke into the mike,

'Neal, can we get a close-up of that with one of the ground cameras?'

Connors looked down at his calendar watch. 'Friday . . .'

'The seventh of September,' said Wedderkind.

'That clinches it. Since we started with Crusoe, we might as well stick to the story. Whatever comes out, that's what we'll call him.'

So Friday it was, after the native companion of Robinson Crusoe, whose name marked the day of his rescue from his savage captors.

'Camera South on main screen . . .

'With the sun behind it, Camera South had the best chance of picking up the details of the black boxlike object that was now emerging from the hatch. Connors watched closely as the telephoto lens zeroed in for a tight side view.

The four 'eyes' grew out on thick curving stalks, arced through a quarter of a circle above the rim of the hatch, then stopped. Connors glanced at the bank of small monitors above the main screen that carried the pictures transmitted by the other cameras. He saw that the 'eyes' were at right angles to each other, and that, between them, they quartered the immediate horizon. It reminded Connors of four cautious soldiers looking out of a foxhole with periscopes.

If the object *was* scanning Crusoe's surroundings the view from the hatch must have been puzzling. To the east was the semicircle of blasted trees, to the west, the bare rocks on the high point of the Ridge. Floating directly overhead was the silver, three-finned balloon with its camera platform, and stretching away on all sides across the barren plateau, the lines of red and white stakes each topped with a blue light. And that was all. There were no men and no machines.

237

Apparently satisfied with the view, the four stalks retracted into the top of the box, which then slid upward out of the hatch on eight rather complicated struts. The box was about three feet high, with sides that tapered outward, then sloped sharply back in at the base. The box measured about four feet across at its widest point.

Connors could now see that the struts were not part of the hatch, they were attached to the base of the eight-sided box. The struts slowly unfolded outward until they touched Crusoe's hull.

'Oh, Jesus . . .' murmured Connors as Friday's black shape became clear.

They were not struts at all. They were eight articulated legs, and the body they now lifted clear of the hatch looked uncomfortably like that of a spider. Beneath him, the inner sphere rotated, closing the inner hatch, then the outer hatch rolled smoothly back out of sight under the surface of the hull. It happened so quickly no one had a chance to time it, but the guess was it took less than five seconds for Crusoe to batten down the hatches.

Fully extended, Friday's legs had a spread of about fourteen feet. His body hung between five and six feet off the ground. The eight side panels of his body had a small honeycomb pattern underneath the black crystal surface. In a curved housing projecting from the body panel facing them were four larger 'eyes' set close together in a diamond pattern. On each side of this eyes pod were two ribbed, tubular feelers like vacuum cleaner hose. The inside pair were short, the outside pair, long. Underneath the body was a multiple array of jointed attachments rather like stunted arms. Some of these appeared to have pincerlike ends.

Just when the research group thought they had seen enough, a line of foot-long black fibres sprouted from the three outer sections of each leg. They were probably tactile sensors that worked like kerb feelers, but they looked like hairs, and increased Friday's unwholesome resemblance to a spider.

'Oh, shit,' groaned Milsom. 'Look at that.'

His voice came over the speaker in the command hut. Spencer had left the mike on. Connors exchanged an amused glance with Allbright.

Wedderkind cleared his throat and spoke into the mike. 'Gentlemen, we're giving this secondary vehicle the code name Friday. Do you have any comments, Vic?'

'Well, I have one piece of good news,' said Tomkin. 'All those of you who don't like spiders can relax. Friday isn't going to eat us, because he's hasn't got a mouth.'

'Or an abdomen,' added Davis.

'Maybe he just likes killing people,' said Milsom.

'Chris, I'm sure we'll all be glad of your sense of humour before this thing is through, but just for the moment, let's keep things serious – okay?'

'Sorry, Arnold.' Milsom looked contritely at the loudspeaker.

'Hold on,' said Spencer. 'We've got some more action here.'

All eyes fastened on the screen as Friday flexed each pair of legs experimentally, wiggled the tool kit under his body, then crawled slowly down Crusoe's gently curving hull and towards the camera. Although he was nearly half a mile away and moving in the opposite direction, it seemed as if he was heading straight for them.

As Friday reached the edge of the hull, he extended his two front legs and touched the earth tentatively. He moved forward a little more and gave it another going over with his long pair of feelers. Apparently reassured, he crawled off the hull, two legs at a time, testing the ground ahead of him at each step. When he was finally clear of the hull, he began to wander around Crusoe in hesitant, ever-widening circles.

As he moved among the red and white striped stakes, he stopped several times to inspect the blue light on top, the wires, and the battery at the bottom.

Whether he was actually 'looking' in any one direction was open to conjecture. They agreed to call the four circular elements in the pod 'eyes' because that was what they looked like. They called the panel with the eye pod the front, because that seemed the most logical place to put them – except that Friday's front, back, and sides were difficult to define. As he wandered around in view of the ground cameras, they saw that Friday could move with equal facility in any direction. In the report, they wrote 'Omnidirectional locomotory capability – which meant the same thing, but would be easier for the people back in Washington to understand.

They also saw that both the top and bottom sections of his body could rotate independently of the centre section to which the legs were attached, so that the eye pod did not always face the direction of movement. The result of this was that Friday appeared at times to be walking sideways or backward, and made it difficult to predict which way he would move from a position of rest.

'That,' said Spencer, 'is one hell of a piece of engineering. See how smoothly he alters course? His limb co-ordination is fantastic. Boy, I'm glad I didn't have to work out that program.'

'There may not be one,' said Page. 'It may not be a machine at all.' As a biochemist, Page had a vested interest in keeping Friday 'alive' for as long as possible.

'Whatever it is, it's beautiful,' said Tomkin. He could already envisage a period of fruitful study ending with a thesis on Friday's locomotion.

Beautiful or not, there was no doubt that compared to

240

Friday's smooth black mechanical perfection, NASA's own Lunar Excursion Module used in the Apollo moon flights looked like a piece of junior school junkyard sculpture made out of Bacofoil and crushed Coca-Cola cans.

Connors swung his chair away from the screens, got up and walked to the window. He glanced outside briefly, then turned around to face Allbright and Wedderkind.

'What do you think?'

'It seems harmless enough,' said Allbright.

'There is no reason why it shouldn't be,' said Wedderkind.

'Well, there's only one way to find out. Somebody is going to have to go out there and show we're friendly.'

'Are you calling for volunteers?' asked Allbright.

'There's no need,' said Connors. 'I want to go myself.' He looked Allbright straight in the eye.

Allbright stared right back. 'I really don't think that is advisable.'

Connors pointed towards the window. 'General, out there is the first animate object, the first sign of life, from beyond Earth. I'm not concerned whether my name gets in the history books or not. I want to be one of the first people to meet it.'

'Mr Connors, my orders regarding your safety – '

'Listen, if Tomkin is right, at least I know I'm not going to get eaten. If this is some kind of vehicle, the worst thing that can happen is that I get run over.'

'Even so, I still think you ought to reconsider your decision. As head of the project – '

'Exactly,' said Connors. 'As head of the project, I make the rules. Rule One says I'm allowed to go out there and meet this thing.'

Allbright stood up. The breadth of his shoulders and

241

his extra height gave him a dominating physical presence. 'In that case, the rules need revising. This is a totally unnecessary risk that I don't think I can allow you to take.'

'General, I don't think this is a situation where you or I need to start throwing our weight around. I've told you what I intend to do. My decision does not endanger the lives of anyone else on this project, and that's all there is to it.' Connors smiled. 'To be honest, if I thought there was any real risk I wouldn't be going.'

Allbright gazed at him for a moment, then said, 'There must be a more sensible way to prove you're in charge.' He looked at Wedderkind for support.

'Don't look at me,' said Wedderkind. 'I want to go out there with him.'

'Very well,' said Allbright, 'You leave me no choice.' He looked at each of them in turn. 'I'll have to come with you.'

Connors couldn't hold back a smile. 'Glad to have you along, General.' He shooks hands with Allbright, and looked at Wedderkind. 'There's just one thing, Arnold. We're going to take this nice and slow. If you pull another one of your *banzai* charges, I'm going to cut your feet off.' Connors put his hand on Wedderkind's shoulder. 'I think it would be best if *you* explained to the research group what we've decided to do. Especially since they're all friends of yours. The General and I will wait for you in his trailer.'

'Thank you very much,' said Wedderkind.

'Take a seat,' said Allbright. 'I plan to have a drink. Would you care to join me?'

'That's why I came,' said Connors. 'Rye with ginger ale if you have it.'

'No ginger. Ice?'

'Okay, that'll be fine.' Connors glanced around the living room of Allbright's trailer. It was as clean as a new pin and in impeccable trim. They must have shipped him the model they used for the catalogue photos.

The sound of voices raised in argument floated over from the research hut. They were obviously taking Wedderkind's news badly.

Allbright handed Connors a cut-glass bucket loaded with three fat fingers of rye.

'Thanks . . .' Connors nodded towards the source of the noise. 'I can't think why they're making so much fuss.'

'Probably for the same reason you did.' Allbright raised his glass. 'To your safe return.'

'And yours.' Connors took a heartwarming swallow and nodded towards the three photographs in the fold-out leather wallet that stood on the window sill. 'Fine-looking family.'

'Yes, I've been very lucky,' said Allbright. You could tell he really meant it, too. 'Do you have any family?'

'I had. A son – Joe . . . he was killed in a car crash when he was eight. My wife was killed too.'

'Must take time to get over a thing like that,' said Allbright.

'Too long,' said Connors. He swirled the ice around in his glass and took another swallow of rye.

The cadet outside the trailer opened the door and let Wedderkind in.

'Drink?' asked Allbright.

'No, thanks. Let's get out there and get it over with.' Wedderkind flashed a sharp look at Connors.

'Be with you in a minute,' said Connors. 'I'm just overcoming my fear of spiders.'

* * *

When Connors stepped down from Allbright's trailer, he found four jeeps lined up in diamond formation. The first was for him to sit in with Allbright and Wedderkind. The next two had the windshields folded down. A bazooka man sat beside the driver-loader. Behind them were two more cadets with M-16s and enough ammunition to start World War Three. The last jeep carried four folded stretchers, a first-aid kit, and two of the NASA medics. The only thing missing were Red Cross armbands.

Connors nodded towards the armed jeeps. 'Aren't we overreacting a little? All we need to show we're friendly is a white flag.'

'Do you think Friday will be able to tell the difference between that and a bazooka?' asked Allbright.

'You have a point there.'

'Perhaps,' said Wedderkind. 'But I must still register a protest. This is a totally inappropriate response.'

'It's a simple precautionary measure in case any of us get injured. The firepower is there in case it's needed to cover our evacuation.'

Wedderkind shook his head. 'Why do all of you have this paranoia? I had the same trouble back in Washington. This is not an invasion, General. This is a landing by a craft from another *civilization*, almost certainly centuries in advance of our own. That means that they are more intelligent than we are, and certainly beyond the need for a display of brute force.'

Allbright didn't turn a hair. 'I don't quite understand how you define brute force, Mr Wedderkind, but this pair is already responsible for the deaths of over *four thousand* people!'

'General, Crusoe didn't make those planes collide with one another. They were piloted by people like you and me.'

244

'Millions of dollars' worth of damage. The destruction of our weather and communications satellites – '

'Deactivation, General. Continuing deactivation. They're still in orbit. Who knows? They may start working again when Crusoe leaves.'

'You're arguing like a Jesuit, Mr Wedderkind. This craft has severely damaged our defensive capability. The Russians only have to – '

'General, you can't expect Crusoe to understand power politics. That's our problem. All he's done is to take precautionary measures to prevent a concerted, hostile, global response. Simple logical precautions that anyone would take if they were landing on a planet inhabited by destructive maniacs like us . . . I don't mean that personally, I'm referring to our general attitude. The fixed belief that power comes out of the barrel of a gun. Force is not going to solve anything in this encounter, General. We have to abandon every prejudice, every misconception, every thought we may have had about an event like this and start completely afresh. The world is poised on the threshold of a new era.'

'That may very well be so,' said Allbright. 'But neither of you are going to set foot across it without this escort. So what's it going to be, gentlemen?' He looked at them both. 'Are you going to ride point with me – or would you rather be locked in and watch the whole thing on TV?'

'Do you really think I could let you get away with that?' asked Connors.

'I'm here to protect you,' said Allbright. 'And that order, as they say, comes right out of the Oval Office.' He smiled. 'So there's no point in making trouble, Mr Connors, especially since you both know neither of you should be going out there in the first place.'

Allbright's habit of being right was beginning to get a

little infuriating. Connors turned to Wedderkind. 'It's up to you, Arnold. What do you want to do – go out there, or file a complaint?'

'Both,' said Wedderkind darkly. He climbed into the back of the jeep. Connors followed. Allbright got in beside the driver. As they were about to move forward, Wedderkind reached out and tapped Allbright's shoulder. Allbright looked around.

'General, can I have your assurance that there is going to be no trigger-happy shooting?'

'The Air Force doesn't train people to be trigger-happy, Mr Wedderkind. No military establishment in the world has higher standards than our academy at Colorado Springs. Take it from me, you'll crack before any of these cadets. Just relax, you're in good hands.' Allbright signalled the driver to move off.

They drove up the path on to the plateau past the sullen research group.

'The natives look hostile,' said Connors. 'I hope you haven't lost too many friends.'

'They're used to politicians fouling things up.' Wedderkind clearly hadn't forgiven Connors for muscling in on what he considered to be an exclusively scientific excursion.

The four jeeps fanned out into a wider diamond pattern and headed slowly towards Crusoe. Friday was continuing his raggedy spiral course and was now moving away from them on the far side of Crusoe.

The monitor hut, which had been following Friday's progress with the aid of their bird's-eye view camera, had given them the grid reference of a point through which Friday was expected to pass. When they reached the selected point, they pulled up in the middle of the twenty-five-yard-wide square, at right angles to Friday's projected path. The two armed jeeps parked in front and behind them. The first-aid jeep stationed itself two squares farther back.

As Friday crawled into view between the lines of stakes, Connors, Allbright and Wedderkind got out of their jeep. The armed cadets took cover behind their vehicles, chambered the first round in their M-16s, selected automatic fire, and loaded the bazookas.

Connors moved into line with the two red and white striped stakes that marked the edge of the square. Allbright was on his left, Wedderkind two yards to his right.

Friday came crawling into view, exactly on course. When he was about forty yards away, Connors took a couple of paces forward. Friday stopped dead in his tracks, then took five small cautious steps forward. The protruding four-eyed panel swivelled around slowly and fixed them with a black, glassy stare.

Connors felt a faint chill of fear ripple up the skin of his back. Reason told him that he was facing a machine, but there was definitely something creepy about Friday's insect-like movements.

To hell with it . . . It was too late for second thoughts. With everyone watching, the only thing to do was move forward. Connors emptied his mind and concentrated on putting one foot firmly in front of the other. Allbright and Wedderkind followed, staying in step and keeping their distance.

Friday froze rock solid across their path.

When he was only five yards away, Connors stopped and waited until the others drew level. Now they were closer, they could hear a veritable symphony of clicking sounds.

Connors looked at Allbright and Wedderkind, then moved slowly forward until he was only ten feet away from Friday. Without quite knowing why, Connors raised his right hand, then, realizing the pointlessness of the gesture, dropped it self-consciously.

Allbright and Wedderkind moved up alongside Connors and faced Friday for a full minute without moving. During that minute, which seemed as if it would never end, Connors felt that every detail of Friday was being engraved on his brain with a red-hot wire. Tomkin was right, Friday didn't have a mouth, but he did have the two pairs of jointed limbs common to the family *Arachnidae* – a short, jointed pair of mandibles for pushing food into their jaws, and a longer multijointed pair of *palpi* – antennae – which they use for feeling out their prey. Both the long and short pairs set on either side of Friday's eye pod seemed to be tubular feelers. They were pointed towards Connors. On the raised end of each feeler he could see a hole opening and closing rapidly.

The clicking noises inside Friday built to a new crescendo, then faded away to nothing. Connors' heart missed a beat as Friday's front left leg twitched, then lifted an inch or two above the ground.

Behind the jeeps, the cadets slipped the safety catches off their loaded weapons, and around the Ridge and in front of the scattered TV monitors everyone held their breath.

Friday's front left leg continued to lift, then very, very slowly, he took three careful steps backward.

For a moment, Connors was unable to react, to understand, then he suddenly felt a great surge of relief. He turned to Wedderkind. 'Did you see that?'

Wedderkind nodded.

Connors looked at Allbright and laughed. 'He's *frightened* of us – isn't that fantastic! When he lifted that foot up I nearly . . .'

'It was quite a moment,' conceded Allbright.

Wedderkind finally found his voice. 'After that, who needs a heart attack?'

'You can say that again.' Connors turned towards the hidden research group and waved to them to come out to look at Friday.

Unfortunately, this impromptu gesture was interpreted as a general invitation to everyone watching. People began swarming on to the Ridge from all directions.

Allbright and Wedderkind waved them back furiously, but in their eagerness to get a close look at Friday, everybody thought they were waving at somebody else. The result was a few frantic minutes of total confusion as the three of them became trapped in a milling crowd that closed in around Friday and, at one point, almost trampled on him.

Friday drew his legs close in against his body, shrank down and 'played dead'.

As soon as they realized the mistake, Allbright's Praetorian Guard of fourth-year cadets started bellowing orders, cutting out the third-year cadets from the crowd. Within a few minutes they had been formed up into their respective squads and doubled off to await Allbright's displeasure.

That left the Air Force technicians and the research group jostling each other for a closer look.

'Mr Harris!' roared Allbright. He waved towards the nearest bunch of technicians. 'I want the names of all these men and I want them off the Ridge. Now!'

'Yes, *sir*!' roared Harris.

The technicians were swiftly weeded out, leaving the civilians in possession of the Ridge.

'Sorry, Arnold.'

Wedderkind gave Connors' shoulder a benign pat. 'Don't worry about it.' Then to make him feel worse he added, 'Just leave the rest to us, okay?'

This, thought Connors, is where a lesser man walks away. He decided to stay right where he was.

The research group backed off to form a semicircle fifteen feet away from Friday, leaving him a clear exit back to Crusoe. He obviously didn't like being crowded. Tiny beads of condensation had formed on the sloping sides of his body – almost as if he was sweating with fear. Wedderkind called up the two Air Force photographers and had them shoot several reels of film. The research group squatted down to scan the details of Friday's construction, discussing their impressions in low voices.

'Why are we all whispering?' asked Milsom.

Since nobody knew why, they all began to speak a little louder.

Milsom called out to Friday. 'Don't mind us, just go on with what you were doing.'

It could only have been pure coincidence, but no sooner were the words out than Friday started clicking. Milsom almost fell over. Friday stretched out his legs and stood up, his body undulating as if on springs. The top half of his body was a good six and a half feet off the ground, his four 'eyes' almost on a level with their own. Complex, compound eyes, as immobile and expression-less as those of a housefly. Dark, unfathomable pools of liquid black in which Connors and the others could see nothing but myriad reflected images of themselves, the earth and the sky.

Friday began to back off. He swivelled his eye pod halfway around towards his line of advance, which created the impression that he was walking sideways.

'Do you think he's going back in?' asked Armenez.

'If he is,' said Wedderkind, 'it's something I want to see.' He ambled towards Crusoe, taking care to give Friday a wide berth. The rest of the research group followed his cue and split up into two groups, some following Wedderkind, the others going around to the left of Friday. Connors and Allbright kept well behind him all the way to the crater.

Reaching the edge of the hull, Friday swivelled his eye pod round to scan the two groups of researchers on either side of him then brought it back to rest on Connors and Allbright. They both halted, waiting to see what he would do next. The two front pincer arms of the 'tool-kit' mounted under his belly slowly unfolded. They held the opposite edges of what looked like a small rectangular metal plaque. Light flared off its highly polished surface as Crusoe placed it carefully on the ground between his front legs.

With that manouvre completed, Friday positioned himself on top of Crusoe with his legs astride the dome. The two hatches opened with a soft swishing sound. He lowered his body halfway in, folded up his legs, and sank out of sight. Within a few seconds, the two spheres rotated on their opposed axes, sealing the entrance to Crusoe under a smooth, unbroken layer of black, diamond-hard crystal.

The research group crowded round Connors, Wedderkind and Allbright as they took a closer look at Friday's calling card. Their curiosity gave way to gasps of astonishment. Neame and Gilligan had both seen the plaque before; Connors and the others had all seen a photograph or drawing of it. Made from a thin sheet of gold-plated aluminium, the plaque measured six by nine inches. It was engraved with various diagrams that included a table of atomic weights, a diagram that showed the relative positions of Earth and the other planets from the sun. Linked to Earth were the stylized naked figures of a naked man and woman.

The plaque had been put aboard the Pioneer 10 spacecraft launched from Cape Kennedy on 3 March 1972 towards the planet Jupiter for a fly-by rendezvous in December 1973. Its course past the huge planet with its mysterious red spot had taken it Uranus then out into deep space.

Pioneer 10, the lonely trailblazer for the triumphantly-successful Voyager II fly-bys of the eighties, was carrying the gold-plated plaque in case, by a trillion to one chance in the next hundred, or next thousand, million years it reached another star system and was pulled into orbit around a planet on which there was intelligent life with a space technology of their own. It would tell them that Mankind had once existed – perhaps might even still be found, reaching out towards the stars.

But now, that message would never reach its unknown destination. Somewhere between Uranus and the uncharted fringe of our solar system, Crusoe and Friday had intercepted Pioneer 10 and, in the first recorded act of space piracy, had taken possession of the plaque – and had returned it to Earth.

Saturday/September 8

THE WHITE HOUSE/WASHINGTON DC

The President viewed the tapes of Friday with considerably more interest than those of Crusoe. He watched Connors' performance on behalf of mankind, then looked across at him with a smile. 'That was a remarkable piece of egocentric behaviour.'

'Somebody had to be first,' said Connors.

'Does the team have any ideas about Friday?' asked the President.

'We're all relieved to find that he's mechanistic,' said

Wedderkind. 'I was beginning to get worried about the problems posed by Crusoe, but now that we've seen the way the hatch operates, I think we're dealing with a fairly straighforward type of spacecraft.'

'And not some diamond-coated cabbage that's about to grow arms.'

Wedderkind looked at the President then eyed Connors. *Et tu, Brute* . . .

Connors accepted the charge philosophically.

'I haven't totally abandoned that hypothesis,' said Wedderkind. 'It's just in cold storage.'

'But at least it's built by somebody,' said the President. 'With a pretty high level of technology. The engineering tolerances on the hatch aren't beyond us, but that crystalline covering – '

'Is it really a black diamond coating?'

'That's what the spectrograph says. But in the hardness test it came out tougher than anything we've got – and that includes the latest synthetic silicates. The idea of its being encased in a giant gemstone is commercially attractive but scientifically irrelevant. It would still be the most valuable thing on Earth if it was made out of Kraft cheese slices.'

'Tell me some more about Friday,' said the President.

'It looks like a fairly straightforward reconnaissance vehicle but with a complex reaction system. It's probably equipped with computer-type reasoning. It might even be linked to a larger electronic brain inside Crusoe. The technology's impressive, but none of us feel too overawed – not at the moment, anyway.'

'But why eight legs?' asked Connors. 'Wouldn't wheels have been a whole lot simpler? And faster?'

'Not necessarily. We would probably opt for that solution because we are wheel-oriented but there are types of terrain where legs would be much more efficient –

especially if developed to Friday's level of mechanical perfection.'

'But how does he work?' asked the President.

'Yes,' said Connors. 'I've spent my life reassured by the idea that giant spiders were a physical impossibility.'

'That's still true,' said Wedderkind. 'You can't just enlarge a spider or any other insect and expect it to work. The weight increases with the scale, and at a certain point the original structure collapses. Friday is a completely different proposition. He's a spiderlike machine. His legs are quite slender. His total weight can't be more than two or three hundred pounds. I imagine four men could lift him quite easily.'

'And how does he move around?'

'Ah – that's just *one* of the sixty-four-dollar questions,' said Wedderkind. 'He's probably powered by very advanced electric batteries.'

'That sort of tool kit he carries underneath,' said the President. 'I noticed he had at least two sets of articulated pincers – in fact they were more like hands.'

Wedderkind nodded. 'Yes. That feature doesn't exist in the insect world. Well, not ours, anyway. It's a unique feature of Man the Toolmaker.'

'I've read somewhere that you can't build an advanced society without it,' said Connors.

'Not an advanced *technological* society.'

'Why did Friday back away from us?' asked Connors.

'You answered that yourself out on the plateau. You said he was frightened of us. In view of our own feelings at the time, it was a natural conclusion, but fear need not be the only reason. It could have been a sign of his peaceful intentions towards us.'

'But if Friday is capable of emotions such as fear and aggression – or in this case nonaggression – he must be alive. And if he's alive, how can he be a machine?' asked Connors.

'Very easily,' said Wedderkind. 'The two states are not incompatible. But if you find the concept too difficult, just think of him as a very sophisticated robot.'

'Okay. How do you propose to verify these ideas?' said the President.

'By continued observation.'

'Do you plan to take him apart?'

'Some of the group would like to try,' said Connors. 'The trouble is we're not sure whether we need a neuro-surgeon or a plumber.'

'A lot will depend on what Friday does next,' said Wedderkind.

'Which could be nothing,' said Connors. 'After almost getting trampled to death the first time out he may decide it's safer to stay inside.'

'He'll be out,' said Wedderkind.

President Lorenzo leaned forward and tapped the clear plastic case Wedderkind had placed on his desk. It contained the plaque that Friday had presented to the research team on Crow Ridge. 'I take it there's no doubt about this?'

'No, we checked,' said Wedderkind. 'It's definitely from Pioneer 10.'

'What d'you make of it?'

Connors deflected the question on to Wedderkind. They had already discussed Friday's surprise package at some length during the flight to Washington. There had been a great deal of speculation but they had failed to reach any meaningful conclusions. Connors thought back to Wedderkind's remark about the difficulty of relating to an alien intelligence. Perhaps there *were* no answers – at least on a level that Man could understand. Perhaps the meaning of this long-awaited encounter was beyond the limits of human comprehension.

Good old Arnold, however, was not about to give up on the case. 'I'm not quite sure . . .' He lit another cigarette and inhaled deeply. 'According to the last data received by the Space-flight Center at Houston, Pioneer 10 was alive and well and on its way out of the solar system. Crusoe and Friday must have hijacked the plaque without altering Pioneer's flight trajectory. It's the only scenario that fits the known data.'

'After Pioneer completed its fly-by of Uranus?'

'That's the gut feeling I have,' said Wedderkind. 'But it could have happened anywhere along the line.'

'Could, uhh – Crusoe have come from one of those planets out there?'

Wedderkind shook his head. 'The chances are next to nil. Compared to Earth, Jupiter, Saturn and Uranus are still in a primitive state of evolution. And conditions get even worse the further out you go. Jupiter, for example, has no solid surface – '

The President cut in. 'How about one of its moons? Aren't some of them almost as big as Mercury?'

'One of them is even bigger. But before the inhabitants of Jupiter could establish a moon-base, they would first have to develop space-flight technology on the planet itself. And that's just not possible. Higher forms of life couldn't exist there.'

'We don't know that for sure,' said Connors.

Wedderkind eyed him and turned back to the President. 'Bob has developed a space conspiracy theory.'

Connors stepped in to explain for himself. 'All I said was we can no longer take anything for granted. Crusoe's arrival is proof that somebody is out there. If Pioneer 10 *was* intercepted then the information it sent back could have been doctored. The same goes for the Surveyor

256

package that was soft-landed on Mars, the Russian Venus probe, and the recent Voyager fly-by of Jupiter, Saturn and Uranus. Let's face it, the pictures and measurements are only sets of figures radioed across space and recorded down here on computer tape.'

The President considered this proposition with a puzzled frown. 'Why would anyone want to beam us a mass of phoney data?'

'To mislead us as to the *real* conditions up there.'

'Is that possible, Arnold?'

Wedderkind favoured Connors with an indulgent smile then answered the President. 'It's an engaging theory. It's true we have no way to verify the integrity of the transmissions but the pictures and data received so far support our previous visual observations and the predictions based on current scientific theories.'

'So what's *your* theory?' insisted the President.

'Everything points to Crusoe and Friday being sent from another star system. Since the technology involved in their construction is way ahead of ours I believe their purpose is to explore all the planets in our solar system. If I was given the job I would start at the edge and work my way in towards the sun.'

'Which was how he ran into Pioneer – and tracked back from there,' suggested the President, anxious to demonstrate that his brain was not, as some unkind critics had suggested, made from *mozzarella*.

'Yes. On the other hand, he may have been around for some time. He could have been camping out on one of Jupiter's or Saturn's moons as you suggested or, alternatively, he might have been in a parking orbit around Uranus or Neptune, or circling the sun – like Halley's comet. Waiting.'

'For what?'

'Some sign of life.' Wedderkind stubbed out his cigarette and dispersed the wreath of smoke around his head.

'You mean . . . some sign of life from intelligent beings who were into space flight . . .'

'That's one possibility.'

Connors realized why the President got so frustrated when he couldn't get 'yes' or 'no' answers. Especially at a time like this with so many other problems crowding in on him. He was clearly wishing he hadn't opened up this particular can of worms.

'I don't get it, Arnold. If Crusoe has been coasting around our solar system for some time, as you suggest, he'd know about Earth. And all the radio and TV traffic would tell him something or someone was down here. Why wait till now?'

'Good point . . .' Wedderkind lit another cigarette. 'I wish I knew the answer. Maybe – until we got into space flight – he didn't think we were worth talking to.'

'There could be another reason,' said Connors. 'Maybe it's because until we launched a craft that could travel out of the solar system we didn't pose a threat to anyone. If the beings who built Crusoe already knew where we were, why remove the plaque from Pioneer 10? You've already accused me of being paranoid but, to my mind, there's only one answer: to stop us from making contact with whoever else might be out there.'

'In that case, why not just destroy the spacecraft?' said Wedderkind. 'If it just disappeared that far from home we would assume it ran into a meteorite or an asteroid.'

'Crusoe and Friday aren't human, Arnold. They may not like killing other machines. In any case they've achieved the same result. Anyone finding Pioneer 10 now will never know where he came from.' Connors smiled and adopted a lighter tone. 'Maybe they're trying to tell us we're looked upon as undesirable aliens who need a

258

special visa before we can emigrate to the United Galactic States.'

Wedderkind gave him a long hard look. 'That may have been meant as a joke but it could be closer to the truth than you think . . .'

CROW RIDGE/MONTANA

At sunrise Crusoe's black dome rotated. The inner sphere spun around on its opposed axis until the two circular hatches were in alignment. Then Friday rose into view, unfolded his legs, and stood astride the dome. Behind him, the sun cleared the tops of the pines and outlined him briefly with burning gold.

Nobody was on the Ridge to greet him, but the TV cameras picked him up, and the night crew in the monitor hut alerted the research group.

Friday spent most of the morning wandering around the plateau, then discovered the collection of prefabs and trailers. It was as he began to explore these that he revealed the unexpected ability to climb up vertical surfaces.

The research group kept him under close observation as he walked from roof to roof, going up and down walls and peering in windows and open doorways. Everyone had been briefed to go on with what they were doing and pretend he wasn't there, but it was difficult to remain completely natural when you found yourself being shadowed by a spider nearly seven feet tall and fourteen feet across.

Friday found his way to the trailer park. There was just enough room for him to walk down between each line. Max was at home, engaged in another interminable round of cards with his off-duty gang. As he studied his hand, he felt someone looking over his shoulder. He turned round to find Friday peering in through the window. Max laid down his hand, got up, switched on the lights, and dropped the blind in Friday's face.

Friday completed his tour of the trailers and the other installations, then headed down to the tree line. Most of the pines covering the flanks of the Ridge grew too close together for him to walk between them easily. He turned back on to the plateau and found the extended dirt road. This he explored all the way down to the gate in the high wire fence. He took a long look at the cadets guarding it, the fence and the vehicles parked among the trees by the side of the road, then shifted into reverse gear and went back on to the plateau.

From there, he moved smoothly over the rocky ground up to the high point of the Ridge. Milsom, Spencer, Wetherby, and Collis, the language scientist, walked up to see what he was doing. They found Friday standing motionless astride the crest from where he had a view of the surrounding country. They sat down some distance away expecting him to swivel around and scan them with his eye pod. Friday didn't react to their presence. Half an hour later when his head did start to rotate, it wasn't in their direction. They could only guess he might be scanning the horizon. They left Friday to enjoy the view and returned to the research hut.

Friday stayed almost motionless on the Ridge till sunset, then he moved gracefully down over the rocks and returned to Crusoe.

In the research hut, the scientists watched the TV monitor as Friday folded himself up and slid in through the two hatches.

'I wonder why he stayed up on top of the Ridge all day?' said Milsom. 'Surely he wasn't just sunning himself.'

'He just seems to be wandering around aimlessly.' Page, the biochemist, never did anything aimlessly.

'I don't agree,' said Spencer. 'He's explored everything that's on the Ridge.'

'Depends what you mean by explore,' said Page. 'He spent half the morning going backward and forward over the roofs. There was absolutely nothing systematic about his movements at all.' Page held up a sheet of paper. 'Here's a plot of his tracks that the monitor hut recorded. It looks like a ball of string that's been got at by a kitten.'

Collis took the sheet of paper from Page. Friday's tangled tracks had been superimposed on a simplified map of Crow Ridge and the installations. Page was right, Friday's movements could hardly be described as systematic. He passed the paper on to the others.

'I don't see anything wrong with it,' said Tomkin. 'It may not be the way *you* would walk around the ridge, but it is the way an insect would.'

'I thought we were agreed Friday was a machine,' said Page. He still hadn't managed to master his disappointment.

'Maybe he was looking for something,' said Milsom.

'Why?' asked Page. 'He didn't collect any soil or rock samples, or any specimens of flora, or any of the dozens of insects running around those rocks out there.'

'Maybe that comes next,' said Collis. 'He obviously wanted to find out more about us first.'

'We couldn't have been all *that* interesting,' said Page. 'He ignored us for most of the day.'

Milsom grinned. 'I sometimes feel that way about people myself.'

'Funny man,' said Page, peevishly.

'Listen,' said Spencer. 'Right now we may have nothing but question marks, but let's not fall into the trap of attributing superman status to that pair out there. They may be products of a highly advanced technology, but they are still two pieces of machinery. A machine's

261

function can be analysed, and if it's been put together, it can be taken apart.'

'How can you talk of taking Crusoe apart?' said Page. 'You can't even dig him up.'

Spencer didn't bother to look at Page. He thought he was a prick. 'Page is right. We haven't been able to dig him up. But if we could get inside him, we may not need to.'

'Inside?' Tomkin looked surprised.

'What do you want to do?' asked Spencer. 'Let them fly away without finding out how they work? If we could crack the secrets of their technology, it might help us leapfrog the next two hundred years.'

'Aren't we in a big enough mess already?'

Milsom jabbed a finger at Collis. 'Don't start hitting us with that classical *shtick*. Whatever technology has gotten us into, it can get us out of.'

'But do we have the right to take Crusoe or Friday apart?' insisted Collis.

'Look, let's forget this ethical crap,' said Neame. 'Let's get down to the practical problems. What are you going to use for a can opener, Dan?'

'Don't you think you ought to wait till Arnold comes back from Washington?' said Collis.

'Exactly,' said Page. And in the meantime, I think you should consult Professor Lovell before you take this any further.' Lovell was the senior member of the group.

'Page,' said Spencer. 'Why don't you fuck off?'

Page rose, tight-lipped, and made a prim exit.

'So what's next?' asked Milsom.

'The first thing we have to do is to get Neal Zabrodski to run us the tapes of Friday going in and out of the hatch. It opens when he stands astride it, and closes as soon as he's inside. What we need to check is whether he stands in exactly the same place each time, and whether he follows a sequence of movements. If he does, there's a chance that he activates the hatch himself. If we can find out how he does it, there's a chance we may be able to duplicate the operation. The rest is simple.'

'Do you really mean you're prepared to go in there?' asked Collis.

'Neil Armstrong and Ed Aldrin landed on the moon without a guaranteed return ticket,' said Spencer.

'I don't mind going in,' said Milsom. He meant it too but, since he was always making jokes, no one took him seriously.

Sunday/September 9

On Sunday, Wedderkind and his wife Lillian went over to lunch with his eldest daughter, her husband, and their four-year-old son. Resisting the attempts of his son-in-law to sell him yet another insurance policy, Wedderkind escaped to the master bedroom and called George York in Baltimore. Wedderkind wanted to know what progress he'd made in collecting the latest data on the Earth's magnetic field.

'It's coming along, Arnold. It's coming along.' That was all York would say on the subject. He did, however, give Wedderkind some information he hadn't bargained for.

'I had an interesting conversation with a friend of mine at the University of Chicago. Lou Corsalero. He knows Al Wetherby.'

'Oh, yes,' said Wedderkind.

'Lou told me he'd been picking up some remarkable underground tremors coming from your direction.'

'And?'

'Well, I phoned Riddell in San Francisco. He confirmed that the epicentre was situated some two thousand feet under Crow Ridge.'

'There's been some movement, but no real boneshakers.'

'Oh, no, it's not the strength of the tremors,' said York. 'It's the frequency. Lou and Riddell both picked up regular groups of pulses with varying strengths and numbers of beats. Four, eight, twelve, eight, eight, four – that kind of thing. One could almost imagine it as some kind of seismic Morse code.'

One could, thought Wedderkind. But from *two thousand* feet down? 'Could you follow this up for me, George?'

'On what scale?'

'Well, to be any use it would have to be on a global basis.'

'Arnold, there are two hundred and forty stations.'

'Yes, but there's a data centre here and one in Europe.'

'They're still processing last year's records.'

'Well, phone around. You can send me the bill. If this *is* a message that Crusoe is drumming out, then there has to be someone to receive it. They may send a message back.'

'Which would enable us to get a fix on their position.'

'Right, George. The epicentres might coincide with the centres of the fade-out waves. In which case those figures of yours might make sense.'

'I can't promise anything.'

'I realize that. Ask Riddell to help. He owes me a favour.'

'He owes me one too.'

'Good. That makes one hundred and twenty stations each. If you pull in Corsalero, you'll only have to check eighty. Less, in fact – you can forget the Russian stations.'

'Okay.'

'There's only one problem, George. You have to get them to help without telling them what's going on.'

'I understand.'

'And think up a good answer about the Crow Ridge tremors. I don't want anyone sending up a research party.'

'Are you asking me to lie to my colleagues?'

'George,' said Wedderkind. 'Isn't that how you got hold of the computer?'

Wedderkind took his grandson for a walk in the park, responding to his happy chatter with grown-up noises that left him free to ponder on the significance of York's latest news. Children, however, are never long denied, and Wedderkind paid for his preoccupation by getting his finger gnawed by a squirrel.

CROW RIDGE/MONTANA

Spencer had the edited tapes of Friday screened several times. His hunch had been correct. In both sets of exits and entrances, Friday positioned himself over the hatch with the tips of his legs in exactly the same place each time. He put his two side pairs of legs in position first, followed by the rear, and then the front. When they were all in position, the two spheres rotated, bringing the two hatches into line. To enter, Friday first folded in the front and rear pairs of legs simultaneously, then the two side pairs. As soon as he sank below the level of the inner hatch, it rotated shut.

When he emerged from Crusoe, he unfolded his legs in the reverse order, the two side pairs first, then the front and rear pairs. When all eight feet were on the points, the inner hatch closed and the dome rotated.

'Let's go and look at the hull.' Spencer waylaid four passing cadets and persuaded them to volunteer their services and the use of their two jeeps. He drove off in the lead vehicle with Milsom, Tomkin, and Collis, and waved to the cadets to follow.

They parked close to Crusoe. Spencer told the four cadets to stay in their jeep, then walked up on to the hull with Milsom, Tomkin, and Collis. Spencer went down on his hands and knees near the dome and took a close look at the smooth black translucent surface. After about ten minutes he found what he was looking for, a small matt-black octagonal patch, almost as big as the palm of his hand and about seven feet from the centre of the domed hatch.

'Here it is. We've got to find seven more of these.'

The others knelt down to examine the patch. It was barely discernible on the black surface.

'If you look at the surface at an angle and get the light reflecting off it, you'll be able to pick it up more easily,' said Spencer. 'There should be one directly opposite me. Spread out around the dome – and be careful not to step on one.'

Milsom, Tomkin, and Collis backed down the hull and spread out cautiously like men who'd suddenly found themselves on thin ice. Spencer waved to the four cadets. They came up on to the hull and huddled around him.

'I want you four to get between the four of us,' explained Spencer. He pointed at the black patch. 'That's what you're looking for. You'll need to look closely, they're pretty hard to see.'

'I've got mine,' said Tomkin. He was now opposite Spencer.

'Okay,' said Spencer. 'Chris, you and Dan should be at right angles to us.'

Milsom and Collis adjusted their positions.

'And you four guys should be halfway in between.'

The cadets edged sideways till the distances were about right.

'Okay, everybody should have one of these patches right under their nose.'

Tomkin sat back on his heels while the others searched for and located their patches.

'Everybody okay?'

They all nodded. Spencer looked around and saw Page and Lovell walking towards them. Page's preoccupation with Lovell's opinion on any matter was not out of deference to Lovell's seniority. Everyone knew that Page was after Lovell's recommendation to help land a well-paid and prestigious research post at the Massachusetts Institute of Technology.

'Okay,' said Spencer. 'Let's get the sequence right. Dan, you and the guy on your right are the front legs.'

'Right,' said Collis.

Spencer turned to the cadet on his left. 'You and Chris here are the rear legs. Do whatever he does.' Spencer looked across at Tomkin. 'We and these two other guys are the side legs, so we go on first.'

'Got it,' said Tomkin.

Spencer turned to the cadet on his right. 'You and I go together, right?'

'Yes, sir,' said CRAWFORD, N.

'Okay,' said Spencer. 'It's the two sides first, then the rear, then the front. Three-second intervals. Get your right foot ready, and when I give you the signal, place it lightly on to the patch.'

'Sir?' It was the cadet on Spencer's left, GIBBS, J.K.

He looked too young even to buy razor blades. 'Could you tell us what you're expecting to happen?'

'Yes, sure. We're hoping that by exerting the right pressure on these patches, we will activate the two spherical hatches. Have you seen any of this on the screens?'

'Yes, sir.'

'Good. Just relax. If it doesn't open, I'll buy you all a drink. If it does, you can all buy me one. Okay, everybody ready?'

They all nodded and each man slid his right foot forward.

'This is like stepping on a land mine to see if it's working,' said Milsom.

Spencer waited till the second hand on his watch reached twelve. 'Sides – now! Rear – now! Front – now!'

The four pairs of feet pressed down on the patches in sequence. Nothing happened.

'Spencer looked across at Collis. 'Can you see any movement? It should start coming up on your side.'

Collis shook his head.

'Maybe they work on an electrical contact of some kind,' suggested Tomkin.

'If they do, we're screwed,' said Spencer. 'Let's try it again, this time with more weight on your right foot.'

Page and Lovell arrived at the edge of Crusoe's hull. 'Do any of you have any clear idea of what you're doing?' asked Lovell.

'Yes, we're trying to add to the sum total of human knowledge,' said Spencer. He came from a rich family, so he didn't need to worry about Lovell's patronage, now *or* later. 'Okay, let's go!'

They pressed down hard on the patches in the same sequence. Nothing.

'Keep it up,' commanded Spencer. 'Move your whole weight on to it.'

Almost a minute passed and nothing happened. Spencer's hopes of a breakthrough started to recede like the picture on a switched-off TV set. Just as he was about to give up, the dome rotated from left to right, exposing the outer hatch, then the second sphere spun around towards him, bringing the inner hatch into line.

'How about that?' Spencer laughed, his face pink with excitement.

'Beautiful,' said Milsom.

Lovell and Page hurried up on to the hull.

'Keep your feet on the patches. Keep 'em hard down,' said Spencer.

They all craned their necks forward and looked into the hatch. The dark, complex well that had contained Friday was empty.

'He must be in another compartment,' said Lovell.

Spencer grinned. 'That's good. It means that when he's outside, there'll be room to move around down there. Okay, gang. Let's see if we can shut this thing. It's front and rear feet off first.'

Collis and Milsom and the two cadets on their right got ready.

Spencer checked his watch. 'I'll give you a countdown of five.'

As he raised his hand to count off the seconds, the two hatches rotated shut of their own accord.

Spencer looked around the ring of faces. 'Okay, who moved?' Nobody answered. 'Okay, everybody back off for a minute.'

They all took a couple of steps back down the hull. Spencer frowned. 'What do you think, Chris?'

'We must have done something wrong. If these *are* pressure pads, they could be highly sensitive. The slightest variation from the norm may trigger off an alarm . . .'

'Or there could be an automatic control that closes the

hatch after a set time.' Spencer looked at his watch. 'Did anyone keep a check on how long it was open?'

Nobody had. 'Listen,' said Milsom. 'If we can open it once, we can open it a second time.'

'You're right,' said Spencer.

'If it's any help, I timed the taped sequence of Friday going back inside,' said Tomkin. 'He takes fifteen seconds to fold the first four legs, fifteen for the second four, and fifteen to slide down below the level of the inner hatch.'

'But the hatch isn't fully open when he starts folding his legs,' said Collis.

'No, that's right,' said Spencer. 'Okay, back on your marks, let's give it a whirl.'

They tried several times to repeat their first success, but the dome didn't budge.

'Doesn't look as if it's going to work,' said Page.

'Keep trying,' said Spencer. *Come on, baby . . . just to wipe that smirk off Page's face.* Nothing moved. 'Okay, let's get it together. Just one more time.'

The two hatches rotated into line. The inner sphere with its complex pattern of struts was still empty.

'Maybe there's a closed cycle as well as an open one,' suggested Tomkin.

'I'm ahead of you,' said Spencer. 'When it closes, we'll try again and keep a close check on the time.' They repeated the operation three times. There *was* an override control on the hatch. Regardless of the pressure on the hull patches, it rotated after forty-five seconds and remained shut for five minutes.

'Forty-five seconds doesn't give you very much time,' said Page.

Spencer grinned at him. 'Are you kidding? You can run a hundred yards in eight and half.'

'You're not seriously thinking of going in there, are you?' asked Lovell.

'No, he's not,' said Milson. 'I am.'

Everyone still thought he was joking.

'Whoever it is will have to wear a space suit,' said Spencer. 'We have no way of knowing the pressure or temperature conditions inside the main hull. This double hatch could be some kind of airlock. We don't even know if we can maintain two-way communication with whoever goes inside.'

Lovell considered the problems. 'This is something that will need a lot of preparation. We'll have to discuss it with Arnold first.'

'Of course,' said Spencer. 'We've got to do it right.'

'But this is a really a big breakthrough.' Lovell patted Spencer on the back. 'Well done.'

'Yes,' said Page. 'Excellent . . .'

Spencer gave a wry grin and shook hands with the four cadets. 'Thanks, fellas. Half past nine in the bar, okay? And forget what I said before. The drinks are on me.'

Milsom took the wheel of the jeep for the short drive back. Spencer sat beside him looking curiously dissatisfied.

The two of them shared a trailer, and much later that night, when Milsom came out of the shower, he found Spencer sitting on the edge of his bunk, deep in thought.

'What's the problem?'

'The hatch . . .'

'Didn't everything work out like you said?'

'Yes. But it shouldn't have.'

Milsom put the towel round his neck like a boxer, sat down opposite Spencer, and reached for a cigarette. 'Shoot.'

'I wanted to try to open the hatch when Friday was inside because, if we had found him folded up in the hatch, it would have meant there was probably no means of access to other parts of the ship.'

'But now we know there is.'

'Right. But with Friday already on board, the hatch *shouldn't* have opened. There should have been a lock on those pressure points. Who *else* would Crusoe want to open up for?'

'Neame seems to think it's us,' Milsom grinned. 'Maybe Crusoe's planning to throw a Tupperware party.'

'Aw, for Pete's sake, Chris! I'm trying to have a serious conversation – '

'Sorry, go ahead.'

'I don't really go for Neame's idea – do you?'

'If I did, I wouldn't be volunteering to go into Crusoe.'

'Then what's his angle?'

Milsom thought about it for a moment, then shrugged. 'Maybe Crusoe isn't as bright as we think he is.'

Spencer nodded slowly. 'Yeah . . . But on the other hand, maybe *we* aren't as bright as we think we are.'

He tried to remember exactly when he had had the first glimmerings of the idea about the hatch. It had come to him that morning. When he had been up on the Ridge with Milsom, Wetherby and Collis . . .

And Friday.

They had sat watching him for two hours. He tried to remember what train of thought had led him to the first ideas about the hatch. It was difficult to filter out the other thought circuits that kept cutting into his retrieval system. The spat with his wife about a new car. There was the letter he should have written to his mother. The sweet smell of his daughter's hair as he'd kissed her good-bye when he'd left for Crow Ridge. And Friday . . .

He'd thought a lot about Friday. Was it possible that Friday had . . . ?

Spencer looked across at Milsom, then decided not to mention that last idea. Instead, he said, 'First thing we have to do is to try and find out if Friday is controlling

Crusoe, or the other way around. We also have to immobilize Friday before going inside – otherwise it could get a little crowded in there.' He paused, then said, 'If we can get a couple of suits up here, are you game to go inside Crusoe with me?'

'How many times do I have to say it?' said Milsom. 'I keep volunteering but no one will take me seriously. Of course I'll come.'

'Good . . .' Spencer lay back on his bunk. 'Let's hope Arnold agrees.'

'It's not just up to him,' said Milsom. 'That guy Connors is bound to stick his oar in. *And* that maniac Allbright.'

Tuesday/September 11

When Connors and Wedderkind got back to Crow Ridge, they saw the videotape record of Spencer's weekend experiment with the hatch. He had also managed to open it the next day while Friday was out on the plateau.

'What makes you think there's going to be any space below the hatch to move around in?' asked Connors.

'There has to be,' said Spencer. 'Friday was inside, but the hatch was empty. From what we managed to see of the framework inside the hatch, it looks as though it contrarotates when the hatch opens so that Friday stays the right way up, then drops down into a lower compartment. Once he's outside the ship, that must leave plenty of room for us.'

'Not necessarily,' said Wedderkind. 'He might remain folded up and be slotted straight into a storage well.'

'In that case, there's no reason why he can't stay folded up inside the hatch.'

'I can think of several,' said Wedderkind. 'We can't preclude the possibility that Friday may be only one of several similar craft. Even two would make more sense. In the case of a malfunction or damage, the hatch would select the serviceable craft. All it would need would be for the outer dome to have a variable axis of rotation. It could then open on to several storage wells.'

'In that case, we'll just have to sit there till you let us out,' said Spencer. 'If Crusoe *is* directing Friday's activity, you may well be right. But consider the reverse possibility – that Friday controls Crusoe. The LEM landed on the moon, but it was the men who stepped out who were running the show. You saw what happened on the tapes. The two domes opened up on *our* signal – as they did on Friday's.'

Instead of shutting himself in at sunset, Friday stayed outside on an extended walk. Wedderkind asked the monitor hut to keep a watchful TV eye trained on him.

Connors, Wedderkind, and Allbright got together with the scientists and engineers in the research hut and discussed Spencer's breakthrough.

They finally agreed on the insertion of one volunteer for a quick preliminary reconnaissance, to see if there was a way into other parts of Crusoe, and to check whether two-way communication was possible. The first move in this plan was to immobilize Friday during one of his walks, and take him to the field lab for examination. With Friday out of the way, the round trip could be made without fear of interruption. If the first insertion was successful and there *was* access into the main part of the hull, they would then insert a two-man team for a more thorough examination of the interior.

There was one big question Connors had in mind that no one asked at the meeting: Would any attempt be made to rescue the first man if he didn't come out as planned? Maybe no one asked because they didn't want to hear the answer – or maybe they already knew what it would be.

When the meeting broke up, Connors and Wedderkind decided to take a walk and breathe in some clear night air. Wedderkind regaled Connors with domestic trivia, mainly about his grandson. Connors sensed what was coming.

'Do you think you and Charly are going to make it?'

'I don't think I'm going to make it with anyone, Arnold.'

Wedderkind had been instrumental in bringing Connors and Charly together. As a would-be matchmaker, he had a vested interest in their relationship. Connors enjoyed rebuffing his fatherly concern but he also found it touching.

'Mmm . . .' Wedderkind lapsed into silence for several yards. 'Is this all because Carol died?'

'Not entirely. We were already divorced when she had the accident.'

'Have you talked to Charly about it?'

'No.'

'Do you want to tell me how it happened?'

'Not really. I know exactly what my hang-up is.'

'Well, go ahead and tell me anyway.'

Connors sighed and assumed a matter-of-fact voice. 'I put my career before my marriage, never came home, ran around with other women. My wife took to drink, had an affair that went sour, decided to leave me, took our son with her, had an accident, he was killed.'

'Was she . . . ?'

'Yes, of course she was drunk. And yes, of course that

was really my fault but – I sued for divorce, she blamed herself for Joe's death, I never forgave her, she kept on drinking. And it all went downhill . . .'

'Did she kill herself or was it an accident?'

'Who knows? The car swerved and went straight into an oncoming truck. That's why I didn't find Weissman's suggestion about the Bodells so funny. Still, I got a partial comeuppance – I had to identify her body. That was something I could have done without . . .' She had left an envelope addressed to him which he had burned without reading the contents. He shook his head. 'It's amazing what you can do to people when you really try.'

'Or when you stop trying,' said Wedderkind. He put his hand on Connors' shoulder. 'I'm glad you finally told me.'

'Yeah, well, that's okay. Just so long as you don't think it makes me feel better.'

'You're not supposed to,' said Wedderkind.

They rounded a corner of the trailer site and almost collided with Friday.

'Jesus Christ!' gasped Connors. He had forgotten that Friday was still wandering around the plateau.

Friday froze with the now characteristic backward movement. Connors stepped back out of sight and leaned against the side of the trailer to recover his composure. Wedderkind stayed where he was.

'Arnold, for God's sake – ' Connors shuddered with revulsion.

'It's okay, he's moving away.' Wedderkind turned to Connors.

'I'm sorry, Arnold. Walking into him in the dark like that just frightened the life out of me.'

Wedderkind patted him on the shoulder. 'If it's any comfort, I wanted to move but my legs wouldn't. Come

276

on back to the trailer. Phil, Alan Wetherby, and Ray Collis are coming over for a nightcap.'

Wedderkind's trailer-made coffee was infinitely superior to the canteen brew. He had also shipped in six real coffee cups and saucers from Washington. 'I know I'm being fussy, but I can't stand the feel of those expanded polystyrene cups.'

'When the oil starts to run out, the disposable cup will become a thing of the past,' said Brecetti.

'In ten years, nothing will be disposable,' said Wetherby. 'We're going to have to start making things that last. I'm even hoping students will start majoring in Repair and Maintenance instead of Business Management.'

'That's enough of your radical chatter.' Wedderkind handed out the coffee and told them about the encounter with Friday. 'I know he's harmless, but he looks hideous in the dark.'

Connors' skin crawled as he thought about it again. 'It's ridiculous, I know. I've seen people pick up spiders and insects and let them run around in their hands – if I had to do that I'd probably pass out. Why are there so many people like me with this totally irrational fear of spiders? It's not through any bad experience, it was there even as a small child.'

'There isn't really an answer to that,' said Collis. 'It's thought that the effects of psychological states, shocks, fears, accidents experienced by pregnant women can be transmitted to the unborn child. It may be the relic of a more primitive animal instinct, a deepseated folk memory from the distant past, that affects some of us more than others. I knew a brave man who would faint if confronted with a snake. And there is always the more comic spectacle of women who leap on to chairs at the sight of a mouse.'

'If this fear was a folk memory, from a time when we had reason to fear spiders, could it be because there were things like Friday around then?' asked Connors.

Wedderkind shrugged. 'If science teaches us anything, it is that anything is possible. Hardly a day passes without some discoveries that challenge what were once the unassailable natural laws on which our knowledge of the physical world is based. Darwin's theory of evolution is under constant attack, the new skull finds in Kenya and elsewhere force us to revise our dating of the appearance of *Homo Erectus* – '

'And there are now the "Black Holes" in space that could conceivably swallow up our entire universe before we solve the riddle of its creation,' said Brecetti.

'You're as comforting as Allbright,' said Connors. 'If the Hellfires don't get us, the Black Holes will.' He stared at his coffee as he stirred in two fatal spoonfuls of sugar, then looked up. 'I've heard this term "folk memory", "race memory" mentioned on odd occasions. Is it conceivable that Crusoe's kind could have been here before?'

'It is if you believe in Divine Intervention,' said Wetherby.

'In the biblical sense – or as discovered by Erich Von Daniken?' asked Connors.

'I think the truth lies buried in his books *and* the Bible,' said Wetherby. 'And in the Talmud, the Torah, the more esoteric religious texts – and in the priceless works that are locked in the cellars of the Vatican.'

'Oh, come on, Al, the Vatican isn't hiding anything,' said Brecetti.

'Papist – ' Wetherby turned to Connors. 'Phil belongs to the evolutionary accident school. A pointless existence in an equally pointless world created by chance out of the chaos of the cosmos.'

'Not quite,' said Brecetti. 'Man has to create his own

278

goals. I happen to believe he would act more constructively in this life if he gave up thinking about the next. There *is* no conscious or spiritual existence beyond the death of the body. Heaven and hell, as Omar Khayyám said, exist here, on Earth. And by the way, Al, I don't subscribe to the Big Bang theory. I'm still wedded to Modified Steady State – despite what Sandage and Gunn say.'

'That makes you a heretic on two counts,' said Wetherby. He turned again to Connors. 'They never learn. Arnold is just as bad.'

'Not true,' said Wedderkind. 'After people started to fall off the Steady State bandwagon, I became a floating voter. I'm even prepared to indulge your fanciful theories.'

'What are they?' asked Connors.

'I think we were given a helping hand,' replied Wetherby. 'But it goes further than that. I think our first visitors gave Earth the Kiss of Life. I believe they seeded the atmosphere to get rid of the choking clouds of methane, the perpetual mists of ammonia. And with the breathable atmosphere came the visible separation of heaven and Earth. It's amazing how, all over the world, there are myths that relate how gods raised the sky from the Earth. Once that was done, the oceans became the spawning grounds for embryo life-forms – the primordial soup. Again, you only have to compare the amazing similarity in the myths. Even primitive tribes produced amazingly sophisticated stories to explain evolution that coincide remarkably with modern theory. But then, I believe that myths are historical events or scientific information recounted so many times that the original meaning has been lost in the telling.'

'But basically, what you're saying is that we are the

279

end product of a gigantic biological engineering project,' said Wedderkind.

'Yes, but the project has a purpose. I think that over the aeons of time since Earth saw its first God-given sunrise, there have been periodic visits to control the evolution of life and the balance of its various forms. For instance, the mass extinction of the dinosaurs was part of that weeding-out process. Its purpose was to enable the mammals to flourish.'

'To give our ancestors elbow room,' said Connors.

'Yes, but perhaps, when a suitable form arose, *homo sapiens* was created by genetic engineering and *not* the slow process of evolution. That could explain why the Darwinists can't find this missing link. If our evolution was artificially accelerated, there wouldn't *be* a direct link with the primates. *Homo erectus* could have been the start of a new experimental line, using some new and borrowed parts. Man *began* with Man.'

'All that does for me is conjure up a picture of a prehistoric Frankenstein,' said Wedderkind.

'That may not be far from the truth,' said Wetherby. 'I've often wondered about the origin of the prehistoric headhunting cults, and ritual human sacrifices – ripping out the heart and organs to offer to the Sun God. Maybe they were a sort of perverted homage, primitive imitations of surgical operations or autopsies, performed by the beings early Man knew as gods, as part of the control process – the search for the perfect mutation. Man could have been a lengthy process of trial and error.'

'Al,' said Brecetti. 'Where this really belongs is in a paperback. No kidding, you'd sell a lot of copies. All these theories fall down on one point. Who helped the people who gave *us* a helping hand? Come on, now, the process *had* to start somewhere.'

'Can you tell me where the universe started?'

'That's a low blow. Don't dodge the question. If, as you say, gods taught us farming, animal husbandry, weaving, mathematics, and gave us the gift of language, where did *they* get this knowledge?'

Wetherby waved his hand in the air. 'It's all part of a continuing process.' He pointed at Collis. 'Ray here believes that the sum total of knowledge in the universe is passing through this room like radio waves. We're unable to receive it because our brains aren't tuned in to the right wavelength.'

'That's not really an answer to my question,' said Brecetti.

'You're not going to get one,' said Wedderkind. 'What kind of a universe does this missionary activity take place in, Al – Big Bang, Modified Steady State or Open?'

'Big Bang . . .' Wetherby pushed a lock of black hair back from his forehead. 'I like the idea of a universe born out of the cataclysmic explosion of the primal atom, spreading out through the infinite depths of space for a brief moment of eternity . . . There are some wonderful lines I came across years ago – I never forgot the words, just the name of the man who wrote them. *Far to the north, in the land called Svithjod, lies a black rock, one hundred miles high and one hundred miles wide. Once every ten thousand years, a little bird flies to the rock and sharpens its beak. When all the rock has been worn away, one second of one day of eternity will have gone by.*'

'That's a telling image,' admitted Connors. 'But where did the primal atom come from?'

'The previous universe,' said Wetherby. 'It expands to a certain point and then collapses back on itself. The entire material universe crushes together with colossal force and creates the next explosion. It goes on like that forever, expanding and contracting rhythmically like a giant heart, beating throughout eternity. Galaxies are created, stars, solar systems, planets cool, primitive life emerges, intelligent creatures evolve and eventually colonize and civilize other planets, orbiting other suns . . .'

'And this colonizing, this teaching process, continues throughout the life span of the universe . . . and begins all over again in the next?' asked Connors.

Wetherby nodded. 'It's a continuing process. An infinite cycle of creation. I think we will even find that Phil's Black Holes are part of this swallowing up process.'

Brecetti looked at Connors. 'These damn geographers are all the same, they stick their noses into everything.'

Connors held out his coffee cup as Wedderkind did the rounds with the pot.

'Sugar?'

'No, I'll take it straight this time. Al, a lot of the myths you mention also say that Man was once immortal. Was this an optional extra that was dropped on the later models? That may sound a little cynical. It's not meant to be.'

Wetherby smiled. 'I think Man was once endowed with some extraordinary mental qualities he has since lost. We all know he's not in such good physical shape as he used to be. Sight, smell, taste weakened, muscles atrophied. Ray has a theory about this that is tied up with the development of language.'

'I don't really think it's relevant,' said Collis.

'Go ahead, Ray, you're quite safe here,' said Wedderkind. 'There are no hairy engineers waiting to beat you on the head with their slide rules.'

Collis paused reluctantly. 'Well – the problem is that if you don't subscribe to the basic beliefs, it tends to sound a little ridiculous.'

'Try me,' said Connors. 'I dumped all my preconceived ideas overboard when this project started.'

Collis swallowed. 'Well – basically, I believe that our present concept of immortality springs from a distant folk memory of Man's early state of grace. By folk memory, I mean a deep-rooted, instinctual memory – part of our genetic makeup that passes through countless generations. I believe there was a period, when Man first walked the Earth, when his whole being was permeated with what we term cosmic consciousness – universal knowledge, if you like – an awareness that the material state of the physical world he perceived about him was only one brief phase in the continuous cycle of creation, of which *he* was a part. Have I lost you?'

'No, go on.'

'Okay. I believe that he was also aware that this same cosmic consciousness permeated the whole world of nature. The rocks, the earth, the sea, the sky above his head. Man was in tune with his surroundings. Everything, in varying degrees, was alive as he was alive.'

'And it was from a memory of this awareness that the later myths of forest, water, and mountain spirits came?' asked Connors.

'Yes. There must have been a point in time when this total awareness of and identification with other animate and inanimate objects began to fade. Man slipped from the spiritual into the material world. Perhaps through genetic changes – by chance, or deliberate mutation – the chain of RNA/DNA molecules lost the vital link. The coded message that endowed Man with this awareness. Once can imagine it, perhaps, as a key, without which crucial circuits in the brain remained locked. Inactive.'

'It is certainly true that one of the universal themes of mythology is the losing of the message that would make Man immortal,' said Wetherby.

'Exactly,' said Collis. 'And Alan will also confirm that there is a growing mass of evidence indicating that highly developed societies flourished in the distant past *without* the art of writing. They may not even have needed language. I believe these people were telepathic. One has only to study language to realize, in spite of its beauty and complexity, what an amazingly imperfect tool it is. And despite all our studies and theories we *still* don't know how language developed. I believe that as Man began to speak and write, he became *less* able to communicate. Gradually, the tremendous telepathic powers in his brain were shut off – or drained away. He no longer identified with the world around him. It became a hostile environment, peopled by dimly remembered spirits that were quickly classified into good and evil. The loss of this awareness meant that he no longer understood his part in the eternal process of creation. Immortality became a distant dream, part of a golden age long past to which he would never return. Man learned to read and write, but in cosmic terms, he became illiterate,' Collis shrugged. 'That's basically it. I'm sorry it took so long. Most people usually find an urgent need to go to the john halfway through.'

'Don't be so defensive, it made sense to me.' Connors stood up and looked at his watch. 'My watch says bedtime, but the caffeine tells me the night's still young.'

'You can always race Arnold to the crater,' said Brecetti.

'Good night, Phil,' said Wedderkind. 'Next time you come, bring your own plastic cup.'

Wetherby's trailer was near Connors'. They walked along in the dark, and looked up at the star-studded sky.

'I wonder which one Crusoe's from . . .' mused Wetherby.

'I didn't know Ray Collis was interested in all that

stuff,' said Connors. 'How long has he been hooked on Rudolf Steiner?'

'I don't know. He doesn't talk about it very much,' said Wetherby. 'Once you start mentioning the spiritual world, most people's eyes start to glaze over.'

'Yeah, well, there're some really nutty ideas around. Ray made it sound simple enough, though I must admit, when anyone mentions cosmic consciousness, I feel like reaching for a baseball bat.'

They arrived at the door of Connors' trailer.

'I've been thinking about Daniel Defoe's story,' said Wetherby. 'Arnold was telling me how Crusoe got his code name.'

'Yes, it was the President's idea.'

'Mmm . . . it's interesting. Most people only remember the story as being about Crusoe and Friday, but there are more characters. In his twenty-seventh year on the island, Crusoe was joined by a Spaniard and another Negro – survivors of a shipwreck – and later by a captain, his mate, and a passenger. Their ship had been seized by the mutinous crew.'

Connors felt a cold ball form in the pit of his stomach. 'I'd forgotten about those other characters. So there were six of them . . .'

'Plus Friday. They recapture the ship from the mutineers and sail back to England.'

'And they all lived happily ever after – '

'Not quite,' said Wetherby. 'You've forgotten Part Two. Not many people read the sequel – it's rather inferior. Eight years later, Crusoe returns with a priest, mechanics and sailors – and Friday, of course. He founds a Christian colony. Poor old Friday gets killed by the cannibals.'

'Does Crusoe stay on the island?' asked Connors.

'No. After Friday's death he goes back to England, and eventually dies.'

'Ah . . . That's interesting,' said Connors. 'It shows how carefully people read stories. I'd completely forgotten that there were more characters besides the cannibals, and I certainly didn't know about the sequel.'

'Yes . . .' Wetherby rubbed his forehead. 'It's curious, I can't think of what prompted me to give you such a pointless piece of information. Oh, well, perhaps it'll come to me in the morning. Good night.'

'Good night, Alan.' Connors went into his trailer. The information may have seemed pointless to Wetherby, but it made chilling sense to Connors. He had had an odd feeling about that code name right from the start. Was it possible that they could be caught up in a space-age version of the story? If so, there were five more . . . characters due to appear. That really *would* be a bizarre twist of fate. And which bit of the story was taking place – Part One, where Crusoe's aim was to get off the island? Or Part Two, when he returned to colonize it?

He told himself the idea was too fantastic and tried to put it out of his mind. What's in a name? The project could have been called ABLE, BAKER, or CHARLEY BROWN but it hadn't. It had been called CRUSOE. And his gut reaction was a signal that his brain knew something it hadn't told him yet.

Wednesday/September 12

CROW RIDGE/MONTANA

Heartened by Friday's apparent timidity, Max and Wedderkind hatched a kidnap plot. Now that the drilling was

286

over, Max had reverted to his real job, which was to act as 'front man' in the Corporation's dealings with outside contractors and local suppliers in nearby Miles City. Whenever possible, however, he preferred to stay up on the Ridge instead of down at the base camp, in the hope of seeing some action.

Connors had been surprised to learn from Wetherby that Max had graduated with honours in geology, and that two of the other Texans had degrees in mining engineering. Their erudition was buried beneath a hefty layer of brawn. Three of them were even bigger than Max, and they all looked as if they had been raised on a steady diet of Saturday-night fistfights.

When Connors had remarked on this one evening in the canteen, Gilligan, another of the engineers, had said, 'You want to take a trip to Butte. The Swedes and the Irish there would make these guys look like marshmallows.' The big mining town lay close up against the Rockies in western Montana. Gilligan had been born there, moving later to Seattle. Unless you were King Kong, Butte sounded like a good place to stay out of. Especially on a Saturday night.

Marshmallows or not, besides being experienced wildcatters, Max and his Texans were expert in handling a wide range of mechanical mining and earth-moving equipment. It was this skill that Wedderkind planned to make use of.

They waited until Friday came out for his morning walk. Then, when he was about two hundred yards from Crusoe, the Texans, under Max's direction, surrounded him with four bulldozers. Friday shrank back to consider the situation, and his body slowly rotated through 360 degrees as his eye pod scanned the huge blades that had suddenly walled him in. There was a gap at each corner large enough for a man to slip through but too narrow for

Friday. He clicked rapidly for about a minute, then attempted to climb up one of the blades. The move had been anticipated. The driver of the bulldozer jiggled the blade up and down and shook Friday off.

Wedderkind and Connors stood on the shaking roof of the cab to watch what was happening. Despite his revulsion, Connors couldn't resist a feeling of sympathy for Friday now that he was hemmed in and apparently helpless.

Wedderkind called down to Max who was by the side of the cab, 'Tell your boys to go easy, we don't want to crush him.'

Max relayed the message through cupped hands.

Retreating from the first blade, Friday doggedly tried to climb the other three walls of his pen, and was shaken off. On the fourth attempt, he almost got over. The driver, a man called T-Bone, raised and lowered the blade in rapid succession as Friday balanced his body on top of the blade and tried to get his four left legs on to the hood of the bulldozer. His four right legs scrabbled over the blade, but each time it thumped back on the ground he lost his grip. In such a precarious position there was a real danger of Friday getting some of his legs crushed.

Wedderkind looked around for Max but couldn't see him. He waved at T-Bone and shouted, 'Let him go – we'll have to find some other way!'

With the noise of all four engines T-Bone didn't hear. Wedderkind called down to Spencer and while he was explaining what he wanted him to do, Max clambered up on to the hood of T-Bone's bulldozer with a long wooden stake. As Friday rocked to and fro, Max got the stake underneath him and sent him tumbling backward off the top of the blade. Connors winced as Friday landed on his head with a sickening thud. For a few seconds, his eight legs waved feebly in the air. Then he folded them two at a time close in against his body, and lay there upside down.

Wedderkind climbed off the top of the cab and ran forward along the hood. 'What did you do that for?' he shouted angrily.

Max looked bewildered. 'I thought the idea was to keep him inside.'

'Yes, but not like that, you clumsy ape!'

Max threw down the stake in disgust and turned to Connors with outspread hands. 'What the hell did I do wrong?'

Wedderkind squeezed through the gap between the right-angled blades of two bulldozers, followed by Spencer, Milsom, Neame, and Tomkin. Connors moved to the hood of the bulldozer on which he had been standing and looked down at Friday.

After what was probably a quiet moment of reflection, Friday extended two of the retractable eyestalks set in the flat top of his body, and tipped it over on to one side. The two legs pinned underneath unfolded like scissor jacks, lifting his body sideways into the air. Pivoting upright, Friday put out his six other legs on the ground and raised himself up to his normal height. He shook the dust from his two eyestalks and retracted them.

'What do we do now?' asked Neame.

'If we can get him to curl up and play dead,' said Wedderkind, 'we can scoop him up on the shovel of one of the small earthmovers, and take him down to the field lab. We should be able to get him through the door sideways – and once he's in, unless he goes berserk, he's going to have a hard time getting out.'

Wedderkind called in some more people until there were twelve of them in a ring around Friday. As they

289

closed in, he shrank down, and then folded his legs neatly against his body.

The bulldozer facing Connors backed away and the earthmover took its place with Wedderkind standing behind Aaron, the driver. Aaron lowered the long-toothed shovel and edged forward. Max jumped down from the hood of the bulldozer and gave the signal to start biting dirt.

Friday tilted sideways as the earth lifted beneath him. Max signalled to the opposing bulldozer to drop its blade into the earth and bring a pile forward to act as a buffer.

Aaron freed the ragged wedge of earth that Friday was sitting on, and carefully angled it up clear of the ground. Spencer and Milsom packed some thick plastic foam sheeting behind Friday, then wrapped a length of thin rope several times around the shovel to make sure Friday didn't fall out. Max signalled Aaron to lift it clear of their heads, then walked over to Connors and Wedderkind.

'Okay, away you go.'

'Thanks,' said Wedderkind. 'I'm sorry I got upset back there. I thought you might have damaged him.'

'What are you gonna do when you get him to the lab, give him a bowl of milk?'

'Well, no, but if and when we decide to take him apart, the idea is to do it scientifically.'

'Okay,' said Max. 'But if you run into any problems, tell me. One of the boys in my crew is an ace with a seven-pound hammer.'

'I'll let you know,' said Wedderkind. He walked away.

Max turned to Connors. 'Lee Ryder . . .' He picked up the wooden stake from the ground. 'I was with him at this fair in Phoenix. He took twenty shots at a '47 Buick. It looked like it'd been run over by a tank.'

Connors smiled.

'Okay, laugh.'

'I'm not laughing, Max.'

'Just tell me, how far have they got with their fancy instruments? Nowhere. Right?'

'Be fair, there were problems when Crusoe was surrounded with a magnetic field and none of their gear was working. Also, I think the idea at the moment is to show we're friendly.'

'Why?' Max jabbed his stake towards Crusoe. 'Hasn't that son of a bitch caused us enough problems?'

'It has, but for the moment, the heat's off.'

'Then why not fix them both for good while we can get at them?'

'Max, we can't risk any drastic action until we know exactly what we're dealing with – or at least have a better idea of the problems than we have now.'

'Who needs it?' said Max. 'It cost me a lot of my friends to learn one thing during the war in 'Nam. Never give the enemy time to dig in. This guy's had enough time to start pouring concrete.'

'We're keeping a close eye on everything, Max, believe me. I'm just as aware of the dangers as you are. That's what my job is – to see this thing doesn't get off the rails.'

'Yeah, okay.' Max nodded wisely. 'I just hope you're still around if and when we have to start shovelling up this pile of shit.'

'I'll be around,' said Connors. 'In the meantime, let's leave it to the scientists.'

'Scientists?' Max snorted. 'Those guys don't even know which end of a test tube to fart into.' He stuck the stake into the ground in front of Connors and stomped off.

There is no way to win this one, thought Connors. This time, he was really the meat in the sandwich. The President had Fraser breathing fire down the back of his neck in Washington, while on Crow Ridge, Allbright was playing the local heavy. And now Max. There would be plenty of people in the country who would share Max's view.

Ranged against them was Wedderkind and the forces of reason – but not necessarily common sense. They were committed to keeping this project alive. Just how far would they go to achieve that objective?

In crossing up the Russians and hiding the truth from the rest of the world, the White House had laid itself wide open to a little discreet blackmail from the scientific community on Crow Ridge. They were sealed off from the outside world, but what about their friends who had kept the press happy with the idea that new, inexplicable solar flares had been the cause of the fade-out? What kind of a deal had Wedderkind done with them?

Connors thought back to his first meeting with the research group at Wright-Patterson AFB, Ohio, and the feeling he had had that the group had known Crusoe was due to arrive. He dismissed the idea yet again, as simple nonscientific paranoia. People were always dreaming of mad scientists plotting to take over the world. They overlooked the fact that most of them were so bad at management that they would never be able to get it together.

That was why God, in his infinite wisdom, had made some men politicians.

The field lab consisted of two facing pairs of prefabricated units linked to a fifth, central unit that ran transversely between them. The four units each housed part of the research group – physics, chemistry, biology, and systems engineering. The central unit was common ground, with various shared facilities, a canteen conference area and a corner for the inevitable paperwork.

Friday was manhandled from the shovel of Aaron's earthmover on to a wooden pallet where he was brushed clean, then a fork-lift truck lifted the pallet through the double doors of the central unit on to a wheeled metal base. Friday's legs were still pulled in tight against his body, and his eyestalks and feelers were fully retracted.

Milsom, who was one of the people pushing the low trolley, had one hand on one of Friday's legs. The black crystal surface felt very cold. When they got Friday to the centre of the room, they saw a thin film of condensation misting his shiny surface.

'Look, he's sweating again. Just like when we first had him surrounded.' Milsom patted one of Friday's sloping side panels. 'Don't worry, baby, this isn't going to hurt.'

'Much,' added Neame.

Spencer felt a cold draught and shivered. 'What happened to the air conditioning?'

Wedderkind, Brecetti, Lovell and the others all became aware of the cold. They didn't need a thermometer to tell them something they could see with their own eyes. Friday was reducing his body temperature.

The thin film of condensation began to turn into creeping patterns of frost over Friday's black body. Wedderkind turned to Milsom. 'Now you know he wasn't sweating, and he wasn't frightened.'

'Shit . . .' said Milsom. 'He's a walking deep freeze.'

Brecetti blew into his hands and rubbed them together. 'How about rustling up some fast heat?' suggested Spencer.

'Good idea,' said Wedderkind. 'Can you get that organized?'

Page, who had gone to get a thermometer from the chemistry unit, said, 'You'd better hurry. The room temperature is minus two degrees centigrade already.'

They left Friday in possession of the central unit and gathered outside the entrance where it was twenty degrees *plus* – a sunny, sixty-eight degrees Fahrenheit.

'Of course the one thing we won't have on the Ridge is a cold suit,' said Wedderkind. 'That would be asking too much.' He buttonholed Milsom. 'Go over to operations, and see if they can get some flown in fast.'

Connors drove up to the field lab in a jeep. 'What are you all doing out here?'

'Take a look inside,' said Wedderkind.

Connors give them all a puzzled glance, pushed open one of the doors to the lab, and gasped as the block of ice-cold air hit him. His lungs felt full of icy needles.

Friday sat on the wooden pallet, his legs still folded in close to his body. Both were now entirely covered in a layer of glittering white frost. He looked like a wedding cake designed by Salvador Dali.

Connors shut the door hurriedly and stepped back outside. He beat his arms across his chest and shivered.

'We can't get near him,' said Wedderkind.

'Isn't there anything you can do to stop it?'

'We're rustling up some gas heating units, and I've sent Milsom to try and organize delivery of some cold suits.'

'Look,' said Page. 'The windows in the side units are misting over.'

Wedderkind tried the handles of the entrance doors, then jerked his hand away as he felt the flesh begin to stick to the metal. The lock was beginning to ice up. Connors cleared a circle of condensation and peered through the panel in the door. Everything inside the central unit was now covered with frost.

Spencer and a cadet came running back with a cylindrical gas turboheater on a wheeled frame. Behind him were six more cadets with another heater and two fat drums of butane.

'How's it going?' asked Spencer breathlessly. Page pointed to the windows. The insides were now an opaque

294

white, and frost was beginning to form on the outside of the glass.

'Shit,' hissed Spencer. 'Aren't those units double glazed?'

Wedderkind took Connors' arm and moved him farther away from the field lab. 'I don't think it would be advisable to go in there until we get the cold suits.'

'What's the temperature in there now?' asked Connors.

'We left all the thermometers inside,' said Page. 'Along with everything else.'

'Okay, let's light these two blowers and shove 'em through the door,' said Spencer.

Brecetti shook his head. 'Complete waste of time. If I had a slide rule I could prove it quickly, but just take my word for it, the number of thermal units those two can put out won't make any difference. If you had fifty perhaps . . .'

'Well, we could at least try,' insisted Spencer.

'Okay,' said Connors. 'Go ahead. There's nothing else we can do.'

They connected up the two turboblowers to the butane drums and lit the ring of gas jets.

'Don't touch the door with your bare hands!' said Wedderkind.

Spencer took the proffered handkerchief, wrapped it round his right hand, and put his own on the left, then grabbed hold of the two handles of the entrance doors. They were frozen solid. He put his shoulder to the door and heaved.

'Can someone lend me a hand to get a little more weight on here?'

'Let me try, sir.' It was one of the cadets. TURNER. The danger hit Wedderkind a fraction too late. As he opened his mouth to cry 'Stop!' Turner hurled himself shoulder first at the doors, burst them open and went crashing through to hit a wall of air at minus triple figures centigrade.

Spencer recoiled as the white cloud of cold air rolled outward. They saw Turner spin round with his mouth open, then fall with outstretched arms against the partially open doors, slamming them shut.

'Jesus Christ!' yelled Spencer. 'Help me get him out.'

Connors grabbed his driver's arm. 'Get the medics!' The cadet leaped into the jeep and roared away.

Wedderkind ran across to the entrance door as four of the cadets who'd brought the heaters got their shoulders to it. 'Get back! It's no good! You'll have to leave him in there!'

One of the cadets grabbed his arms with polite firmness. 'Would you mind standing aside, sir?'

The cadets put their shoulders to the doors and got them partly open Another white cloud of cold air swirled around them.

'Don't breathe in!' cried Wedderkind.

Connors, Spencer, and Page passed the two turboblowers up to the cadets by the doorway to pour in what heat they could, while Shanklin dragged Turner out. Spencer kicked both doors shut.

Wedderkind knelt over Turner. The moisture on his skin had formed into tiny crystals of ice, and his lips were blue. His friends crowded around him. Spencer loosed a stream of remorseful obscenities. Wedderkind stood up.

'Is he going to be all right, sir?'

Wedderkind shook his head.

'That's crazy – he has to be.' One of the cadets began to knead Turner's chest. He looked up. 'Doesn't anybody know what to do?'

Connors took Wedderkind aside. 'What happened to him?'

'His lungs froze solid. That's what happened. Stopped his circulation, like that.' Wedderkind snapped his fingers.

A jeep screeched to a halt behind them and the emergency medical team piled out. The young doctor tried to revive Turner's heart with an injection of digitalis, pounding it with his fist, artificial respiration, mouth-to-mouth resuscitation, but it was all quite useless. Turner had died as he stepped through the door. The medics pulled a stretcher from the back of the jeep, put Turner on it, and covered him with a blanket.

Wedderkind pointed to Shanklin, the cadet who had gone in to pull out Turner.

'You'd better take this young man with you. He's going to need some fast treatment for frostbite.'

'Right,' said the young doctor. Shanklin was ushered aboard the jeep. Turner's body was loaded on the back.

Wedderkind watched them drive away. 'It's all my fault. I saw it happening and just didn't shout fast enough.'

'No, it's mine,' said Spencer. 'If I'd tried harder to open the door – '

'It might have been you under that blanket,' said Connors.

The outside walls of the field lab units were now covered with an opaque layer of white frost like that on the windows.

There was a series of sliding noises from inside the lab, a clatter of things falling, glass smashing. Spencer picked up Turner's hard hat and smashed one of the windows in the door to the central unit. Cold white air spilled out through the hole. Spencer edged up to the window. The inside of the central unit was a complete shambles.

As his body temperature had plunged past zero, Friday had turned himself into a supermagnet, exerting a colossal force that had dragged everything metallic towards him.

They broke the windows in the four wings of the field lab and found the same chaos. Everything was covered with frost. Expensive and fragile equipment stuck out bizarrely from the walls in the corner of the room where each one joined the central unit. The force of the attraction had even sheared tools from the benches where they had iced up.

'Everything's in a dreadful mess,' said Page. 'It'll take weeks to build it all up again.'

'*And* demagnetize everything,' said Lovell.

'Oh, dear, yes, of course,' said Page.

There were more crashing noises as other bits of equipment broke free from the thin grip of ice and flew across the room towards Friday.

'At least we know how these two generate their magnetic fields,' said Wedderkind.

'Great,' said Connors. 'But what do we do now?'

'I think we ought to let him out before he does any more damage.'

They got Aaron to knock both ends of the central unit with the shovel of his earthmover. The intense cold inside rolled out chilling the outside air into small white clouds that drifted around the watching research group. They could now see clear through the shattered central unit. Friday was wedged in by a pile of miscellaneous metal objects – racks, chairs, filing cabinets.

Pushing out his folded legs, Friday calmly created enough room in the middle of the frozen junkheap to stretch them. He had obviously switched off the current which had turned him into a supermagnet. Climbing over the mess, he walked out of the far end of the hut and up on to the plateau. From there, he headed up on to the crest of the Ridge and wandered about in his usual aimless fashion until his white frosted shape thawed out completely.

Back at the field lab the research group began the task of putting the place in order, with the help of a cadet work detail. It was a messy job. All the paper work became soggy as it thawed out and had to be either thrown away or carefully dried. Everything else had to be wiped down. Every item of equipment that contained ferromagnetic or diamagnetic elements was found to be strongly magnetized, and any two objects placed less than three feet apart promptly slid together.

Connors and Wedderkind drove down to the base camp medical unit to see how Shanklin was. They found him heavily bandaged and under treatment for severe frostbite. His hands, face, and feet were badly swollen. Surgery was inevitable.

The news had already been broken to Allbright when they went to see him in the operations hut.

'I'm sorry about that boy Turner,' said Connors. 'And Shanklin – hell, that's just dreadful. They told us he's going to lose all his fingers and most of his face.'

'I've spoken to the other cadets involved,' said Allbright. 'It seems that the accident was as much, if not more, due to their zeal as to anyone else's misjudgement.'

'Nevertheless,' insisted Connors. 'it was *my* misjudgement.'

'No, I'm more to blame than you are,' said Wedderkind. 'I knew exactly what the dangers were. I just didn't react quickly enough.'

'None of us want to cause the death of any of the people on this project,' said Allbright. 'Especially these young men whose lives are full of promise. But if you fail to act decisively, you fail the men under your command. You've just lost your first soldier, Mr Connors. Believe me, losing the second is no easier.'

* * *

Max joined Connors and Wedderkind at their supper table. He hadn't been asked, but then Max was like that. He unloaded his supper, dropped the tray against the leg of the table, and made a mess of the ashtray with his cigar stub.

'Didn't go too well today, huh?' Max filled his big, square jaw with food.

'Not too well,' said Connors.

'We're having problems immobilizing him,' said Wedderkind.

'You're also having problems getting near him,' said Max.

'That's partly due to our limitations,' said Wedderkind. 'The human body only functions efficiently within a very limited temperature range. From about minus ten degrees to plus forty degrees centigrade. We can survive in temperatures in excess of that fifty-degree range, but we have to insulate ourselves.'

'If we'd had the cold suits you might have been okay then.'

'We could have got near Friday,' said Wedderkind. 'But when he turned on the magnetic field, we couldn't put a screwdriver near him without losing control of it.'

'Yeah, I saw the mess,' said Max. 'What's the plan now? You gonna try the big trip?'

'The space suits are on their way,' said Connors. 'We still need to be able to keep Friday out of the way while we get in and out.'

'I could drop the blade of a bulldozer on him,' offered Max. 'Pin him to the ground.'

'Max, until we know whether this thing is alive or not, we're trying not to damage him.'

'He's already killed one guy.'

'Friday didn't kill him, the cold air did.'

300

Max eyed Connors and chewed another mouthful slowly. 'Your father must have been a lawyer,' he said.

Saturday/September 15

It took two days of intensive work to straighten out the field lab, but most of the magnetized equipment had to be replaced. While work was still in progress, the two space suits that Spencer had ordered arrived from Cape Canaveral, Florida, along with a brace of NASA technicians.

Spencer dressed up in one of the suits and was then loaded with the bulky backpack that contained the life-support systems. The suit and pack had been designed for optimum performance in zero-gravity or lunar-g conditions where everything weighed one-sixth of its weight on Earth. Spencer found it was a lot to carry around. It was clear that if anything went wrong while one or more of them was inside Crusoe, they wouldn't be able to get out in a hurry.

Davis, the biologist, and Tomkin, the zoologist, were satisfied that Friday was continuing to explore every corner of his immediate environment, and was keeping them all under close observation. Collis, the language scientist, who, in many people's view, was totally superfluous to requirements, had got together with Alan Wetherby. For several days now, they had been running through the videotapes of Friday trying to spot any sequence of limb or antenna movements that could be even remotely construed as a signal. In conjunction with the videotapes, they were also studying the recordings of

301

Friday's rapid clicking noises, made with the help of a long-range cannon mike.

Collis, who had carried out analytical studies in connection with the Navy's dolphin research program, was well aware of the enormity of the task facing them. The chances of communicating with Friday – establishing what was known as 'interspecies interlock' – were virtually nil.

On the technical side, at least, some small progress had been made. After a careful examination of the contents of the wrecked field lab, it was clear that Friday could drop his body temperature from its normal thirty degrees centigrade to Absolute Zero – minus 273 degrees centigrade. The inevitable question was, if he could drop his temperature that far, how *high* could he raise it? He was turning out to be a far more sophisticated package than they had originally thought, but this new capability fitted in with the idea of Friday as the mobile, all-purpose unit of a planetary probe. If he was to function on Mercury, he would need to lower his body temperature. The same would apply on Venus. And, conversely, he would need to produce heat to withstand the bleak cold of the surface of Pluto, the planet farthest from the sun.

But what about the differing forces of gravity within our solar system? From measurements of the tracks left in the soil, Friday's weight had been estimated at three hundred pounds. Although they had no way of discovering the load-bearing characteristics of the black crystal, Neame had produced calculations to show that Friday's legs were just thick enough to support his weight. To withstand Jupiter's crushing atmospheric pressure – a million Earth atmospheres, plus a force of gravity 2.7 times that of Earth – Friday's legs would have to be as thick as tree trunks. Perhaps Crusoe contained another vehicle specially adapted for exploring high-gravity planets.

Lovell came up with another idea. If Friday could raise and lower his temperature, perhaps he could also vary his weight, in which case the loading on his structure would remain constant. It would not be necessary to change his atomic structure. The weightlessness could be achieved by a condition of minus-g, an antigravity mechanism, working on the principle of magnetic repulsion. Practical experiments had already shown that a train could be floated on a magnetic cushion and then driven forward by linear induction motors.

Lovell's suggestion was based on the theory that he and Brecetti were redeveloping, which was that Crusoe *was* harnessing the Earth's magnetic field rather than producing his own. According to this line of thought, Friday could perhaps harness planetary g-forces in the same way.

'But wait a minute,' said Connors. 'If he can adopt an antigravity state to walk around on planets like Jupiter, he could also use it on this one and – just float away.'

Lovell raised a thick pair of grey eyebrows and tilted his head to one side. 'Yes, he could.'

Connors turned to Wedderkind. 'So we haven't just got to fence him in, we've got to be ready to sit on him as well.'

'We can't exclude that possibility.'

Connors considered the situation for a moment. 'How far are you prepared to go to immobilize Friday?'

'Anything short of physical damage,' said Wedderkind. 'At least until we have an opportunity to look inside Crusoe.'

'I don't get it,' said Max. 'Why do you guys keep pussyfooting around? The only way to find out how this thing works is to take it apart. It's got to be done sooner or later so why not now?'

Wedderkind took off his glasses and began to wipe the

lenses. 'Max, I don't think there is a person in this room who doesn't want to examine this pair, right down to the last molecule.'

He replaced his glasses carefully. 'The fundamental question is, should we interfere with the functional integrity of these two craft, before we gain some inkling of their mission? Earth may be just one port of call on a voyage of exploration that could include our whole solar system – or even our galaxy. Perhaps what we *should* be thinking about is what evidence we could provide Crusoe and Friday with as proof of our existence, the extent of our civilization. Artefacts, a record of Man's history and his achievements for them to take back to their point of origin.'

'Now that's a real cultural can of worms you just opened up,' said Connors. 'We could spend the rest of the century arguing over what we were going to load them up with. Poulenc or Patti Page? Hamlet or Mike Hammer?'

'If they are mindreaders, maybe they know everything we know,' said Brecetti. 'Including the people you just mentioned.'

'So that saves us one problem,' said Wedderkind. 'We're still left with the one we started with. We are always calculating the time it would take us to travel to Alpha Centauri, but suppose they came from a more distant star? Maybe a hundred thousand light years away. In galactic terms, that's just around the corner. They could have started travelling before the dawn of Man. What right have we to interrupt that journey?'

'Good point,' said Connors. 'I don't know how to answer that.' He looked at the others, ending with Max.

Max studied the chewed end of his cigar, then shrugged. 'Don't look at me,' he said. 'I just dig the holes round here.'

'True,' said Connors. 'But now you know what the problems are, how about coming up with a few practical suggestions? If we could pin Friday down, say for a week, that would give us time to get a good crack at Crusoe. Right, Arnold?'

'Yes, we might not even need that long.'

'Exactly,' said Connors. 'I think the answer's going to be a combination of science, cunning and brute force.'

Max stood up, put his hard hat on and pointed his cigar at Connors. 'I'll take that as a compliment.'

Sunday/September 16

CROW RIDGE/MONTANA

In the self-defensive art of jujitsu, the strength of the attacker is employed to defeat him. It was this idea that triggered the plan Max and Wedderkind came up with. Like Max, the plan had a straightforward, brutal effectiveness that made Wedderkind wince. But the chances of success looked good. It was cheap, and required little preparation. Best of all, it used Friday's own power to spring the trap.

Connors approved the plan, told Allbright what was happening and secured his agreement. Wedderkind and the research group had still not worked out whether Crusoe was controlling Friday or vice versa, but there had been no reaction by Crusoe to the previous attempt to hijack Friday, so there was no reason to expect trouble now.

The titanium steel frame required was put together in the workshop by Air Force technicians, loaded on to a jeep and left covered with a tarpaulin.

305

On another jeep they fixed a remote-controlled TV camera on a pylon mounting, and wired it to a twenty-one-inch monitor. Both faced backward, and the screen of the TV set was flush with the rear of the vehicle.

Spencer and the other systems engineers went to work on Crusoe's hatch. They replaced their own unscientific feet with a set of adjustable weights and, in a series of controlled experiments, got the two spheres opening to order.

The technicians then built a tubular steel frame which fitted on to the hull around the dome. The frame was held in place by suction pads and ballast. Fitted to the frame were precisely weighted 'feet' linked to a timing device and operated by compressed air.

All the frame operator had to do was throw a lever and the eight 'feet' planted themselves on the pads in the correct sequence and with the required pressure. Connors and Wedderkind went up on to the hull to watch it being tested. It worked perfectly. When the pressure was applied, Crusoe opened up obediently, the two spheres rotating into line with a quiet, smooth hiss.

The next step was a more thorough examination of the hatch. Two of the monitor hut technicians drove out with a portable videotape recorder and TV camera. The plan was to lower the camera into the hatch so that every detail could be recorded and studied carefully. All that showed up on the screen was a dancing pattern of dots and lines. A magnetic field within the hull was interfering with the magnetic elements in the TV system.

'*Scheisse*,' said Wedderkind, in a rare outburst of temper.

'Will some photographs do?' asked Connors.

'They'll have to, but this means that we won't be able to run a TV camera or a radio inside the hull and *that* means we won't know what is happening until whoever goes in comes out.'

Nicholas, one of the Air Force photographers, brought his camera bag up on to the hull. He took a good look inside the hatch to make an estimate of the available light and set his Hasselblad for 1/50th at F/11. He fitted a long bulb release and mounted it on a tripod. The spheres rotated shut. Spencer waited five minutes, then opened Crusoe up again. Nicholas turned the camera tripod upside down, lowered it into the hatch, and splayed the legs wide apart so that they rested against the rim of the hatch. He took the first picture, then moved the tripod legs round to take a second picture. With each succeeding exposure, the movement of the working parts became more and more sluggish.

Spencer, who was on the hull operating the foot-frame for Nicholas, allowed his mind to wander from the stopwatch to Nicholas' exposure problems. Without any warning, the override cycle cut in, and the two hatches started to close with the tripod and Hasselblad hanging down inside. Nicholas managed to grab one leg of the tripod but lost his balance as the dome rotated under his feet. Before he could pull the camera clear, the outer and inner rims of the hatch slid one over the other, shearing through the heavy tubular legs of the tripod like a florist's scissors through daisy stalks.

Spencer helped Nicholas to his feet. 'Are you okay?' Nicholas nodded, white-faced. 'You're lucky you didn't have your arm in there.'

As soon as the five-minute closed cycle had expired, Spencer rotated the hatches open again. Nicholas wired a Nikon for flash, and whacked off two rolls of film looking down into the black crystal interior of the inner sphere. The prints were sharp, but black on black is difficult to photograph.

The partial failure of the photographic sortie was reported to Wedderkind. The answer, he suggested, was to find someone who could draw.

Davis, the biologist, turned out to be the fastest pencil on the site. He was, as he said, really better at flowers, but his scientific background and trained powers of observation put him ahead of the other two artists they discovered, a cadet who was good at caricatures, and a technician who'd done a stint in the background department of MGM's cartoon studios before joining the Air Force.

Davis went to work, with the four systems engineers taking it in turn to look over his shoulder to aid him in interpreting the mechanical details.

Later that night, they sat down around a table in the operations room and studied Davis' sketches and the pictures Nicholas had managed to take from the outside.

Milsom pointed out to Connors the circular structure that lined the interior of the hatch. 'We're pretty certain that this whole section contrarotates as the sphere spins shut.'

'So that Friday stays the right way up.'

'Yes. His legs fold in and engage these eight vertical sections. They must act like guide rails in which he slides up and down.'

'How?' asked Connors.

'Probably by magnetic repulsion and attraction,' said Milsom. 'From this disc . . .' He picked up another of Davis' drawings and pointed to a raised disc at the bottom of the sphere directly opposite the circular hatch.

'Is that forty-five-second override on the hatch going to be a problem?' asked Connors.

'It doesn't make things any easier,' said Neame. 'We plan to build a wooden platform over the dome with a hole in the middle so as we can get straight into the

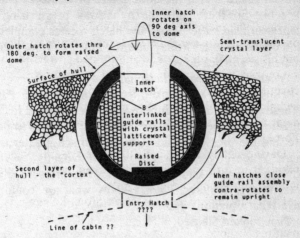

SECTION THROUGH HATCH
Drawing by Neame based on Davis' sketches

Inner hatch rotates on 90 deg axis to dome

Outer hatch rotates thru 180 deg. to form raised dome

Semi-translucent crystal layer

Surface of hull

Inner hatch

8 Interlinked guide rails with crystal latticework supports

Raised Disc

Second layer of hull - the "cortex"

When hatches close guide rail assembly contra-rotates to remain upright

Entry Hatch ????

Line of cabin ??

hatch. Forty-five seconds gives us ample time to get somebody in and out of the hatch.'

'A lot depends on what footholds we can find inside,' said Spencer. 'It's ten feet from the lip of the hatch to the bottom of the inner sphere.'

'How about lifting tackle on an overhead beam?' suggested Gilligan. He was also from NASA. 'We could use a clip-on helicopter rescue harness and just pull them straight out.'

'Feasible?' asked Connors.

'Yes, that'll work,' said Spencer.

'But before we get that far, there are several important measurements that need to be made with the nonelectrical instrument package that Professor Lovell, Jo Armenez, and I have assembled,' said Page. 'It will give us an atmospheric analysis, pressure, temperature, internal gravity – and the direction and degree of movement of the inner hatch.'

'It must be an airlock,' said Spencer. 'Which Crusoe pressurizes to match the atmosphere of whatever planet he's on. So there must be a halfway pressurizing or depressurizing stage before the hatch rotates completely and opens up to let Friday into the hull . . . I bet there's some real goodies down there.'

'Yeah,' said Milsom. 'I can hardly wait.'

'Haven't you overlooked something?' asked Page. 'These space suits you propose using are designed for use at zero atmospheric pressure. What do you plan to do if we find the pressure inside Crusoe is much greater than ours? Whoever goes in will be crushed to death.'

'You're right,' said Wedderkind. 'The pressure *is* the vital factor. Frankly, I don't know what we could do given that situation.'

Page looked pleased.

That evening, when it came to the choice of who was going to dress up in space suits, Milsom found that there was no rush to draw straws. Several people had apparently decided this was one occasion when losing was smarter. Connors and Wedderkind processed the list of possibles.

The real standout choices were among the engineers. Some years before, Milsom, Spencer, Vincent, and Gilligan had all been selected for astronaut training, then had been dropped from the course as NASA cut back its manned-flight program.

Milsom, the first in line, was single. Spencer had volunteered but was married. So was Gilligan, but as he had no family, he had offered to go in the Number Two spot – if they couldn't find anyone else. Vincent and Hadden, the two Air Force engineers, had both been primed by Allbright. Vincent was single, Hadden the father of four.

'So it looks like Milsom as eager beaver, Vincent

as Number Two, with Gilligan as backup man,' said Connors.

Once Friday had been immobilized, they would have forty-eight hours to explore Crusoe's interior. That was the longest single period Friday had spent on one of his walks. There was no way to predict what might happen if that time was exceeded. Friday's failure to return might trigger off a whole new mission sequence, including takeoff. The idea was to get in, explore as much of the interior as possible, then get out before the deadline expired.

That at least was the thinking on Sunday night.

Monday/September 17

CROW RIDGE/MONTANA

At dawn, the air was crisp with autumn prairie freshness. On the horizon, layers of Disney-pink clouds were spiked on the rays of the rising sun.

Connors smelled the coffee as part of his dream before he woke up to find Wedderkind shaking him.

'He's out.'

Connors yawned hugely, stretched, then sat up on one elbow. Wedderkind had brought him a breakfast tray.

'Great,' yawned Connors. He hauled himself up straight.

Wedderkind put the tray on Connors' lap, switched on the TV monitor and sat down. Friday stood astride the dome taking the morning air.

Connors drained his orange juice, sampled the scrambled egg, then pushed it aside and tried the coffee.

311

It was Arnold's, and tasted good. 'Anything on last night's tapes?'

'No . . . Oh, by the way,' said Wedderkind. 'I got word that a guy at the University of Chicago has filtered out some rhythmically pulsed tremors. They seem to be coming from this direction. It might be of some interest. Since Al Wetherby knows him I've sent him over there to look at the recordings. I hope that's okay.'

'It's your department,' said Connors. 'Are you going up on to the plateau or are you going to watch from the operations room?'

'I'll go up, I think.'

'I'll stick with the multiscreens. You get a better all-around view. Have I got time for a shower?'

'That depends on Friday.'

'Okay . . .' Connors got out of his bunk and wrapped himself in a bathrobe. 'If I'm not there, start without me.'

'Keep your fingers crossed,' said Wedderkind.

Connors smiled. 'When you've thought of everything including prayers, that's the only thing you *can* do.'

The cadet driver of the TV jeep waited until Friday had walked down off Crusoe's hull, then switched on the camera and drove slowly in front of Friday. The camera picked him up and transferred his image to the screen. Friday stopped in his tracks as he saw it, then moved after the jeep as it cruised towards the point selected for the ambush.

The cadet pulled up in position with his eye on his rearview mirror and kept the motor running. Friday hung around the back of the jeep looking at himself on the TV screen.

When Connors arrived at the operations room, Allbright was already sitting in front of the double bank

312

of screens. On the top left-hand screen was the picture of Friday looking at himself.

Connors sat down. 'I wonder what he's thinking.'

'Yes,' said Allbright. 'This could be the first time Friday has seen himself. He may not know what he looks like – or even that he exists. I wonder how his data circuits will handle that discovery.'

'If he blew a fuse, it would save us a lot of trouble,' said Connors. 'But that's an interesting point you've raised. Why don't you mention it to Arnold?'

Allbright smiled. 'I'm sure it must have already occurred to him.' He turned his attention back to the monitor screens.

Down in the heavy-vehicle parking area, four bull-dozers were making a cartridge start. Max was driving one of them. Fifty yards away from the TV jeep, four earthmovers were parked with their raised shovels full of earth. Two of Max's riggers were hosing water over the earth. Nearby were several man-high mounds of loose soil.

Friday seemed fascinated by his electronic image. He raised his two front legs, and saw his TV double do the same. As Max's bulldozer chugged up on to the plateau, the four top 'eyes' popped out on their stalks to get a clear view over the jeep. Max was nearly two hundred yards away and heading across the front of the TV jeep. The 'eyes' sank back into Friday's head.

Max circled around behind the group of earthmovers and parked the bulldozer with the engine running. The two riggers started to hose water on to the mounds of loose soil.

The jeep carrying the steel frame pulled up fifty yards to the right of Friday with its rear facing him. The three other jeeps took up similar positions at right angles to one another and all facing away from Friday.

From a point halfway up to the crest of the Ridge, Wedderkind watched the vehicles move into position. He focused his binoculars on Friday. Friday's attention still seemed to be focused on his colour TV image. Wedderkind swallowed and nodded to Spencer.

Spencer spoke into a two-way radio. 'Okay, all stations, time to commercial break is ten seconds, starting now – '

The driver of the TV jeep eased off the hand brake, and selected four-wheel forward drive. The three other drivers selected four-wheel reverse gear and looked back over their shoulders. They'd rehearsed this move throughout the previous day, and had written off two jeeps in the process.

'. . . Five, four, three, two, one, *go!*'

The four jeep drivers clamped a lead foot on to the accelerator and shot backward towards Friday as the TV jeep roared away in a right-hand curve. Max put the bulldozer into top gear and clanked noisily out of hiding.

The four jeeps braked simultaneously and slid backward to form a neat box around Friday. In a flash, his legs contracted inward and he crouched down in a tight bundle. Four of the eight men seized the steel frame from the jeep – a four-sided pyramid with a flat top and a diagonal mesh of thick bars.

As they dropped the cage over Friday the second group quickly pinned the cage to the ground by driving in two-foot-long steel stakes with sledgehammers.

Before the stakes were halfway in, icy condensation started to collect around Friday. The cage began to frost over as his temperature plummeted. The men hurled the sledgehammers into the jeeps and retreated to a safe distance as Max arrived with the bulldozer.

Aided by hand signals, Max hammered the stakes into the ground with the edge of the bulldozer's blade. The

314

blade turned white as ground frost formed in a spreading circle around the cage.

Max backed the bulldozer away and waved the earthmovers forward. The four vehicles fanned out and curved in towards Friday at right angles to one another. The loads of earth in their shovels had been hosed into mud, and as it poured into and over the icy cage, it froze solid.

Shovels empty, they headed back to the piles of earth, loaded up, and returned to heap it over the freezing mass that had engulfed the cage. An ice-cold mist drifted round them as they tamped the earth down with the flat of their shovels.

Half an hour later, Friday was buried under a flattened mound of earth twelve feet high and thirty feet wide. The steel cage had been designed to restrict his movements, and to stop him from being crushed. The four bulldozers tidied up the mound, then reversed up the frozen slopes to park back to back on top.

Connors drove up to view the final result with Allbright and Wedderkind. Max climbed down from his bulldozer and pulled off his furlined parka as he walked over to them. Behind him, the bulldozers started to ice over.

'Do you think it's going to work?' asked Connors.

'It should.' Max pulled a cigar out of his shirt pocket. He lit the cigar, then rolled it between his teeth to the corner of his mouth. 'If he keeps on freezing, he's locked solid, and if he heats up, he'll bake himself into a steel-lined brick.' Max grinned. 'If he can get out of that, he's Houdini.'

It was a great curtain line, but it was Friday who had the last word. As they were driving away, they heard a series of sharp, metallic clinks followed by dull, metallic clunks. They stopped, turned back and circled the frosty mound.

The sharp clinks had been made by heavy metal castings fracturing in Friday's sub-sub-zero temperature. The dull clunks had been the sound of the deep-frozen bulldozers collapsing into four untidy lopsided heaps.

With the aid of Davis' sketches and some frantic forty-five-second bursts with a measuring tape, Vincent and Hadden obtained enough information to build a frame that could be quickly locked into the eight guide rails inside the hatch.

Professor Lovell's non-electric instrument package, which had a quaint eighteenth-century look, was attached to a special mounting inside the frame. If the frame revolved, the mounting would remain horizontal, recording the movement of the inner hatch.

A wooden platform had been built to fit around the dome and over the foot-frame that opened it. On the platform, two inverted-V uprights supported a crossbeam. A rope and pulley were attached to the beam to lower Milsom in and haul him smoothly out of the hatch.

Following the swift amputation of the photographer's tripod by the closing hatch, a tape-recorder alarm system had been installed just outside Crusoe's skin-deep magnetic field; the system broadcast an amplified voice countdown during the forty-five seconds the hatch was open. The tape was triggered by the opening of the hatch itself. Ten seconds before it was due to close, an alarm bell rang for five seconds, followed by a final five-four-three-two-one voice count to rotation.

Lovell, Armenez, and Page double-checked the instruments and adjusted the settings. Then Vincent and Hadden lowered the package to arm's length inside the hatch and locked it into the black crystal guide rails.

'. . . Five-four-three-two-one-rotation.'

The instrument package was left inside the hatch for

fifteen minutes and then was taken back to the field lab. When Wedderkind saw the results of the test, he asked Lovell to check the instruments and run the test again.

Wedderkind joined Connors in the operations hut.

'Any luck?'

'We've got some results,' said Wedderkind. 'That may not be the same thing.' He sat down with a sigh. 'The framework in the inner sphere *does* contrarotate. That means Friday stays the right way up when the two hatches spin around. The inner sphere rotates through one hundred and eighty degrees. The hatch ends up facing downward.'

'Good. Does the outer sphere rotate so that both hatches are in line again?'

'We think it does. That's one of the things Milsom will have to confirm.'

'How about air pressure?'

'There isn't any. The inner sphere makes a quarter turn, there's a sixty-second depressurization cycle. When the air pressure reaches zero, it makes another quarter turn, presumably to line up with the outer hatch to make an entrance into the hull.'

'But there's no air at all.'

'No air, no noxious gases, no anything. A total vacuum.'

Connors frowned. 'Is that how it should be?'

Wedderkind shrugged. 'Machines have no need for air. In fact a sterile, dust-free, airless temperature-controlled environment would permit mechanical devices to function at peak efficiency for – well, forever.'

'So that reinforces our theory that both Friday and Crusoe are machines.'

'Ye-es . . .'

'How about temperature?'

317

'Minus two hundred and seventy-one degrees centigrade.'

Connors looked surprised. 'Absolute zero?'

'No, but that figure is interesting. It's the temperature of outer space measured in terms of black body radiation. Absolute zero is two hundred and seventy-three degrees centigrade. Point one five to be exact.'

'Arnold, after minus thirty, cold is cold. Okay, so we've got zero pressure and zero temperature. Anything else?'

'Yes, we've got zero gravity as well. A condition of weightlessness. Milsom's going to be able to float around inside that hatch the way the astronauts did inside Skylab.'

'But that's crazy. How . . . ?'

'Lovell's running another test right now.'

'But is it possible?'

Wedderkind tapped back his glasses. 'Do you remember that idea Phil Brecetti and Lovell had? That in certain situations Friday might utilize antigravity to counteract planetary g-forces? What Crusoe seems to have done is to create an internal field whose strength equals our own force of gravity. The result is zero-g. If it was any more, he'd start to float.'

'But what use is that?'

'Well, not much for any machine function that depends on gravity or friction, but zero-g would improve the overall environment for certain other types of machinery. The mechanical force required to move parts is virtually nil, friction is eliminated. This reduces your power requirements, consequently your power source lasts longer.'

'Except that you're burning up power generating the antigravity field.'

'Not in outer space,' said Wedderkind. 'Only on a

318

planet. And there, Crusoe may simply reverse the existing gravitational field.'

'You mean in the way that Brecetti said he could be using the Earth's magnetic field to produce the cutoff zone he put around himself when he landed?'

'Yes. He and Lovell now think that the black crystal coating on his hull could be acting as some kind of condenser. The whole idea relates quite well to the Universal Field Theory.'

'Great, but don't start opening that can of neutrinos. Let's stick to the hatch. Have you told Milsom about this?'

'No, I'm waiting for the results of the second test.'

The results of the second test merely confirmed the first. Zero pressure, zero temperature, zero gravity. It did at least solve one thing. There would no longer be a weight problem with the bulky life-support pack. And Milsom didn't have to worry about accidentally falling out of the hatch, when it turned upside down.

Tuesday/September 18

CROW RIDGE/MONTANA

When Connors arrived at the medical unit, Milsom was already dressed in the space suit. The two NASA technicians who had been flown up with the suits put the helmet over Milsom's head and locked it into the collar of the suit. He checked the closure of the gold-plated visor, then lifted it up again. Milsom grinned at Connors.

'How do you feel?'

'Great. If you're interested, the autographs are two dollars fifty cents plus tax.'

Connors shook Milsom's gloved hand. 'I'll buy one when you come back.'

'In that case, I'd better give you the name of my agent,' said Milsom.

Connors returned to the command hut and sat down in front of the bank of TV screens that covered the activity around the hatch.

Waiting like a hanging party on the hull platform were Max and his three biggest roughnecks. They would be hauling Milsom out on the rope. Neame and Gilligan would help guide Milsom down into the hatch, Vincent and Hadden were operating the foot-frame to open it, and Spencer was there to co-ordinate the whole operation.

The thing that had threatened to stymie Milsom's trip was the lack of a suitable light source. Crusoe's skintight cutoff zone made it impossible to use electrical power, and the total vacuum inside the hatch prevented the use of any simple chemical combustion process. The research group finally came up with a light paddle, the size and shape of a table-tennis bat, and coated on both sides with a supercharged luminous compound. It would provide a dim light source by which Milsom could see if there was a way into the hull.

A parachute harness had been modified to take a chest-mounted ring through which the lifting hook could be clipped. Neame and Gilligan strapped Milsom into it, then guided his arms through the straps of the life-support pack. One of the NASA technicians connected the pack to the suit and checked that all the systems were working.

Spencer clipped the lifting hook to Milsom's chest, then patted him on the shoulder. 'Take it easy. Stay out of trouble.'

'I'll only be gone five minutes.'

Spencer grinned. 'Somehow that doesn't have the same ring as Neil Armstrong's "one small step" speech.'

Milsom pulled down his gold visor. Sunlight flared off the mirrored surface.

'Okay, Max. He's all yours,' said Spencer.

Max's crew hauled Milsom four feet into the air. Steadied by Neame and Gilligan, Milsom swung out over the top of the dome. Vincent pulled the lever which set the eight 'feet' down on the hull pressure points. The dome rotated and the two circular hatches spun into alignment. On Spencer's wave, Milsom was lowered smoothly into the black crystal well. Spencer, Neame, and Gilligan leaned over and watched Milsom unclip the rope.

'Forty seconds to rotation . . .'

They pulled up the rope. Milsom found handholds and footholds on the honeycombed framework that supported the guide rails and leaned back against one side of the well. He looked up at them and gave them a thumbs-up sign. His dark, golden mask made him look like a one-eyed plump white grub.

The alarm bell jangled from the loudspeaker, then ten seconds later the hatch closed as the two spheres rotated into the hull.

Connors sat back in his chair and breathed out heavily. He looked at his watch. 11:05. Wedderkind lit a cigarette.

Connors turned to Allbright. 'This must be a bit like waiting for a squadron to return from a mission.'

'A bit,' said Allbright.

At 11:10, Vincent rotated the hatches. Spencer, Neame, and Gilligan looked down into the well and were relieved to see that Milsom was still in one piece. He was crouching down at the bottom of the well.

Spencer turned to Max. 'He's okay.' He passed the rope down to Milsom hand over hand.

Milsom made no move to clip the lifting hook on to his harness.

'What's wrong with him?' asked Neame.

'I don't know,' said Gilligan. 'Maybe he's hurt himself.'

Spencer turned angrily on Gilligan. 'How the hell could he do that? The guide rails don't move when the hatch rotates.'

'I don't know how,' said Gilligan. 'Maybe he lost his grip when normal gravity returned. If he was upside down – '

'Listen, he didn't fall on his fucking head. He can see us, for Christ's sake – look!' Spencer swung the rope towards Milsom. The hook clacked against the visor of his helmet. Milsom shrank back and pushed the rope away.

'Chris!' Spencer banged his fist against his chest. 'Clip on the hook!'

Milsom waved his arm – not towards the rope, but to them.

'Twenty seconds to rotation . . .'

Max, Vincent, and Hadden joined them at the hatch and looked down at Milsom. Milsom seemed to shrink away at the sight of them, but waved his arm again.

'Fifteen seconds to rotation . . .'

'What the hell is he trying to say?' asked Max. 'Does he want us to come in after him?'

'That's what it looks like,' said Neame.

Max turned to Gilligan. 'You're right. He has fallen on his fucking head.'

The alarm bell sounded. Max yanked the rope out of the well. Milsom was still beckoning to them when the hatch closed.

Connors watched Spencer run down the hull towards

the communications jeep. He stood in front of the TV camera and came into close-up on Screen 5.

'Arnold, we've got a little problem here. I don't know how much of it you were able to get on the overhead camera.'

'We got some of it. Most of the time your heads were in the way.'

'Yeah, well, we were trying to see what was wrong. Something's happened to him. We don't know what.'

'Could he have broken his arms?'

'No. His arms move okay, and his reflexes seem normal. He's waving to us. He just won't hook up the line so we can pull him out.'

'What do you plan to do?'

'Well, we're going to rotate in five minutes and try again.'

'Okay. What was it that Max said? We didn't quite catch it.'

'He said it looked as if Chris wanted us to come into the hatch.'

'It could mean he wanted help.'

'Yes, I know, but he actually had the lifting hook in his hand. All he had to do was clip it on but he pushed it away. And when all six of us were round the hatch he kind of backed down away from us, almost as if he were frightened. I don't understand it.'

'Neither do I,' said Wedderkind. 'Give it another try.'

'Oh, hell, yes,' said Spencer. 'We're not just going to leave him in there.' He went back up on to the hull platform.

Wedderkind eyed Connors and Allbright and stuck out a doubtful lip. 'I don't like it.'

'Max is up there,' said Allbright. 'He'll figure out something.'

Max did. At 11:16 the two hatches swung back into

line. Milsom was still there, crouching down in the bottom of the well. He beckoned to Spencer. They dropped the rope down to him. Milsom took hold of the rope but made no attempt to clip the hook to his chest. He waved to Spencer again.

'Chris!' roared Spencer. 'The hook! Clip on the hook!' He mimed the action, thumping his fist against his chest.

Milsom didn't respond. It was impossible to see his face behind the reflecting surface of the visor. There was nothing but a circle of sky edged by their own bodies and enclosed by the dark interior of the sphere.

'Thirty-five seconds to rotation . . .'

'Move aside,' said Max. He grabbed hold of the rope and turned to his crew. 'Okay, I'm going in to hook up this son of a bitch, so get a good grip on that rope. When I shout, I want to come out of there faster than a cork out of a champagne bottle. Right?'

'Max – ' began Spencer.

Max began to slide down the rope. 'If you want to help, get on the other end of this thing.'

'Okay, we'll get it,' said Vincent. He and Hadden joined Max's three roughnecks on the rope.

As Max landed beside Milsom, Spencer saw that Milsom had wound the loose end of the rope around the bottom of two of the guide rails and had snapped the hook back on to the line. Max grabbed Milsom, heaved him aside, and began to unravel the rope.

'Max!' yelled Spencer.

Max half-turned and threw up an arm to protect himself as Milsom dropped a loop of the rope around his arm and neck, yanked it tight, then fell on top of him like an ungainly white bear. Max hit out with his fists, knees and feet, but the multi-layered insulation of the suit absorbed the force of his blows.

'Twenty seconds to rotation . . .'

Max hurled Milsom away from him and managed to loosen the rope around his throat and arm before Milsom came back at him. Max had unclipped the hook from the rope, but the rope itself was still twisted around the guide rails. Milsom fell against him, arms outstretched. It was clear he wasn't trying to hit Max, he was just trying to hold him down to keep him from leaving the hatch.

'Fifteen seconds to rotation . . .'

'For Christ's sake!' yelled Max. 'Doesn't anyone have a knife or a gun up there! Why don't you shoot this son of a bitch!' Max sent Milsom crashing against the other side of the well. Without his space helmet, Milsom's skull would have been fractured.

With the rope still locked around the guide rails, the only thing Max could do was climb out hand over hand. Max jumped at the rope and as his hands closed round it, he swung his legs up and booted Milsom in the chest.

In the same split second that Max's feet connected, the alarm bell began to ring and the rope party made their fatal mistake. As they felt Max's weight on the rope, they hauled in on the other end. Instead of hanging straight down into the centre of the well, the rope snapped taut and kinked around the edge of the hatch to where Milsom had fastened it at the bottom of the guide rails.

With the last ten seconds ticking away in slow motion, Spencer saw Milsom fall back from the blow and Max twist around on the rope and lose his foothold.

'Down a bit!' yelled Spencer.

The rope crew let out two feet of rope. It was one foot too many. That extra twelve inches put Max back within Milsom's reach. As Max reached up to haul himself out by his hands alone, Milsom flung both arms round Max's legs and hung on. Milsom, plus the suit, plus the life-support pack was too much even for Max's muscles. He hung on to the rope but couldn't bend his arm to get any higher. The veins knotted under the skin of his head and neck.

Spencer stood paralysed with the alarm bell jangling in his ears. Max's hands were clenched around the rope just below the bottom rim of the hatch – just an arm's length away. Spencer did not dare reach down and grab Max's hand. If the hatches closed, the twelve-inch-thick crystal rims would cut through his arm like an electric meat slicer. The alarm bell stopped ringing.

'Five – '

Spencer saw Max's left hand scrabble over the smooth rim of the inner hatch.

'Four – '

The fingernails tried to find a hold in the impossibly fine joint between the inner and outer spheres.

'Three – '

Max's hands began to slip backward on the rope.

'Two – '

His face contorted with rage as he launched himself upward, flexing his body back and forth like a marlin on a line in one last desperate effort to shake himself free of Milsom.

'One – '

Max got one hand on top of the other.

'Rotation . . .'

'You stupid mother – '

The two circular hatches slid across each other eclipsing the rest of Max's curse at the same time as they cut the rope.

Connors sat staring at the monitors, unable to accept that he had just witnessed the last thirty-five seconds of Max's life. It was just not possible. On Screen 3 Spencer was on his knees pounding on the dome with his fist.

Connors knew what the answer would be but he had to ask. 'Does Max have a chance?'

Wedderkind shook his head silently. He took off his glasses and began to wipe the lenses, head bowed.

'What will happen? Will it be – ?'

'Quick?' Allbright eyed Connors. 'That hatch depressurizes in sixty seconds. As the air is exhausted he'll suffocate, and as the pressure drops to zero, the blood in his veins will boil.'

Connors winced. 'Jesus . . .'

'I think Max knew the risk he was taking,' said Wedderkind.

'Yes,' said Allbright. 'The one thing he didn't foresee was that Milsom would try and keep him in there.'

'And anchor the rope to keep us from pulling Max out.' Connors cursed sharply under his breath. 'It's stupid. He should have had a safety rope around him.'

'Yes, he should have. It's easy to think of what could have been done. Someone on the platform could have gone in to help Max with Milsom. They might have ended up getting killed as well.'

'Why?' asked Wedderkind. He put his glasses back on. 'Why would Milsom want to do such a thing? He must have known what would happen to Max.' He lifted his hands. 'It just doesn't make sense. Milsom was . . .'

I know what you mean, thought Connors. Always making jokes. This one had turned sour.

Spencer came back on Screen 5. His face was pale, his voice tense but controlled. 'Arnold, we're going to rotate again at eleven twenty-two just to see what the situation is.'

'Max doesn't have a chance, Dan.'

'I know, but we just can't leave Chris in there. If he's gone crazy, it's our fault. Maybe if two people had gone in on separate ropes – '

327

'Dan, now it's happened, all of us have got a dozen better ways of doing it. Believe me, we feel just as bad about it as you do.'

Connors took over the mike. 'Let's just get one thing clear, Dan. Next time, if Chris won't come out on his own, nobody goes in or tries to help in any way. Is that clear?'

'Yes,' said Spencer. Clear but unwelcome.

The hatches were rotated at 11:22. The inner sphere was empty. The only trace that remained of Max and Milsom was the severed length of rope still attached to the bottom end of the guide rails.

The hatch party returned from the plateau and came over with the rest of the research group to the operations room. They sat behind Connors, Allbright, and Wedderkind and gloomily watched the taped replay of Milsom's entry into the hatch and Max's rescue attempt. Spencer sat with his head in his hands during the last part.

Connors swung his chair around to face the hatch party. 'Okay, let's talk this through and see what we can come up with. Milsom is shut inside the hatch. For five minutes, he is in a zero-pressure, zero-gravity situation. He's protected by his space suit so nothing can happen to him physically. But *something* happened, obviously. He experienced something that made him frightened to come out – made him frightened of you.'

Connors held up a hand to forestall Wedderkind. 'Okay, let's allow for the fact that we might have misinterpreted his feelings. Perhaps he *wasn't* frightened. He didn't *want* to come out. At least there's no argument about that. Yet he wanted *you* to go in and join him – even though without suits, that was impossible. Fatal.'

'He may have meant only me,' said Spencer. 'We had planned to go in together.'

'In that case, why did he hang on to Max?' asked

328

Wedderkind. 'Chris must have known what would happen if Max was trapped inside the hatch.'

'I can't explain why Chris did that.'

'Somebody or something must have got to him,' said Connors. 'If it was bad news, the natural reaction would be to get out and warn us. But he stayed inside. That could be because he'd become part of that bad news himself. Infected, contaminated in some way. He may have thought that if he stayed inside, he could stop it spreading to *us*.'

'Perhaps it wasn't Milsom we saw,' said Page.

Oh, Mel Fraser would love you, thought Connors. He held back a smile but Page sensed his scepticism.

'You did suggest he might have been got at.'

'I did, but if Crusoe was going to use Chris for some kind of takeover bid, he would be no use stuck inside the hatch.'

'Except as bait,' said Spencer. 'That backpack will keep him alive for eight hours. As long as there's a chance of rescuing him, we have to keep trying.'

'But Crusoe had no way of knowing that,' said Connors. 'We could just leave Chris in there.'

'But you won't,' said Spencer.

'We will, if I decide that's the best thing to do,' said Connors. He felt the chill, negative vibrations of the group.

'Could I come in with a comment?' It was Ray Collis, the language scientist. 'What we haven't considered is the possibility that what Chris Milsom discovered was not *bad* news, but good news.'

Good news? Connors found the idea faintly ridiculous.

Collis seemed to share his opinion. He cleared his throat nervously. 'If Milsom wouldn't leave Crusoe, it might have been because being inside was infinitely preferable to being outside. It would also explain why he

329

beckoned to the others in an effort to get them to join him.'

'If it was that fantastic, why didn't he come out and tell us all about it?' asked Connors.

'There could be two reasons. The first is that Milsom may have been unsure he would be able to get back inside – it's possible we might have tried to prevent him. The second is that perhaps whatever he experienced is something impossible to communicate in words. It may be something that has to be experienced in order to be understood.'

'Okay,' said Connors. 'Why couldn't he come out and tell us that?'

'I don't know,' said Collis. 'Maybe the hatch is like a turnstile. You can only go through it one way. He may have undergone an irreversible mental process that makes a return to our world impossible.'

'Are you also saying that this – process – was so good Milsom was prepared to share it with Max even if it killed him?'

'That *is* a problem,' admitted Collis. 'I'm not dodging the question. I can only imagine that in relation to the benefits conferred by the experience, Max's physical death was probably irrelevant.'

'I doubt if it was to Max,' said Allbright.

'Nor to any of us, General, on this side of the hatch.'

Connors exchanged a long look with Wedderkind and wondered why he hadn't said anything. Did he agree? He turned back to Collis. 'That's quite a hefty spiritual kite you're flying, Ray.'

Collis shrugged. 'The physical sciences can't provide all the answers. If you find the word "spiritual" upsetting, consider it as a metaphysical experience.'

'It doesn't make much difference,' said Connors. 'The only way we can verify your theory is for us to follow

Chris through the hatch – in the way the children of Hamelin followed the Pied Piper into the mountain. When do we stop, when there are none of us left?'

'That could be the reason why we were allowed to open the hatch in the first place,' said Collis. 'But how many of us are prepared to risk losing this uncertain life in search of good news in the next?'

'Exactly,' said Connors. 'It's a nice idea, Ray, but I don't think it gets us any nearer to solving our immediate problem – which is what to do about Chris.' He looked at his watch. 'He's got enough oxygen till seven – is that right?'

'Yes. But seven is the absolute limit,' said Spencer.

'Okay, I suggest the best thing for you to do is to rotate the hatch every fifteen minutes starting at twelve-thirty, just in case Chris reappears. Anything to add, Arnold?'

'No, that's fine.'

Connors patted Spencer on the shoulder and walked with him to the door. 'I know how you feel, but don't take the whole thing on yourself.' He dropped his voice. 'One other thing. If you'd been on that rope with ten seconds to go and Milsom around your feet, *I* wouldn't have stuck my arm in that hatch – and Max wouldn't have either.'

Spencer bit his lip on what he was going to say and nodded instead.

The meeting broke up, leaving Connors alone with Allbright and Wedderkind. Connors called the monitor hut and got them to pipe in a second replay of the whole disastrous sequence. As he watched Max's life end for a third time, Connors thought about Collis' idea. It was interesting, but not the kind of thing he could take to the President. He swung his chair away from the screens and found Wedderkind watching him.

331

'Had any more thoughts?'

'Yes,' said Connors. 'I was thinking that if I was asked to describe our progress on this project, I'd say that every time we open one can of beans, all we find inside it is another can.'

'We have two decisions to make,' said Connors. 'One, do we go for a second insertion, and two, should we tie the next candidate down to keep him from leaving the hatch?' Connors sat back while Allbright and Wedderkind mulled over their answers.

'Number Two is easier,' said Wedderkind. 'We could lock our man into a safety harness anchored to the guide rails.'

'It sounds like a real ball and chain job.'

'It would have to be.'

'I think we're getting a little off course,' said Allbright. 'If whoever goes into the hatch becomes so deranged as to require this treatment then it may be safer for us to leave him there.'

'Does that mean you think we shouldn't try to find out what happened to Milsom?'

'It would cut down our casualty rate – and it might save us a lot of problems,' said Allbright.

'General, Milsom's disappearance means that there *is* a way into Crusoe. It means there is a chance for us to try and unlock some of its secrets. For a scientist, that prospect is irresistible. That hatch is like the doorway to a twentieth-century version of Aladdin's cave. A treasure house of technology. Why, just the power unit alone might provide the answer to our energy problems. And think what it would mean to the Air Force if we could discover how Crusoe causes the radar fade-out.'

'I'm glad you finally agree with me, Arnold.' Connors

tried not to smile at Wedderkind's political somersault.
'Let's get back to basics. Do we go for a second insertion?'

'Yes, I'll go.'

'Arnold, you're not going anywhere. If you had to carry that backpack you'd need an armour-plated truss.'

Wedderkind's mouth turned sour.

'General?'

'You have one more space suit and two volunteers.'

'That was yesterday.'

'Then let's check them out.'

Checking out the backup men took hardly any time at all. Neither Vincent nor Gilligan wanted to try out the hatch. Since Vincent was a civilian Air Force employee, Allbright couldn't make it an order even if he had wanted to, and Gilligan wasn't even on the payroll. That left the USAF technicians and the five squads of cadets. Connors was mulling over Allbright's offer to call for volunteers when Spencer arrived and got him off the hook.

'Are you sure you want to go?'

'Yes. It's not a snap decision. Chris and I planned to go in together way before you started picking names out of a hat.'

'It wasn't that haphazard. You have a family.'

'So had Max.'

'You need a better reason than that for volunteering.'

'I'm not volunteering, I'm laying it on the line. The other three only had six months' astronaut training. I had a full year.'

'That was three years ago,' said Wedderkind.

'The project owes me this trip. I was the one who opened the hatch.'

'No one can argue with that.'

'Besides which, I know Chris better than anyone else here. If he needs handling, I'm the best person to do it.'

'Arnold?'

333

Spencer didn't give him a chance. 'Arnold knows I've got the qualifications and the medics can tell you I'm fit enough.'

And pushy, too. Connors turned to Allbright. 'Would you like to try and get a word in edgeways?'

Allbright looked at his watch. It was nearly two o'clock. 'How are things out there?'

'There's no sign of Chris. We've decided to rotate the hatch every half hour instead of every fifteen minutes. We don't want to jam up the works. Those two spheres have probably spun round more times this morning than they have in the last ten years.'

Allbright looked at Connors. His eyes said it all.

'Okay, Dan. Stand by. We'll let you know.'

'If I'm going to go, I'd better start getting into that suit. It takes time.'

'I'm not making any promises,' said Connors. 'But if you want to try it on for size, go ahead.'

'I'll need Arnold's authorization.'

'And he'll need mine,' said Connors. 'Tell them to phone me.'

Spencer left.

'What do you think, General? Should we go again?'

'Let me ask you a question. If you lose Spencer, will you try a third insertion, and after that a fourth, fifth, and sixth?'

'No. I think I'd probably stop right there. How would the Air Force evaluate this kind of situation?'

'Well, in the planning of any operation, you establish what we call an acceptable loss rate of men and aeroplanes. It usually bears a direct relationship to the strategic or tactical value of the operation. On this project, we don't know how much there is to discover, so it's difficult to assess the value of any particular mission. In that kind of situation, one has to set an arbitrary figure.

334

You appear to feel that, in this case, the acceptable loss rate is three. In the circumstances I've described, it might be argued that even that is one too many. I'm sure Mr Wedderkind understands what I mean.'

'I know we could draw a blank or hit a bonanza,' said Wedderkind. 'Whether either is worth another life, I can't say. If one is going to be coldly scientific, one can't draw any firm conclusions from Milsom's reactions. A sample of one is useless. The experiment has to be repeated. What happened to Max, regrettably, doesn't count. We have to try again.'

'That's what I think,' said Connors. 'General?'

Before Allbright could answer, the phone rang. It was the medical unit. They wanted to know whether they should put Spencer in the space suit.

'Yes,' said Connors.

Wedderkind put the phone back on the hook. 'Do you think we've made the right decision?'

'He's fit, he's qualified, he feels responsible – and he'll never forgive us if we say "No",' said Connors. 'Let him go.'

When Spencer was ready, Connors drove over to the medical unit with Wedderkind.

'Does it fit?' asked Connors.

'Tailor-made.'

'Dan,' said Wedderkind, 'once that hatch closes, you are going to find yourself, quite literally, in the dark. None of us knows what happens in there, so you're going to have to play this whole thing by ear. What we want you to do is to stay inside the hatch – unless some unforeseeable condition makes that impossible.'

'Don't worry, I'll hang on tight.'

'Good. You're due to insert at fifteen-thirty. We'll rotate at fifteen thirty-five, at which time we expect to lift you out. Now – ' Wedderkind spread his hands. 'If something *does* begin to go wrong, ah, perhaps there may be some degree of physical or mental disorientation, ah – '

'I know what you're trying to say,' said Spencer.

'Good. What we want you to do is write down as much as you can on this.'

Page showed Spencer a clipboard with a pad of black paper. A chubby pen was attached to the board by a plastic line. 'This may be the world's first luminous pen,' said Page. 'It's really more like an oversized eyedropper. You squeeze out the paste as you write. Write in largish capitals. The paper is porous to prevent it smudging, and the edge of the clipboard is luminous so you can see where to write.'

Spencer tried out the pen.

'We are going to hang this pad inside the well,' said Wedderkind. 'If, for any reason, there is not enough time to write whole words, we want you to use this simple code: X – for danger. O – no danger, keep opening hatch. L – internal light source. M – contact with Chris. If Chris is alive, put a circle around the M. If you find a way into Crusoe, put a dot inside the O. If you find no way in, put a line across it. Have you got that?'

'Yes. Supposing I do make contact with Chris and find he's in a bad situation? Can I leave the hatch to help him?'

'The answer is "No" – but I'm probably wasting my breath telling you that. Naturally we want both of you out safely. The really important thing is to give us as much information as you can. That's absolutely vital. Don't let us down, Dan.'

'Okay. I'll do my best.'

On the hull platform, a new snap-shut lifting hook had been fitted on to the severed rope. Spencer clipped it on to the chest loop of his safety harness. The time was 15:28.

Neame had taken over command of the hatch party. He patted Spencer's shoulder. 'Just hang on tight to those rails and stay loose.'

Spencer lowered the visor of his helmet. The NASA suit technician checked the life-support pack and watched closely as Spencer pressurized his suit.

15:29. In the operations room, Connors sat half-turned away from the bank of screens. He had thought about going up on to the platform but had decided to stay out of the way. On either side of him, Allbright and Wedderkind remained annoyingly calm, their eyes fastened on the main screen.

At 15:30, Vincent rotated the two spheres and Spencer was lowered in through the circular hatch. As the rope was hauled clear, Neame leaned in and fastened the black notepad and pen to the top of the guide rails where it could be easily retrieved.

'Twenty-five seconds to rotation . . .' With Max's death, Neal Zabrodski's tape-recorded voice had acquired a sinister, relentless quality.

Spencer found handholds and footholds on the guide rail supports and pulled himself clear of the raised disc on the floor of the sphere. In a few seconds it would swing around up over his head.

'Twenty seconds to rotation . . .'

What *are* we doing? Connors asked himself. He had come to regard Crusoe as a huge, half-buried technological, cultural – even intellectual – time bomb slowly ticking away in their midst. And there they were, tinkering around with it like a bunch of blind ants.

For the scientists, the project was a Fourth of July treat but Connors was convinced that none of them were within a million miles of understanding the how, what, and why of Crusoe.

The alarm bell rang. Ten seconds.

'Five-four-three-two-one-*rotation* . . .'

As the hatches moved out of line, Connors saw Spencer raise his right thumb.

Spencer saw the circle of daylight become lemon-shaped, then rapidly diminish and disappear in under a second. An impenetrable darkness filled the sphere. He looked up and saw the luminous pale green line that marked the edge of the clipboard. The burden of his backpack and the weight of his body began to ebb away as the hatch became an integral part of Crusoe's zero-gravity field. Spencer reached up and touched the pad with his finger. The pad floated away from him, slowly rotating on the end of its invisible line.

Gradually, his eyes became accustomed to the darkness. He could now see the dim outlines of the guide rails that lined the well, and above his head, he could make out the raised disc that had been at the bottom of the sphere before rotation. The glow was not coming from there, it was coming through the circular hatch, now under his feet.

Very carefully, he turned head over heels to investigate the source of the light. They had been right. Both spheres rotated to bring the hatches into line, giving access to Crusoe's interior.

He inched his way down one of the guide rails towards the light filtering through the five-foot-wide hatch. There was no point in plunging through headfirst until he saw the layout. Perhaps he might see Chris down there. Or was it *up* there? As Spencer clung to the thick, double rim of the hatch, he began to lose his sense of direction.

The light was coming from stars. Millions upon millions of stars . . .

Spencer retreated back inside the hatch. Something was happening inside his head. He could hear voices calling to him soundlessly. His whole body seemed to be cooling, his heartbeat was almost imperceptible. Breathing was no longer necessary. He became aware of the texture and depth of his skin, the porous structure of his cheekbones. He could feel, three-dimensionally, each tooth in his skull and jaw, every bone in his body, held together by tendons and interwoven, fibrous muscle. It was as if his mind's eye had become an electron microscope through which, in one blinding glimpse, every particle of his cumbersome physical self had been revealed.

Spencer knew that his consciousness was expanding, knew that, at any moment, his mind would break free from his body, knew why Milsom had hung on to Max – and why he himself could not return. Wedderkind's words echoed faintly out of a past that seemed to be receding from him at the speed of light. A message . . . He had promised to leave a message. Spencer unclipped the luminous pen and wrote swiftly in large capital letters, using the prearranged code, then added four brief words. They were pitifully inadequate, but someone might understand. Ray Collis perhaps . . .

Spencer let go of the pen and the clipboard, turned over, and eased himself down towards the circular hatch in the bottom of the sphere. Beyond, the stars were glowing with a clarity and brilliance he had never seen before. He floated, arms outstretched, braced against the rim of the hatch and felt his brain swell up and press for a brief, frightening moment against the inside of his skull. It was the last physical sensation his brain recorded, for, as Spencer launched his body headfirst into eternity, his mind mushroomed painlessly through the top of his skull and soared unhindered into the cool, welcoming stillness of infinite space.

At 15:36, Vincent rotated the spheres. The two hatches slid into line. The well was empty. Spencer had gone. Neame reached in and pulled out the clipboard. The squeezy pen dangled on its cord. That, at least, was one good sign. Neame wrapped the clipboard in a polyethylene bag and sent it down to the monitor hut.

Zabrodski made a videotape of Spencer's luminous message and piped it in to the main screen in the operations room. Neame's hatch party had stayed on Crusoe. The rest of the research group clustered around Connors, Allbright, and Wedderkind, and studied the words on the screen.

$$\underline{\odot} - L - \text{\textcircled{\scriptsize M}}$$
$$\text{\textcircled{\scriptsize MX}}$$

SPACE-ANSWER
EVERYTHING
FOLLOW

'The first part is simple enough. No danger. He's emphasized that by underlining the circle,' said Wedderkind.

'What was the dot, Arnold?'

'That means a way into Crusoe. L – that's good. An internal light source. The magnetic field that is making life difficult for us could be localized around the area of the hatch, to act as a barrier. Like invisible armour plate.'

'SPACE – what does that mean?' asked Connors. 'Room to move around inside the hull?'

'It could be. We talked about the possibility that the hatch might only open on to a storage well into which Friday would be slotted in his folded position.'

'ANSWER . . . ?'

'I don't quite get that,' said Wedderkind. 'He could mean he found the answer to Milsom's disappearance. Or you could read it as ANSWER EVERYTHING.'

'ANSWER *to* EVERYTHING.' suggested Brecetti.

'To what?' asked Lovell. 'Crusoe's mission? It hardly seems likely after five minutes.'

'Perhaps EVERYTHING is by itself,' said Collis. 'Access to everything inside Crusoe. Below the hatch is SPACE where the ANSWER to the questions about Crusoe can be found. The space provides access to EVERYTHING within it.'

'And FOLLOW?' asked Connors.

'That can be read as an injunction – he wants us to follow him, or it could mean he had decided to follow Chris' trail.'

'The M is for Milsom,' said Wedderkind. 'The circle around it means Chris is still alive. That explains why Dan left the hatch.'

Connors tapped the circled MX. 'What about this? Does it mean that Max is alive too?'

Wedderkind raised his eyebrows in sync with his shoulders. 'If we are to accept the logic of the rest of the message, the answer to that is "yes".'

'Which we know is impossible.'

'Unless the instrument readings were wrong.'

'That's impossible too,' said Page. 'We double-checked. We couldn't have made a mistake.'

Wedderkind shook his head. 'There is no way Max could survive in a total vacuum. No way.'

Collis began with an apologetic smile. 'What you really

mean is that there is no way Max could survive in the physical sense.'

'That's the only way that counts,' said Allbright sharply.

Collis looked hurt. 'Nevertheless he may still exist in some paranormal state.'

'If that *is* the explanation,' said Connors. 'then it probably means we've lost Dan too.'

Allbright pointed at the TV screen. 'Mr Collis, are you suggesting this a message from the other side?'

'General, I'm not sure where, or *who* it's from.'

'Well, I'm sure of one thing,' said Connors. 'No one else is going in.'

Neame's hatch party continued to rotate the two spheres every half hour. Just before six that evening, Connors drove up on to the Ridge with Allbright. They went up on to the hull platform and gazed down into the black empty well.

'Thirty seconds to rotation . . .'

'How long can they hold out now?' asked Connors.

'Chris' oxygen will run out in an hour. Dan's will last till eleven-thirty tonight. I've spoken to Arnold. We're going to rotate every half hour till seven-thirty, then every hour after that.'

'And if there's nothing at eleven-thirty?'

'We'll make one last try at midnight, then we'll wrap it up,' said Neame.

Connors wasn't sure that he wanted Milsom and Spencer rescued. Despite their instructions, Spencer had left the hatch. Milsom's behaviour was baffling, and if Spencer did bring him out, there was the question of his responsibility for Max's death. Collis' suggestion of some paranormal influence was difficult to grasp, and only sounded like more trouble.

Connors knew he was falling into the old earthbound

science fiction trap, but if Milsom and Spencer *did* reappear with discernible internal modifications, then he, Allbright, and Wedderkind might have to take the decision to destroy them. Yes . . . It would be a lot easier all around if Milsom and Spencer kept their heads down.

Connors turned to Max's three roughnecks. 'I guess you'd like a break.'

'If you can ship out somethin' to eat, we just as soon hang on. Hell, we ain't hauled a thing out of there yet.' It was Lee Ryder, the one who liked slugging cars with a sledgehammer.

'Of course.'

'Oh, another thing,' said Lee. 'We heard a buzz that Max might still be in one piece down there. Is that straight?'

'I wish it were,' said Connors.

'No chance, huh?'

'Not even a million to one, Lee.'

Lee nodded soberly, then jerked his thumb at Crusoe. 'Max never reckoned much on fooling around with this damn thing . . . Yep . . . 'course, I guess you and the Fat Man must have the next step in mind, but if those two don't come out by midnight, I'd fill that hatch full of nitro and stand back. When he tips that over, it'll blow his ass right out of the ground.'

'Stick around,' said Connors. 'We may end up doing just that.'

Wednesday/September 19

Although Spencer's oxygen supply had run out at 11:30 P.M., Neame decided to open the hatches again at midnight. They clamped the eight 'feet' on to the hull pressure points. Nothing happened. The dome stayed shut.

Neame's voice came over the loudspeaker in the command hut. 'No joy, Arnold. No sign of Dan or the others – and it also looks as if we've developed a malfunction on the hatch.'

'Yes, I noticed that. Is the foot-frame still sequencing correctly?'

'Yes. The pressure level's okay and there's no misalignment of the frame. It must be some kind of internal glitch.'

'Okay, wrap it up for tonight, Rog. We'll take another look at this whole thing tomorrow morning.'

It could have been Crusoe's way of telling them that there was no point in waiting for Spencer. On the other hand, having overheard Lee Ryder's explosive suggestion, Crusoe might have decided to batten down the hatches rather than have them filled with nitroglycerine.

The TV cameras covered the hatch party as they trailed disconsolately down Crusoe's hull and climbed into the waiting jeeps. Connors turned to Wedderkind.

'I've been thinking about Spencer's message again. If the instrument readings *were* wrong and Max *was* alive, is it conceivable that Crusoe could be holding the three of them hostage until we release Friday?'

'That thought had occurred to me,' said Wedderkind.

344

'But if we accept that possibility, we have to accept that Crusoe is operating on a much higher level of reasoning than we originally thought.'

'Let's assume he is. Could his actions still be the product of a machine intelligence?'

Wedderkind pursed his lips. 'It depends on how you define "machine intelligence". With the progress in biochemical computers, it's becoming increasingly difficult to draw a dividing line between the input-output potential of so-called "electronic" brains and their biological counterparts.'

'You'll have to give me that again, Arnold. After midnight my brain turns into a pumpkin.'

'What I'm suggesting,' said Wedderkind, 'is that a machine intelligence from an advanced civilization could quite easily match our own brain functions. In some areas, it may even outperform us. It may, for example, be capable of monitoring our own cerebral activity – '

'Yes. I must admit that does worry me.'

'That's because thought police and human robots were all invented here. Telepathic contact doesn't have to be malevolent, it can be a simple practical tool. For instance in this present situation, it would increase his chances of survival if Crusoe were able to understand the logic – or lack of it – behind our reactions. Initially, Crusoe will have been programmed in the same way as our own computers, that is by feeding in control data – mission orders, if you like – and mechanical data that would enable him to diagnose malfunctions and repair himself. But he could also be programmed to acquire data. I don't just mean recording planetary temperatures and pressures. Crusoe may have the capability to *learn* – to develop and expand his own consciousness. And he may not have an "Off" switch.'

Connors stared at him, then shook his head slowly.

'You keep coming out with these awesome speculations. A few weeks ago, you had us up to our armpits in melted icecaps. I don't know whether I can take more bad news.'

'I'm sorry. In a situation like this, we have to keep the data we acquire under constant review, consider all the implications, the possibilities.'

'But they keep multiplying,' complained Connors. 'Maybe it's my fault. I shouldn't ask so many questions.'

'I wonder how you'd feel if I *did* hide the truth from you,' said Wedderkind.

'You mean if this was the end of the world?' Connors smiled. 'I thought about that when the comet Kohoutek was on its way past – and what a great nonevent that was . . . Anyway, if some astronomer had worked out that it was going to hit us smack on the Tropic of Cancer, knock a hole in Honolulu and send the Pacific rolling all the way to Maine, I think I might have preferred not to know. If I *had* known, what could I have done about it? Nothing. Better to go on. The world could have fallen apart if we'd just sat around waiting – and the calculations might have turned out to be wrong. I read somewhere a marvellous saying: "*If the world were to end tomorrow, I would still plant my apple tree today.*" I can't quite remember who said it, but he was right. Otherwise, our existence is meaningless.'

'All the same,' said Wedderkind, 'I think you'd be as mad as hell if you hadn't been told what was going to happen.'

'Nobody's perfect.'

'Don't you think scientists have a duty to warn the world about something like this?'

'I think it's vital to know that we're running out of oil, or polluting the ocean, or making the air unbreathable. It depends on the scale of the disaster and the speed at which it's likely to happen.'

346

'But shouldn't people know in advance so they can make plans to survive?'

'You mean another Noah's Ark? Take to the hills with the Bible, a book club edition of Shakespeare and the Boy Scout Manual? It's going to get a little crowded. And if you told people, who would take any notice? Groups of nuts have been rushing up mountains with canoes and cans of soup every year since I can remember, only to find four weeks later that they've picked the wrong year. Nobody takes that kind of prediction seriously.'

'Not predictions, perhaps, but supposing there was proof?'

'Proof? Proof is when it happens. How can anyone really know about this kind of thing? Didn't Brecetti say that we had reached a point where the physical laws that underpin our scientific view of the universe may prove to be completely fallacious?'

'Some of them may require modification,' admitted Wedderkind. 'But let's suppose there *was* proof. Incontrovertible evidence. Would the world be better served if that knowledge were shared by only a few people?'

Connors smiled. 'Do you really believe that old intellectual pipe dream? The scientist, the philosopher, painter, poet, the surgeon, architect, and engineer? The elitist group who will preserve all that is good in our society and build anew? The trouble with that idea is that it is the power elite who decides who is to survive and they always put themselves at the top of the list. I know, for instance, that if nuclear war breaks out while I'm working at the White House, I've got six months' guaranteed five-star bed and board in the Presidential fallout bunker. Morally, though, I have no more right to survive than any one of the millions of people who voted in the man I'm working for.'

'What would you find more acceptable, survival of the fittest?'

'That was Nature's solution before we started to interfere. No favours. Everyone starts even.'

'Not quite. Natural selection favours a physical elite. The blind, the old and the infirm wouldn't stand a chance.'

'If they are poor, black, and live south of the Sahara, what kind of chance do they have now?'

'True . . .' Wedderkind looked at Connors for a moment. 'I wonder, if it came to the crunch, whether you'd really be so fairminded.'

Connors got up with a grin. 'Listen, if the world has to come to an end, make it early in the New Year. That's when I get the worst bills.'

'And ruin the January sales? That's when Lillian does most of our shopping.'

Connors spread out his hands. 'That's the trouble with Armageddon. Whatever you arrange, it is bound to inconvenience somebody.' He looked at his watch. 'Jesus, it's twenty past one . . . When do you plan to start digging up Friday?'

'About eight. I'm putting Max's boys on to it.'

'Do you really think there is a chance Crusoe will be willing to trade?'

'I wouldn't put money on it, but what else can we do?'

Connors patted Wedderkind on the shoulder. 'You're right. Good night, Arnold.'

'Sweet dreams, *boychik*. And don't worry. Everything's going to turn out fine.'

Connors opened the door and stepped down from the hut. The fall night air was crisp and clean and scented with pine. The sound of bullets ricocheted from the nearby monitor hut where the duty crew sat watching a late-late Western. Overhead, the jet-black sky glittered

like the jewellery counter at Tiffany's. Don't worry? The
man had to be kidding . . . Connors showered and went
to bed with a bizarre craving for the apricot pancakes his
Hungarian grandmother used to make.

In the morning, Max's widowed crew of roughnecks
cleared the shattered bulldozers from the top of Friday's
burial mound with the replacement machines, then carefully shaved the excess earth away. Underneath, the mud
had dried into a solid lump that crumbled at the touch of
the steel blade. It was no longer frozen solid, nor had it
been baked hard. Friday had either changed his mind
once he found out he was trapped, or he must have
known they were going to dig him out and had decided to
make life easier for everyone.

Connors and Wedderkind drove up on to the plateau
as the roughnecks began to uncover the steel cage. Inside
the cage, parts of Friday could be seen where lumps of
mud had crumbled away through the steel mesh. Lee,
Aaron, T-Bone, and Fish crowbarred up the hooked steel
spikes that pinned the cage to the ground while Cab and
Dixie hooked up the hose and got the pressure pump
going. Lee took over the nozzle end and washed off
Friday's mud overcoat.

'He looks okay,' said Connors.

Wedderkind nodded and walked over to take a closer
look with Neame, Gilligan, Tomkin, Davis, and Page.
Vincent and Hadden were over on Crusoe's hull with a
squad of cadets clearing away the wooden platform and
foot-frame from around the dome so that Friday could
open up the hatch in the normal way.

Friday lay tilted over at a slight angle with his eight
legs folded tightly in against his body. He looked undamaged. The group backed off and formed a half circle. For
about fifteen minutes there was no movement, no sign of

life. Then the Air Force technician with the cannon mike picked up something in his earphones.

'I've got some faint clicking sounds coming through.' He twiddled a couple of knobs on his tape recorder and nodded. 'It's increasing in volume.'

Friday was back in the game.

Five minutes later he started to unfold with slow, jerky movements. After what seemed an age, he got all eight feet on the ground, hoisted his body into the air, then hesitantly flexed each leg as if he had a cramp in every joint. When his limb movements were smoothed out, Friday popped up the four curving eyestalks and rotated the top and bottom sections of his body in opposite directions.

Lee dropped down on one knee and hosed the dirt off Friday's folded tool kit. As the water sprayed over his belly and up under his legs, the four eyestalks shrank halfway in, then slowly eased out again. Lee waved to Cab to cut the motor on the pump and turned to Wedderkind.

'Okay, there he is. Have fun.' He rolled the hose away.

Apparently satisfied that all systems were at 'go', Friday retracted the eyestalks and upped his body temperature to steam off the trickling rivulets of water. As soon as he was dry, the foot-long sensor hairs sprouted from the lower sections of each leg. Friday fixed each one of the watching group with his eye pod and his four hoselike feelers, then skirted carefully around them and wandered off towards the crest of the ridge.

Connors watched him make a wide curve around the bulldozers and Max's roughnecks. He turned to Wedderkind. 'Wasn't he supposed to go back to Crusoe and let the others out?'

'That was the general idea. Don't worry, he'll go back eventually.'

Friday picked his way up over the rocks, zigzagging across the slope in his usual aimless fashion, pausing now and then to examine something on the ground. Twice during the ascent, his eye pod swivelled around to gaze at the group.

'I don't get it,' said Gilligan.

'Perhaps he has a fixed mission sequence for each walk,' suggested Neame. 'Trapping him in the cage may have been like putting your hand in front of a battery-operated toy car. When you lift your hand away it just goes right on the way it was going.'

'Didn't he do more or less the same thing after he froze the field lab?' asked Connors.

'Yes, he did.'

'Seeing as how he's put us to so much trouble, I'd say that was downright rude.'

Connors turned to find Lee Ryder and the other roughnecks behind him. They must have walked over and heard the last part of the conversation.

Connors smiled. 'I know how you feel, Lee. What do you want to do, Arnold, clear the Ridge?'

'We might as well. We can keep them both on camera and come up again when Friday goes back in.'

Vincent and Hadden walked over from Crusoe to join them. Everything had been stripped off the hull.

'I thought we were going to see some action,' said Vincent.

'Sorry,' said Neame. 'Big anticlimax. He's gone off for another Sermon on the Mount.'

'Great . . . I could have had another hour in bed.'

'Let's grab some breakfast,' said Hadden.

'Okay. Oh, Lee, if your guys could get those wrecked bulldozers down to the workshops, our people could have a crack at repairing them.'

'Sure, we'll get on that right away.'

Vincent and Hadden and the rest of the research group drove off in two of the waiting jeeps. Friday reached the top of the Ridge and climbed on his favourite rock.

'Are you coming back?' asked Wedderkind.

Connors' attention was focused on Friday. 'I wonder what he's doing up there . . .' He turned to Wedderkind. 'How about a little walk first?'

'Sure . . .'

They found a couple of rocks just below the crest on the western slope of the Ridge and sat down about ten yards away from Friday. The eye pod swivelled round at their approach, stayed on them for about five minutes after they had sat down, then appeared to lose interest.

West of the Ridge, the ground fell away towards the head of a dry river whose course ran southward to join the Yellowstone between Forsyth and Miles City. On the other side of the riverbed lay another vast stretch of rolling high-plains country. A brief flash of sunlight from a moving windshield signalled the position of an invisible pickup travelling along a distant back road.

Connors pictured the driver of the pickup, a rancher, probably, with his radio tuned into the local radio station, totally unaware of what was happening five miles to his right on Crow Ridge. Even to Connors, who had lived with the situation from the beginning, it still seemed incredible that here he was, in the second half of September, sitting on a hillside in the middle of Montana less than thirty feet from a wayward lump of machinery from another star system.

'I wonder how people will react when this story gets out,' said Connors.

'Do you think it ever will?' Wedderkind asked.

'It's bound to eventually.' Connors smiled. 'Ever since this thing started, I've been expecting chartered busloads of flag-waving delegates from groups like the Okefenokee

352

Flying Saucer Society to land on our doorstep. If this visit has proved anything, it is that none of these nuts are really in touch with whoever's out there.'

'They may have got a message telling them to keep quiet,' said Wedderkind.

'Stop trying to frighten me. I know the idea was to keep this thing under wraps, but it's still pretty amazing that the media haven't got on to it yet.'

Wedderkind shrugged. 'It took the bloodhounds of the press six months to discover Reagan had been shipping arms to the Iranians.'

'Yes . . . But suppose Crusoe decides to break out by tunnelling under the wire? Or if Friday freaks out on an antigravity trip, as Brecetti and Lovell suggested? That's what I'm really worried about. I mean, that would really blow this thing wide open.'

'Well, to tell you the truth, Bob, I'd feel a lot happier if a few more people *did* know what was going on.'

'Why?'

'You'll accuse me of being paranoid if I tell you.'

'No, I won't, I promise.'

'Okay. At the back of my mind I have a nagging feeling that there could be someone planning a very simple solution to all the problems associated with Crusoe.'

'How?' asked Connors.

'Oh, by, say, accidentally obliterating Crow Ridge. To make sure of destroying Crusoe, one would have to use something fairly potent.' Wedderkind's black-button eyes locked on to Connors to catch the slightest reaction.

'Have you discussed this with anybody?'

'Ah . . . Let's say I discovered some of my colleagues share my uneasiness.'

'I see. Just who do you visualize as being behind a thing like this – the President?' asked Connors.

'If the President had set up a plan like this, you would know about it.'

'I would hope so,' said Connors.

'In which case, you'd tell me.'

'That's a reasonable assumption. So who's Big X?'

'Listen, Bob, don't be coy. You can count on the fingers of one thumb the people who've got the balls to set up a deal like this.'

'Fraser . . . Do you think it's Fraser who could be planning to take out Crusoe?'

'Not just Crusoe, the whole project. Everything. Everybody.'

Connors' eyes didn't leave Wedderkind's. 'That's a pretty drastic solution.'

Wedderkind shrugged. 'Are you saying it's impossible?'

'I hope so – otherwise it would mean that I'd be at the top of the casualty list.'

'Or in charge of it.'

'Me? Why would Fraser let me off the hook?'

'This doesn't have to be Fraser's plan,' said Wedderkind. 'It could be yours.'

'Now you *are* being paranoid,' said Connors. 'Christ Almighty, do you really think I'd pull a stunt like that?'

Wedderkind cocked a finger at him. 'That's exactly what St Peter said when told by Jesus that he would deny him three times.'

Connors grinned. 'You disappoint me, Arnold. I didn't realize that you saw yourself as the betrayed Messiah on this project.'

'I don't,' said Wedderkind. 'It's against my religion. I was just testing you out, *boychik*.' Normally, Fraser was never far from Connors' mind. His crucial hesitations, and the reluctance to mention Fraser's name had confirmed Wedderkind's suspicions. There *was* a plan. And Connors

354

knew about it. *Nyehh . . . let them keep their secrets. Let them play with their bombs. It wouldn't change anything.*

Connors glanced away and looked out across the empty grassland beyond the river. How, he asked himself, could Wedderkind have heard of Operation CAMPFIRE? For him to have just plucked the same idea out of the air seemed to be stretching coincidence *too* far. Wait a minute . . . Connors' brain backtracked. Plucked the idea out of the air . . . They had virtually accepted that Crusoe had established some form of telepathic contact. Was he also passing on everybody's secrets?

Just after eleven o'clock in the morning, Friday jerked out of his trance. For a full five minutes he clicked away like a convention of castanet players, then headed back down the hill towards Crusoe.

In contrast to his zigzag ascent, Friday's descent was on a straight line back to Crusoe. As they only had two legs each, Connors and Wedderkind took the long way down and, consequently, were a hundred yards behind him by the time he reached the level ground and entered the grid.

Connors paused on the slope and saw that their jeep had gone. It didn't matter. Their return would have been picked up by one or more of the TV cameras covering Friday so someone would be on their way to pick them up. Down over on their left, four of Max's men in their telltale bright orange hard hats were hitching a towline to the last of the shattered bulldozers. Back in Rockville, everyone would probably be watching a TV set to see if Crusoe's hatch would open for Friday. If it did, there was a chance Crusoe might also cough up Milsom, Max, and Spencer. Connors privately rated their chances of a return ticket as slim to nonexistent but whatever happened, the project would continue.

In the monitor hut, Neal Zabrodski was heading up the six-man day shift. Seated in front of the bank of TV monitors, Neal saw Friday heading through the grid towards Crusoe. Connors and Wedderkind were still picking their way down from the crest. He glanced at the bottom left-hand screen and saw six men climb into a jeep and drive of towards Rockville.

Neal picked up the phone and called the transport section. 'Have you got the White Knight's wheels down there?'

'Yeah, it's parked outside.'

'Okay, get it up on the Ridge. He's on his way down the hill.'

As Neal hung up, the top sergeant on his right pointed up to the middle screen of the bottom bank of five. 'Where are those guys going?'

Neal looked up. Moving through the grid was the jeep with the six men aboard. Instead of driving down from the plateau, it had turned eastward towards Crusoe and parallel with Friday.

'Give me a close-up on that.'

The sergeant hit the traverse button of the camera to the east of Crusoe and closed in tight on the jeep with the zoom lens. Neal put the picture on the main screen. It was Max's six roughnecks. He couldn't remember the name of the driver, but the man next to him was Lee Ryder. He had a sledgehammer across his lap.

Neal leaned towards the mike and switched it to Allbright in the command hut. 'Sir? We seem to have some unscheduled activity on Screens 5 and 8.'

'Thank you, Mr Zabrodski, I have the situation in view.'

Connors and Wedderkind reached the bottom of the hill at the same time as their own jeep bounced on to the plateau. It came racing towards them, then slid the last

356

five yards with all four wheels locked by the brakes. KINNER, D. J., was at the wheel. He had been Connors' driver all week. Kinner seemed to be under the impression that everyone in the White House hurtled about their business at the speed of sound. Consequently, he drove Connors around as if he was out to win the Indianapolis 500.

Allbright watched the TV screen. The roughnecks' jeep turned towards Friday. When he was quite sure what was going to happen, he glanced up at his senior cadet commander. 'Make sure it doesn't get out of hand, Mr Harris.'

Wedderkind climbed into the back of the jeep. Connors got in the front beside Kinner and put one foot up on the dashboard. Kinner looked across at him expectantly, his right arm braced against the gear lever for a racing start.

'Tag along behind Friday.'

Kinner gunned the motor.

'Just keep it nice and slow,' said Connors. 'We've got all day.'

The words were no sooner out of his mouth when the roughnecks' jeep roared across their front and smacked into Friday at forty miles an hour. In the split second before they collided, Friday managed to dart a half pace backward so that instead of mowing him down, the jeep struck him a glancing blow, buckling his two front left legs and hurling him sideways into one of the grid posts. As Friday crashed against it, the thick post snapped over on top of him like a broken matchstick.

'Jesus Christ!' said Connors.

Behind him, Wedderkind cried out sharply as if in pain. '*Meshuggener!*'

Over his shoulder, Connors saw three jeeploads of cadets put daylight under their wheels as they shot up the

357

slope and on to the plateau. 'It's okay, look, there's some help on the way.'

The roughnecks' jeep slid to a halt. Lee and the four others in the back piled out with sledgehammers and watched as T-Bone put his foot on the gas pedal and reversed in four-wheel drive.

Connors grabbed Kinner's arm. 'Can you block that jeep?'

'Yes, sir-r-r,' said Kinner. He stepped on the gas so hard he nearly lost his distinguished passengers overboard. Ahead of them, Friday struggled to his feet but before he could move out of the way, T-Bone ploughed backward over Friday's front right leg and rammed into his feelers and eye pod with a sickening crunch.

'Hang on tight!' yelled Kinner.

As T-Bone curved away backward over the uneven ground, Kinner hit him with a glancing blow that shot T-Bone out of his seat and put his jeep into a slow roll. Connors was better braced for the impact. While Wedderkind was still picking himself up off the floor, Connors thumped Kinner on the back and dropped out of the jeep.

'Don't stop till you get to Rockville.'

The cadet put his foot down and carried Wedderkind out of cursing range. Connors ran back to the roughnecks.

'Okay, just hold everything right there!'

Lee Ryder pointed a huge finger at him. 'Shut your ass, Connors.'

As Aaron and Fish blocked off Connors, T-Bone ran limping from the overturned jeep.

'Better hurry, Lee. We've got trouble from the Air Force.'

'No sweat,' said Lee. 'We've got them outnumbered.'

Lee, Cab, and Dixie only had about thirty seconds before the cadets surrounded them, but to Connors it seemed like thirty minutes as Friday was struck with a rapid series of massive, alternating blows every third one of which was delivered by Lee with the force of a huge piledriver.

When the cadets made their grab, Connors tensed up in anticipation of a barroom brawl. Nothing happened. Lee just dropped his sledgehammer and offered no resistance. The other five did the same. Connors pushed his way through to confront Lee.

'Do you realize you may have just screwed up this whole operation?'

'Tough shit . . .' growled T-Bone.

Connors ignored him. 'But why, Lee? I mean, what were you trying to prove?'

'Nothin'. I just wanted to get in a few licks for Max.' Lee stared back at Connors.

Connors looked at the other five. *A few licks for Max* . . . It was as simple as that. They were all quite unrepentant. And with good cause. What the hell could he hit them with, destroying extraterrestrial property? The worst that could happen would be losing their jobs with the CIA. Big deal . . . 'Get them out of here,' he said wearily.

Connors turned to look at Friday. His black crystal skin had caved in like the laminated windshield of a car. Patches of frost had formed on the three unbroken body panels and two of his legs. The battering had obviously knocked his cooling system out of action. Kinner returned with Wedderkind, Tompkin, and Davis. Neame and the three other engineers were in a second jeep behind them. They got out to survey the damage.

'*Meesemachine die verbrecher* . . . how could we hire such people?'

'There wasn't a lot I could do, Arnold.'

359

'Well, you tried, anyway . . .' Wedderkind gave Connors a perfunctory pat on the back.

Thanks a bunch . . .

Friday hauled himself more or less upright and began to crawl back towards Crusoe, trailing his three broken legs behind him. The four feelers were flattened and twisted. The eye pod had taken a brutal battering.

Wedderkind turned to Tompkin. 'What do you think, Vic? Is he going to make it?'

Tompkin looked doubtful. 'I would guess that whoever designed Friday must have envisaged the possibility of his losing a leg or two. It's the damage to the carapace, eye pod, and pedipalps that may be more serious.'

'There's also the small problem of how he is going to open the hatch without the right number of serviceable feet,' said Connors.

'I would think that situation must have been foreseen too,' said Tompkin. 'In any case, we'll soon know the answer.'

Friday lurched sideways and blundered into a stake. He backed off, felt his way around it, then zigzagged off to the right of Crusoe and walked slap into another stake.

'They must have blinded him,' said Davis.

'Savages,' muttered Wedderkind. 'Savages . . .'

Connors thought back to what Wetherby had said about the characters in Robinson Crusoe, and the savages who had finally succeeded in killing Friday. Was this the role that Man had been assigned in this updated version of the story?

'You're all talking as if he's alive,' said Neame. 'It's a repair problem. Crusoe's bound to have a few spare parts tucked away somewhere.'

'Is that all you feel about it?' snapped Wedderkind.

'Well, I don't feel any moral outrage, Arnold. It's just a piece of machinery. I admit that I no more enjoy seeing him smashed up than I would enjoy watching those goons go ape over a computer or a Steinway concert grand. But I don't look on him as one of the family.'

'Maybe you should,' said Wedderkind. 'Maybe we all should.' He turned his back on them and hurried after Friday.

'I think we're crazy to let him go back to Crusoe.'

Connors looked at Gilligan. 'Why?'

'Because now this has happened, Crusoe may not feel like swapping Dan, Chris, and Max. In fact, the three of them may not be hostages at all.'

'What are they?'

'Specimens – in which case, I think we deserve a specimen too.'

They got into the jeeps and drove over to Crusoe. Wedderkind was standing at the edge of the hull already. Despite what Neame had said, Connors had come to regard Friday as something more than a machine. Faced with the sight of this broken body struggling towards safety, Connors' feelings were a mixture of sympathy and fear. Within him, there was a desire to help. Yet, at the same time, he felt exultant at the near destruction of this object which stirred up a host of irrational fears within him.

Friday dragged himself over to Crusoe and climbed up towards the dome like a rundown clockwork toy. Halfway up the curving hull, his remaining right legs locked solid and his two undamaged left legs buckled under him. Friday keeled over in slow motion, then slid sideways down the hull onto the earth at the rim of the spacecraft.

Connors eyed Neame. 'Looks as if he's here to stay.'

Friday didn't move as they crowded around him. Tompkin hooked a stethoscope into his ears and sounded him out carefully. He looked up at Wedderkind and shook his head.

361

'Great . . .' muttered Neame to Gilligan. 'Now we can take him apart.'

Another jeep carrying Brecetti, Lovell, Armenez, and Page pulled up behind them. They joined the group and surveyed the damage.

'Look,' said Page. 'He's turning grey.'

Page was right. A grey opaque film was spreading outward from the damaged body panels, dulling the deep brilliance of the black crystal the way a cataract clouds a human eye.

'Arnold, can we take him over to the lab?' asked Neame.

Wedderkind nodded. Gilligan waved to the driver of the nearest jeep and got him to back up. Dark brown blotches started to appear on Friday's greying skin.

'You'd better hurry,' said Page. 'It looks as if that crystalline coating is unstable. If he's made of organic . . .'

'Don't say it,' said Neame. 'You'll bring us bad luck. Jess, Lew, give us a hand with this thing.'

Vincent and Hadden moved to help Neame and Gilligan.

'Okay, spread out. Get a grip under the body somewhere and lift on three, right? One, two, three – '

Gilligan was holding two of the stiffened right legs at the point where they joined the body. When they were halfway to the jeep, both legs snapped clean off.

'Goddammit, Steve, the idea is to get this thing back in one piece.' The words were no sooner out when the eye pod Neame was holding sheared away from the body. Before anyone could grab him, Friday slipped out of Vincent and Hadden's grasp, hit the ground and split apart like a cheap plaster ornament.

'I thought that might happen', said Page.

Neame turned on Page with a snarl. 'Listen, if you're

such a fucking wise guy, why don't you help pick this thing up?'

'Gentlemen, please!' protested Lovell.

'Creep . . .' muttered Neame.

'Cool it,' said Connors. 'If you guys don't get this together fast, we'll need a vacuum cleaner.'

Neame and the others turned back to look at Friday's fractured body. Whatever had been packed inside had collapsed into a meaningless junkheap of gooey crystals, honeycombed with decay. Brown blotches spread rapidly through Friday's greying skin, then spots of dark, fungoid yellow began devouring the brown. But as always, there was a twist. Friday was not only decomposing, he was disappearing.

Connors sniffed the air. 'I know that smell . . . what is it?'

'Jasmine,' said Davis.

Connors shook his head. 'Crazy . . .' He watched the group slide Friday's fragments into clear plastic bags and place them carefully on a thick sheet of foam in the back of one of the jeeps. Neame spent several minutes manoeuvring a leg segment into a bag. Although it was heavily pitted with brown and yellow blotches, he managed to get it as far as the jeep in one piece, but as he laid it down it crumbled apart like a dried corn husk. Neame thumped the side of the jeep in anger and jarred some more fragments into dust.

'That was a dumb thing to do,' said Gilligan. He had just spent ten minutes picking up those particular pieces.

Neame slapped a hand to his forehead. 'Jeez, I'm sorry, Steve. Hell, this whole thing's pointless.'

'Not completely,' said Page. 'Microscopic and chemical tests of the fragments will at least give some indication of what Friday was made of.'

'That's where you're wrong, the process hasn't stopped.

363

Look – ' Neame held up a small bag of powdered fragments, ' – it's still decaying. It's even started to eat away the plastic bag.'

'Has anybody got any ideas on what we can do?' asked Wedderkind.

'What *can* we do?' said Neame. 'We're screwed both ways. If we drive back to the lab too fast the fragments will shake to pieces. If we drive too slowly, there'll be nothing left by the time we get there.'

Connors turned to Page and Armenez. 'I think it'd be a good idea if you got this batch over to the lab while these guys pick up the rest.'

Page was already in the jeep before Connors had finished speaking. Armenez helped Neame lay a second sheet of foam over the bagged fragments, then climbed aboard. Neame went back to help the others.

A fast drive across the plateau was normally a real boneshaker but with some prompt pathfinding by Page the ride back to the lab was almost as smooth as Sonja Henie on ice. Unfortunately, almost was not quite good enough. When Page and Armenez peeled back the top layer of plastic foam, there was nothing left. Friday's decaying fragments had gnawed through the plastic bags and had gouged out deep holes in the foam layer underneath before eating themselves out of existence.

The remaining consignment was conveyed with equal care and speed but, once again, only the plastic bags made it as far as the field lab. A microscopic analysis and tests on the bags, the pitted foam sheet, and the soil on to which Friday had fallen revealed nothing. No new chemical compounds, no mutant molecules, no alien organisms. Nothing that could tell them how he was made or how he moved or whether he had ever been, technically, alive.

Even in his manner of dying, Friday had still managed to outsmart them.

Connors left Wedderkind to commiserate with the research group. He found Allbright about to have lunch in his trailer and was invited to join him.

'I'd like to thank you for straightening out that situation on the plateau.'

'I wish we could have got there sooner,' said Allbright.

'Yes . . .' Connors pressed his lips together. 'Still – I don't think any of us anticipated this kind of reaction from anyone on the project.'

'I should have.'

'Perhaps,' said Connors. 'I think we were lucky you managed to lay hands on three jeeploads of cadets so quickly.'

'Yes . . .' Allbright's eyes didn't waver.

'And we have at least learned one thing from this fiasco. When it came to the crunch, Friday was surprisingly vulnerable.'

It was this discovery that had spurred Connors into some fertile speculation. Crusoe and Friday had both demonstrated an uncanny ability to render useless most of Man's most sophisticated technology, yet Crusoe had been brought to the surface by good old-fashioned gelignite stuffed down a hole in the ground, and Friday had been run over by an automobile. In spite of the much-quoted idea of a telepathic link, neither Crusoe nor Friday appeared to have been forewarned of the roughnecks' intentions – or to have been able to turn them off the idea. Admittedly that was in line with Wedderkind's theory of a benign mental contact, which used suggestion, not coercion. And yet, and yet . . . The knowledge that Crusoe, if he had wanted to, *could* have immobilized the roughnecks' jeep with his force field slapped a big, complicated question mark over everything.

'Do you think Crusoe might respond to the same treatment?' asked Allbright.

'He might,' said Connors. 'I imagine a lot would depend on how big a stick you hit him with. Lee Ryder suggested filling Crusoe's inner hatch with nitroglycerine, which would detonate when the spheres rotated but before the inner sphere had time to depressurize. Crusoe must have heard him, because after the time Spencer's oxygen supply ran out, the hatches never opened again.'

'Do I gather from what you say that "brute force" is now an acceptable concept?'

'It's never been unacceptable to me, General. I've always regarded its controlled application as one of the options open to us in this type of situation. However, I think Arnold and the others may have some trouble taking the idea on board. But there are ways around that.'

'Several,' said Allbright. 'What do you want me to do about Max's roughnecks?'

'Where are they now?'

'Under guard in one of the trailers.'

'I'll call up McKenna and have them transferred. If they stay here, some of the research group may try and put litmus paper in their cornflakes.' Connors swore quietly to himself. 'I don't understand how dummies like that could be recruited by the CIA.'

'They all had good combat records,' said Allbright.

'Yes, I know, but the point is they still fouled up.'

'Maybe they did, but the net result is that we now only have one problem instead of two.'

'I wish I felt so optimistic,' said Connors. 'Crusoe could be full of those damn things, and the next one out may not be so cuddly.'

'So what do you plan to do?'

Connors finished the piece of steak he had on his fork

before replying. 'If we set aside the people killed in the air crashes, we've lost four men. One killed, three missing and presumed dead, another has lost half his face and all his fingers, and six more have just hammered their way out of the CIA pension fund. Okay . . . we can argue that our casualties are due to our own clumsiness. Crusoe isn't rampaging up and down the countryside dispensing death and disaster but it poses a threat all the same. There's the constant possibility of another prolonged period of fade-out. Arnold still maintains that the problems created by Crusoe stem purely from his self-protective posture. He may be right. There's still no percentage in it for us. Scientifically, Crusoe may be the greatest thing since sliced bread, but politically, militarily and economically, he is a total, unmitigated disaster.'

Allbright smiled. 'I appreciate your concern. I was under the impression you might have been pleased to see some of the hawks humbled.'

'There's one thing you should never forget, General. To get his half of the Nobel Peace Prize, Kissinger bombed Le Duc Tho all the way from Hanoi to Paris. It's no secret that I'm one hundred per cent behind the President's drive to remove the threat of a nuclear holocaust and see an end to all wars – but don't get me wrong. This nation must remain strong – but that strength is meaningless unless America also occupies the moral high-ground.' He grinned. 'Until we reach that lofty position, I believe in carrying a lead-weighted olive branch.'

'Okay, you're reclassified. What next?'

Connors pushed his plate away and draped an arm over the back of his chair. 'I know, deep down, that this is the most fantastic thing that ever happened to any of us, but when you consider the problems it's landed us with, I mean, really – who needs it?'

Certainly not the Air Force. Which was probably why Allbright didn't say anything. He didn't need to.

Connors leaned forward on the table. 'I'm flying back to Washington later today with a new batch of tapes. In my report to the President, I will recommend termination of the Crusoe Project.'

'Immediately?'

'I'm prepared to give Arnold's team another week. There's always the chance that they may come up with something.'

'Does the research group know of this decision?'

'Not yet. I'll break the news to them when it's official.'

'And then?'

Connors smiled. 'I imagine the ball will be in your court.'

'I don't quite understand,' said Allbright.

'Well, we just can't leave him here to become a tourist attraction,' said Connors. 'We're going to have to blow him out of the ground. The problem is, we don't know what we're letting ourselves in for. It's impossible to predict how Crusoe will react to an attempt to destroy him – although he didn't exactly rush in to defend Friday. But if we go in, we have to get it right first time. We may only get one bite at this apple – so we can't piddle around with high explosives. It's going to have to be a nuke. Right?'

'The situation may call for that type of response,' admitted Allbright.

'It will,' said Connors. 'And since SAC holds the major part of our nuclear arsenal, you'll be delivering the package.'

'We would if the President ordered us to.'

'General, the President has told me about Operation CAMPFIRE. I think you helped Mel Fraser set that up. You

368

weren't co-opted on to this project just to twiddle your thumbs on Crow Ridge.'

Allbright allowed himself a half smile. He got up from the table. 'Would you like some whisky with that coffee?'

'Do we have something to celebrate?'

Allbright took out two of his heavy cut-glass tumblers and held one up. 'Beautiful, aren't they? French crystal. Present from my daughter.' He dropped in some ice, swamped it with rye and returned to the table.

Connors raised his glass. 'To CAMPFIRE . . .'

Allbright swallowed half of his rye, then set his glass carefully down on the table. 'What do you know about Commissar?'

'Nothing,' said Connors. 'Is it something you think I should know about?'

'I think it would help.' Allbright refuelled with another shot of rye. 'During the last, three-week fade-out, which began the day Crusoe landed – '

'That's history,' said Connors.

'Well, during those three weeks, the SR-71s of SAC's 9th Strategic Reconnaissance Wing flew photographic missions over Russia and China every day.'

Built by Lockheed, and flown in secret for three years, the SR-71 Blackbird was a space-age replacement for the U-2 spy plane of the Eisenhower era. Two huge turbojets rammed the Blackbird along at well over two thousand miles an hour at eighty thousand feet. Without radar, there was no Russian plane that could get near it.

'Wasn't that a little provocative?'

Allbright shrugged. 'Their radar was out along with ours. They had no way of spotting us.'

'Except when the fade-out ended. You had no way of knowing when that was going to be.'

'It was a calculated risk. We overflew from north to south so as to cut down the time we were in their air

369

space. With our reconnaissance satellites out of action, we had to know what they were doing, just in case they had not been entirely honest with you.'

'And did you discover anything of interest?'

'Yes,' said Allbright. 'In the set of pictures taken on the thirty-first of August.'

'The day Crusoe surfaced – and the fade-out began to lift . . . Oh, Christ, don't tell me the Russians have got one of these things too.'

Allbright nodded. 'Confirmation came through on Monday. Same size, same shape. Code name Commissar.'

'Jesus . . .' Connors was hit by a wave of depression. 'Where has it landed?'

'Kazakhstan. Southwest of Lake Balkash.'

'That must be almost bang in the middle of Asia,' said Connors, trying to visualize the map.

'It is. The Sinkiang Province of China is just to the east, Afghanistan to the south. What's even more interesting is that the landing site is on almost the same latitude as Crow Ridge and on the reciprocal longitude. They both lie on a great circle route passing through the poles.'

'And there's absolutely no doubt about this?'

'None at all. And they know it's there, too. The pictures show three big transport helicopters, a couple of small Mi-2s and eleven military vehicles including four large trucks with camouflage netting.'

Okay, thought Connors, so we didn't tell the Russians about Crusoe. They had still double-crossed us. Fraser was right not to trust them . . . 'Why weren't we told about this on Monday?' he asked.

'You'll have to take that up with the Defense Department. I've put my job on the line by telling you, but right now it's already at risk – along with yours.'

'Yes . . .' Fraser probably wanted to keep Commissar a secret because he was still having nightmares about

370

Wedderkind getting together with other scientists and forming some kind of international pressure group. Connors could picture Samuels over at the Defense Intelligence Agency, beavering around, making sure every possible contact was wired for sound. 'I appreciate you sticking your neck out. What made you decide to tell me?'

'Your decision to terminate the project,' said Allbright. 'I had a feeling you'd come down on the right side of the fence.'

Yes, thought Connors. But in face of this latest jolt, which side was that? And what was the best thing to do now – push ahead and take out Crusoe, or come clean with the Russians and set up some joint plan of action? Connors emptied his glass and held it out to Allbright. 'Mind if I go around again?'

Allbright took the glass and refilled it.

'Whoever found that picture of the spacecraft must have been pretty surprised.'

Allbright shook his head. 'The photo interpreter didn't realize what she was looking at. She thought it was a geodesic dome erected to cover something else. We didn't tell her what it really was.'

'I wish you hadn't told *me*,' said Connors. He raised his glass to Allbright and took a stiff shot. It blunted his sharp attack of nervous digestion.

'To Commissar,' said Allbright. 'It's not every day we find a spacecraft.'

'No,' said Connors. 'Just every three weeks.'

Allbright greeted this with a quiet smile. 'There's something else I think I should tell you. When the President told me who I'd be working with, I asked a friend in the Pentagon to get me some background material on you. They also threw in your flying training record. I was impressed. You could have been quite a hot shot. The Navy lost a good man.'

'They probably saved themselves a few aeroplanes,' said Connors. He shook his head, remembering a particularly close shave that, even now, caused a shiver to run down his spine whenever it came to mind – usually when he lay in bed, trying to get to sleep. 'All that was a long, long time ago.'

'It was indeed,' said Allbright aimiably. 'In fact, you weren't even called Connors then.'

'That's right,' replied Connors, without the slightest trace of embarrassment. 'The thing was, I always had to keep spelling my other name.'

Connors and Wedderkind left Crow Ridge just after 1 P.M. At the base camp, they went through the regular medical checks. By now, the NASA team had streamlined their techniques and the careful processing only took thirty-five minutes instead of the original sixty. Apparently satisfied that Connors and Wedderkind were still 100 per cent human, the NASA team passed them through the gate into the outside world.

At Glasgow AFB, the now-familiar Jetstar was waiting to take them back to Washington.

The moment they became airborne, Connors unstrapped his wristwatch and wound it forward to 5:15 P.M. Washington time.

He looked across the table at Wedderkind and wondered if he had any inkling that he was preparing to sell the project down the river. He tried to analyse his decision. Was it fear – or frustration at their failure to make any headway? But then, what gave them the right to expect they could understand everything the universe contained?

The Jetstar's captain ducked through the door from the

flight deck and walked down to where Connors and Wedderkind were sitting. 'Ah – I thought you might like to know we just lost our radar and UHF frequencies.'

Connors exchanged a startled glance with Wedderkind, then looked back at the captain. 'Fade-out?'

The captain nodded. 'Yes. Looks like it's back again. But don't worry, we shouldn't have too much of a problem. We still have short-wave and medium-wave band radio links.'

'That may take care of us,' said Connors. 'But all hell must be breaking loose in Chicago, New York, and Washington.'

'Oh, God, yes,' said Wedderkind. 'I hope this doesn't turn into another day of disaster.'

'It won't be as bad. The airlines have all cut back their schedules.'

'Do you want us to push on, or divert to the nearest Air Force Base?' asked the captain.

'Do you think you can make it?'

The captain grinned at Connors. 'If I didn't, I wouldn't give you the option. The way I read it, by the time we get into Washington air space everything else should be on the ground – one way or the other.'

'How's the weather up ahead?' asked Connors.

'Pretty good. There shouldn't be too much trouble if everyone sticks to the emergency procedures.'

'Yes, *if*,' said Connors. 'Still – I think we ought to try for Washington. Okay, Arnold?'

'Sure, go ahead. You know my philosophy. When your time comes it comes – whether you're in the air or in the bathtub.'

Connors nodded to the pilot. 'We're in your hands.'

'Okay. We're going to take her up to thirty-five thousand to keep well clear of the mess. I'll keep you posted on any further deterioration.'

'Thanks.' Connors watched the captain go back on to the flight deck. He looked at Wedderkind. 'The last fade-out was to cover Crusoe's landing. What does this new one signify – takeoff?'

'Perhaps.'

'Is that the best you can do?'

'I'm not a mindreader, Bob. He could be preparing to leave. Is that what you want him to do?'

'I think it would save us a lot of trouble,' said Connors. It was a seductive scenario. Crusoe would go away. The project would be quietly buried and everyone would just go home. The world need never know about his visit. There would be no need for any dramatic decisions on Connors' part. He would be freed from that Montana rockpile that hung round his neck like the Ancient Mariner's albatross. He could go back to the relatively simple earthly traumas of the White House, go to sleep without worrying, go on vacation with Charly.

'It would also rob Man of the chance of finding out the truth about himself,' said Wedderkind. 'Crusoe could hold the key to the questions we've been asking for centuries. Don't you want to know the answers?'

Not really, Arnold, thought Connors. He was tired of the constant speculation, frustrated by the lack of tangible progress and, above all, frightened by Crusoe's disruptive powers and the dangerous situation created by his continuing presence. And on a more personal level, a grasp of the cosmic realities wasn't going to remove the small wart on the back of his neck, reduce the astronomical bill he'd recently received from the power company, or replace the handle that had fallen off his freezer. Arnold had this insane idea that if they tried hard enough and long enough, the secrets of the universe would be revealed to them. Connors didn't want to understand. He didn't want to know the answers. Knowing would make life too difficult. Impossible. But there was no point in telling Wedderkind that.

'Of course I want to know,' said Connors. 'Isn't that what this whole operation's about?'

CROW RIDGE/MONTANA

The manner of Friday's death gave the research group plenty to talk about, and they decided to reassemble the hull platform around the hatch to see if it would still open. Within a few seconds of the decision being voiced Crusoe blanketed the whole of the Ridge with a new improved force field that shut off everything from the overhead TV cameras to Allbright's electric iron.

It caught them totally unprepared, and it took a couple of hours to get everything straightened out and for everybody to get used to the idea and to the scale of the problem. This new cutoff zone was no five-hundred-yard affair. It had immobilized a couple of jeeps three miles away on the dirt road up to the Ridge.

THE WHITE HOUSE/WASHINGTON DC

When Connors arrived at the White House a few minutes after nine o'clock, he found that nearly everybody except the duty staff had gone home. Marion Wilson, however, was still at her typewriter. She told him that the President was upstairs in his private apartment and that Connors was expected.

'Did the fade-out give you any problems?'

'It was a little bit hairy on the way in,' admitted Connors. 'But by the time we got to Washington, the emergency procedures were in force. Has the boss had an up-to-date situation report?'

'Yes,' said Marion.

'Have there been many bad accidents?'

'Not too many. The airlines have shut down again. The State Department has been in contact with our embassies, and Defense got a roundup from our overseas bases. The fade-out is worldwide and building. People are stranded everywhere.'

'Yeah, the last two months haven't been too good for the travel business,' said Connors. He flicked a corner of the pile of papers next to Marion's typewriter. 'Looks like you're going to be here all night.'

Marion peeked at Connors over the top of her glasses. 'In that case, we may yet have breakfast together.'

'My office or yours?' asked Connors.

'Make it the canteen,' said Marion. 'What the hell, let's tell the world.'

Connors went up to the President's apartment. The President shook his hand and took him through into his study.

'Marion told me you've had a situation report.'

The President nodded. 'Yes. Mel Fraser tells me the characteristics of the fade-out are the same as before.'

'That's good. It means we've got about a week before we lose the medium waves and twelve days before the last of the long-wave transmissions are wiped out. That should give us plenty of time to get ourselves organized.'

'What was Arnold's reaction?'

'He's worried, obviously. I tried to drag out a prediction that this new burst of interference was a prelude to Crusoe's departure, but Arnold wouldn't commit himself. How could he? He didn't ask to be written in as the oracle on this project. The interesting thing is that a lot of his guesses have been right on the nose. He was right about Crusoe radiating ultraviolet light, for example.'

'What are his views about this telepathic contact with Crusoe?'

376

The question took Connors by surprise, but he managed not to show it. 'Where did you get that story from?'

'I think it was something Allbright mentioned to Fraser.'

'That must have brought back the colour to his cheeks. Hell, I've come back here to recommmend termination. If I'd been brainwashed, I'd be telling you everything was under control.'

'Yes, I suppose you would . . .'

'It's true the idea's been kicked around on the Ridge,' said Connors. 'But so have a lot of other outlandish ideas. Whatever any of us may have thought previously, that one was finally killed yesterday – along with Friday.' Connors related how Friday, long considered an immovable object, had met the irresistible force of Lee Ryder's sledgehammer. 'And God knows, it wasn't as if they didn't telegraph their intentions. Friday just didn't get the message until the jeep ran him over.'

'So they *are* vulnerable.'

'Friday was. We thought he was made from the same virtually indestructible material as Crusoe, but he caved in like a cheap tin toy – and then evaporated. Crusoe, though, is something else. He's built like a bank vault. But even they've been blown open from time to time.'

The President eyed Connors. 'Are you suggesting we give Crusoe the same treatment?'

'Yes,' said Connors. 'That's the easy part. The hard part is deciding just how we are going to do it. But maybe someone's already thought about that . . .'

'Yes . . . do you think we ought to wait to see if Crusoe is going to take off?'

'No. I think we ought to move right ahead. If it takes off before we're ready, then so much the better.'

'Have you discussed this decision with Arnold?'

'No, just Allbright. Arnold's bound to scream a little

when I break the news, but there's nothing we can do about that. Ordinarily he's tuned in on the political realities, but this time he seems to have got carried away. I don't like going behind his back, but . . .' Connors shrugged.

The President smiled. 'You can always blame the decision on me.'

'Don't worry,' said Connors cheerfully. 'I will.'

'Where is Arnold, by the way?'

'He had to go up to Baltimore with his wife. It's either his sister or sister-in-law who's sick. I can't remember.'

'Oh . . . that's a pity,' said the President. 'I was going to ask him what happened to his contacts with the Russians.'

'Karamatov went home,' said Connors. 'And the Kremlin took everyone else's phone off the hook.'

The President nodded, consulted a notebook on his desk and dialled a number. Connors heard it ring four times before it was answered. 'Hello, Mel?'

Connors wondered how long the President had been calling Fraser at his home number.

'Mel, I've got Bob with me. He's put in an action recommendation which ties in with our thinking on the Crusoe Project. I think it's about time you two got together on this . . . Okay, how soon can you get over here? . . . Good, bring Chuck Clayson along. Oh, and Mel, I want to brief Bob on Commissar. Make sure you have all the information with you . . . Right, we'll meet in my downstairs office.' The President put down the phone.

'Commissar?'

'It's the code name we've assigned to a second craft that landed in Russia.'

Connors did his best to look surprised.

Arnold Wedderkind had a late supper with his wife Lillian at their home in Washington, looked at the latest pictures of his grandson, then took a quick nap while she drove him to Baltimore in the pouring rain. Wetherby was waiting for them at Wedderkind's sister-in-law's house.

Wetherby borrowed the sister-in-law's car, drove around to the alley at the back of the house, and picked up Wedderkind.

'You don't really think anyone's following us, do you?'

'I don't know,' said Wedderkind. 'I just have an odd feeling that someone's plotting something and that we could be in danger.'

'Who, the research group?'

'Not all of them. You won't be involved.'

Wetherby smiled. 'You've been reading the coffee grounds again . . .'

'Has anything new come in?'

'Yes, you're in luck,' said Wetherby, 'Phillippe Kerjac just sent us the data from the *Prince Albert*.'

Named after the royal Monegasque patron of oceanography, the *Prince Albert* was a French research ship operating in the Indian Ocean.

'Does it fit into the pattern?' asked Wedderkind.

'George is just finding out now. He's over in the research block. It's not far, but we'd better drive there. I know you hate getting wet.'

From experience, Wedderkind knew that by Wetherby's standard of measurement, not far meant anything up to three miles. Years ago, when he'd first met Wetherby in London, he had found himself striding beside him across Hampstead Heath without a coat, with the winddriven midsummer rain cutting into them horizontally. He had never forgotten Wetherby turning to him with a happy grin and saying, 'Marvellous, isn't it?' There were a lot of Englishmen like that.

It was a mile and a half to the research block. The rain had stopped by the time they got there. Wetherby unlocked the front door and led the way down to the basement and through the double set of doors into the faintly antiseptic environment that housed the computer.

'I loathe these damn things,' said Wetherby. 'But they really are amazing. Wait till you see what George has produced.'

York was sitting in front of a large twenty-one-inch visual display screen. Below it was an IBM keyboard which he was using to interrogate the computer. He gave them a little wave as they walked in but didn't get up.

'Hi, Arnold. Got some real goodies here for you.'

'That's what I've come to see.'

'We've fed Shirley the various measurements of the magnetic field – declination, horizontal and vertical intensity, etcetera, together with the geographical co-ordinates of the measuring station,' explained York. Shirley was his pet name for the computer. 'She then plots these on a map of the world and joins up the points of equal force or variation giving us a magnetic contour map.'

York keyed a short message to the computer.

A series of bright green contour lines began to curve across a map of the world.

'This map shows the magnetic declination. The lines connect points of equal variation of compass north from true, or geographic, north. This was the situation on August first. You can see the situation is fairly normal. There's the usual bunching of the lines in the high latitudes round the two poles. Now – ' York punched some more keys. 'What we've done is to feed in the data we've gathered in the last six weeks. I asked Shirley to interpolate the changes on an hourly basis and project the results at twenty-four frames a second. The result is rather like an animated film. The whole sequence lasts forty-two seconds. Yell out if there's any point you want to stop at and take a closer look. Okay?'

'Yes,' said Wedderkind.

'Okay, hang on to your hat. The double figures top right of screen show the date, by the way.' York pressed the start button. The date numerals began to build like the digital clock at an Olympic track event. At first, the lines hardly moved, then on the tenth of August, they began to shift and sway across the map, finally breaking apart and reforming into a totally new pattern. Wedderkind stared at the map in disbelief.

York grinned. 'It's pretty wild, isn't it?'

'Makes a real mess of compass navigation,' said Wetherby. 'Fortunately it's been superseded by other systems.'

'I've never seen anything like it,' said Wedderkind.

'There's never *been* anything like it,' said York.

In the last thirty days, the north and south magnetic poles had shifted east and west respectively to align themselves with the geographic poles. The movement, as such, was not unusual. During severe magnetic storms, magnetic north had been known to wander up to two hundred miles across the Arctic wastes, and since the beginning of the century, it had moved several hundred miles nearer true north. This was the first time, however, since observations began in the 1800s that both poles had coincided so precisely.

What was even more remarkable was that now the magnetic contour lines converged on six *more* 'polar' regions. Two of them were on the equator, one south of the Caroline Islands in the Pacific, the other on the reciprocal longitude off the coast of West Africa. Of the other four, two lay 45 degrees south of the equator, in the southern Indian Ocean, and in the Pacific off the southern province of Chile. The other two, on the same opposing lines of longitude, were sited 47 degrees north of the equator. Despite the bare outlines of the map, Wedderkind recognized the locations – Lake Balkash in the Soviet Republic of Kazakhstan, and Crow Ridge, Montana.

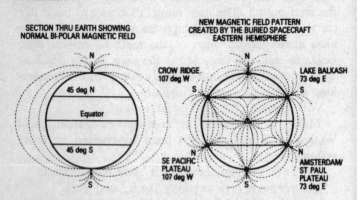

SECTION THRU EARTH SHOWING
NORMAL BI-POLAR MAGNETIC FIELD

NEW MAGNETIC FIELD PATTERN
CREATED BY THE BURIED SPACECRAFT
EASTERN HEMISPHERE

45 deg N
Equator
45 deg S

CROW RIDGE
107 deg W

LAKE BALKASH
73 deg E

SE PACIFIC
PLATEAU
107 deg W

AMSTERDAM/
ST PAUL
PLATEAU
73 deg E

To simplify comparison, Magnetic North and South Poles on normal Earth Field is aligned with the Geographic North and South Poles – as demonstrated by Professor York on September 19th. Pattern created by new magnetic sub-poles is simplified version of York's computer display and does not show field anomalies created by ferromagnetic deposits within the Earth's crust

The equatorial north-seeking sub-pole shown on the diagram is situated at 17 deg W, in the Romanche Gap, southwest of Freetown. In the western hemisphere, the opposing south-seeking sub-pole lies on the equator at 163 deg E, in the Carolines, between Kapingemarangi and Nauru, and the magnetic field pattern shown in the diagram is inverted.

Wetherby tapped the screen with his finger. 'Interesting pattern . . . If you ignore the terrestrial poles, these six points are all situated at approximately ninety degrees of arc from one another.'

'Three are north poles and three are south,' said York. 'It's as if we had four dipole magnets intersecting each other within the Earth's core. The whole thing dovetails together quite beautifully.'

That was one way of describing it, thought Wedderkind. But whatever emotive words one used, the facts were staring out of York's map. Crusoe had arrived with five companions. They had split up like the multiple warheads of a nuclear rocket, had landed in a geometrically precise pattern, and had buried themselves under cover of the second fade-out. After a three-week period of incubation, they had burrowed back up through the Earth's crust. But during that three weeks, they had harnessed the Earth's magnetic field, and had used it to spin their own alien web around the globe. Crusoe and his companions *knew* how to control one of the mysterious, primal forces of the universe. Wedderkind wondered how he could break the news to Connors.

'As far as I can see, the only problem is that four of these six sub-poles appear to be under water. Doesn't that ruin your theory?'

Wedderkind snapped out of his reverie to answer York. 'Not necessarily. Now we are more sure of the approximate locations, we can get a more accurate fix on the sites and check the seabed with submersibles. Al, how deep is it in those places?'

'Six to nine thousand feet.' Wetherby waved at the screen. 'They are all on undersea mountain ridges.'

'Will we need the help of the Navy?'

'Yes. They're funding most of the research by the privately-owned submersibles.'

'Which means Fraser is bound to get his grubby hands on it,' said Wedderkind.

'It's not going to stop there,' said Wetherby. 'There are quite a few craft that can operate at these depths but they are not all American. You'll probably have to let the French in on this. Apart from their experience, that site in the Indian Ocean is in the middle of a group of islands that belongs to them. And this one here below the Carolines could also be a problem. There are two islands nearby, one administered by Australia, and the other by us.'

'And the one off Chile?'

'That's just empty ocean. The same applies to this other one here in the Atlantic.' Wetherby tapped the screen. 'This is rapidly becoming a United Nations exercise.'

'I'm not averse to spreading the load,' said Wedderkind. 'This situation transcends the interests of national security, but what chance is there of concerted international action? Right from the beginning we set up a bilateral deal with the Russians, which neither of us had any intention of honouring. Both sides were hoping to make contact first in order to cream off any scientific or technical knowhow that could put them ahead. Not one of my contacts over there has put out so much as a squeak – and we've behaved just as badly.'

'We didn't have a lot of choice,' said Wetherby. 'Connors made the position quite clear – our silence was a precondition for joining the project.'

'Bob's a good boy,' said Wedderkind. 'But he doesn't always think for himself – although usually, he thinks of nothing else. I don't know whether we would be safer to tell the world what is happening. We're already running a risk concealing information from our *own* masters.'

York grinned. 'What are you going to do, Arnold? If you want to push this thing any further, you're going to *have* to tell people what they are looking for.'

'I know.' Wedderkind frowned. 'I need some time to think about it. George, how do these new sub-poles fit in with what we know about the coded earth tremors?'

'They correlate almost exactly,' replied York. He cleared the screen and tapped out a new order to the computer. Shirley set up six small circles on the map. 'These are the new sub-poles you saw on the previous projection. I'll now key in the epicentres of the coded tremors . . .'

York tapped out a five-part code on the keyboard. Six green crosses blipped on to the screen. Some were off centre, but all were within the green circles.

'These seismographic readings provide a more accurate fix on the landing sites – if that's what they are.'

In Wedderkind's mind, there was no longer any room for doubt. Six spacecraft had landed in an almost precise pattern around the globe, had sent underground messages to one another to signal their position and safe arrival, and had woven the Earth's magentic field into a new pattern. But for what purpose?

Wedderkind knew that the answer would not be found in York's computer, or at the White House. It was waiting for him on Crow Ridge.

CROW RIDGE/MONTANA

About ten o'clock in the evening, Page thought he might take a walk. He had read all the scientific journals and beaten everybody at chess, and conversation was hard to find. Everyone seemed to be sunk in gloomy contemplation.

Page noted the disagreeable behaviour of his colleagues in his diary and locked it in his briefcase. He wrapped carefully around his neck the woollen scarf his mother had knitted and tucked it into the front of his short topcoat, then stepped out of the trailer into the bright moonlight.

Page walked along the path to Rockville, then cut up the slope and headed southward across the plateau.

Ahead of him, Crusoe's huge black curving shape rose out of the ground. Page stopped. There was something not quite right, something different about Crusoe. He walked slowly around the hull, then realized what it was. The proportions had altered. Crusoe's hull was higher in relation to its width, and the domed hatch on top seemed to be smaller, flatter somehow . . .

As Page continued to circle Crusoe, the moonlight revealed that the hull was no longer one smooth, continuous, curved surface. He could see a faint edge where two planes joined one another. Page walked up on to the hull and went down on one knee to catch the light at the right angle. He found three more edges. They marked the joints between four curved, triangular-shaped surfaces. The angular difference was slight, but unmistakable. Crusoe was changing shape and – Page bent an ear to the hull – he was doing it to music. A high-pitched, continuous, tinkling sound like a cascade of crystals, and beneath it, a deep, wavering hum. Page hurried happily across the plateau to announce the news to Professor Lovell. The others could wait till morning.

Thursday/September 20

WASHINGTON DC

Wedderkind was in the middle of breakfast when the specially-installed scrambler phone rang in his study. It was Lovell, phoning from the base camp on Highway 22.

Lovell told him about Page's discovery.

'Are you absolutely sure?'

'Yes,' said Lovell. 'Neame and the other engineers are out taking measurements now.'

'Okay, stay where you are. I'll call you back.'

Wedderkind picked up his house phone and keyed in Charlotte Annhauser's number. 'Hello, Charly? It's

Arnold. Listen, I realize it's rather an indiscreet question at this time in the morning, but is Bob there?'

'Yes, hang on, he's in the shower.' Charly's voice was filled with laughter.

Connors came on the line. 'Hi, what's new?'

'I just had a call from Lovell.'

'Uh-huh . . .'

'From the base camp.'

'What was he doing down there?'

'Using the only available phone. Crusoe blacked out the whole Ridge at three o'clock yesterday afternoon. About half an hour before we got word that radar wavelengths had been hit by the fade-out.'

'How bad – I mean, how big is it?'

'The cutoff zone? About seven miles in diameter.'

'Jesus wept.'

'It's all right. Don't panic, there's no problem at the moment. The only people without power are up on the Ridge. Nobody in the surrounding area is affected. The edge of the cutoff zone is still nearly four miles clear of the base camp.'

'Is that the good news or the bad news?'

'The good news. Our friend has developed growing pains.'

Connors felt a cold shiver run up his spine. 'Christ, what does it mean, Arnold?'

'I don't know. It may be the good news you've been waiting for. Lovell said the dome appears to be shrinking back into the hull. Taking an optimistic view, one could interpret that as an indication that Crusoe was battening down the hatches, so to speak – prior to takeoff.' Wedderkind didn't pass on the news that Crusoe's hull had grown several feet higher. 'In Allbright's language, it would be described as "adopting flight configuration".'

'You'd better make sure someone tells him that,' said

Connors. Charly draped a towel over his dripping head and went back into the kitchen.

'What do you think we ought to do?'

'Well, I realize that you can't say too much on the phone,' said Wedderkind. 'I'd like to get back to the Ridge right away to see what the problems are. What are the chances of getting a plane back this morning?'

'There's one on standby at Andrews Field. All you have to do is call Greg and he'll arrange a pickup. But what about the meeting? We're heading into big trouble.'

'Over the fade-out?'

'Over everything.'

'What's happening? Is Fraser moving in for the kill?'

'He could be. And frankly, we don't have a lot to stop him with. All we have to throw back is a catalogue of failures and a barrage of question marks.'

'Okay, we've bungled it. I picked some of the best brains in the country and they screwed up. Fraser couldn't have picked a team that would have done any better. This isn't just an inert lump of machinery. Crusoe's *resisting* analysis. He's sabotaged our research efforts, ruined our instruments, and robbed us of electric power. No one can carry out any meaningful research under conditions like that. All one can produce is armchair theories.'

'Arnold, I know what the difficulties have been. The point is, where do we go from here?'

'We keep trying, of course. The alternative is unthinkable. In fact, there is no alternative.'

'But what about the fade-out?'

'The fade-out, the fade-out . . . My God, is that the only thing people can think about?' said Wedderkind heatedly. 'There is still some radio communication possible. All right, so there is some temporary inconvenience. Look on the bright side – at least it's impossible to start

World War Three, we're spared the daily drivel being pumped out on TV, and a few hundred people who might have been killed in aeroplanes will – '

' – get the chance to die in automobile accidents,' said Connors. 'Okay, I'm convinced. What do you want me to do, Arnold?'

'Stall them. We need more time to find out what Crusoe is up to. You can flimflam Fraser.'

'Yes, sure. Did you turn up anything of interest in Baltimore?'

'Nothing conclusive,' said Wedderkind. 'We're still working on the data. But it looks interesting.'

'In what way?'

'Well, there are indications of some large directional variations in the Earth's magnetic field. It confirms our hunch that Crusoe could be using the Earth's field as a source of power.'

'To generate the cutoff zone and the fade-out?'

'Yes. The trouble is, since we don't know how the Earth's field is generated, there's little chance of being able to cut off his power supply.'

No, thought Connors. But if you can't get at the flashlight battery, you can always try removing the bulb. 'What do you want me to say, Arnold?'

'As little as possible.'

'There's no point in hiding anything.'

'I'm not trying to hide anything,' said Wedderkind. 'In any case, Allbright will probably have semaphored the news to Fraser. Just put the best possible construction on it, that's all. Don't let Fraser stampede the Old Man.'

'Into what?'

'Into trying to destroy Crusoe. For God's sake, Bob, I'm not *that* naïve. I know how Mel Fraser's mind works. He's not going to come up with any *constructive* suggestions.'

'Okay, Arnold,' said Connors. 'I'll do my best to hold the line. But watch your step.'

'I'll call you as soon as I've assessed the situation on the Ridge.'

'Fine. If I'm not in the office, leave a message with Greg.'

'Okay.' Wedderkind hung up.

Connors went back under the shower. It had all worked out rather well. The meeting Wedderkind would miss had been cancelled anyway. All the decisions had been made the night before. While Wedderkind was winging his way westward, Connors would be heading eastward, with Mel Fraser, aboard Air Force One. To Moscow. With a message from the President of the United States and copies of the pictures the Air Force had taken of the second spacecraft in Kazakhstan.

CROW RIDGE/MONTANA

The dawn examination of the hull by the research group revealed some startling changes.There was no longer any visible line separating the sinking dome and the hull. The two shapes now flowed together to form one continuous surface. The shadowy pressure patches that had once activated the hatch were no longer visible on Crusoe's black crystal skin, and the hull had grown four and a half feet taller overnight.

Below the skin, a dull blue light flickered at irregular intervals, zigzagging through the convoluted pattern of the cortex. Prompted by Page, the group listened to the noise coming from the hull, the first anyone could remember Crusoe making. To Davis, it sounded like the tinkling noise made by Japanese wind chimes.

Page explained that what they were hearing were

stress sounds produced by the hull as Crusoe's crystalline structure rearranged itself into a new shape.

While the purpose of the change caused a certain amount of speculation, what mystified everybody was how Crusoe could change his shape at all. Previously, they had imagined that the diamond-hard hull must have been moulded from a liquid silicate, then machined to its final shape. Now, they had to accept that the hull was composed of organic crystals with a controlled growth pattern to match changes in function. It was an incredible, mind-boggling piece of technology – like making a two-seat Italian sports car that could turn itself into a Greyhound bus. It was against all the rules, but there it was, happening right before their eyes.

The current theory was that Crusoe generated the cutoff zone as protection during transitional phases when he was vulnerable. If so, the fact that he had slapped a seven-mile cutoff zone on them must mean that the face-lift he was undergoing was a major event. The big question was, how long was it going to take? Although nearly sixteen hours had elapsed since the force field had appeared, people were still wandering around with a stunned look on their faces suffering from what Gilligan had termed 'electro-deprivation'. The more serious cases, he maintained, kept vainly turning switches on and off in the hope of finding something that worked.

The loss of power had put things back to the way they had been on the day of their arrival. Cautious of the mysterious cutoff zone around Crusoe, transport had been abandoned at the embryo gatehouse, and cooking, heat, and light had been provided by compressed gas cylinders. Then slowly, as the limits of the cutoff zone had been defined and later, when the zone disappeared, more and more electrically-powered equipment had been installed on the Ridge until they had become as dependent on it as was the world outside.

As a consequence, they had found themselves painfully short of emergency lighting, but the evening had been illuminated by a celebration blackout barbecue-and-beer-can special.

Deprived of the video recording equipment, the research group arranged for one of the photographers to cover Crusoe with the aid of a camera built before the age of the silicon chip and went in search of breakfast. The butane cylinders hadn't come up from Miles City but the baker's truck had. The coffee was hot, the bacon had the sweet tang of woodsmoke just as in the best days at summer camp, and all in all there didn't seem too much wrong with the world.

Vincent and Neame shoved two tables together for the group to sit around, Davis brought a trayful of steaming coffee cups and Tomkin and Page brought the food.

'Right, gentlemen,' said Lovell. 'Arnold will be back on the Ridge in a few hours. Let's compare notes and see if we can present him with some sort of coherent picture.'

Wedderkind and Wetherby arrived back on the Ridge just after midday. A light plane hired from the Miles City air-taxi outfit set them down on an improvised airstrip behind Broken Mill, and from there, one of the converted diesels had given them a noisy ride all the way up to the plateau. The first thing Wedderkind did was to take a look at Crusoe.

When Crusoe had surfaced, his hull had measured about seventy feet across, curving gently to a height of fifteen feet in the centre, and topped by a shallow dome, which they had found to be the exposed portion of the spherical hatch unit.

Now, Crusoe's hull was over twenty feet high, and it

seemed to have grown wider, too. The four curving surfaces that made up the hull were now quite clearly defined.

'My God,' muttered Wedderkind. 'This is absolutely fantastic. Do we have any idea what the rate of growth is?'

'We'll have a better idea tonight,' said Page. 'We're taking a series of still pictures at fifteen-minute intervals throughout the day. I think they'll prove that the growth rate is accelerating.'

'I can give you the dimensional changes so far, Arnold . . .' Neame leafed through his notebook. 'At midday, the overall height was twenty-three feet, base diameter eighty feet. The domed hatch now only measures four feet across – that's a 60 per cent decrease in size. Except that it's not shrinking as Page originally thought, the whole spherical hatch unit is retracting into the hull.'

'But the really important thing is the *rate* of change,' insisted Page. 'Assuming growth started yesterday when Crusoe generated the new cutoff zone, he grew four and a half feet taller in the first fifteen hours, and another three and a half feet in the last *six*.'

'Which means if he continues to grow at the same rate for the next couple of days, we can expect something spectacular,' said Wedderkind. He pulled out his pocket calculator, punched two digits, then swore quietly as the display failed to light up. He put the inert lump of electronic wizardry away and listened to the tinkling noise coming from Crusoe's hull. As he peered through the semitranslucent outer skin, a wisp of blue light zigzagged through the darkness below. He laid a hand on the hull. 'This whole thing is alive with vibrations.'

'The whole Ridge is,' said Neame. 'Didn't it wake any of you up last night?'

'The trailer was rattling a bit this morning,' admitted Brecetti.

'I don't just mean that. There were two definite tremors last night – at three o'clock, then at five. Did nobody feel it? A small double shock. Ba-boomm . . .'

Just as the others were about to shake their heads, the ground shuddered under their feet. Ba-boomm . . .

'Just like that,' said Neame.

Wedderkind backed several yards away from the hull and took a long look at Crusoe. 'You know, ever since we failed to dig up this character, I've always assumed that there was as much of him under the ground as there was above it, but he may have been growing downward even longer than he's been growing up.' He turned to Wetherby. 'Do you remember how the remaining charges, in those two rings Max drilled, exploded when Crusoe surfaced? It puzzled me at the time. Your joke about him putting down roots may turn out to be true after all.'

'If it is,' said Wetherby, 'I don't know whether being right is going to provide much consolation.'

They began to walk back across the plateau to Rockville. When they were halfway across, Allbright, flanked by two of his aides, rode up on his palomino. He dismounted to greet Wedderkind and walked along with him and the others. Apparently he'd ridden down to the highway to make some calls over the unaffected base camp phone.

'Just how big is the cutout zone?' asked Wedderkind.

'We estimate it has a radius of about three and a half miles,' said Lovell.

'Although the edge of the zone is still well clear of the highway, I decided to stop using helicopters,' said Allbright. 'We could land on the highway, but the airstrip at Broken Mill provides an extra margin of safety.'

394

Wedderkind smiled. 'A wise move.'

'It's very much an after-the-event precaution,' said Allbright. 'We were fortunate there was no flight activity in the area when Crusoe laid the new cutoff zone on us. That's the real danger with this thing, there's no warning when it's coming. The other problem is – just how much bigger is it going to get?'

'General, there's no way I can answer that. I'm trying to work out why he needs this much protection. He's already blacked out a pretty colossal area. Speaking for myself, I certainly don't anticipate it getting any bigger.'

'Good,' said Allbright. 'I'm counting on that.' He looked at his watch. 'Could we meet in the command hut at two? There are one or two points I think we ought to discuss.'

'All right, General,' said Wedderkind. 'I'll see you there.'

Allbright remounted, gave them an informal salute and wheeled away followed by his two senior cadets.

'Fortunately we're still the only people in the cutout zone,' said Lovell. 'So things aren't as difficult as they might have been.'

'Are the problems the same?' asked Wedderkind.

'Yes,' said Neame. 'We're back to square one.'

'What happened to the generator trucks?'

'They went up like fireworks,' said Neame.

'But there is one interesting anomaly,' said Brecetti. 'This time, the surging phenomena affect currents only above two hundred and fifty microvolts.'

'Crusoe must have wanted to spare us at least one headache,' said Neame. 'Remember the dizziness and nausea that affected people around the crater when we first arrived?'

Brecetti, Collis, and Wetherby went back with Wedderkind to his trailer. Wedderkind had brought a small, folding, camper's gas stove back with him. He made some of his good coffee and handed it around.

'I didn't like to say anything in front of Allbright, but did nothing strike you about that figure of nearly seven miles for the diameter of the new cutout zone?' asked Brecetti.

'Nothing,' said Wedderkind. 'Apart from the fact that the metric equivalent is eleven kilometres. Unless you're attaching a mystical significance to the number seven.'

'There's nothing mystical about it. The maximum diameter of the *original* cutout zone was established at a little over twelve hundred yards. That's about point-six-nine of a mile. Does that ring a bell?'

'No. Not a tinkle.'

'Point-six-nine miles is one hundredth of one degree of arc – '

'Ah, of course,' said Wetherby. 'Degrees of longitude . . .'

'Yes – measured at the equator. The new cutout zone is ten times as big as the old one.'

'And you think that if there's any further enlargement, it will multiply by ten again?' asked Wedderkind.

'Yes, to sixty-nine miles. But it's a big "if".'

'Then six hundred and ninety, six thousand nine hundred, and so on,' suggested Wetherby.

'Yes,' said Brecetti. 'It's just a theoretical progression, but all you'd need is one more step and – '

'And the whole world would be covered . . .' Wedderkind exchanged glances with Wetherby.

'It'd be an interesting situation,' said Brecetti.

'But why, Phil?' asked Collis. 'I can see some reason for Crusoe protecting himself by a seven-mile cutoff zone during takeoff. It could be regarded as a critical manoeuvre. But what would be the point of depriving the whole world of electricity? It would be catastrophic.'

'That's true, but we could adapt – eventually.'

'Some of us might,' said Wedderkind. 'Industry would collapse, water wouldn't reach the cities, sewage would flood into the streets, food supplies would run out –'

'And within a week, there'd be total chaos,' said Brecetti. 'I'm not anticipating anything on that scale. I was merely pointing out the dimensional relationship between the old and new cutoff zone and what *appears* to be the unit of measurement.'

'Yes, thanks, I see that . . .' Wedderkind patted Brecetti on the shoulder. Brecetti didn't know, of course, that York's computer had come up with the possible locations of five other craft. If they all acted together, each producing a cutoff zone six thousand nine hundred miles in diameter, they could switch off most of the world. Permanently. To Wedderkind, that made a whole lot more sense than a formation takeoff.

As he sipped from his cup, the hot coffee steamed up his glasses. Wedderkind took them off and dried the lenses with his handkerchief. He squinted at Wetherby with small, naked eyes that looked curiously vulnerable. Wetherby got the message and nodded.

Wedderkind replaced his glasses and tapped the bridge into place on his nose. 'Al and I got some information from George York in Baltimore last night that we'd like to share with you. I'm not sure what to make of it. The important thing is to decide what we are going to do about it.'

Wedderkind told Brecetti and Collis about the possibility that there could be five more landing sites and the changes in the Earth's magnetic field. It took them both a few minutes to get used to the idea.

'So far, I've remained steadfastly optimistic,' said Wedderkind. 'But whichever way you look at it, one is a visit but six . . .'

'Sounds more like a lynch party,' said Brecetti.

'The point is, we can't keep this to ourselves much longer,' said Wedderkind. 'In fact, I'm going to have to tell Bob. We're going to have to confess to the Russians that we double-crossed them – and that we know they double-crossed us too.'

'We could always pretend we just found Crusoe,' said Collis.

Wedderkind smiled. 'You're learning fast, Ray.' The smile was replaced by a frown. 'I wonder what Allbright wants to talk about?'

'I think he wants to move everybody off the Ridge and down to the base camp,' said Brecetti. 'He's concerned about these continuing earth tremors.'

'So am I,' said Collis. 'They're not violent, but if Crusoe keeps on growing . . . why take the risk? Especially now that we're completely cut off up here.'

'Yes, I can see the problems,' said Wedderkind. 'But whatever the risks, I think it's vital for some of us to remain here for as long as possible.'

'Why?' asked Collis.

'Because once we move off the Ridge, we might not be allowed back.'

Brecetti nodded soberly. 'Neame told me he'd heard that there was a rumour going around among the Air Force technicians that the project was going to be terminated.'

'It wouldn't surprise me,' said Wedderkind. 'That three-week fade-out really rocked everybody back in Washington. Up here on the Ridge, we've been concerned with the purely scientific view. Even so, I don't have to remind you of the wider implications. And the dangers – on all kinds of levels. Bob has done his best on our behalf, but Fraser has been cutting the ground away from under him. I know Bob. He never tries to defend

398

an untenable position. This new fade-out has put the pressure back on again. He may well have recommended termination.'

'Without telling you?' Collis looked surprised.

'Why tell me first when he can tell me afterward and blame someone else for the decision?' said Wedderkind. 'I don't mind. After all, I've been holding out on him.'

'I thought you were friends,' said Collis.

'We are,' said Wedderkind. 'I didn't want him to worry.'

'But Arnold, even if they send us all home, they still have to get rid of Crusoe. What are they going to try to do, blow him up?' asked Wetherby.

'I imagine they'll try.'

'And are you going to stand by and let them?'

It was Brecetti who replied for Wedderkind. 'What's the alternative, Alan – link arms around the hull and sing "We shall not be moved"?'

'No, but Arnold has access to the President,' said Wetherby. 'He could go to see him and explain what we've discovered, and urge him to postpone any decision to end the project.'

'Al,' said Wedderkind. 'You know what the reaction to Crusoe has been. What do you think they're going to say when I tell them there could be five more? Bob is going to go bananas. Up to now I've steadfastly believed Crusoe's presence to be essentially harmless. I still do. But supposing the cutoff zone does *spread*? Should we just stand by and let it happen, or should we warn people, and at least give them the chance to try to stop it?'

'What could they do?' asked Wetherby.

'Nothing,' said Brecetti. 'And there's nowhere anyone can go to avoid it. In any case there's no need to alarm people unnecessarily. Let's wait to see if the cutout zone gets any bigger. There'll still be plenty of time to warn Washington.'

'What do you think, Ray?'

'I think it's madness to hold back on this information. I think you ought to tell Connors that there could be more than one landing site and where you think they are – and also pass on Phil's gloomiest prediction. Regardless of what Connors or Fraser or both of them together are plotting behind our back.'

'Al?'

Wetherby grimaced thoughtfully. 'I think I agree with Ray. Since I can't see any advantage in concealing the information, honesty would seem to be the best policy. I also think it might be time for our group to get ready to head for the hills. The journey may turn out to be totally unnecessary, but it will be a useful exercise.'

'If only to prove how pathetically impractical the whole idea is,' said Collis.

'Don't agree,' said Wetherby. 'Noah's Ark. Lot and his daughters warned to flee the destruction of Sodom and Gomorrah. Admirable biblical precedents. And historically, we have the example of the early monasteries acting as centres of knowledge during the Dark Ages.'

'But surely, if we're contemplating the possibility of dislocation on – well, let's just say a continental scale – wouldn't it be better for all of us to try to work together instead of hiving ourselves off into selfish little splinter survival groups?'

'Now that *is* impractical, Ray,' said Wetherby. 'Faced with a prolonged breakdown of the type Phil has theorized, it would be impossible to maintain the present structure of society and the same geographical groupings. Without twentieth-century communications we'd have to revert to decentralized authority. And without electrical power, we'd find ourselves back in an America of the

1870s with bizarre outcroppings of twentieth-century gas, diesel, and chemical technology. Pioneer railroad America before the days of the telegraph, with modern diesels pounding the tracks at one hundred miles an hour. Diesel cars and trucks, light aircraft like the German planes of the late thirties – maybe even simple jets. All with primitive cockpit instruments operated by air and hydraulic pressure. Communication with the ground would have to be done by waggling the wings. And if the six magnetic sub-poles York has discovered ever become a permanent feature, then compass navigation will become a real tour de force . . .'

As an ex-RAF navigator, Wetherby found the problem especially appealing. He paused to consider the perspectives he had opened up. 'As a matter of fact, you know, it could be jolly exciting.'

Wedderkind checked the time and finished his coffee. 'I think I'll take the diesel down to the base camp and phone Bob before I talk to Allbright.' He turned back in the doorway of the trailer and smiled at Wetherby. 'Living on the edge of the Chicago campus has certainly sharpened *your* sense of survival.'

Wedderkind arrived back on the Ridge some twelve minutes after he was due to meet Allbright in the command hut.

'Sorry I'm late. I was down at the base camp trying to contact Bob Connors.'

'But he wasn't in Washington.'

'No . . .' Wedderkind took the offered chair.

Allbright sat down behind a spartan desk, the top of which was as trim and ordered as a barrack square.

'What was it you wanted to see me about?'

'Evacuation.'

'Partial or total, and on whose orders, General?'

'Phased and temporary,' said Allbright. 'And it's not an order, just a suggestion. Starting with all nonessential personnel. In view of what is happening – and what may be about to happen – it would seem to be a sensible precaution. Especially as the cutoff zone has virtually brought all research activity to a halt.'

'I agree there's not a lot we can do up here at the moment,' said Wedderkind. 'I wouldn't oppose a reduction in numbers. I assume you're proposing to transfer them to the base camp?'

'That would be the first step,' said Allbright. 'If we accept the idea that Crusoe is preparing for takeoff, then according to your theory, he should revert to his fluorescent state. That will mean he'll be beaming out a large amount of ultraviolet radiation. I don't think it's a good idea to have this campsite crowded with spectators when that happens.'

'No, that's right.'

'Good. Now as you know, before any of us can leave this area, all Ridge personnel have to be checked out by the base camp medical unit. That process takes thirty-five minutes per person. Deducting our recent losses, we're left with a total strength of three hundred and twelve men, including yourself and Mr Connors. The unit can process two cases simultaneously, giving us a total processing time of around ninety hours. That's three and three-quarter days, assuming the unit works nonstop. Given a sudden emergency, we could find ourselves with a big tailback.'

'There's the emergency medical unit on the Ridge, and NASA could always draft in more staff,' said Wedderkind . 'But in any case, General, is it *really* necessary to have all your people processed? You and I, Bob Connors, and Alan Wetherby have all been given a clean bill of health. Not once, but several times. If anybody on the project had been taken over by a parasitic host, or were incubating a virulent extraterrestrial plague, surely we would have been contaminated too.'

'I don't think our medical opinions carry much weight,' said Allbright. 'Washington's fears are understandable, the Defense Department directive is quite specific, and I don't have the authority to countermand the order.' Allbright allowed himself a quiet smile. 'I also think it's time we stopped pretending.'

Wedderkind frowned. 'I don't understand what you're getting at.'

'Oh, come now, Mr Wedderkind. Do I *really* have to put it into words?'

'It might help.'

'I wonder . . .' Allbright looked squarely at Wedderkind. 'I was referring to the fact that you and I both know that everyone on the Ridge has, in varying degrees, been affected by the contact with Crusoe.'

'Well, obviously, we're bound to be changed in some way by this experience.'

'Of course,' said Allbright. 'But I'm not referring to a change in attitudes. I'm talking about a physiological change that hasn't been detected yet by the base camp medics. That opens up . . . how can I put it . . . new areas of understanding?'

Wedderkind didn't say anything. He didn't need to. The other way was so much easier. He relaxed his defence and let his mind interlock with Allbright's.

WEDDERKIND: HAVE YOU TOLD ANYONE? *Allbright: No. I thought it might be misinterpreted. I was reluctant to believe it myself.* AFRAID? *At the beginning, yes. I was afraid I might be losing control over my own actions. Now I realize that nothing else has changed.* NOTHING. WE STILL HAVE OUR FREE WILL. ONLY OUR PERCEPTION HAS INCREASED. CRUSOE HAS UNLOCKED THE CLOSED DOORS IN OUR MINDS.

BUT WE ARE STILL LIMITED. WE CANNOT COMMUNICATE IF EITHER OF US REFUSES INTERLOCK. *Perhaps that will change with time. Do you think Crusoe has been interlocking with us?* YES. I BELIEVE HE WAS IN CONTACT WITH SOME OF US WHILE HE WAS STILL IN ORBIT. *Feeding us with ideas?* YES, BUT ON A LEVEL BEYOND OUR PRESENT DEGREE OF PERCEPTION. I AM UNABLE TO DISTINGUISH HIS THOUGHTS FROM MY OWN. *So, in fact, we could be completely under Crusoe's control.* HOW CAN YOU THINK THAT WHEN YOU HAVE HELPED PLAN HIS DESTRUCTION? *That's true, but we could still be deluding ourselves. The idea that we still retain total freedom of action could be just an illusion. Covert mind control was the one thing that the people in Washington feared.* ALL GOVERNMENTS FEAR IT BECAUSE THEY KNOW, SUBCONSCIOUSLY, IT IS A POWER THEY WOULD LIKE TO POSSESS — AND MISUSE, TO BLUDGEON US INTO CONFORMITY. THERE IS NOTHING TO FEAR. WE ARE AS WE HAVE ALWAYS BEEN. THE POWER IS WITHIN ALL OF US. ONLY NOW, SOME OF US ARE ABLE TO USE IT. *But why set us apart from the rest? And why me? I am committed to destroying Crusoe. Why arm his enemies?* PERHAPS HE KNOWS YOU BETTER THAN YOU KNOW YOURSELF. IT MAY BE BECAUSE WE WERE AMONG THE FIRST TO MAKE CONTACT WITH CRUSOE — OR THE FORCE HE IS RELAYING. WE ARE NOT THE ONLY ONES AFFECTED. I CAN SENSE A GROWING AWARENESS AMONG EVERYONE ON THE RIDGE. PEOPLE TRYING TO UNDERSTAND WHAT IS HAPPENING WITHIN THEM. *Is Connors aware?* ONLY PARTLY. HIS MIND IS STILL CLOUDED. I CAN FEEL THAT HE KNOWS SOMETHING IS HAPPENING TO HIM BUT HE IS TRYING TO FIGHT IT. IT WORRIES HIM. *And many of the others too. The degree of awareness varies from person to person. It is as if they had been handed a strange tool without any explanation on how to use it – or what to use it for.* YES. THE ONLY DIFFERENCE BETWEEN US AND THE OTHERS IS THAT WE HAVE BEEN QUICKER TO UNDERSTAND ITS

POTENTIALITIES, AND TO USE THEM. I KNOW THAT COLLIS
AND BRECETTI ARE ALMOST AT THE SAME POINT, BUT I HAVE
NOT TRIED TO CONTACT THEM BECAUSE IT IS STILL TOO
DANGEROUS. IT IS BETTER TO WAIT. THERE WILL BE PLENTY
OF TIME AFTERWARD. *There may not be any 'afterward'.*I
CAN'T ACCEPT THAT. THERE HAS TO BE. OTHERWISE THERE
WOULD BE NO REASON FOR OUR EXISTENCE OR CRUSOE.

The exchange widened out to include other ideas,
attitudes and experiences, and as they progressed towards
a deeper understanding, Allbright unexpectedly revealed
a terrifying vision that had lain inside his brain like a
hidden cancer for years.

*Countless explosive chain reactions, fusing into one
enormous, apocalyptic, cleansing fireball that would wipe
the diseased, the poverty-stricken, the overpopulated, bur-
densome nations of the world clean off the face of God's
Earth. Society would start again. Start anew. The rotten
would perish. The sane would survive. And so would the
strong. Enough to build a new America. A clean, straightforward, simple America, that his father had known and
that he, himself, had seen corrupted . . .*

Wedderkind was so disturbed by the discovery that he
lapsed back into speech. 'Did you really want that to
happen?'

'It was a nightmare wish that stayed with me a long
time,' admitted Allbright. 'It may have been because of
my job. When you are near the apex of the command
system that controls the most powerful, most destructive
force the world has ever known . . .'

'I know. One tends to develop a Jupiter complex.
Scientists are sometimes afflicted with it too,' said Wedderkind. 'And now – ?'

'Now I realize that there are other ways by which the
same end result can be achieved.'

'But less bloodily.'

'That depends very much on how people react,' said Allbright. 'Things may go badly if you rely on people's willingness to make great sacrifices. The kind of change you and I are talking about will be viewed by most people as a global catastrophe – and no doubt they will react accordingly.'

'And will you still go ahead as planned?'

'Of course. There's no other alternative.'

'Even though you may be risking your life?'

Allbright shrugged. 'That's nothing new. We are all condemned to die from the moment we're born. It's what you do in between that counts. If I refused to carry out my orders, it could put the lives of everyone on the project at risk.'

'You're right. I hadn't thought of that.'

'In any case, neither you or I have the right to allow Crusoe to impose his ideas on the rest of the world. If it was put to the vote what do you think the verdict would be?'

'How often has the majority been right?' asked Wedderkind. 'There was no room for the democratic process in your own thermonuclear solution.'

'My personal feelings are irrelevant, Mr Wedderkind. I took an oath of allegiance to serve my country. Crusoe's presence may be benign, but neither you or I have absolute proof of that. Whatever benefits Crusoe may have come here to bestow on us – and already, we both know of one – his presence and power threaten the authority of the government that the people of the United States elected, and that I serve. Regardless of any other considerations, for that reason alone, if the order comes, I *have* to act.'

'Oh, it will come, General. It's inevitable. We are all prisoners of the system. I know the present situation is fraught with danger, but I'm praying for your efforts to be rewarded with total failure – and also for your safe return. Even if it is only to arrest me for treason.'

Allbright smiled. 'If it does prove impossible to destroy Crusoe, I hope, for your sake, I *do* survive, Mr Wedderkind. You're going to need people like me.'

Despite the apparently frank exchange, Wedderkind had been aware that Allbright was blocking off certain areas within his mind that held information he was not ready to share. In visual terms, the sensation was rather like driving along a freeway in clear weather and then suddenly running into a dense bank of dark grey fog that blots out all sight, sound, and movement. With practice, it might be possible to probe through the mental barriers into the concealed areas. Allbright must have experienced something similar, because Wedderkind had, himself, made a strenuous effort to hold back his knowledge of the possible existence of other landing sites.

He realized that he would have to work hard to develop his reawakened telepathic powers. In particular, Wedderkind foresaw an urgent need to perfect a blocking technique that employed a diversionary segment of irrelevant experience to screen off the knowledge he wished to conceal rather than the telltale 'fog'. If he was going to find himself surrounded by a host of open-minded telepaths, a little mild deception might come in handy . . .

AIR FORCE ONE/WASHINGTON-MOSCOW

With Connors and Fraser aboard, and Colonel Buzz Bricker at the controls, Air Force One took off from Andrews AFB at 10 A.M. Thursday and headed eastward across the Atlantic on a route that would pass over the Azores.

It was the first time Connors had been face to face with Fraser for more than an hour without a table between them. The President had intended him to go alone, but after their midnight meeting, Fraser had asked to go along on the trip. This time, at least, they were agreed on the course of action to follow.

Before leaving, Connors had reread the background material Greg Mitchell had compiled on Fraser. Just reading about him had been an exhausting experience. Not content with collecting good grades in law and economics, Fraser had been a star football player at Oregon State, had served with distinction in the Marines, played good golf, had helped crew one of the yachts in the 1970 America's Cup Race, was a keen fisherman, strong swimmer, ran three miles every morning, and enjoyed chopping down trees with an axe.

Connors had never played football, couldn't bear golf, preferred boats with engines, found his fish in restaurants, could just keep himself afloat with a floundering breast stroke, had lately been having problems running up his own stairs, and the nearest he'd got to an axe in the last twenty years was a stereo version of 'Woodchopper's Ball'. Still, his record was not one of total failure. With single-minded determination, Connors *had* made the UCLA tennis team but only because he was even more determined to make the women's singles champion. At the end of the season she had announced her engagement to a thirty-year-old dentist. Totally disgusted, Connors abandoned sports and went back to the college library and the more rewarding pursuit of girls with glasses.

Connors had viewed the forty-eight-hour trip with mixed feelings, but fortunately, Fraser had brought four Defense Department aides with him. Apart from some initial desultory conversation, Fraser spent a lot of the trip working with his aides on a sackful of papers. It gave Connors time to review the files on Crusoe, CAMPFIRE, and Commissar, and to work out exactly what he was going to say to the Russians. He reflected for a moment on the curious way in which his life had been dogged by the letter C: the choice of his own surname; California, the state in which he'd spent his first years in America; the name of his first wife and the name of the girl he might yet marry – and now Crusoe . . .

Just after the Azores had drifted past the starboard wing, Fraser left his shirt-sleeved colleagues and came over to Connors. 'May I join you?'

'Sure . . .'

Fraser sat down and loosened his striped tie. 'Boy, have we got problems . . .'

'The fade-out?'

'Yeah . . . when those short waves go, the shit really hits the fan.'

'Yes, I can imagine.'

'I wonder if you can,' said Fraser.

'I've been on the NSC and the Special Action Group for two years,' said Connors. 'That does give me some idea of the workings of the military establishment.'

'Do you realize that without radar and radio it's practically impossible to hold this country together, let alone defend it? And globally, by the time that last three-week fade-out ended, we'd lost our grip on the whole situation. But I mean totally. If the Russians hadn't played it straight down the middle – '

'At least I got that bit right,' said Connors. 'They're in as bad shape as we are.'

'Don't kid yourself,' growled Fraser. 'They're not geared up the way we are. Do you know how many of their tanks have radios? One in four.'

'But at least their Red ant heaps didn't swarm all over us.'

'Not last time. But don't write off that possibility. We don't know how long this new fade-out is going to last –

or whether the Russians will go along with us. If these guys sense an opportunity to screw us, they will. Look at the way they covered up the second spacecraft.'

'And the way we broke the agreement to ban reconnaissance overflights. That's going to take some explaining when I lay the photographs of Commissar on the table.'

'You'll think of something,' said Fraser. 'Listen, the only reason they didn't try it was because they don't have anything to match the SR-71A. The dummies went *banco* on photographic satellites. Fat lot of good that did them. And what about Crusoe? You and the Old Man led the big clam-up on that.'

'Weren't we right?'

'Absolutely. It just proves my point. When it comes down to the real nitty-gritty, all this talk about trust and mutual understanding between us and the Russians turn, out to be plain hogwash.'

'You know why we decided to keep quiet. Crusoe's landing created an entirely new situation. We didn't know how *we* would react, let alone the Russians. Especially under the impact of the fade-out. That altered the whole balance of power that formed the basis of the agreements we'd reached.'

'My words to the President exactly,' said Fraser. 'Except that in my opinion, the agreements aren't worth the paper they're written on. I put my faith in a big gun and a strong dollar.'

'Yes . . . the trouble is, we don't seem to be able to have both.'

Fraser didn't say anything. Winning congressional approval of his Defense budget was just *one* of his current problems. And now, with the renewed fade-out, the billions of dollars already invested in advanced electronic-based weapons systems was looking, at least temporarily, like a total write-off. Without a big gun, and with the dollar weakening under the economic impact of the fade-out, the only way for the United States to avoid trouble was to make friends and influence people. And that meant using the relationships people like Connors had helped the President build with the Communists.

'Do you think they're going to buy this bluff of yours?' asked Fraser.

'I think we have a more than even chance.'

'Well, if it comes off, it will be one hell of a double play.' There was a hint of grudging admiration in Fraser's voice. 'Still, I suppose you people understand better than we do just how their minds work.'

Connors ignored this veiled reference to his middle-European origins. He had, after all, only been six years old when following the collapse of the 1956 Hungarian uprising, his parents had brought him to America after a perilous crossing of the Austrian border under fire from a Red Army patrol that had killed three other refugees travelling with them. 'The point is this, if the Russians do agree with our proposition, can you guarantee that a nuclear bomb is going to destroy these spacecraft?'

'What else do you suggest we use?' asked Fraser.

'But is a fifty-kiloton weapon going to be big enough?'

'The Russians can use what they like,' said Fraser. 'We've calculated the size we need. What do you want us to do, use fifty megatons and destroy half of the midwest?'

'No. I trust your experts. It's just that we may only get one bite at the apple.'

'What makes you say that?' asked Fraser.

'I don't know. It was just a thought.'

Fraser grinned. 'Crusoe's finally got you worried too.'

'There's never been a time when I wasn't worried,' said Connors. 'Even so, I think it was right to give Arnold and his boys a chance to try to find out something about it.'

Fraser shook his head. 'We should have blown it up in orbit. We had a whole week while it was circling around. Our radar was locked on to it, there was no fade-out. We couldn't have missed.'

'It still could have been dangerous. Supposing Crusoe had been stuffed with radioactive cobalt? The debris could have poisoned the atmosphere and killed us all.'

'Could we be in any greater danger than we are now?' asked Fraser.

'But Mel, with what we know now, do you honestly believe that we could have blown Crusoe up before he landed? Our satellites were knocked out by a burst of radiation. A missile could have been deactivated in the same way.'

'I'm not prepared to consider that kind of proposition,' said Fraser. 'If we allow ourselves to think for one moment that Crusoe is indestructible, then we might as well all jump out of the window.'

'Oh, come on, Mel,' said Connors. 'I'm with you one hundred per cent on this, but if we're going to drop a nuclear bomb on him, we *have* to consider the possibility that it's not going to blow him out of the ground. That means considering that the fade-out might not be a prelude to takeoff but a permanent fixture. I know the problems would be gigantic, but we could adapt. We'd find *some* kind of solution. We'd have to. It certainly wouldn't be the end of the world.'

Fraser eyed him. 'All I can say is you've got a funny view of it. You remember we asked the Hudson Institute to prepare various scenarios on the basis of a prolonged fade-out?'

Connors nodded.

'I got a sneak preview of their preliminary assessments,' said Fraser. 'Catastrophic . . .'

'In that case everything had better go according to

plan,' said Connors. 'If the Russians play ball, by next Friday we'll have seen the last of Crusoe and an end of our uncertainties.'

'That moment can't come soon enough for me.'

'Weren't you *ever* curious to know more about Crusoe?' asked Connors. 'I find it amazing that you never wanted to come to Crow Ridge and take a firsthand look at Crusoe and Friday. After all, an event like this is not likely to happen again, not in our lifetimes anyway.'

Fraser shrugged. 'The tapes were good enough for me. The President wanted to go but I advised him against it. What good did it do you? You practically shook hands with Friday. Are you any the wiser?'

It was Connors' turn to shrug.

Fraser smiled. 'What are you pleading, the Fifth Amendment? Relax. According to the medical reports you're still R. J. Connors.'

'It's curious how you're really bugged by that idea,' said Connors. 'Don't tell me you seriously thought that Crusoe might gain control of the people on the project?'

'It was something we considered. I guess you think I'm pretty stupid.'

'Far from it,' said Connors. 'But do you really think that the universe is only populated by beings intent on destroying this world? Do you think a peaceful visit is impossible?'

'Is that how you'd describe what we're currently experiencing? Do you remember our argument over the mad dog theory right at the beginning of all this? Crusoe isn't just an ordinary piece of space hardware. It's got a brain. There's an alien intelligence at work. You've seen the pictures of that second layer.'

'The cortex . . . yes, but we just used that word to describe its appearance. There's no proof that it functions as a brain. And there's still no *conclusive* proof that

413

Crusoe's reactions are anything more than high-grade, computer-directed reflexes.'

'I don't care if he's running on a clockwork motor,' said Fraser. 'He still made assholes out of the research group. Right from the start I knew this was going to be bad news. I predicted it. I was against letting it land. But nobody listened to me . . .'

'That's true,' said Connors. 'I was just thinking how you turned out to be absolutely right about Crusoe being the source of that first twenty-minute fade-out.'

'I just had a hunch.'

'Yes, I know, but it was still pretty amazing. I mean you were wrong about it being a Russian spacecraft, yet you still stuck your neck out even though you knew they couldn't have built a plasma-powered space-vehicle without Arnold or one of his friends at the Fermi Institute hearing about it.'

'Yeah, I know. I knew it didn't add up, but something at the back of my mind told me I was right,' said Fraser.

'Even though Arnold's people and the Air Force scientists all said it was freak solar radiation . . .'

'There were those figures for the fade-out times,' said Fraser. 'Which showed the shock wave moving around the earth.'

'Yes, but *you* asked for that data to be collected.'

'And it proved what I'd been saying all along. Crusoe *was* the cause of the fade-out.'

'Yes. Several of us have been right,' said Connors. 'I suggested that the interference could come from within the earth. The fade-out *did* continue while Crusoe was underground. Arnold suggested that Crusoe might grow. He *is* growing – into a different shape.'

Fraser looked at Connors thoughtfully. 'What are you trying to say, that I've been got at too?'

'I'm not suggesting anyone's been got at,' said Connors.

'That's one of your ideas. I'm just trying to point out that if you *are* right, Crusoe may have got to some of us while he was in orbit. Which means that now he's on the ground, he could reach out a lot further than Crow Ridge.'

'Yeah . . .'

It gave Connors considerable pleasure to watch Fraser's furtive contemplation of the possibility that his own mind might have been contaminated.

'Have you mentioned this idea to anybody?'

'No,' said Connors.

'Good. Maybe, just for the moment, we ought to keep it to ourselves.'

'Sure,' said Connors. 'We don't want to alarm anybody.'

'No . . . did the President, ah, you know – I mean, did he ever come up with any ideas about Crusoe?'

'No,' said Connors. 'He just thought of the code name.'

'Yeah . . . As a matter of fact, now I come to think of it, Gene Samuels may have suggested that stuff about the fade-out to me. I just presented it at the meeting. That's the way I think it happened.'

'It doesn't matter which of you it was,' said Connors. 'After all, Arnold, Allbright, and I have all been cleared more than once by the base camp unit. We're not affected in any way, so why should either of you be? Still . . . if you are worried, all you need do is have Gene go through the same checkup.'

'Yeah . . .'

Connors had never taken Wedderkind's suggestion of a possible extermination plot very seriously. Nevertheless, he hadn't forgotten what the President had said about CAMPFIRE. '*If it proved necessary, the strike would include everything and everybody on the Ridge . . .*' As far as Connors knew, the medical evidence showed that Crusoe hadn't infected their minds or bodies *or* their environment but there was always a chance that, once formed, the idea could still be lurking at the back of someone's mind. By suggesting to Fraser the possibility of a random telepathic contact over unlimited distances, Connors hoped to take the heat off the people on the Ridge once and for all. He was even more anxious to put himself in the clear – especially as he was becoming more and more convinced that he was starting to hear voices . . .

Jean Seagren appeared in the aisle. 'Would you gentlemen like some coffee, or something a little stronger?'

'Why not,' said Fraser. 'Give me a rye with plenty of ice in it, but make sure it floats. We're not going to get a decent drink over there.'

'I'll just have a coffee,' said Connors. He looked back at Fraser. 'What is it with you and Russians? Do you really hate them that much?'

'I'm not exactly in love with them,' said Fraser.

'Does that mean you think I am?'

'I think you're looking at the world through rose-coloured glasses,' said Fraser. 'But then when it comes to foreign policy, I know you have me filed under "B" for Backwoodsman.'

'And what am I, a Red agent?'

'I wouldn't classify you as a bleeding heart, but all the same I think you're way off base. I understand what you're trying to do. I'm not looking for a fight with the Russians either. But by God, I want to make sure that they never try and pick a fight with us.'

'Do you think they could afford to?' asked Connors. 'And even if we win, what would we be left with? If we threw away three-quarters of our nuclear arsenals we'd still both have enough to commit global suicide. That kind of war is unwinnable. Do you really want your grandchildren's children to grow up in cities ringed with antiballistic missile systems? We have to continue building towards a lasting peace – but on an entirely different foundation. That means creating relationships based on a new understanding of the global realities, economic, social, and political. It means reconciling our own aims and aspirations with those of the rest of the world.'

'And you think the President's "most favoured nation" trade policies with Russia and China are going to help keep the peace?'

'Yes, I do.'

'Pie in the sky,' snorted Fraser. 'The Reds are never going to give up. They're going to keep chipping away at us, and you're playing right into their hands. Trading with these guys is like handing them a loaded revolver. Don't kid yourself it works both ways, it only works to *their* advantage. Hell, we've used economic pressure on South America long enough. You only have to consider how our own foreign policy decisions have been influenced by the commercial lobbies. Supposing a big chunk of our industry was relying on orders from China and Russia and those contracts meant the difference between boom and bust? We've already got problems with communist insurgents in Thailand, Indonesia and the Philippines. What the hell would we do if Moscow or Peking came out of the closet and openly supported a take-over bid? Cancel the grain contracts, the chemical plants and construction deals? Throw our people out of work? You'd be able to stand on Capitol Hill and hear the sound of banks foreclosing all the way from Texas to North Dakota. Can you imagine the howls of pain we'd get from the Treasury? Not to mention Congress. There be more lobbyists on our back than flies on a cow's teat.

'The Reds don't have this problem. They rule from the top down. Okay, there may be some argument over policy behind closed doors but once it's hammered out that's it. They just hand down the tablets of stone to rubber-stamp legislatures who are so used to applauding, they'd give a standing ovation to news of their own execution. They got it all sewn up. They have complete control of the media and, at the first sign of unrest they can call on the police and the army to come to the aid of the party.

'Democracies don't operate like that. You pay a price for freedom. Liberty for the individual is an idea I subscribe to but it makes this country ungovernable. Back in the old days, if you were a Jew in Russia, or part of an oppressed minority anywhere else you voted with your feet. And once you got here if you didn't like it in the East you headed West. But nowadays, there's no place to go. Anyone with a beef hangs a placard round his neck and takes to the streets or starts learning how to make bombs. There are guys out there pushing every nutbrain idea you can think of, from Learn To Love The Ku Klux Klan to Five Million Cokeheads Can't Be Wrong.

'With everybody fighting for their own corner, it's impossible to arrive at a consensus on what is in the national interest. Result? Lame-duck presidents, hamstrung administrations. Wheels and deals. Trade-offs and sell-outs. Shift and drift. Whenever there's a choice people always go for the soft option. It's human nature. We've had it too good too long. Americans want tomorrow today and they want it on easy terms with no down payments.

'That's the difference between us and them. Those guys in Moscow and Peking can put their consumer dreams on hold whenever they want. If it comes to the crunch, they can even throw their economies into reverse. Russia and China don't need our technology to survive. They can replace it with ideology. Take it from me, they're happy to pick our brains, and we've got idiots falling over themselves to make a swift buck. What they don't realize is that they're selling our country short.'

'Do you mean that we shouldn't trade with them at all?'

'Damn right. We don't need them. They need us. They need our currency to buy goods, our grain, our meat. They can't even feed themselves. You may think it's only a few million bushels of wheat or another chemical plant but what you're *really* doing is bolstering communism. Supporting a government whose avowed aim is the overthrow of America. The free world. Democracy. Yet all they have to do is give you people in the White House a bottle of vodka and you're ready to rush out and kiss Lenin's tomb. But nothing has changed. Every shipment of Russian bullion is just another gold nail in our coffin. For Chrissakes, when are you guys going to wise up? These people are the *enemy*!'

Jean Seagren returned with Fraser's rye and Connors' coffee on a tray. Connors pulled down the folding table from the back of the seat in front and took the offered cup.

'Sugar?'

'No, I'm feeling strong-willed today.' He fumbled in his pocket for his sweeteners. On the pack it stated clearly 'No aftertaste.' Another lie. The world was full of them.

Fraser watched Seagren move out of the cabin, then leaned confidentially towards Connors. 'If you're ever in the market, that little lady is a fantastic piece of ass . . .'

Friday/September 21

Colonel Buzz Bricker, Air Force One's captain, came down the aisle. One would have expected the President's pilot to look like John Wayne with wings. Bricker was under six feet and looked like a sharp-eyed accountant, just back from a vacation in Bahamas. He had fifteen thousand faultless hours in his logbook and one of the best instrument ratings in the Air Force.

'Hi,' said Connors.

Bricker sat down beside him. 'Where's Fraser?'

'He's lying down. He's another one of these people who can sleep anywhere. How's it going up front?'

Bricker grimaced. 'Not too bad. We used our inertial navigation systems to get across the water, spot-checking every hour with sun shots. At the moment we still have radio contact with ground stations on the medium wave bands, and I don't know whether you know or not, but the Navy has a line of picket ships strung out across the Atlantic.'

'Ah . . . that's comforting.'

'Yeah, they're keeping station a hundred miles apart. Means we don't have too far to paddle. They gave us the weather up ahead. Thank God we had INS – our compasses are totally out of whack. At one point, they were indicating magnetic north as somewhere down on the equator.' Bricker grinned. 'At least we didn't have to worry about a midair collision. I bet the sky hasn't been this empty since Lindbergh flew over in 1927.'

'That suits me,' said Connors. 'I used to enjoy all this

420

when I was training with the Navy. When I think back on some of the things I did . . . I must have been out of my mind. I guess I'm getting too old. All I want to do now is stay on the ground. That must seem crazy to you.'

Bricker shook his head. 'I know a lot of guys who are happy flying desks. They do their minimum numbers of hours to keep their rating and that's it. I'm happy to keep going – especially with the job I've got.' He smiled. 'I've made all the mistakes I'm going to make – and got away with it. All I've got to worry about now is some other damn fool making a mistake.'

They slipped through a couple more time zones and landed at the big US Air Force base outside Frankfurt. It was just after midnight, local time. Connors walked up to the nose door to get a breath of fresh air while the plane was being refuelled.

Bricker emerged from the flight deck. 'I'd better go and dig our two Russians out of the officer's mess, then we'll press on to the Motherland. I won't rush. When I'm using Eyeballs Mark Two, I prefer to land in daylight.'

'I hope they know we're coming,' said Connors.

'Don't worry,' said Bricker. He pointed at the window. 'It's bullet-proof glass.'

Because of the radar breakdown the Russians had suggested that it might be a good idea if Air Force One's crew had some help from a Russian navigator and a radio operator. To the White House, it seemed like an offer they couldn't refuse.

The two crewmen had flown into Frankfurt in the late afternoon aboard a Russian Air Force Tupolev Tu-26, a sharp, sleek, supersonic bomber known to NATO as the Backfire-B. In service with the Russian equivalent of SAC, the Tu-26 was Moscow's answer to the US Air Force's Rockwell B-1B. It's face was familiar but very few people outside the Iron Curtain had seen the real thing and practically the whole base turned out to take a look at it.

The Tupolev's crew must have had the bomb bay loaded with roubles, because they aimed straight for the base PX, negotiated a fast rate of exchange, piled up three jeeps with crates of Coca-Cola, bourbon, nylons, Polaroid cameras, cartons of Marlboro cigarettes and every available copy of *Penthouse, Popular Science*, and *Practical Mechanix*, rushed back to the bomber, stowed everything aboard, shook hands all round, yelled '*Dosvidanya!*' through the cockpit window, and headed for the runway while the Base Intelligence Officer was putting the fourth reel of film in his camera.

Connors closed his eyes as Air Force One angled up into the darkness and set about the task of persuading his biological clock that it really *was* 2 A.M. and not time for a dry martini. He fell asleep as Air Force One entered the air corridor that crossed East Germany and Poland. When he woke up, he found Fraser shaking his shoulder.

'Uh, what – oh . . . are we there?'

'Nearly.' Fraser poked a finger towards the window.

Connors blinked himself awake and looked to see what Fraser was pointing at. Gleaming sharply against the violet-grey of the predawn sky, two silver Mig-25 jets with red stars on their shark-fin tails were stacked up just beyond and behind Air Force One's starboard wing. Fraser moved to the window seat in front of Connors.

The nearest of the two twin-tailed fighters had the number 074 stencilled in large black figures on the fuselage just ahead of the cockpit. His wingman's number was 069. Connors could see, quite clearly, the two pilots strapped into their ejector seats. Both of them had red and white striped crash helmets with raised green visors, and oxygen masks covering the lower half of their faces. They could easily have been Americans. But instead of being raised on a farm in Iowa, 074 might have grown up among the grain of a *kolkhoz* outside Kiev, and 069, instead of coming from Atlanta, might be a boy from Odessa who was crazy about flying . . .

Fraser's aides were looking out of windows a few seats ahead of Connors. The nearest one straightened up and called back to Fraser. 'Do you see those air-to-air missiles under the wings?'

'Yeah,' said Fraser. 'Hell, that first guy's so close I could pick him off with a forty-five.'

Connors waved to the nearest Mig and the Russian pilot raised a gloved hand in reply.

Fraser poked his head over the top of the seat. 'See that? The bastard's waving at us!'

Ahead, the horizontal layer of cloud that lined the horizon was rimmed with gold. Connors sat back and closed his eyes, while Air Force One and its escort cruised serenely towards the morning.

MOSCOW/RUSSIA

The flat, olive-drab countryside to the west of Moscow was shrouded with low-lying mist as Bricker lined up Air Force One with the runway at Domodedovo and began a long, slow letdown. When they were about five miles out from the runway, with flaps out and undercarriage down, 074 waggled his wings, then both Migs peeled off in a climbing turn to the right.

They landed at 5:45 A.M. Friday, local time, and were guided to the far corner of the parking apron, where a four-car convoy of black Lincoln Continentals was waiting with a police motorcycle escort. The newest of the Lincolns was from the American Embassy. The others, all

1984 models, were flying small red hammer-and-sickle flags. While the steps were being wheeled into place, Connors looked out of one of the cabin windows on the port side and saw that the First Secretary from the American Embassy was among the small group waiting to meet them. Connors scanned their faces and recognized a senior member of the Soviet Praesidium, an Army general from Marshal Rudenkov's staff, and Tibor, one of the Kremlin's regular interpreters who always had a fund of scurrilous political jokes that on anyone else's lips would have guaranteed the teller a one-way ticket to Siberia.

Buzz Bricker came off the flight deck. 'Did you see those Mig-25s? Beautiful. Two thousand plus in top gear.'

'Were they checking up on us?' asked Connors.

'Either that or to make sure nobody jumped us. There were two more ahead of us on the port side. They picked us up just after we crossed over the border from Poland.'

Fraser came up the aisle followed by his four aides. 'Did you see that they were armed?' he asked Bricker. 'And close too. I could practically count the rivets.'

Connors let Fraser go out of the door first. Fraser paused at the top of the steps and surveyed the scene. The flags on the black limousines were almost the only bright spots of colour.

'Lincolns,' he grunted. 'They can't build a decent car of their own.'

Connors raised his hand in greeting and they began to walk down the steps. About fifty yards away a plump, middle-aged woman in a white head scarf and a faded blue cotton work coat was sweeping the concrete apron with a wide broom.

Fraser nudged Connors. 'See that? If they ever took over, that could be your mother out there.'

'I know,' said Connors. 'And the food here is terrible too.'

After the welcoming round of handshakes and introductions, Connors and Fraser exchanged a fast 'hello and good-bye' with the American First Secretary and drove off with the Russians. Apart from Fraser's four aides, the US party included NASA director Chris Matson, head of the US half of the stalled Joint Study Group, and Dan Chaliapin, the White House Russian interpreter. Connors could have translated anything Fraser wanted to say but Fraser obviously wanted to hear what Connors had to say, in English.

The convoy of Lincolns drove into Moscow, through an almost deserted Red Square past the Kremlin, and out into the wooded countryside on the other side of town. Some of the leaves on the larch trees that lined the road were beginning to turn yellow. The convoy swung left on to a side road, paused at a checkpoint manned by soldiers from one of the crack Guards regiments, then entered a fenced and heavily-guarded estate. They drove on for another mile through dense woodland and arrived at a large, beautifully restored, white-painted *dacha* complete with verandah and wood-shingle roof. Long, slanting shafts of morning sunlight cut through the backdrop of trees and spread pools of golden fire over the carpet of tall wild grasses.

Alekseii Leonovich, First Secretary of the Communist Party and Russian Premier, came out on to the verandah with Marshal Rudenkov as Connors' party spilled out of both sides of the Lincolns. There was a second round of smiles and handshakes. Connors noticed that Rudenkov was not wearing his usual chestful of medals.

Fraser cast a woodman's eye over the view from the verandah, then turned to Connors. 'Not bad . . . This is my kind of country.'

Connors smiled. 'If you're nice to them, they might let you cut down a few trees.'

Fraser eyed him but didn't say anything.

Inside the *dacha*, breakfast had been laid on a long table covered with an ornately-embroidered linen tablecloth. Spotless silver cutlery lay gleaming on either side of blue and white plates, and down the centre of the table were crystal bowls of flowers and fruit and baskets of fresh, crusty bread.

Leonovich and Marshal Rudenkov took the centre seats facing the windows on to the verandah and invited the others to take their places at the table. Connors was placed opposite Leonovich, Fraser faced the Marshal. Six buxom waitresses with yellow headscarves and white aprons over yellow dresses poured everyone a glass of freshly-squeezed orange juice.

Premier Leonovich raised his glass. Tibor stood up and translated for him. 'Gentlemen, it's a little early for vodka – even in Russia. I will spare you the usual lengthy diplomatic expressions of goodwill. I welcome you to my home and my table as friends. Let us drink to continued peace, trust, and friendship between our two great countries. May it be an example for the rest of the world to follow.'

Connors raised his glass and drank with the rest of them. The Soviet Premier's toast was doubly ironic. If God had a sense of humour, thought Connors, he would make us all choke to death. But it was not to be; the tangy juice from the sunbaked Georgian SSR slipped safely down their lying throats.

The breakfast turned out to be a leisurely forty-five-minute affair during which the conversation touched on every conceivable topic except the one that they had flown eight thousand miles to discuss. Connors made all the right noises, listened with half an ear, and made last-minute mental revisions in the carefully-prepared message he had come to deliver on behalf of the President.

The first meeting was confined to Premier Leonovich, Marshal Rudenkov, Connors, Fraser and the two interpreters. Leonovich led the way into a large book-lined study redolent with the scent of pine. Six round-backed chairs with deep-buttoned red leather seats and a table draped with red baize stood in the middle of the room on an Astrakhan carpet that covered most of the polished wood floor. The room was spotlessly clean but still managed to look lived in. Tibor carefully closed the waxed pine doors behind them.

'It's a little primitive,' said Leonovich. 'But I can't stand being cooped up in the Kremlin during the summer. My wife still prefers the Black Sea.' He pulled a lace-edged blind down over the window to take the edge off the sun.

Tibor translated for Fraser's benefit.

Leonovich gestured to Connors and Fraser to take the chairs opposite himself and Rudenkov. Chaliapin and Tibor sat between them. Fraser opened his briefcase and took out a bulky manila envelope bearing the stamp of the Defense Department, placed it on the table in front of him and sat back with folded arms.

Premier Leonovich and Marshal Rudenkov looked at the manila envelope and then at each other. Rudenkov pulled a pack of Camels out of a side pocket and offered a smoke to Fraser. Fraser shook his head. Rudenkov lit himself a cigarette and left the pack on the table. Tibor got up and brought him an ashtray.

Premier Leonovich clasped his hands together on the table and smiled at Connors. 'Now – what is it you want to talk to us about?'

With Dan Chaliapin translating, Connors began by

427

recapping the efforts made by the President to promote a better understanding between the two countries, the trade agreements, and the slow but perceptible progress towards a reduction in nuclear arms. He then moved on to review the effects of the first twenty-minute fade-out, the defensive alert, and the prompt, frank exchange of information that led to the identification of the spacecraft, Connors' visit to Moscow with Wedderkind, the agreement on a continuing exchange of information, the proposal for a two-nation search operation and the setting up of a Joint Study Group to evaluate the spacecraft if it was found. It was at this point that the world had been hit by the second, three-week fade-out which, after twelve days, had made *all* radio communication impossible. The effect on both their countries, and the other developed nations, had been shattering. But far from bringing America and Russia into closer co-operation, it had set them apart. Russia had closed her frontiers, had stopped all traffic, incoming and outgoing, all movement of people including embassy staffs, and cut all postal and telecommunication links. America's press and that of the Western world had fully publicized the troubling impact of the fade-out on their countries. But no one knew what was happening in Russia or how they had been affected. This situation had, obviously, caused the American government great concern. Leonovich nodded soberly.

'Which is why,' continued Connors, 'I have come here to confess. In spite of the agreement banning extraterritorial troop movements, the reinforcement or transfer of naval units already at sea, and the covert penetration of each other's air space, the American Government airlifted a division of Marines to Diego Garcia – to protect our interests in the Persian Gulf.'

Rudenkov puffed calmly at his cigarette. He looked amused. 'Do you think one was enough?'

'It was purely a precautionary measure,' said Connors. He smiled back at Rudenkov. 'It's also a very small island. But I am afraid that's the least of our transgressions. I have to tell you, with great regret, that the President has discovered that the Air Force has been flying continuous high-altitude photoreconnaissance missions over the Soviet Union throughout the whole three-week period of the second fade-out.'

Premier Leonovich and Marshal Rudenkov exchanged another glance.

'Go on,' said Leonovich.

'I authorized the overflights,' said Fraser. 'I believed it was my duty to do so on the grounds of national security, and the President has given his retrospective approval to my actions. It wasn't just your country; we also covered China.'

'So did we,' grunted Rudenkov.

'That doesn't excuse our actions in relation to the Soviet Union,' said Connors. 'We broke two of the specific fade-out agreements. I can only hope you can view this lack of faith as a temporary aberration. We were hit hard by the fade-out – and we panicked.'

The Soviet Premier shrugged. 'It's understandable, in the circumstances. We were also worried.' He nodded towards Rudenkov. 'These military men are sometimes hard to control. I can't even stop this one smoking. However, I don't think we need let these events stand in the way of our future co-operation.'

'No,' said Connors. 'That's very important.' He picked up the large manila envelope. 'You see, we find ourselves in a very difficult position. In breaking our word, we found that you had also broken yours.' He pulled out a sheaf of large black and white photographs, split them roughly into two equal piles and laid them in front of Leonovich and Rudenkov.

Premier Leonovich reached inside his jacket and pulled out a spectacle case. He put on a pair of half-lens reading glasses and examined the photographs that Connors had placed in front of him, then exchanged his pile with Rudenkov.

Rudenkov nodded in admiration. 'They're sharp. You've got good cameras.' He pointed out something on one of the pictures to Leonovich, then looked at Fraser. 'These pictures must have been taken on the thirty-first of August.'

Fraser nodded. 'And the first of September.'

Rudenkov raised an eyebrow but said nothing.

'We believe that the circular object in the photographs is the extraterrestrial craft our two countries located in orbit at the beginning of August,' said Connors. 'And we also believe it is the probable source of the atmospheric interference currently affecting radio communications.'

'I see,' said Leonovich. 'What did your President say when he saw these photographs?'

'He was concerned by your failure to communicate news of the landing of this craft in the Soviet Union, and worried that you might not have fully appreciated the dangers arising from your actions. He asked me to convey an urgent message to you, expressing that concern,' said Connors. 'I think it would be best if we read you his own words.'

Connors reached down into the briefcase by his chair and pulled out a stiff blue leather folder bearing the seal of the President of the United States. He gave a Xerox copy of the letter to Fraser, then opened the folder and passed it to Dan Chaliapin. The folder contained two mounted sheets of the President's notepaper on which his letter had been typed in both languages. He had signed both copies.

Dan looked at the first few lines, cleared his throat,

wiped his mouth with a handkerchief and began to read in his deep, rich Russian voice. '"To Soviet Premier Alekseii Vasilievich Leonovich. Dear Friend: Certain evidence has been presented to me which proves, beyond all doubt, that, for the last three weeks at least, units of your Army and Air Force have been aware of, and have concealed, the presence of an extraterrestrial craft in the Kazakhstan Soviet Socialist Republic. A copy of this evidence is presented with this letter.

'"In view of your past co-operation in forging closer relationships between our two countries I am saddened by the prospect that you and your colleagues in the Soviet government are actively involved in the continuing concealment of this craft – an act which is in direct breach of the verbal agreement concluded in Moscow on August eighth by representatives of our two governments.

'"You cannot be unaware of the serious, worldwide effects of the second prolonged fade-out, which, since Wednesday of this week, now face us again. The evidence I have, and which must also be shared by the Russian units involved, shows that the fade-out is directly related to the presence of the spacecraft, and that we face the constant threat of further periods of disruption for as long as the spacecraft is allowed to remain in your country. I am sure you would not wish to prolong the present situation.

'"Every hour that the fade-out is allowed to continue damages the relationship between our two countries, disrupts our economy, and creates an intolerable pressure on our system of law and order. It dangerously upsets the present balance of military power and, due to the breakdown in our command-control systems, inevitably increases the risk of an accidental and indiscriminate nuclear war between us.

'"In these circumstances, I cannot remain indifferent

to the effects of the fade-out on the rest of the world and I am sure you are also aware of your responsibility to the international community. I therefore urge you to make immediate preparations to remove this threat to world peace and stability by the most appropriate means at your disposal and in consultation with my representatives. Failure to act speedily could precipitate a situation in which we may be forced to take unilateral action to remove the spacecraft. Both of us know that the consequences of such an action would be incalculable. I beg you to act now and save us all – "'

Yours et cetera, et cetera . . .

Chaliapin passed the open folder to the Soviet Premier. He glanced through the Russian text, then shut the folder. He took off his glasses and looked at Connors.

'As you probably helped write this, would you say this was a threat?'

'No,' said Connors. 'It's an appeal to reason, for an end to mistrust, and for a return to honest negotiations.'

'Well, no one can doubt the sincerity of your President,' said Leonovich. 'And it would be pointless for us to try and deny this evidence. It's clear that we made several grave errors of judgement.'

'That's true,' said Connors. He wasn't going to press for a stronger admission of guilt. The Russians were on the hook. That was all that mattered. 'But that need not stop us from working together again. If you believe this object is the source of the fade-out, we must destroy it before it destroys us.'

Premier Leonovich ran a finger over the embossed seal on the cover of the folder. 'What would the President like us to do, drop a bomb on it?'

'If it's feasible,' said Connors. 'That's one of the things our team has come to discuss. But first, we should like to know more about it. Have either of you seen it?'

'The Marshal has,' said Leonovich.

'We've given it the code name Commissar,' said Fraser.

'Hah! Well chosen.' Rudenkov lit another cigarette and smiled broadly. 'Like all commissars, he's been making life very difficult.'

Connors was aware that both he and Leonovich appeared quite unabashed at being confronted with proof of their deception, and he couldn't figure out why. It looked as if the double play was going to work, but it all seemed to be going too easily . . .

'Is it a spacecraft?' asked Connors. Both he and Fraser had to act as if they knew nothing about it.

'It's a craft of some kind,' admitted Rudenkov. 'But it didn't land. It came out of the ground.'

'You mean you think it landed somewhere else and burrowed its way towards Lake Balkash?'

'It's a possibility that's been considered,' said Rudenkov. 'You'll have to talk to someone like Grigorienko for the scientific view. Not that our scientists know all that much. They're as baffled as the rest of us.'

'So, what is the situation?' asked Connors.

Rudenkov took a long pull on his cigarette. 'In a large nutshell, it's this: on the twenty-seventh of August, thirty-eight coal miners were trapped five hundred metres underground when a series of mine shafts collapsed – due apparently to a severe earth tremor. Four days later, a circular, incandescent object, twenty-five metres in diameter and five metres tall, surfaced in a deserted area southwest of Lake Balkash. Two days after surfacing, all atmospheric interference had terminated.'

'How far away was the coal mine?' asked Connors.

'About six hundred and fifty kilometres, north of the craft's present position.'

Connors looked at Fraser. If the two incidents were related, as the Russians seemed to think, Commissar had obviously landed in the wrong place and had been burning his way through the earth to his allotted position at about six and a half kilometres an hour.

'Did you find the craft's original landing point?'

Premier Leonovich shook his head. 'An aerial search has been made, but, so far, we have found nothing. I'm told it's possible that it may have landed in some other country.' He smiled. 'It could have been America.'

Connors' heart missed a beat. He looked surprised. 'America?'

'Why not?' said Leonovich. 'If it can travel six hundred kilometres why not six thousand?'

Connors thought it was time to switch back to Rudenkov. 'What happened after it surfaced?'

'On cooling,' continued Rudenkov, 'the object was seen to be made of a semitranslucent black crystal. The shape was like an overturned saucer. The material defied conventional analysis but the tests proved it to be of exceptional hardness. Approximately one metre below the surface, a second layer of material with a moulded surface pattern like the human brain was observed. There were no hatches, panels or protuberances of any kind. All attempts to excavate the object were repulsed by a strong magnetic field, generation of heat, ultrasonic waves, or by generation of a force field that neutralized all electrical apparatus.' Rudenkov smiled. 'You can see I have memorized the reports quite well. Two days ago, radar transmissions were once again interrupted, and a force field with a diameter of eleven kilometres was generated around the object. In addition to these two problems, there are indications that the object is growing.'

'Growing?' Connors did his best to look puzzled.

It all sounded depressingly familiar except for two important points. Commissar had no spherical hatch, and thus contained no equivalent of Friday. Connors knew

434

that Commissar's present position was almost exactly on the same latitude as Crusoe, and on the reciprocal longitude. It hinted at some kind of pattern, a symmetry, but did it mean anything more than a tidy mind, as Wetherby had suggested?

'Once you knew where it was,' said Connors, 'why did you conceal it from us?'

'That was a temporary arrangement,' replied Leonovich. 'Some of our people thought it might prove technically advantageous to try to find the mechanism by which Commissar, as you call it, impeded radar transmissions.' He smiled. 'I'm sure, if the situation had been reversed, some of your people would have suggested a similar cover-up.'

'It's possible,' said Connors. 'But the fact remains that, wherever it landed, Commissar surfaced inside the borders of the Soviet Union.'

Leonovich pursed his lips and nodded in slow agreement. Marshal Rudenkov leaned over to Tibor and whispered behind his hand. Tibor got up and left the room.

Rudenkov wagged a finger at Fraser. 'Sending your planes over was not a wise thing to do. Our air and rocket forces were on a full war alert for the whole three weeks. One slip and we would have all been finished.'

'If we hadn't taken the chance, we would never have known you had double-crossed us,' said Fraser aimiably.

Connors winced, then relaxed as Chaliapin tactfully translated 'double-crossed' as 'something to hide'. Tibor returned with a heavy brown briefcase.

Rudenkov unlocked it and pulled out a bulky green file untidily stuffed with papers and tied with blue tape. He began to pick at the knot with blunt fingers. 'I'm glad we have this chance to speak frankly,' he said. 'I think it's about time we got this game over with. The truth is this spacecraft has given us a big headache as well. You may

435

have had problems, but you haven't got the Chinese sitting on your back doorstep. We've already done some thinking on how best to get rid of this thing, but, as you know, that is only half the problem.' Rudenkov finally got the knot undone. He untied the file and removed a large brown envelope.

Connors recognized the colour and felt a chill premonition of disaster.

Premier Leonovich laid his hand on the blue leather folder containing the President's message. 'My friend, I think you should take this back. We have both broken our word in a patriotic attempt to protect our two countries, but there is no longer anything to be gained by continuing this deception. It's time for a fresh start.' Leonovich pushed the folder across the table to Connors. 'If you genuinely wish to resume *honest* negotiations, then you could begin by explaining this.' The Soviet Premier took the envelope from Marshal Rudenkov and dropped it on top of the one that Fraser had brought from the Defense Department in Washington. They were identical.

Fraser stared at the two envelopes with stunned disbelief. Connors picked up the top one, read the name and address printed in the top left-hand corner and offered it to Fraser.

'Since it's from your office, maybe you'd better open it.'

Fraser took it from him and untucked the flap. 'How did you get hold of this?'

Rudenkov shrugged. 'Through a friend . . .'

Inside were a dozen ten-by-twelve-inch black and white photographs. They had all been printed with a US Air Force serial number and the words 'TOP SECRET' in white in the bottom right-hand corner, and on the back, stamped in red, were the words 'Department of Defense'.

The pictures included oblique aerial shots of the crater on Crow Ridge, Crusoe, Friday, views of the Rockville buildings and trailer site, and the base camp on Highway 22. Fraser and Connors had both seen some of the photos before. They formed part of a series taken by a special Air Force unit documenting the Crusoe project.

Fraser slid the photographs towards Connors. 'They even got a picture of you.'

Connors looked down at the photographs but didn't pick them up. He opened his mouth to say something but the words remained locked in his throat. As he sat back helplessly, Rudenkov slapped the table and roared with good-natured laughter.

It was the first time Connors had been caught lying since he'd stolen money from his mother's purse at the age of eight. The lies hadn't stopped, of course, but the shock and humiliation of that first exposure had brought out the secretive side of his character. Over the years, nourished by success, the carefully-planned deceptions and smooth-tongued explanations had grown in complexity, and somewhere along the line, he had begun to lie to himself. The silken yarn of deceit had become so closely interwoven with the raw thread of truth it was impossible to distinguish one from the other.

Coming to America, the street-level crash course in communication, competing against the homegrown boys on the block, using his native cunning wherever he lacked physical strength, citizenship, changing his name, recreating the past – it had all helped spin a protective cocoon around himself. This time, he had been well and truly nailed. The photographs in front of him, supplied by a Red well-wisher in Washington, had exposed him for what he was, the principal agent and instigator of a deliberate attempt by the government of one nation to deceive another – a nation with whom he had worked for years in a genuine effort to achieve better relations.

He'd come a long way from the case of the missing fifty cents but the pain he felt was as fresh as it had been thirty years ago. Connors took a deep breath and started again. 'What is it you want to know?'

'Everything,' said Leonovich. 'Our friend has kept us well informed on the Crusoe Project but we'd like to hear it again from you.'

The only way out of that situation was to tell the truth. It would be an interesting experience. 'I think this would be a good time to bring in the rest of our team,' said Connors.

'Good . . . we'll move next door.' Leonovich stood up. Connors and the others followed suit.

Marshal Rudenkov approached Fraser with an amused twinkle in his eye and said, in heavily-accented English, 'No more double-cross – finish, okay?' He held out his hand.

'Okay . . .'

'Good.' Rudenkov gripped Fraser's hand and pumped it up and down as if he was trying to raise water from a fifty-foot well. He picked up his pack of Camel cigarettes and showed it to Fraser. 'American fantastic. You – we fight German together. Is good. Now we fight again.' Then speaking in rapid Russian, with Tibor translating, Rudenkov said, 'If we don't get rid of these two black-heads soon, we will all end up planting rice.' He made a swift hammer movement with his fist. 'I think it's vital we hit them both at the same time.'

'I agree,' said Fraser. 'It's our only chance.'

Marshal Rudenkov patted Fraser on the arm and walked out of the study with Premier Leonovich. Tibor followed.

'It looks as if we struck out with all bases loaded,' said Chaliapin.

Connors smiled. 'Don't worry, Dan. We may still come out even at the end of the series.' He put the President's rejected message back in his briefcase and wondered how to pull himself clear of the wreckage. They'd achieved their objective – Russian co-operation – but his artful plan had fallen flat on its face, casting doubts on the President's integrity and badly weakening his own credibility as a negotiator with the Russians. It could even mean an end to his usefulness. Yet there was still no joy in it for Fraser, for it was the photographs stolen by someone with access to highly sensitive areas of the Defense Department that had demolished their negotiating position. Whoever it was had to be on, or close to, the Crusoe Project. All the photographs connected with the Project were processed in the mobile lab on Crow Ridge, then forwarded to the Defense Department for strictly limited 'eyes only' distribution.

Fraser picked up the stolen envelope. 'When I get back, I swear I'm going to track down the son of a bitch who did this. I don't care if I have to take the Pentagon apart brick by brick.' He slipped it into his case and snapped down the locks. 'Otherwise we might as well give them the keys to the whole fucking building.'

'It looks as if they've already got them,' said Connors.

CROW RIDGE/MONTANA

Throughout the rest of Thursday, Crusoe continued to change shape, and by Friday morning, the last vestiges of the dome had disappeared. The spherical hatch was completely enclosed within the black crystal hull. The hull itself now had the profile of a shallow, smooth-tipped Islamic dome made up of four curving sections. Neame

439

supervised the dawn survey and reported that Crusoe was now thirty-three and a half feet tall and eighty-six feet wide. He had grown some ten and a half feet taller in the last eighteen hours. The figures were plotted on a graph. It showed that the growth curve, although still rising steeply, was beginning to arc over to the right. It was an encouraging sign. If the line continued to curve into a sloping S-shape, it meant that the growth rate would slacken and then peter out altogether as Crusoe reached his full height.

'Can you project the curve to give us some idea of where that point might be?' asked Wedderkind.

'Not yet,' said Neame. 'We really need to plot a couple more measurements on the graph before we can extrapolate with any degree of accuracy.'

'I don't think we ought to overlook the possibility that if the curve *does* level out, the period of zero growth might merely be a prelude to a new growth cycle,' said Page.

'Page,' said Neame. 'I'm really getting pissed off with you – '

'Now, gentlemen, gentlemen,' began Lovell.

Neame ignored him. 'The only time you come alive is when you're spreading bad news. If you really want to tell us something, how about telling us how this thing does what it's doing? You're supposed to be a chemist. Shouldn't you be coming up with the answers?'

'I've taken *my* share of the work as far as I can,' huffed Page. 'My reports and analyses are all complete. I don't see why I should be made responsible for other people's incompetence.'

'In other words,' said Neame, 'you've got no fucking idea what's happening.'

'Okay, okay, that's enough,' said Wedderkind. 'Let's

just hold it right there.' He moved in between Neame and Page.

'Totally unnecessary,' muttered Lovell. 'I've rarely seen such infantile behaviour – '

'Yes, okay, Mike,' said Wedderkind. Lovell, the senior, grey-haired member of the team, preferred a calmer, contemplative, pipe-smoking approach to all problems, no matter how pressing. 'I guess we're all getting a little jumpy – '

'Disgraceful . . .' Lovell was still puffing away in the background.

'Mike . . .' Wedderkind silenced him with a look. 'It's only natural in view of what's happened. The loss of three colleagues, the continued frustration of our research efforts and now, the tension due to the general deterioration of conditions here on the Ridge and the lack of sleep. Let's just keep calm and keep it together.' Wedderkind turned to Neame. 'I don't think any of us can tell you what's happening, Rog. I certainly can't – in fact, I think it's time to admit that we are all way out of our depth. The best we can do is watch, in the hope of understanding something.'

Neame nodded and began to simmer down.

'What do you want to do?' asked Wedderkind. 'Go on checking at twelve-hour intervals?'

'Yes. It'll save us getting up in the middle of the night,' said Neame. 'Not that we're going to get much sleep with those tremors.'

'No . . . I think I ought to mention that General Allbright has suggested that because of the tremors, the cutoff zone and the, ah – general air of uncertainty, we should begin a partial evacuation of the Ridge, starting with nonessential personnel. If any of you feel you fall into that category, let me know after breakfast.'

'Do we just put down our own names, or can we

441

suggest other people?' Neame's question was aimed at Wedderkind, but his eyes were on Page.

At 6 P.M. Neame went out again with his team to check Crusoe's measurements. They found that Crusoe had grown five feet taller and four feet wider since their dawn survey. He was now thirty-nine feet tall and ninety feet wide. The ground around the base of the hull had been fractured and pushed back as his width had increased. The spherical hatch was now almost completely swallowed up by the underlying cortex which, as far as they could tell, was still its original size.

The new measurements were plotted on the graph and they showed that the growth rate was continuing to slacken.

'What do you think, Rog?' asked Wedderkind.

'Well, if we take the optimistic view, he could stabilize at a height of anything between fifty and sixty feet, somewhere around Tuesday or Wednesday. You can see the curve I've projected, but it's still just a guess. The line between the dawn plot and this evening's is not curving over to the right all *that* much.'

'No, but it's going to have to start soon,' mused Wedderkind. 'The Ridge isn't big enough for both of us.'

'There's something else that's bugging us,' said Gilligan, one of the other three remaining engineers. 'The angular difference between the four curved surfaces of the hull.'

'What about it?' asked Wedderkind.

'It's increasing.'

'So – ?'

'Well, I know we have to accept the fact that Crusoe can grow, even if we don't know how, but with all this talk about a possible takeoff surely the logical end result would be a tall, streamlined shape.'

'Yes,' said Vincent. 'Like the nose cone of a rocket.'

442

'With a circular cross section,' said Hadden.

'But it's not happening,' said Neame. 'This cat's growing corners.'

While the research group was busy discussing these latest observations, one of the Corporation's converted diesels came up to collect another batch of cadets for medical processing. The driver had a message for Allbright from the base camp. A cadet took it over to the command hut on horseback. Allbright was going over details of the temporary evacuation with his two senior cadets, Harris and Cameron, and Kirkonnen, the senior Air Force technician.

Allbright read the brief message. It was the signal he'd been waiting for. 'Mr Harris, I'm going to leave you to supervise the rest of the evacuation to the base camp area.' He looked at his watch. 'I have to go to Washington. The Defense Department has cancelled all further medical checks so you may need to modify the timetable we've set up.'

'Yes, sir.'

'Any further movement orders for Air Force personnel will come through the Corporation's office manager down at the base camp. In the meantime, I expect you and Mr Cameron to give Mr Wedderkind and Mr Connors your full co-operation. Is that understood?'

'Yes, sir,' said Harris. 'Shall I call up a diesel?'

'No. It's a beautiful evening, I think I'll ride over to Broken Mill. If you'd care to escort me, we'll leave in thirty minutes.'

Harris, Cameron, and Kirkonnen were already on their feet before Allbright was halfway out of his chair. He pocketed his silver fountain pen, picked up the folding leather picture wallet containing the colour portraits of his wife, son, and daughter, and shook hands with Kirkonnen.

'Good-bye, Mr Kirkonnen. In case I don't get back in time to see you off, I'd like you to convey my thanks and appreciation to your team.'

'Thank you, sir. Does this mean the project is closing down?'

'I won't know till I get to Washington, Mr Kirkonnen. So until it's official, I'd like you to kill any rumours to that effect. It might turn out that you'll be here longer than you expect.'

'I understand, sir.'

'Good luck . . .' Allbright turned to his senior cadets. 'A pack horse for the baggage, Mr Harris.'

'Yes, sir.'

The guard detail turned out to salute Allbright as he rode through the main gate followed by Harris and Cameron. The pack horse, with Allbright's two Air Force-blue duffel bags, was hitched to Cameron's saddle. Allbright turned off the dirt road and headed down into the pines on the north flank of the Ridge. After fifteen minutes of weaving and ducking under branches, the pines thinned out and they rode into the open country east of Bodell's shack. It was unfenced prairie with a sparse covering of buffalo grass and patches of sweet-smelling sage.

Allbright heeled his horse into a canter and moved ahead, kicking up a line of dust that hung, glowing, in the still evening air. Harris and Cameron swung out on either side and stayed with him. To their left, the September sun had dropped into the last quarter of the sky, turning the distant sandstone buttes into slabs of gold. To their right, spaced-out lines of small, flat-bottomed heaps of cloud floated towards the North Dakota line.

A Twin Comanche from the Miles City air-taxi outfit

was waiting at the highway end of the emergency grass strip, and the posse of small boys who'd followed the arrival and departure of Connors was perched on the fence near the parked aeroplane. Some of them wore brown stetsons that were nearly as big as they were.

Allbright dismounted and patted his horse's neck and nose while Cameron loaded his baggage aboard the aeroplane. Allbright handed the reins to Harris.

'Would you ride him back, Mr Harris?'

'It will be a pleasure, sir.'

'And when it's time, make sure he gets clear.'

'Yes, sir. Good luck.'

'Thank you, Mr Harris. We may all need some of that.' Allbright shook hands with him and ducked through the fence. Both engines of the Twin Comanche were already running. Allbright shook hands with Cameron, then climbed on to the low wing and settled in beside the pilot. He pulled the door shut and buckled himself into his seat. As he looked up, he found the pilot looking at him in surprise.

'Well, I'll be damned . . . what the hell're you doing in this neck of the woods, General?'

'Just visiting,' said Allbright. There was no point in denying his identity. He had no idea who the grizzled, square-faced pilot was. 'Where did we meet?'

'In the war. I was flying B-52s with the 92nd out of Guam. You paid us a visit with General Westmoreland. October '73. Just before we came back to the States. You flew with us on our last mission over 'Nam.'

'Ahh . . . yes.'

The pilot grinned. 'It's okay, you don't have to try and remember me. We weren't introduced then. The name's Korvin. I made major before I came out.'

Korvin took a good look around and pushed the throttles wide open. Cameron, who had moved ahead of

445

the aeroplane on the port side, gave them a double thumbs-up signal. Korvin replied with a raised hand, then released the brakes. The Twin Comanche gathered speed quickly, bumping gently over the uneven ground, then lifted into the air. Korvin retracted the undercarriage and flaps, trimmed the aircraft into a steady climb and banked gently around towards the north.

They levelled out at fifteen hundred feet. Korvin leaned towards Allbright and tapped the compass. 'When I flew up from Miles City, according to that, I was flying south. There's a big magnetic disturbance in this area. It's been getting worse in the past few weeks. The papers say there's trouble all over. I guess that's why the Air Force is up on Crow Ridge.'

'Are there many people down at Miles City who share that view?' asked Allbright.

'A few,' said Korvin. He made a slight adjustment to the rudder trim.

'Then I think it's your duty to straighten them out, Major. I can assure you that there are no Air Force units operating in the area of Broken Mill – and I also think that you've got me mixed up with someone else. Do you read me?'

'Loud and clear,' said Korvin. He smiled. 'You don't have to worry about me, General. The CIA put our outfit on the payroll several weeks ago. Best thing that ever happened to us. First thing we did was put a down payment on this aeroplane. I don't care who's up on the Ridge. I just hope they stay there till we make enough to buy ourselves another twin.'

Back on Crow Ridge, the news of Allbright's departure filtered through to the research group around nine that evening when people were starting to light the acetylene lamps. Page put his nose against the windows of

446

Allbright's trailer and returned to report it stripped of all signs of occupation.

'I thought I saw him ride off with Harris and Cameron.'

'Maybe the *Herr General* has moved into the base camp,' said Neame.

'What did you do?' asked Gilligan. 'Put him down as NEP?' The term 'non-essential personnel' had been quickly abbreviated to its three initials.

'He's gone to Washington,' said Wedderkind, then hurriedly added, 'at least, I imagine that's, er – where he's gone.'

'Why didn't you go with him?' asked Brecetti.

'Phil, his trip may be nothing to do with the project,' said Wedderkind. 'Allbright has been made a member of the National Security Council. They may be reviewing the current situation. Or maybe the Russians have been up to something.'

'Oh, marvellous, that's all we need,' said Collis.

'A bit odd, though,' said Lovell. 'He could at least have said good-bye to you. The way these Air Force people behave sometimes, we might as well not be here.'

Wedderkind shrugged but didn't say anything. Allbright *had* said good-bye to him – Crow Ridge style . . .

Saturday/September 22

With Washington's National Airport closed, the sky over the city was completely empty. Greg Mitchell looked at his watch. 7:26 A.M. . . . Air Force One's ETA at Andrews Field was 07:30. Gene Samuels nudged Greg's

447

arm and pointed to a tiny grey speck which slowly grew wings and engines and then resolved itself into a Boeing 707. Air Force One. Bricker floated her in over the masts of the approach lights and dropped the nosewheel on to the centre line of the runway at precisely 07:30.

Connors and Fraser said good-bye to the seven-man flight crew and led the other passengers down the steps.

'Good trip?' asked Greg.

Connors patted his arm. 'The best I can say is that it all worked out beautifully in the worst possible way. I'll fill you in later.' He turned to the two Russians who'd followed them out of the aeroplane and introduced them to Gene Samuels and Greg.

Vasily Grigorienko, Chris Matson's opposite number, and General Yevgeny Golubev, Rudenkov's senior aides, had both been at the meetings in the Soviet Premier's *dacha*. In his civilian clothes, Golubev looked like Lee J. Cobb in a 1947 gangster movie. The two Russians had come over as observers to meet Wedderkind and the research group, and to monitor the attack on Crusoe. Chris Matson had stayed on in Moscow and would fly out to Kazakhstan to perform a similar function when he was joined by the second US observer. Arkhip Karamatov, the Russian liaison man who had worked with Matson at NASA's Houston headquarters, would be hosting his stay in the USSR. Connors and Fraser had discussed who should be the Number Two man on the return flight but had not made a final choice. Connors had a feeling that their indecision stemmed from the unpredictable outcome of the attack. Deep down, they weren't sure whether to send the right man or someone they wanted to get rid of.

'Did you get the hotel fixed up?' asked Connors.

'Yes, it's all set,' said Greg. 'I'll stick with them, and when you're ready I'll bring 'em over to the White House.'

'Good. The General would like to go downtown. I think he wants to buy a new suit.'

'Off the rack?'

'Whatever he wants. Just don't take him to Arnold's nephew.'

Greg laughed. Connors looked around and signalled to Dan Chaliapin. 'Dan, I know you could do with some sleep, but could you go with these guys?'

'Yes, certainly.'

'In that case, can you round up our Cossacks and get them into the second car in the line?' asked Greg. 'I'd like to make tracks before the traffic builds up.'

The shiny, olive-drab Presidential helicopter provided and flown by the Army whisked Connors and the others across town to the lawn of the White House.

THE WHITE HOUSE/WASHINGTON DC

Connors, Fraser, and Samuels left the Department of Defense aides downstairs and went up to see the President. General Allbright and the three Joint Chiefs of Staff – General Wills, Air Force General Clayson, and Admiral Garrison – were already in the room. Everyone looked eager to hear the outcome of their visit to Moscow.

Connors gave them the good news first: a firm Russian agreement to attack Commissar on Wednesday the twenty-sixth of September. Time over target, 6 A.M. But in Kazakhstan the clock was running thirteen hours ahead of Crow Ridge. If the attacks were to be synchronized, time over the target in Montana would be 5 P.M., Tuesday, the twenty-fifth of September. The Russians had also accepted the American proposal to send observers to review the Russian research findings on Commissar and to watch the nuclear explosion.

'That's good,' said the President. 'But it's sooner than

I expected.' He swivelled his chair towards Fraser. 'With all this latest trouble can we be ready to go on Tuesday?'

'No problem. We would have preferred to go in the morning but we gave them first choice.'

'Yes, of course. Good move.'

'It still gives us nearly four hours of daylight.'

Allbright caught the President's questioning glance. 'Both crews are now at full alert status. They have flown daily practice missions over the target for the last two weeks. I'm sure they could fly the route blindfold. And the bombardiers have put up impressive scores in training. The only thing that can stop us is bad weather and heavy cloud over the target, but all the forecasts for the area are looking good.'

'That's also why the Russians want to go by midweek,' said Fraser.

'And everything's covered – I mean you don't anticipate any last-minute hangups with electromechanical problems?'

'No, sir,' said Allbright. 'The new cutoff zone reaches an altitude of thirty-seven thousand feet. If you can imagine it, it's like a transparent circular bowl stuck upside down over Crow Ridge. We'll be flying at an altitude of fifty thousand feet, well clear of the effects of the cutoff zone. An optical bombsight replaces the normal computerized radar system, and of course our normal radio communication and direction-finding equipment is out. We'll be using our inertial navigation system to get us there.'

'The bomb itself is rigged to detonate on impact,' said Fraser. 'The major change is a switch from the thirteen-stage electrical arming sequence to a simpler, manual one. It's additional insurance.'

'What about the Russians?' asked the President.

'They'd already been making preparations before we

turned up with our, ah – proposition,' said Fraser. 'To a large extent their thinking parallels ours. As you'd expect.'

'Still, if they were in a jam, we could always offer them our reserve aircraft. I suppose we've got more than one of these modified bombs, haven't we?'

'Yes,' said Fraser. He shot a glance at Connors.

'I think they've got that side of things pretty well in hand,' said Connors.

'I'd like to have been there when you laid those pictures of Commissar on the table,' said the President.

'It was quite a moment,' said Connors. 'Maybe we could come back on that when we've got CAMPFIRE sewn up.'

'Sure . . .' The President saw that Allbright wanted to say something. 'Go ahead, Mitch.'

'Thank you, sir. In order to provide maximum security I would like to fly with the selected crew on the mission against Crow Ridge.'

Connors could see from Fraser's expression that the request was unexpected.

The President looked undecided. 'What do you think, Chuck?'

'Well, sir, if – in his judgement – Mitch thinks it's necessary, I'd be prepared to agree.'

'Mel?'

'I'd like to ask why he *does* think it necessary. You picked these two crews, Mitch. Don't you trust them?'

'Implicitly. But in spite of all our preparations, we're flying a mission into the unknown. In World War Two, it was the practice for squadron commanders to lead the toughest missions. I regard this as a similar situation. We may not get a second chance. I want to go along to ensure that, whatever happens, the attack is pressed home – all the way.'

451

Allbright's manner was firm, his voice quietly matter-of-fact. Nobody said anything immediately, but Connors was sure that they all had the same thought in their heads. Something else from World War Two – when Japanese pilots flew their planes straight into the US carriers. If things got rough, Allbright intended to make a kamikaze attack on Crusoe by riding the big B-52 all the way down to the Ridge.

'Okay, Mitch,' said Fraser. 'You handle it whichever way you want.'

'Thanks.'

'Evacuation,' said Connors.

General Wills pulled the cigar from his mouth. 'That's my department. I'm putting in a mechanized airborne unit to clear and seal off a circular area with a twenty-mile radius around Crow Ridge. We're also calling out the local National Guard detachment from Miles City and we've already alerted the State evacuation agency.'

As one of the states with a heavy concentration of Minuteman 3 ICBM silos, Montana was one of the prime targets for Russian missiles, and in 1974 planning had begun to cover the speedy mass evacuation and relocation of a major part of the population in the event of imminent nuclear war.

'What reason are you giving for the evacuation – and how are you going to keep it out of the newspapers?' asked the President. 'Won't the place be full of out-of-state tourists at this time of the year?'

'There're not too many in eastern Montana,' said Wills. 'Most of them head up to the area around Fort Peck or stay close to the Yellowstone. Both are well clear of the evacuation area. But it will mean closing Highway 22, the main north-south link. Our cover story is quite straightforward – a top-secret, prototype nuclear-powered rocket went out of control during orbital tests and crashed

452

on Crow Ridge. Cause – the short, sharp burst of deep-space radiation that triggered the first fade-out. Problem – the nuclear reactor was not destroyed in the landing. Air Force scientists have been working in an effort to dismantle the reactor, have failed, and there is now the risk of an imminent explosion followed by radioactive fall-out. Hence the evacuation.'

'Well, it would convince me,' said the President. 'How about the troops involved?'

'They will be briefed with exactly the same story,' said Wills. 'We don't want a lot of conflicting information flying around. It could start a panic.'

The President nodded. 'That's true. We have to do everything we can to contain this thing.'

'I think you ought to tell the people you are evacuating that it was a *Russian* nuclear-powered rocket,' said Connors. 'You could then brief the press and stress the vital importance of not letting the Russians know we've got hold of it. It will give us a good reason for having kept the whole situation under wraps and it also shifts the blame for the evacuation, subsequent damage, and general inconvenience off our backs and on to theirs. And since no one in his patriotic mind will print a word of what's going on, the Russians won't have the opportunity to deny it. And when it's over, we have a better than even chance that the press will go along with whatever statement we put out.'

They all considered the proposition. It will be, vowed Connors, my last deception.

'It's kind of sneaky, but it certainly takes the heat off us.' The President looked for signs of opposition. There didn't appear to be any. 'Is that okay, Vernon?'

'Anything that makes life easier,' said Wills. 'But compensation will still have to be paid out of federal funds.'

'Sure, no question,' said Connors. 'We're not going to start an international lawsuit for damages.'

'Okay, let's go with that,' said the President. 'When do you plan to start?'

'The order will go out as soon as this meeting is concluded,' said Wills. 'The National Guard units were alerted yesterday and told to report this morning for a snap tactical exercise. Evacuation is scheduled to be completed by twenty-four hundred hours Sunday. That's a clear forty-one hours before Chuck's B-52 arrives over the Ridge.'

'I still have to break the news to the people on the project,' said Connors.

'You can do that on the telephone from here,' said the President.

'Well, with respect – and with your permission – I'd like to make one last trip out there. The only phone line working is into the base camp. I wouldn't like Arnold and the others to get the news secondhand.'

'All you're doing is adding one more person to the list of people to be evacuated. Your job is over now.'

'I feel I owe it to them,' insisted Connors. 'And my job won't be over until they are clear and there's nothing left on Crow Ridge except a big hole in the ground.'

'Okay, do it your way,' said the President. 'I don't want any of my staff feeling emotionally deprived.'

'Thanks,' Connors turned to Fraser. 'What are the arrangements for evacuating the Ridge and the base camp?'

'They'll be moving out under their own steam,' said Fraser. 'The Corporation will see that everybody gets clear well ahead of time.'

Connors turned to McKenna. 'Does that mean your front man out there is in charge?'

'Yes, Rizzik, the office manager down at the base camp.

454

He'll make sure that there is adequate transportation. But technically, he's just servicing the Ridge. Until the Crusoe Project officially closes down, the man out there giving the orders is Wedderkind – that is until you get there.'

'Got it. I imagine he and the research group will want to hang on until the last possible minute. We can start by getting most of the Air Force units away first. The biggest snag will be the time we need for medical processing.'

'You don't need to worry about that,' said Fraser. 'When I sent the signal from Moscow recalling General Allbright to Washington, I also countermanded the quarantine order covering Ridge personnel. It was clear from the negative results of the several tests on yourself and General Allbright that there was no health hazard, either physical or mental, to any of the people in contact with Crusoe, and that further widespread testing would be time-consuming and would prove equally negative.'

'That's good.'

'Yeah, but that doesn't mean your people can fool around until the last minute,' growled Wills. 'It may only take half an hour to move those trucks twenty miles, but I suggest you clear the area by midnight Monday. That will give us from first light on Tuesday till midday for our helicopters to make a final check of the fire zone. Anyone still in there after that gets a free ticket to the barbecue.'

'Have you got that, Bob? I don't want us to get into a cliff-hanger situation by a last-minute pursuit of scientific knowledge.'

'Or a sit-down strike by Arnold and his boys,' said Fraser.

'That's why I want to go out there.' Connors smiled at the President. 'My biggest worry is that when they hear what's coming, someone may get killed in the rush. But if there is any argument, I'm sure General Allbright's cadets will give me a hand to carry away any protesters.'

'No problem,' said Allbright. 'You'll have their full support.'

'When do you plan to go out there?' asked the President.

'I thought I'd go early on Sunday,' said Connors. 'I only managed a brief nap on the way out. I'd like to grab four good hours before I get into this.'

'Sure, I understand. Okay, it looks as if we're in good shape,' said the President. He stood up, bringing everyone else with him. 'Let's move ahead with the final phase of Operation CAMPFIRE. Vernon, do you want to start by getting your show on the road?'

'I'll go back to the Pentagon and send the signal now,' said Wills.

'Make sure your people are briefed the way Bob has suggested.

'Yes, sir.'

The President shook Allbright's hand. 'Good luck and good hunting.'

Allbright left with the three Joint Chiefs of Staff. McKenna and Samuels started to head for the door before they caught Fraser's signal to stay. The President returned to his swivel chair behind the heavy desk and motioned them to sit down again.

'Now . . . what did the Russians say when you hit them with the pictures of Commissar?'

Connors looked at Fraser. 'Ah, Mel – maybe it would be better if you took it from here.'

As Fraser described the way the Russians had trumped their hand with pictures of Crusoe, the President's frown deepened. He sank back into his big wing chair and pinched the bridge of his nose.

'In one sense, it doesn't affect our position,' continued

456

Fraser. 'We achieved our basic objective – a joint attack on Crusoe and Commissar.'

'And in every other sense they made dummies out of us,' said the President. He appeared to have entirely forgotten that it was his own loaded response to a question put to him by Fraser on Friday, August tenth, that had initiated the whole Crusoe cover-up. Nobody seemed to think it was an appropriate moment to remind him.

'How in hell am I ever going to be able to face these guys again? How am I going to get them to believe anything that I say – or that *any* of us say?' He flashed a sharp glance at Connors and picked up the blue leather folder containing his message that Premier Leonovich had rejected. 'It's humiliating . . . If we'd played it square with them from the start, I would never have got sucked into signing this garbage.' The President tossed the folder aside.

'That's not quite fair,' said Fraser. 'It was a good plan. And it would have worked if someone involved with this project – and probably from my department – hadn't fed those photographs to the Russians.'

Connors was surprised by Fraser's unexpected leap to his defence.

'I'm more worried about some of the other things he might have got his hands on,' said Samuels. 'Like the reports on the effect of the fade-out on our operational capabilities.'

'That's your problem. Just find the leak, plug it, and send me an estimate of the damage.' The President turned back to Fraser. 'I know Bob thought it was a good plan. Naturally, it was his idea. But it was a gamble, Mel. You know that as well as I do. However I don't want to get dragged into an argument about that. The point is the plan didn't work and it's got my name on it.'

'I did have a long talk with Premier Leonovich before we left,' said Connors. 'I think I managed to convince him that the whole thing was my idea. And that it was only with the greatest reluctance that you put your name to the document. When the dust settles, I think you'll find that we managed to carve most of the blame away from you. We'll come out of this all right.'

'Well, I know *I* will,' said the President pointedly.

Connors tried but couldn't remember a day when his fortunes had slipped so badly. It was clear that whatever he said, he had no hope of winning this particular exchange, even though, this time, Fraser was in there rooting for him.

'Is there anything else, or have I had all today's bad news?'

'There are a couple more points, but I wouldn't call it bad news,' said Connors. 'As part of the deal, the Russians want two of their people to meet Arnold's research group and monitor the attack on Crusoe. We brought them back with us.'

'Great. What would you like me to do – ask them over for tea?'

'That's entirely up to you. Their visit is being kept a secret.'

'Are they important?'

'Grigorienko's a big noise at Star City. He was the man the Russians named as head of their half of the Joint Study Group. General Golubev is one of Rudenkov's senior aides. Chris Matson, whom we left over there, pulls the same weight as Grigorienko. We need to send someone to match the General.'

The President didn't hesitate. 'Garrison can go. It will give the Navy a chance to do something useful for a change.'

As an ex-Navy man, Connors recognized it as a parting shot aimed at him – below the waterline.

By Saturday morning, the angular difference between the planes of the four curving sections had increased even more. One of the Air Force photographers was lifted skyward on the defunct TV camera platform of the balloon to get some overhead shots of the hull. His pictures, processed down at the base camp, showed that Crusoe's originally circular plan view was looking decidedly square. His height had increased a further four and three-quarters feet, and his width was now ninety-three feet. Plotted on Neame's graph, the figures showed that Crusoe's growth rate was slackening, but there was still no sign of it levelling out.

The photographs were passed around the table in the research hut for everyone to look at. Wetherby frowned at one of the plan views and a side view for a long time and said, 'I know this may sound crazy but I think Crusoe's turning into a pyramid.'

Wedderkind took the pictures back from Wetherby and had another look for himself. The hull was still too curved for him to visualize it as clearly as Wetherby had, but the idea triggered off a whole new set of possibilities.

Pyramid cults had existed since the dawn of history and the pyramid remained a potent symbol of arcane magic. In recent years, scientists had become aware that, as a form, the pyramid possessed peculiar physical properties that they were at a loss to explain. It had been demonstrated that the pyramid could arrest the process of decay, perhaps even alter the nature of Time itself. It seemed to act as a focal point, a condenser, for what modern students of the ancient mysteries believed were the elemental life forces permeating the universe. Whatever the truth might be, a new pyramid was growing on the Ridge. If they were lucky, if Crusoe withstood the planned attack, and if they themselves survived what would inevitably follow, the answers to their questions might be found within it.

Wedderkind walked up on to the plateau with Wetherby, Collis, and Brecetti and took a long look at Crusoe.

'The engineers were right about the shape,' said Brecetti. 'He's not getting ready to move, he's settling in.'

'Are you sorry?' asked Wedderkind.

'I think "worried" might be a better word. If the enlarged cutoff zone is not to cover Crusoe during takeoff, then we have to ask ourselves – what *is* it for?'

'Perhaps it's to protect him from whatever our friends may be planning to do. We've accepted the fact that he can anticipate our actions – and possibly even read our minds. He may also have established a direct line with the White House.'

'True. And if there are *six* landing sites, as York's researchers indicate, no doubt they'll all take similar precautions and cut off all the power. The world isn't ready for a change of this magnitude, Arnold.'

'Phil, the world couldn't survive it,' said Collis.

'In fact,' continued Brecetti, 'the world isn't ready for any change at all, although God knows it badly needs a new sense of direction.'

'That's why I think it's inevitable that we will try to destroy Crusoe,' said Wedderkind. 'Even at the risk of destroying our own future. The majority of people would prefer to trade it for some more of the present.'

'You're right,' said Collis. 'I never thought I'd find myself siding with the forces of reaction. When you asked me to join the project and explained the kind of opposition we had lined up against us, I really saw it in terms of "us" and "them". But now, I don't mind telling you, I'm scared as hell. I don't want anything earthshattering to happen. I've just finished paying for my house, we've finally got the kids into a decent school, my wife's found a beautiful summer cabin in Minnesota – '

'You're lucky,' said Brecetti. 'We're still looking.'

Wedderkind looked at Wetherby. 'See what I mean? Multiply Ray by two hundred million and you've got America's answer. It was Fraser who had the right attitude from the start. Man doesn't like mysteries. He has to unravel them. He feels threatened by events he doesn't understand – because in his divine arrogance, he believes he can understand everything. And because there standing in front of us is a finite object to be measured and photographed and fiddled around with, we believe we must be able to understand that too. But perhaps the pyramid that Crusoe is becoming is just the physical tip of a metaphysical iceberg – the meaning and importance of which we are failing to grasp because, at the moment, we lack the necessary degree of perception.' Wedderkind hoped he might trigger off a telepathic contact with his last few words, but no one came through.

'I did suggest something along these lines after we lost Milsom and Spencer,' muttered Collis.

'That's true,' said Wedderkind. 'And your words fell on stony ground. And here you are, our psychic apostle of the paranormal, running for cover.'

'Put it down to an overdeveloped sense of my domestic responsibilities. Hell, you're a grandfather. Can you honestly say you'd be happy to consign your family to the kind of chaos Phil has predicted?'

'No, of course not,' said Wedderkind. They began to walk slowly towards Crusoe.

'Well, it's reassuring to know you haven't become totally detached from reality. Our present society may not be all that brilliant, but there will be no bright future

461

for any of us if all the lights go out. And yet you still haven't told Washington about this, or the other sites. And you didn't recommend termination.'

'I couldn't contact Bob.'

'Allbright could have passed on a message,' said Collis.

'I know, but it could have got into the wrong hands. I'll try and get through to Bob later. As for not recommending termination, that's true. But there were plenty of other people eager to make that decision for me. I couldn't do it. Not because I'd lost touch with reality, but because I was trying to grasp the new reality that Crusoe's presence had imposed upon us. It's also true that I held back information. I wanted to gain as much time as possible. To give us a chance to understand. If I had passed on everything we knew or suspected it wouldn't have made any difference.'

'You sound very pessimistic,' said Brecetti.

'Not really, Phil, just full of regret. Two hundred years ago Crusoe and his companions could have landed on Earth and everything would have been fine. There was nothing to be affected by the fade-out and nothing that could be cut off by Crusoe's force field. It would have been a fascinating encounter – the intellectual curiosity of the eighteenth-century mind and a space-age culture from beyond the millennium. There might have been time for Crusoe to get his message across. Our trouble is we have too big an investment to protect.'

'Yes, but it's not just the system,' said Brecetti. 'The scientific community is threatened too. When something like Crusoe starts defying our natural laws, the whole scientific house of cards threatens to come crashing down around our heads. We can only explain what is happening in terms of what we already know. But if the basic principles on which that knowledge is founded are rendered obsolete, we have to throw all the textbooks out of the window and start again.'

'And that could be very inconvenient,' said Wetherby.

'It would ruin a lot of reputations.'

'And make publishers a fortune. What would you do with your Nobel Prize, Phil, hand it back?'

'It's okay for you to smile, you English bum,' said Brecetti. 'How would you geographers feel if someone produced conclusive proof that the Earth was flat?'

'It's a potent combination,' said Wedderkind. 'When Man is inconvenienced by something he doesn't understand, he reacts in the only way he knows how. And all the reasoned argument in the world isn't going to stop him.'

They reached Crusoe and paused to consider his shape. He was now over forty-five feet tall – three times his original height. The position of the cortex, now buried deep within the huge angular block of crystal, could only be gauged by the blue wisps of light that flickered fitfully across its surface. Wedderkind listened once more to the sounds coming from within the hull, then stood back and looked up at Crusoe.

'It's curious. This sudden growth cycle – the sheer size of this thing – is so overpowering, yet the sound it's making is so innocuous. I don't know how it affects you but I find it calming – almost soporific . . .'

Brecetti nodded. 'I know what you mean. It's a pity he cut off our power; we could have recorded it. The tinkling sound and the underlying hum both have slight variations in pitch. It produces an interesting counterpoint.'

'That's right. Almost melodic.' Wedderkind turned to Collis and Wetherby. 'Does it do anything for you?'

Wetherby shrugged. 'Not really, but then I'm tone deaf.'

'Ray?'

'I'm more concerned about the percussion section in

the basement,' said Collis. 'Can't you feel the ground beating under your feet? It's fantastic.'

'It's oscillating at a pretty high frequency, but the vibrations aren't all that strong,' said Wetherby.

'You must have thick-soled shoes on,' said Collis. 'What's setting them off, the growth cycle?'

'Most probably. He's loosening up the ground to give himself room to move.'

'So those earth tremors that have been keeping us awake mean that Crusoe's also growing *underground*.'

'Not necessarily,' said Wetherby. 'Eastern Montana often gets an odd tremor or two.' He smiled at Collis. 'I share your reservations over what might be about to happen, Ray, but there's no point in worrying. Look on the bright side. At least we're not about to be subjugated by seven-foot-tall spiders.'

'I don't think we were ever in danger of that, Al,' said Wedderkind. 'I've been going over everything that happened with Friday and I think I've worked out what he was.'

'And what was that?' asked Wetherby.

'A toy.'

'A *toy*?' Wetherby looked surprised.

'Oh, come on, Arnold, you've got to be kidding,' said Brecetti.

'No, I'm serious, Phil. I think Crusoe gave him to us to play with. To examine and evaluate, to try to take apart. To occupy our minds while Crusoe got on with the real business of settling in. It's not so crazy when you think about it. And it would explain why Crusoe didn't protect Friday with a cutoff zone when Max's roughnecks attacked it. Friday was expendable. It was our reactions that Crusoe was interested in. The way we handled Friday would have told Crusoe a great deal about us, in the way a child psychiatrist can judge the development of an infant by watching him at play.'

'Assuming he's interested in us at all,' said Brecetti.

'I don't think you really doubt that.'

'Okay, let's accept it, the next question is – what kind of interest? Clinical, or fatherly? There's a big difference. You once lectured us about the use of downgrading terminology. We may have committed a psychological error in upgrading both these artefacts by conferring human status on them. Crusoe, Friday, he, him . . . Perhaps it would have been smarter to call them X-One and X-Two.' Brecetti waved towards Crusoe. 'Instead of coming here, as you imply, to sit in judgement upon us, this . . . thing might be nothing more than a superbly animated gizmo whose sole purpose is to analyse the atmospheric gases, pressure, and humidity, measure our magnetic field, check soil content and acidity, probe the geological structure of the Earth's crust, observe the flora and fauna, and puzzle over the curiously eccentric behaviour of a small group of carbon-based vertebrate bipeds. To Crusoe, we may be nothing more than grotesquely shaped packets of water, iron, copper, calcium, and other assorted minerals, salts and vitamins, wrapped in varying percentages of animals, vegetable, and synthetic fibres.'

'I don't know quite what you mean by grotesquely shaped, but I hope it isn't me,' said Wedderkind. 'It's a nice idea, Phil, but I have a feeling you're whistling in the dark. You know there's more to it than that.'

'Yes,' said Wetherby. 'What about all that business with the hatch – and Spencer's message?'

Brecetti didn't reply.

'I think we were being offered an easy way to find out what Crusoe was all about, ' said Wedderkind.

'I agree,' said Collis. 'But the trouble is, Crusoe was only selling one-way tickets.'

Sunday/September 23

The Pontiac from the White House car pool arrived outside Connors' door at a quarter to six. Charly helped Connors into his coat and handed him his briefcase. She was wearing his bathrobe.

'This is almost like being married,' she said.

'Yeah . . . what does it feel like?'

Charly put her arms around his neck and kissed him. 'Mmm . . . I guess I could get used to it. But if we were going to stay here, I'd want to have a Philippine couple living in. Or some Vietnamese boat-people. They're cheaper, but of course there's the communication problem.'

'Yes. And it's not just with Vietnamese . . .' Connors picked up his zipped travel bag. 'Will you remember to mail that cheque to the power company for me?'

'Sure.' Charly hugged him once more before letting go.

'And turn everything off before you leave?'

'Of course.'

'Okay . . . well, g'bye, Charly. I'll call you when I get back. I'm not quite sure when that'll be. Take care.'

'You too.' Charly gave him a wifely peck on the mouth and hid behind the front door as she opened it.

Connors walked down the path without looking back.

The driver started the car. 'Do you want to go straight to Andrews Field?'

'No, I want to stop off at the Rochester Towers.'

The driver pulled into the hotel forecourt and stopped alongside Greg. Greg dropped his luggage into the trunk and got in beside Connors. Dan Chaliapin and the two Russians were sitting in another green Pontiac parked just ahead of them.

'All set?'

'Yes, fine.' Greg leaned towards the driver. 'They're going to follow us.'

They cleared the car in front and turned left into the street. Both pavements were lined with cars but there was little other traffic. At the intersection the driver swung right and headed down towards Fifteenth Street.

'Did the General get fixed up?'

'Yes. A discreet dark grey worsted. Conservative cut. Amazing. Put these guys in the right clothes and they wouldn't look out of place on the board of the Chase Manhattan.'

GLASGOW AFB/MONTANA

Their plane left Washington at 6:30 A.M., arriving at Glasgow AFB, Montana, at 8 P.M., local time. Colonel Zwickert, the Base Commander, and Major Jessup, the SAC Communications link man between Crow Ridge and Washington, were there to meet them. General Allbright had briefed Zwickert on the project shortly after the Air Force had got their hands on the Ridge.

Grigorienko and General Golubev changed into crisp new sets of olive-drab fatigues. Supplied by the Air Force, the uniforms came complete with stencilled name tags, red bands around the epaulettes and, in the case of the General, five gold stars on the cap and collar.

One of the yellow Corporation helicopters lifted them over to the civilian airport at the town of Glasgow, some eighteen miles south of the base. The Twin Comanche from the Miles City air-taxi outfit touched down a few seconds after they did. Harvey Korvin was at the controls. Connors saw him do a marvellous double take as Golubev and Grigorienko climbed in and began talking to each other in Russian.

The word about Connors' aquaphobia had obviously got around, because Korvin's flight path was angled clear of the Fort Peck dam. Once across the Missouri, he followed Highway 24 south through McCone County. Ahead, Connors could see the T-junction where Highway 24 met the east-west road running from Sydney to Lewistown. If they flew more or less straight on, they would pick up Highway 22 angling in from the northwest, and Broken Mill would be just off the starboard wing. Korvin crossed the T-junction at a height of two thousand feet. It was one of those days when you could see forever. The sky was clear and cloudless.

'What's that place on the right?' asked Connors.

'Van Norman,' said Korvin. 'That creek running almost underneath us is called the Little Dry.' As he said it, both engines of the Twin Comanche coughed and died.

Connors' heart missed a beat as the steady comforting roar was replaced by the soft whistle of air over the wings.

Red warning lights indicating power failure flared up along the top of the instrument panel and then faded abruptly. The needles of the flight instrument wavered and dropped to zero. Korvin switched on the emergency battery power supply, checked the fuel and ignition switches, primed the fuel pumps, and looked expectantly at the engines. The propellers continued to windmill but the engines didn't start.

'What in hell's happening here . . . ?' muttered Korvin.

Connors knew. He looked back at Greg. 'Is it the electrics?' he asked Korvin.

'Yeah, everything's blown,' said Korvin.

This is impossible, thought Connors. They were over thirty miles away from Crow Ridge. But it was the only explanation. The cutoff zone had expanded – and they had flown right into it. From high up, the ground looked deceptively smooth. But if they didn't pick the right spot, there could be no second try . . .

Korvin pulled on fifteen degrees of flap, pumped down the undercarriage, and turned into wind. 'Sorry about this, folks. Just tighten your seat belts, sit back, and relax. We'll all walk away from this one.'

BROKEN MILL/MONTANA

Deputy Carl Volkert left Forsyth before eight, crossed over the Yellowstone, and drove north along the unsurfaced back road that climbed into the badlands north of the river. About twenty miles out, the road began to snake between sloping buttes topped with piles of flat weathered sandstone. Volkert broke out on to the higher part of the plain and got a chance to push the patrol car up to sixty-five. He rocked along with his left elbow out of the window, whistling tunelessly.

He topped a shallow rise and saw about two hundred head of cattle moving south over the range to his left. The herd had five outriders, and following it on the road were three pickups, one towing a trailer, and two Army trucks. All the vehicles were loaded with bedding and furniture.

Volkert swung off the road to take a closer look at the herd and recognized the horned-H brand of the Hiller ranch on the steers. The nearest cowboy turned out to be a teen-age girl. One of the Hiller boys rode up to him.

Volkert pushed back his stetson and grinned. 'Where the hell are you going – Australia?'

'No, the Army's movin' everyone clear of the Ridge. We got word the whole shootin' match is going right up in the air. They're evacuating everybody from here all the way to Cohagen.'

'Hell, I didn't know that. How long's it been goin' on?'

'Got word yesterday mornin'. They gave us till midnight tonight. Whole thing's top secret.'

Volkert smiled. 'It was till they told you. Where's the rest of your stock?'

'The Army trucked 'em out yesterday. We're heading down to Ma's cousin's place near Cartersville. Where're you aimin' for?'

'Broken Mill. Official business.'

The Hiller boy grinned broadly. 'Well, you're gonna have to do it standin' up. I was over there yesterday. Most of the widow lady's stuff was already packed and out in the yard.'

Volkert pointed at him. 'Ross, next time you go through town, make sure you drive nice an' slow.'

Volkert got back on the dirt road and headed towards the loaded pickup. Two of them had the wives and kids aboard. Old Man Hiller was hauling the trailer. He leaned out of the window and waved to Volkert as he pulled up alongside him.

'Where're you headin'?'

'Broken Mill.'

'You may not get through. They're settin' up road blocks back there.'

'That's okay. Official business. Who's the girl you got back there?'

'She's from Miles City. There's two of 'em out there. Bid for them at the last Jaycee's slave auction.' Hiller chuckled. 'They thought they was comin' to clean out the kitchen. And you know what? Dang me if they ain't handlin' those steers almost as good as my two hands.'

'Where's your other boy?'

'National Guard called him out on Friday.' Hiller chuckled again. 'Went down to Miles City yesterday morning, put on his uniform, and got himself detailed back to the ranch with a bunch of GIs to help move some of the hay. We're gonna need that this winter.'

'How big do they say this blast's going to be?'

The smile faded from Hiller's face. 'Gonna take out our whole ranch. Probably burn off all the grass too. Won't be nothin' left of that. They say we can move back in again in three weeks' time. But, hell – what to? And you know who's behind all this? The damn Rooshians. That's who it is.'

'Yeah, the government ought to do somethin' about that,' said Volkert.

'Oh, that side's okay. The way they're talkin' we're gonna get paid twice over – but goddammit, I already had the place burned down once. We just got it all put back together. Makes me madder'n hell.'

'Maggie must be pretty upset too.'

'That's only the half of it. What about the land? Forty years we've been workin' that. They say it won't, but how do they know this blast ain't gonna poison everythin'?'

'I guess we just have to hope the government knows what it's doin',' said Volkert. He drove on.

As he reached the abandoned site of the old post office at Maudlin and turned east towards Highway 22, an Army helicopter swooped low over the roof of the patrol car, circled round and hovered alongside long enough to read the words 'County Sheriff's Office' on the side of the car. The copilot of the Iroquois gave him a thumbs-up as they lifted up and banked away to the left.

Volkert parked outside Annie's Mercantile and General Store and went in to buy his usual Sunday gift of ice cream. Most of the goods had been cleared from the

471

shelves and packed into cartons piled up on the floor, but the big deep freeze cabinet was still humming quietly to keep itself cool. Annie came through from the house and put a bundle of bedding on top of a wooden crate full of pots and pans.

'Still open for business?'

'For as long as we're here,' said Annie. 'If you can find it, you can buy it.'

'Know where they're takin' you?'

'I did hear somebody say Jordan. You come to pick up Laura?'

'I just dropped by to see if she was okay. Give me a pint of that strawberry ripple.'

The clock in the store started to strike nine. Volkert glanced up at the wall but there was only a white circle where the clock had been. The chimes were drowned out by the deep-throated roar of a heavy truck.

Volkert peered out of the window. 'They come for you already?'

Annie didn't look round. 'That's one of the diesels from Crow Ridge. 'Spect there'll be a plane comin' in soon.'

Annie went over to the freezer. As she opened the lid to get out the ice cream, the freezer's motor stopped.

'Now what in the world do you think's wrong with that?'

'Sign in the window's gone out too,' said Volkert. He switched on the neon tube hanging from the roof of the long poky store. It didn't light up. 'Must be a power line down.'

'I'll go and start the jenny,' said Annie. 'I've got three hundred dollars' worth of food in there and I got meat down in the cellar. Don't know we're going to get that away without spoiling.' She wrapped up the ice cream in a couple of sheets of the *Miles City Star*. 'A dollar.'

Volkert paid and stepped outside. Sid Lindstrom, Annie's husband, was thumping one of the two old pumps in front of the store. He'd been gassing up a beige Subaru station wagon with Idaho plates. It was crammed with a family all wearing stetsons. Volkert walked over.

'No use beating it, Sid. You got a power line out. Annie's down starting the generator.'

'Hope she remembers the tank's empty.' Lindstrom turned to the big red-faced driver of the Subaru. 'Back up over to the hand pump there and I'll give you the other five.'

The driver turned the ignition key. The Subaru's starter motor turned over, the engine fired briefly, then died. The driver pushed back the brim of his stetson and tried again. This time nothing happened. Volkert stepped in front of the car.

'Switch on your headlights.'

The lights came on, flared up to a bright yellow four or five times, then cut out.

Volkert slapped the hood and walked back to the car window. 'Okay, switch 'em off. I hope you ain't in a hurry to get anywhere.'

'Why?' asked the driver.

''Cos we got all kinds of trouble,' said Volkert. He handed the driver the pack of strawberry ripple. 'Here – give your kids some ice cream.'

Volkert walked across the road. Laura, the widow he'd come to visit, lived in a big corrugated aluminium trailer set on a concrete base. The curtains had been taken down from the windows. Furniture was piled in the front yard. Volkert went inside.

'Hi . . .'

'Hi, Carl. Won't be no Sunday dinner today.'

'Yeah, I know. Why didn't you call me?'

473

'Couldn't say nothin' to nobody. Didn't they tell you this whole thing is top secret?'

'Yeah, sure. Everything okay?'

Laura nodded. 'We had soldiers here yesterday helpin' out.' She closed the door of an empty cupboard. 'They're comin' back for us later today.'

'Maybe,' said Volkert. 'But whatever happens, don't worry. I'll see you get out okay. Where are the boys?'

'They're around somewhere. Probably over on the fence waitin' to see the plane come in.'

Volkert went back over the road to where the yellow Crow Ridge diesel was parked with its motor idling. It had one of the prefab units loaded on its trailer. Three young men with blue helmets were sitting in the cab.

'Hi,' said Volkert. 'You expecting somebody?'

'Yeah, in about ten minutes,' said the nearest blue hat. He had the name LARSEN stencilled on a white tag over his breast pocket.

'Well, they may be in trouble,' said Volkert. 'You know that problem you had on the Ridge?'

'I'm not too sure what you're talking about,' said Larsen.

'Listen, sonny, don't bullshit me,' said Volkert. 'I was the one that found that hole up there. Damn near got my ass burned off. There was nothing able to move around up there, right?'

'Right,' said Larsen.'

'Well, you've got the same problem right here. Happened just a few minutes ago.'

Larsen looked at the other two cadets in the cab. They all jumped out. One of them climbed up on top of the roof of the trailer with a pair of binoculars and searched the sky to the north.

'See anything?' asked Larsen.

'Nope . . .'

474

'Well, take a good look all the way round. See if you can spot any of those Army helicopters we saw.'

The cadet on the roof of the trailer made a thorough 360-degree search. 'Nothing up here but me and the birds,' he reported.

Larsen banged his fist on the wing of the truck. 'Boy – this is really going to bitch things up.'

'Where're your people coming from?' asked Volkert.

'Glasgow over to Fort Peck, then due south. If they've gone down, they can't be more than thirty miles away.'

'Means they could be up near Van Norman . . .'

'Do you know this area?' asked Larsen.

'I can find m'way around,' said Volkert. 'Want me to come with you?'

'That would be great.' Larsen called up to the cadet on the trailer roof, 'Bail out, Zip. We're gonna drive north, look for the plane, and see how far this thing has spread.'

The cadet jumped off the roof of the trailer.

Volkert hurried back to his car, pulled his Winchester from the pocket under the front seat, and grabbed a box of shotgun shells from under the dash. The truck swung around in a wide circle and stopped opposite the store. Sid and the driver of the Jap station wagon had the hood up and their hands full of wires. The rest of the family were still wedged in the car.

The driver spotted Volkert. 'Hey, wait a minute – '

'Stick around,' said Volkert. He ran across the road and squeezed into the cab of the truck.

The kids, perched patiently on the fence waiting for the plane to skim over their heads, watched as the truck turned north on to the highway. Annie came out of the store.

'Sid! Have you been messin' with that jenny again?'

Lindstrom didn't move his head out from under the

Subaru's hood. 'Did you fill her up?' He checked the lead to the distributor.

''Course I did. I've tried just about everything to get it started and I'm getting nowhere fast.' Annie folded her arms and stayed on the step.

'Be with you in a minute . . .' Lindstrom checked along the bulkhead in front of the windshield. 'Why, it looks like you've got a fuse gone there. That's what the trouble is . . .'

Laura walked across the wide baked-earth street. 'Did Carl say where he was goin'?'

'Nope,' said Annie. 'He just grabbed his shotgun and took off with those three boys up towards Cohagen.'

'Oh . . .' Laura looked puzzled. 'He didn't say anythin' much but I had the feelin' somethin' had gone wrong. Listen, is your phone okay? Mine just went dead.'

'I'll go and check. Maybe the Army cut it . . . Did you hear that, Sid? Laura's phone's out.'

'Be with you in a minute,' said Lindstrom. He turned to the driver. 'See that? Every goddarn fuse has blown clean out. Now just how do you suppose that happened?'

CROW RIDGE/MONTANA

Rizzik, the CIA man running the base camp, sent one of the diesels up to the Ridge with a message for Wedderkind. He was in the command hut. He looked at the message and passed it without comment to Brecetti.

It read: 'All electric power failed at 9 A.M. No radio or telephone contact with Glasgow AFB or Miles City. Await instructions.'

Brecetti passed it to Lovell. 'Maybe you'd better let the others know about this.'

Lovell read the message. 'Mmm. I take it this means we now have an even larger cutoff zone?'

'It does,' said Wedderkind.

'That should present us with a few interesting problems.' Lovell pocketed the message and left.

'Sixty-nine point one miles?'

'Give or take a few yards,' said Brecetti. 'Do you want to put ten dollars on it?'

'No, thanks. You've cleaned me out too often.' Wedderkind led Brecetti into Allbright's empty office and studied the large map on the wall. Wedderkind checked the scale of the map. 'We may be in luck, but only for the moment. It looks as if the edge of the new zone will still be on the north bank of the Yellowstone.'

'Leaving Miles City in the clear.'

'Yes – but only just.' Wedderkind looped one end of his handkerchief around a finger and the other around a ballpoint pen. He measured off thirty-five miles and drew a circle around Crow Ridge.

As predicted, the edge of the circle fell short of Miles City but overlapped the airport and several small settlements between Miles City and Forsyth. The biggest place within the enlarged cutoff zone was Cohagen, about twenty-five miles north of Crow Ridge. Population, two hundred and fifty.

Brecetti tapped the name on the map. 'They must be wondering what hit them.'

'So must Bob. He was due at Broken Mill at ten minutes past nine.'

'My God, yes – of course. Would the plane be all right?'

'It depends which part he was flying over. I saw some really desolate country south of the Fort Peck reservoir. One of the pilots told me it could take two days to walk out of the area. Provided you land in one piece. It'll be a light aircraft so the control problem won't be acute. All they'll lose is their power and instruments. The weather's good. They should get down okay.'

'Hadn't we better send out a search party?'

'It's probably already gone, but we can check with the base camp,' said Wedderkind. 'They'll have sent a diesel up to Broken Mill. Those cadets are pretty bright. I'd be very surprised if they hadn't already got it together. Do you want to drive down with me?'

NATIONAL GUARD ARMORY/MILES CITY/MONTANA

Up until 9 A.M. Sunday morning, Army Colonel Reese, commander of the airborne unit spearheading the evacuation, had been pretty well pleased with the way things had been going. All the ranches and farmsteads in the designated area had been contacted during Saturday morning. They had all been briefed on the situation, and arrangements had been made over the transport each family would require to move their personal belongings, furniture, and livestock. Estimates had been made of the number of military personnel required to assist in loading and moving all transportable items. Departure times had been scheduled. People living in wheeled trailer homes had already been towed clear of the fire zone and resited in the camping and recreation areas north of Jordan. Checkpoints were being set up and detour signs posted. Eight helicopters were patrolling the area and liaising with the ground units. With their normal radio equipment rendered inoperative by the fade-out, the Army was maintaining contact with medium-wave sets. Since anyone with a transistor radio could listen in, they were using cryptic code words, transmitting on one channel and receiving on another. Sunday was going to be Colonel Reese's big day. The remaining evacuees would be packed and waiting for the Army trucks that were already on their way. The ground and air units would move into position, sealing off the 1,250-square-mile area. The Air Force units and CIA personnel would leave Crow Ridge. The stage would be set for the final phase of Operation CAMPFIRE.

By 09:45 hours, it was clear that the Pentagon's plans had begun to misfire. Colonel Reese tore up the laconic progress report he had planned to send to General Wills and sent a more urgent signal to Washington. It read: 'All radio contact lost with CAMPFIRE units north of Miles City. Air and ground transportation in same area inoperative due to unknown electromechanical fault. Telephone links severed. Please advise.'

To his second-in-command Colonel Reese said, 'Round up all the horses you can find in Miles City.'

USAF SPECIAL WEAPONS CENTER/KIRTLAND AFB/NEW MEXICO

At about the same time Connors was bracing himself for a forced landing on the banks of the Little Dry, the two-seat F-4H Phantom bringing General Allbright from Nebraska touched down at the desert airbase east of Albuquerque and popped its striped, slatted dragchute. Allbright dropped into the Base Commander's office, then drove over to the far side of the airfield where the two huge B-52s selected for Operation CAMPFIRE were stationed next to a guarded bunker containing the specially-modified nuclear bombs.

Known as SAC's 'long rifle', the B-52 first entered service in June 1955. Now, over three decades later, it still formed the backbone of SAC's manned bomber force. One hundred and fifty-five feet long and with a wing span of 185 feet, eight engines, and a tall tail like a jib of a windjammer, the B-52 had gone from model B to H, each variant getting heavier, flying farther and faster,

479

and capable of carrying more clout to Mother Russia. Firebreak One and Two were Model Gs, built by Boeing at Wichita.

Alongside the aircraft was a temporary trailer encampment housing the two six-man air crews and the ground crews that had flown in to keep the planes serviced and ready for the special assignment that had kept them separated from the rest of the huge base for the last five weeks.

Alternately winners and runners-up in the last two annual SAC bombing competitions, both crews had been personally briefed by the President, Fraser, and Allbright on the purpose and importance of the mission and, as Connors had suspected, had been prepared to take out the Ridge in the event of a sudden crisis that might have made evacuation impossible.

The waiting period had been spent in intensive practice bombing runs over a simulated target deep inside the White Sands missile range near Alamogordo to enable the bombardiers to perfect their handling of the obsolete but now-vital optical bombsight. Every day, as Allbright had told the President, they had flown over Crow Ridge without anyone below knowing they were there. Swallowed up in the unbroken blue of the sky at over forty thousand feet, the B-52's approach is silent, and invisible to the naked eye.

At 10 A.M., Clayson came on the line from Washington and told Allbright about the enlarged cutoff zone that Reese had reported – without knowing what it was. Allbright summoned the two air crews and their crew chiefs, the SAC controllers, and the Air Force engineers who had modified the arming mechanism of the bombs. Dressed in an impeccable flying suit, with a blue scarf around his throat, he sat on the edge of the table and watched the twenty-six men file into the operations trailer.

Most of them he'd known personally before Operation CAMPFIRE, and since then he'd made a point of getting to know the others. The atmosphere was relaxed and friendly, yet tinged with respect.

Allbright stood up. 'Okay, sit down, gentlemen. I'm glad to see the desert air has done you some good. Anyone who wants a permanent posting to this sandpit should see me afterward. Now – I've just got word of a new situation which has a bearing on our mission, so let's start with a quick look at the overall picture.'

He picked up a stick of chalk and turned to the blackboard. '*TARGET* – CRUSOE . . . and as you now know, COMMISSAR . . . *TIME* – 5 P.M., twenty-fifth and 6 A.M., twenty-sixth . . .' Underneath, Allbright wrote '*FADE-OUT* – GLOBAL. We're now beginning to lose medium-wave transmissions. If the conditions of the previous fade-out are duplicated, we can expect total loss of all radio communications by next Sunday. Telephone line transmissions are being hit by static but they are still the best alternative method of communication.

'*MAG FIELD* – HEAVY DISTURBANCE . . . Anyone who's tried to find his way around with a compass will already know about this. Reports coming in from geophysical research organizations indicate that the whole of the Earth's magnetic field is temporarily disoriented. We've also recently had confirmation that there is, at present, a magnetic south sub-pole centred on Crow Ridge. There is a similar polarization around the second site in Kazakhstan. Up to now, INS has spared us from the navigational problems posed by these disturbances. Apart from that – and the fact that there are no civilian airlines operating – everything is perfectly normal – '

There was some quiet laughter and muttered asides from his audience.

481

'Except in our neck of the woods,' continued Allbright. He wrote '*CUTOFF ZONE*' under the other headings, then pointed to the words with the chalk. 'Last Wednesday, when the fade-out returned to wipe out our radar and UHF/VHF frequencies, the radius of the cutoff zone around Crusoe jumped from zero to 3.5 miles. At approximately 0900 hours this morning, that radius increased to *thirty-five* miles . . .'

As Allbright wrote the figures up on the blackboard, he heard a rustle of consternation behind him. He turned to face the roomful of men. 'The Russians confirm that the same conditions exist around Commissar.'

Colonel Rick Westland, Commander of Firebreak One, leaned forward. 'Does that mean that there's a total loss of electromotive power within that entire area?'

'Above two hundred and fifty microvolts,' said Allbright. 'Crusoe is now enclosed in an electrically dead circular zone, seventy miles in diameter, and rising in a semicircle to a height of thirty-five miles.' He moved to a clear part of the blackboard and drew a semicircle standing on a baseline and put a dot in the middle of the line. 'So, gentlemen, the question is – without power from the generators or the backup batteries, and all your aircraft electrical systems inoperative, can you still fly through this new cutoff zone and hit your target with the required degree of accuracy?'

There was a moment's uneasy silence, then the air crews started muttering among themselves and soon the SAC controllers in the front row turned around and started putting in their two cents' worth. When they reached a consensus, Colonel William 'Smokey' Stover stood up.

'Okay, Smokey, what's the verdict?'

'It's a tough ball of wax. Let's start with the good news. The engines will keep running, and so will the engine-driven fuel pumps. Basically they're gravity fed so there's no problem. The other EDPs will give us hydraulic power and we'll have the PCUs. And that's about it. The bad news – first, we lose all the flight instruments except for the standby ASI, VSI, and pressure-sensitive altimeter – not very accurate. Autopilot will be out, plus main electric trim. We'll have to hand-trim. No intercom between crew stations, we'll have to use sign language – that's going to be sensational on the run-in to the target. All the engine instruments will be out so we'll have no idea how they're running. There'll be no engine overheat warning light and no engine fire extinguishers. No warning lights of any kind and in fact, we're not going to be able to switch anything on *or* off. No fuel booster pumps, which we need to prevent engine surge at altitude – and best of all, if we do flame out, we can't restart the engines. Oh – we have one other cockpit instrument working, our E.2B compass. But that's only accurate to ten degrees and with the mag field distortions, it's shot to hell. The real pig – we lose our Inertial Navigation System once we hit the zone. The only way we can keep on course is to map-read our way over those last thirty-five miles – from forty thousand feet . . .' Stover sat down.

'Is it hard to pick out the Ridge from that height?' asked Allbright.

'Well, sir, it depends on the atmospheric conditions.' It was the bombardier of Firebreak One who had stood up. 'Above twenty thousand, the whole of that area becomes a solid slab of OD.'

'But don't the trees on the Ridge help?'

'Yes, sir, they do, but as I've said, it depends on the conditions. If there is any haze or low patchy cloud you'd have to abort.'

'How about bombing from a lower altitude?' asked one of the SAC controllers.

'Oh, fantastic,' said Stover. 'A zero-length fuse on fifty kilotons from under forty thousand? That's gonna roast our fannies.'

'How about somebody flying a desk in at low level?' asked an unidentifiable voice from the back.

'Okay, then put in a delayed-action fuse.' The SAC controller looked a little miffed.

'Too risky,' said one of the USAF engineers. 'We've gone right back to basics with this weapon. A time fuse is just one more thing that could go wrong.'

'And it would take too long,' said the man next to him.

'So how does that leave us?' asked Allbright.

'Crabbing sideways, sir.' Westland, the Firebreak One commander, stood up. 'We don't have an artificial horizon, or a turn-and-bank indicator, no Doppler to measure drift. We can fly – but how do we fly accurately enough to give you a CEP of under fifty yards?'

'Can't you hold it on a heading with the E.2B compass?'

'No, sir, the magnetic field deviations are making the E.2B oscillate from side to side.'

'Got it . . . that's quite a problem.'

One of the engineers who hadn't spoken stood up. 'It sounds crazy, but I think we're gonna have to rig up one of those old open cockpit speaking tubes for the pilot and the bombardier.'

'Remember we're on oxygen,' said Stover. 'We also need to change the instruments by the aiming panel.'

Electronically guided to the target, the B-52's bomb load was normally unloaded with clinical precision on to a radar image of the target. It enabled the aircraft to bomb accurately through solid cloud, but even in clear weather the crews rarely, if ever, saw what their bombs were hitting.

Firebreak One and Two had been fitted with a perspex panel under the nose so that the bombardier could use the optical bombsight. Beside it had been fixed an electrically-powered altimeter and an air speed indicator. They now had to be changed for the older types of instruments that worked solely by air pressure. Everyone was aware that the whole precisely-planned operation was rapidly becoming a hit-or-miss affair.

'There is one way around some of these problems, sir.' It was Joe Mischak, electronic warfare officer aboard Firebreak Two. With none of his gear working and nothing to do, he probably had had a little more time to think. 'We could mark the target with two crossed lines of flares, and lay a line of flares to guide us on the run-in – and also beyond the target to give the pilots something to fly on.'

'That'll work,' said Stover. 'But who's going to stay behind and light them? The Crusoe Project people are supposed to move out by midday tomorrow. I don't know of any flares that can stay lit for, what – seventeen hours? Unless you're planning to use the Olympic flame.'

'Why not? You could use oildrums,' said Mischak.

'Never last,' said Westland.

'And if they did, they'd cover the whole fuckin' area in smoke,' said Stover. 'Sorry, sir.'

'That's okay, Smokey,' said Allbright. 'Total freedom of expression is what this thing's all about. Mischak's idea will work. Let someone else worry about who's going to light them. The roads are going to be empty, it's not going to take all that long to drive twenty miles.'

Mischak stood up, vindicated. 'You could link the flares in series so that as one burned out, it would ignite the next. That would give everyone time to move out.'

The bombardier of Firebreak One stood up again. 'Could we add some white smoke pots to give us a last-minute check on wind speed and direction to help us calculate drift?'

485

Allbright nodded. His eyes searched out the other bombardier. 'Are you happy about the arrangements?'

'Yes, sir. It should put us in there with an even chance.'

'We need better odds than that,' said Allbright. 'We may only get one shot at this.'

Stover stood up. 'Sir, we've been coming on strong with a lot of negative waves but it's only because a lot of stress has been laid on hitting this thing right between the eyes. On behalf of both crews, I just want to say that as long as that aeroplane'll fly, we're gonna press on in and do our damnedest to lay one on him.'

'If I'd doubted that for one moment,' said Allbright, 'none of you would be here.'

There was a knock on the door of the trailer and an SAC officer came in with a loaded slide projector. 'I've got the pictures you were expecting, sir.'

'That's good. Set them up on that stand at the back.' Allbright pulled down the projection screen in front of the blackboard. 'Blinds, please.'

As the room darkened, the first slide flashed on to the screen and was rapidly focused. It was an early view of Crusoe.

'I want to show you these few pictures because the size of the cutoff zone is not our only problem,' said Allbright. 'You're all familiar with this object from our earlier briefing sessions. The next picture I'm going to show you is how Crusoe looked at 06:00 hours this morning.'

CROW RIDGE/MONTANA

Connors stepped down from the diesel's trailer unit and stared up at Crusoe. When he'd left on Wednesday, Crusoe had been a saucer-shaped disc fifteen feet high. Now, towering above him, was a gleaming black crystal pyramid over fifty feet high and nearly a hundred feet wide at the base. It was just . . . He turned to Greg as he came alongside. From Greg's expression, it was obvious he didn't believe it either.

'This is fantastic,' said Greg. 'What happened to the thing in the photographs?'

'This *is* the thing in the photographs.'

'But that's impossible.'

'Greg, where this son of a bitch is concerned, nothing's impossible.'

They were joined by General Golubev, Grigorienko, Dan Chaliapin and Harvey Korvin. Connors waved towards the pyramid and said, in Russian, 'I'd like you to meet Crusoe.'

'Jesus Christ,' said Korvin. 'What the hell are you guys building here?'

'Ain't nothin' to do with them, no, sir – that whole shebang's come right out of the ground.'

Connors looked around. Volkert was behind him. Larsen and the other two cadets dropped out of the cab and stood looking at Crusoe. They'd been on base camp detail all week, so it was news to them too.

'You mean . . . ?' Korvin sounded like Admiral Garrison.

'That's right,' said Connors.

'Jesus Christ . . .'

Connors turned to Volkert. 'You cottoned on to it pretty fast.'

Volkert grinned. 'Found the hole, didn't I? Had strangers knockin' on m'door tellin' me to keep m'mouth shut. All you guys from Washington in three-hundred-dollar suits. Ol' Harv here gits himself a brand new aeroplane when for years he's bin holdin' 'em together with gum. Shit – we ain't all as dumb as you city folks think we are.'

Connors heard a shout and saw Wedderkind hurrying

across the plateau followed by several members of the research group. He grabbed Connors' hand.

'Thank God . . .'

'My last trip, Arnold. From now on I'm travelling by train.' Connors pointed to Korvin. 'This is the man who got us down in one piece.'

'Hell, it was nothing,' said Korvin.

Wedderkind nodded towards Crusoe. 'Isn't he beautiful?'

'Arnold, he frightens the hell out of me. Christ – he must be over fifty feet high.'

'Fifty-two and a half feet. That was at twelve o'clock. Neame's been measuring him twice a day. The graph shows the growth rate is slowing down.'

'Good. We're going to slow it even further. Five o'clock, Tuesday afternoon, Allbright's boys are going to drop a bomb on it.'

Wedderkind looked at him for a moment, then gave a quiet shrug. 'I suppose it had to happen sooner or later. What about all the people living around here?'

'The Army's evacuating everybody within a radius of twenty miles. At least they were until the cutoff zone expanded.'

'Did you find out how far it had spread?'

'Yes, the zone stops halfway between Cohagen and Jordan, so that means there's no power between here and Miles City.'

'Yes, that's exactly what Brecetti predicted.'

'You mean you knew this was going to happen?'

'Not definitely. It was just another of our gloom-and-doom theories. I've been trying to get hold of you since I got back here on Thursday.' Wedderkind explained Brecetti's hunch that the cutoff zone might go on expanding. 'The next time it will be nearly seven hundred miles across. It will take out half the state.'

'Oh – tremendous . . .' Connors fought back a rising wave of panic. If he had listened to the President, he could be sitting safely in his office doing all this by phone. But if Brecetti was right, where *was* the safest place to be? He tuned back in to Wedderkind. 'How long was it between the first jump on Wednesday and this morning's?'

'Ninety hours.'

'So what does that give us, ninety hours before it jumps again?'

'That depends on the kind of mathematical progression the time interval is based upon. The period between the jumps could get shorter.'

'Or longer. For Christ's sake, Arnold, if the area he's blacking out is getting bigger, he must need *more* time to generate the power, not *less*!'

'Yes, that's a reasonable assumption – but it doesn't necessarily follow. The next jump will tell us if we're working against the clock.'

'When that happens, we'll be in an even bigger mess than we are now. Let's assume we've got ninety hours, it still gives us plenty of leeway.'

'That's true. But there was another reason why I wanted to contact you,' said Wedderkind. 'The magnetic field research Al Wetherby started with York up in Baltimore seems to indicate there could be another landing site, in Russia.'

'There is,' said Connors. 'But don't worry about it. We've got that all buttoned up. The site is in Kazakhstan, the craft's code name is Commissar. It came out of the ground. It hasn't got a hatch. It's growing, and the Russian Air Force is going to take it out at the same time as we hit Crusoe.' He smiled. 'You look surprised.'

'I am.'

'Arnold, you aren't the only one who's been sitting on

information. There've been a lot of guys beavering away behind the woodwork. Come and meet the General.'

Wedderkind decided to let Connors enjoy his brief moment of triumph. Now that there was definite confirmation of the Russian site, there would be plenty of time to tell him about the four others . . .

When Golubev and Grigorienko had seen all there was to see, Connors decided to dispatch them back to Glasgow AFB with Dan Chaliapin, the White House interpreter. Lovell, Page, and Gilligan, one of the engineers, were detailed to go with them, taking all the videotapes of Crusoe and Friday.

While they were getting ready to leave, Wedderkind got together with Brecetti, Wetherby, and Collis in his trailer.

'This is a sad moment. You all know the situation. Washington has decided to blow the whistle on the project. It may work but it may not. In which case it'll be time to head for the hills – ' Wedderkind held up his hand to halt Collis. 'I know you don't agree, Ray, but we all planned for this emergency a long time ago. We've kept the group together, a lot of us are on the project. A week from now you may all be cursing me but the fresh air isn't going to do our families any harm.'

'Okay, Arnold. Do you want me to handle the East Coast group?'

'Yes. Al will work out of Chicago. There's an Air Force plane flying back to Washington. It'll drop you off on the way.' Wedderkind turned to Brecetti. 'I've arranged with Bob for an Air Force plane to fly you to California to, ah – collect some seismic data . . .'

'Got it. What are you and the others going to do?'

'We'll go when they evacuate the Ridge. Don't worry about us, *you'll* be the ones in danger. If the cutoff zone

490

spreads there'll be nothing moving, so get your groups out of the cities as fast as you can. We'll join you just as soon as possible.'

'But how will we keep in touch?' asked Collis.

Wedderkind put a hand on his shoulder. 'Don't worry, Ray. If you think hard enough, that problem will solve itself.'

Connors was in the command hut talking to Greg when Volkert put his head around the door.

'Mind if I make a suggestion?'

'No, go ahead.'

'It's about that truck to Glasgow. Be a good idea to send two in case you have a breakdown.'

'Yes, good idea.'

'Another thing – best if we was to head back up the Van Norman cutoff on to the Fort Peck highway. There's some people up at Cohagen who might not take too kindly at us drivin' through without stoppin'. What with the evacuation story an' all this trouble, things could get a mite touchy if they found we had a couple of real live Rooshians aboard.'

'I'm glad you thought of that. I take it you plan to go with them?'

'Might as well,' said Volkert. 'Could we stop off at Broken Mill and pick up the few folks that're there? Some of 'em's practically kin.'

'Sure. But don't put them in the same truck as the General.'

'Thanks, I appreciate that.'

Connors shrugged. 'You got me out of a hole. Could you ask Larsen to come in here?'

Volkert left. Connors picked up the small blue sheets of paper that lay beside Greg's portable typewriter.

'How's it going?'

'Nearly finished,' said Greg. 'You must have more of the President's notepaper than he has.'

'Always comes in handy. And in this case it's legal. He gave me letters of authority, remember?'

'I'm surprised he didn't ask for them back.'

'So am I,' said Connors. 'That's either a good sign – '

'Or he forgot.'

'Just keep punching those keys.' Connors began to sign the letters.

Greg finished number twelve, passed it to Connors, and packed away his typewriter. 'What do you want me to tell the President?'

'Everything. Make sure Fraser, Clayson, and General Wills know what's happening too. Tell them I've made contact with Colonel Reese in Miles City and have loaned him nine of the diesels to round up the remaining evacuees and stranded Army units, and that we only have three to move out all the people on the project. Explain that without headlights we're slowed down to almost walking pace after dark but that we'll still do our best to get everybody clear by noon tomorrow. And don't forget to explain what Brecetti said about the cutoff zone.'

'No. That's the real killer.'

'And get hold of that guy York. If I know Arnold, he's probably sitting on more bad news.'

'Anything else?' asked Greg.

'Yes . . . if I were you, I'd catch a bad case of flu and take off for a few days.'

'Where to?'

'Anywhere, just so long as it's out of town,' said Connors.'

'You don't really think the cutoff zone'll spread that far, do you?'

'No, but if it does, the last place you want to be stuck is in the middle of Washington.'

'What about the President?'

'Good question. Get him to go to Camp David. In which case, forget the flu and go with him. You can have my seat in the bunker.'

'Bob – is it really this serious – or are you putting me on?'

'I wish I was, Greg. I wish Phil Brecetti would turn out to be the greatest joker of all time. I wish I could wake up and find this was a bad dream.'

'What about the girls in the office – and all my *friends*?'

'Nobody has more than one of those,' said Connors. 'Two at the outside. Look, contact whoever you want but be careful what you say. After all, next Friday we may be back to the dull routine and wondering what all the fuss was about.'

'I wish I could have that in writing.'

'Whatever you do, for God's sake don't start a panic. If that happens, all hell'll break loose, the roads will jam up, and nobody'll get out.'

Larsen knocked and came in. 'The diesels are loaded and ready to go, sir.'

'Good.' Connors folded up two of the blue sheets of paper and handed them to Larsen. 'Keep one of these and give the other to the senior cadet in charge of the other diesel. Those two vehicles are now moving on the authority of the President of the United States. Nobody – repeat, *nobody* – commandeers them. Understood?'

'Yes, sir.'

'Right. I want a six-man squad to ride with each vehicle, all armed with M-16s. If you get into a tight situation use your head first. If that doesn't work, open fire.'

'Yes, sir.' Larsen picked up Greg's baggage and went out.

Connors went out to the diesels and said good-bye to

the two Russians. 'I'll join you in time to see the fireworks. Look after them, Dan.'

'Of course. See you tomorrow.' Chaliapin climbed aboard.

Connors gripped Greg's hand. 'Good luck.'

'You know, in all these last-minute instructions, there's one name you haven't mentioned,' said Greg. 'Charly.'

'That's right.'

'Well, don't you want me to say anything to her?'

Connors put a hand on the back of Greg's shoulder. 'You're right. The question is, what . . . ?' He chewed his lip for a moment then snapped his fingers. 'Her parents have a big motor yacht moored on the Potomac. It's not in the Kashoggi class but it still costs more to run that you and I earn in a year. Call her up, tell her to drop whatever she's doing and head down river with her folks.'

'Where to?'

'Out to sea. Bermuda. Florida – well, maybe not Florida. But you know what I mean. Anywhere so long as it's . . .' He waved dismissively. 'Forget it. They'll never make it. If anything's going to happen, it might as well be in the luxury of their own home.'

Greg gave him a narrow-eyed look then climbed aboard.

'Take care of yourself, huh?'

'You too,' said Greg.

Connors watched the two diesels drive away. Cadets were loading the third in preparation for the final evacuation of the Ridge. The plan was for everybody to spend the last night down at the base camp and then move out when the rest of the fire zone was finally cleared.

Connors went over to the driver and gave him a letter of authority. 'Make sure this stays with the truck. And keep that motor running for as long as possible. We've got to conserve those starting cartridges.'

Throughout the rest of the morning and afternoon of Sunday, the Air Force engineers worked feverishly to replace the instruments beside the optical bombsight in Firebreak One and Two, and to perfect a simple intercom system for the pilot and bombardier. Only one aircraft would be used in the attack but the other would be crewed, fuelled and bombed-up, ready to go in case the first had to abort due to mechanical failure.

While the modifications proceeded at Kirtland, airmen from Holloman AFB, on the eastern edge of the White Sands Range, replaced the seventy-foot aiming circle with a new target one hundred feet square. Around it, they set up a mile-long cruciform pattern of flares, with a run-in and run-out line to enable the pilot to track accurately. They added black smoke pots and retired in the gathering dusk, ready to ignite the flares electrically at dawn the next day.

Wedderkind found Connors standing looking at Crusoe. 'You still haven't told me how Larsen found you.'

'Nothing to it, Arnold.' Connors started to walk slowly across the plateau. Wedderkind fell into step behind him. 'After Korvin put us down, we stuck a note on the windshield and walked a couple of miles to the nearest ranch. They gave us a lift in a covered wagon.'

'You're joking.'

'No, it's true. None of their pickups were working. This was a real, genuine, honest-to-goodness horse-drawn covered wagon. Normally it only comes out once a year for the Bucking Horse Sale Parade down at Miles City. General Golubev was knocked out by it. It turned out he was crazy about Westerns. Greg climbed up one of the buttes and saw the traffic still moving along the east-west highway. Volkert guided Larsen along those dirt roads by the Little Dry and overtook us as we were heading north for Van Norman.' Connors smiled. 'It was funny in a way. I left Washington in a five-hundred-mile-an-hour jet, only to end up behind four horses with my legs hanging down over the tailgate of a wagon. It gave me time to think – mainly about how uncomfortable it was.'

They walked up towards the crest of the Ridge.

'Last time we were up here, we had Friday sitting behind us,' said Connors.'

'Yes,' said Wedderkind. 'I miss him.'

They reached the weathered slabs of rock at the top and looked out across the land to the southwest. Connors saw a distant group of riders, probably some of the National Guardsmen Reese had sent in to scout for stragglers.

'You know, in spite of these last-minute, ulcer-making hangups, in a curious kind of way I feel – glad to be back. That must sound absolutely crazy.'

'Not really,' said Wedderkind. 'Do you know why?'

'No. I just feel . . . different.'

'Must be the Ridge. Did you know that Al Wetherby found out that Crow Ridge was regarded by both the Crows and the Apaches as a "good medicine place"?'

'No . . .'

Wedderkind turned to look at Crusoe. 'I've been thinking about what you told me about Commissar coming out of the ground. When we got the first indications of another site, I immediately thought that Crusoe must be one part of a spacecraft that split up on entering the atmosphere like one of our MIRV missiles.'

'Isn't that what happened? One landed in the middle of North America and the other almost in the middle of

Europe and Asia. The two places where most of the action is.'

'The other possibility is that the spacecraft split up once it was underground. Each part travelling to its appointed position by burning its way through the Earth's crust.'

'Arnold, we know Crusoe demonstrated that capability, but the distances involved are enormous.'

'I know,' said Wedderkind. 'That leads me to my latest theory – that Crusoe and Commissar *didn't* land.'

'Say that again?'

'They didn't land. They were here all the time, buried deep within the Earth. Lying dormant.'

'And – ?'

'The blue-white disc of light that the people of Broken Mill caught a glimpse of could have been a separate energizing unit – that landed to reactivate Crusoe and Commissar. Do you remember Wetherby telling us that legend of the Incas where God sends men underground to the regions of the Earth they are to occupy?'

'Yes, I do.'

'There was another he told me. From Australia. The aborigines there revere the Great Green Ant God. They believe it is a spiritual being that laid down the pattern for the development of human beings – and that can still influence their lives. There's an area of hallowed ground they call the Dreaming Place of the Green Ants and they believe that if it is desecrated, man-eating monsters will emerge to ravage the world. Don't you think there're some interesting similarities?'

'Well, I suppose you could confuse Friday with an ant. But even though he gave me the creeps, he was hardly out to ravage the world.'

'Maybe it's *us* who will emerge as the man-eating monsters.'

'Well, I'm not going to dispute our proven and infinite capacity for destruction. We also have an equally great potential for good. But that's beside the point. Commissar didn't have a hatch – *or* a Friday.'

'And there was no Russian sighting report of a descending blue-white disc of light, even though it was night time in Russia when whatever it was entered the atmosphere and landed on Crow Ridge,' said Wedderkind.

'So you see Crusoe as the central character?'

'Yes. And if you want to continue the analogy, the others are playing bit parts.'

'Others?' From the beginning Connors had steadfastly tried to ignore the possibility.

'Bob, I *know* it's been on your mind ever since the President coined the code word.'

'But surely – not *six*?'

'Now that we know there's one in Russia, it means that the computer picture York and Al Wetherby produced is right. And since Fraser's going to haul him in you might as well know. Yes – it now looks as if there *are* six sites, four of them underwater, and arranged in a neat pattern, on the equator, forty-five to forty-seven degrees above and below it, and all ninety degrees of arc from one another.'

'And are they all magnetic sub-poles like Crow Ridge?'

'Well, York's magnetic data coverage was incomplete so he had to interpolate a lot of the figures. But, yes – they're all polarizing the existing field, and drawing it into a new pattern around the existing north and south magnetic poles.'

'Wow . . . If you're right about Crusoe lying dormant, it gives this situation a kind of – permanent quality. How long have you been sitting on this?'

'Not long. We've suspected the possibility for some

weeks, but I was trying to get some harder evidence. I didn't want to come to you with yet another theory.'

'And it was the Air Force that came up with the proof.'

'And even they didn't tell you about it officially.'

'No, everyone had their own angle . . . Boy, when Mel Fraser hears about this he's going to go bananas.'

Wedderkind smiled. 'That's exactly how I said you'd react when you got the news. But you've taken it rather well.'

'I ran out of my supply of the cold sweat of fear on the way down to that forced landing by the Little Dry. But I can see Fraser coming after you with a knife.' It was Connors' turn to smile. 'After the way I blew out in Russia, maybe it would be a good idea if we both stayed out of Washington for a while.'

Connors looked at his watch. 5 P.M. . . . In forty-eight hours one of Allbright's B-52s would hit Crusoe with the ultimate weapon, and then the whole wearisome discussion of what he was and whether he'd sprung out of the ground or from under God's armpit would become totally academic.

'Come on, Arnold, let's clear out of here.' Connors started down from the crest of the Ridge. 'And if you're hiding anything else, save it till after the bomb goes off. I'll be able to take it then.'

Monday/September 24

BASE CAMP/HIGHWAY 22/MONTANA

In the small hours of Monday morning, nearly everyone at the base camp was woken up by what sounded like a fast freight passing at right angles underneath the highway. The ground shook so violently that some people, sleeping on the edge of their bunks, woke up on their way to the floor. People spilled out of their trailers and clustered together in an effort to find out what was happening. When a search confirmed that the ground was still in one piece under their feet and that there was no visible damage, most of them drifted back to their trailers and tried to grab another couple of hours' sleep. Wedderkind put on his dressing gown and slippers and prowled about in the darkness puffing endless cigarettes.

At about five o'clock, Connors stumbled out of bed, decided he didn't need to shave, and yawned his way across to the canteen and the delicious smell of coffee, frying bacon, and hot fried eggs. At least Crusoe hadn't been able to stop them cooking with gas. Wedderkind joined him, drinking his coffee with an obvious lack of enthusiasm.

'I thought you had your own pot.'

'I left it in my trailer up on the Ridge,' said Wedderkind. 'Do you want to go up and have a look?'

'For your coffee pot?'

'No. To see what all that noise was about.'

'Okay, Arnold. But the idea is for everybody to be moving *away* from the Ridge, not back on to it.'

When Neame heard of the projected trip, he asked if he could come along to check if Crusoe had grown any more. Vincent and Hadden offered to hold the other end of the tape, and in the end it was decided to take along ten of the cadets just in case they needed some help. Before they left, Connors got together with Harris and Cameron, the two senior cadets in charge of the Crow Ridge evacuation, and Bill Rizzik, the CIA front-office manager of the base camp.

'Have we got all our vehicles back now?'

500

'Eight,' said Rizzik. 'There are still two with Reese at Miles City and two up at the airstrip at Jordan – the new pickup point for Glasgow.'

'All with cadet crews?'

'Yes,' said Harris. 'And they all have Presidential passes.'

'Okay, load up as many of your people as you can. Leave me about twenty-five, and ship the rest up to the airbase at Glasgow for transfer to Colorado.' Connors turned to Rizzik. 'How about your people?'

'We'll go the same way. There're only a dozen of us, plus the NASA medical team. What about their equipment? Some of it's pretty fancy.'

'Better leave them till last just in case someone breaks a fingernail. If there's any transport to spare, we can think about moving hardware then.'

'Right . . .'

Connors shook Rizzik's hand. 'Bill, if I don't see you again, good luck. And thanks for covering us.'

'It's what I'm paid for. First thing I'm going to do when I get back home is go around the house and switch everything on.'

Kinner drove Connors' party up to the Ridge. He was a little slower with the truck than he was with the jeep. When they got up to the gate, they found their way was barred by an enormous block of black crystal that had grown out of the hillside. The block, which had thrust its way straight out of the side of the slope, had uprooted several pines, demolished the flimsy wooden gatehouse that had been directly in its path, shattered a concrete post and driven straight through the heavy tube-metal and wire-mesh gate.

Connors stepped back and took a good look at the block. He estimated it was about ten feet high and twelve feet wide. The front edge was cut back in a series of nine steps at an angle of 45 degrees. There wasn't a mark on it. He put a hand on the crystal. It was warm, and he could hear a humming sound that seemed to be coming from inside.

Connors exchanged a look with Wedderkind. 'He really is full of last-minute surprises.'

They clambered over the smashed gate.

'Hey, look, steps,' said Kinner. He climbed up them, and walked along the top of the block to the point where it entered the slope. 'Trouble is they don't go anywhere.'

Wedderkind dispatched the cadets to check all sides of the Ridge. They found that Crusoe had pushed twelve stepped blocks sideways out of the Ridge. Four, one of which had demolished the gatehouse, faced North, South, East and West, and were on a higher level than the other eight which radiated out at 45-degree intervals. Connors walked down and looked at two or three of them with Wedderkind, then returned to Crusoe.

Neame, Vincent, and Hadden completed their measurements. Crusoe was now fifty-six and a half feet tall, with a base measurement just a few inches short of one hundred feet. The last trace of his curving lines had disappeared and he was a pure pyramid of solid black crystal. The light flickering over the buried cortex was like an angry swarm of blue fireflies.

THE WHITE HOUSE/WASHINGTON DC

The news Greg brought back from Montana sparked off a series of meetings which went on almost until dawn. The President slept for a couple of hours, showered, shaved and then went back to his office to meet Fraser, General Wills, and General Clayson.

Faced with the horrendous possibility that Crusoe's cutoff zone could expand to engulf the whole of the

United States, the President had asked the state governors to call out all National Guard units, and had secretly put the three Armed Forces on full alert. Throughout the night, by road, rail and air, troops had been moved into position around the major urban areas of the nation. If the worst happened, their task would be to seal off the cities, preventing an uncontrolled mass exodus into the open country beyond.

'Everything now hangs on the outcome of this air attack,' said Fraser. 'If the cutoff zone is expanding at ninety-hour intervals, then we're in the clear. Any other kind of situation is unthinkable. I've been going over the various contingency plans with my people most of the night and there's no way we can cover it. We have plans for survival after a nuclear war, civil defence organizations in each state, fallout shelters to house one hundred and ninety-five million people, emergency rations to last sixty-five million people fourteen days – but every plan is predicated on having emergency power available. Apart from those twelve converted trucks out in Montana and the freaks with their hang-gliders, there won't be one fucking thing able to move! There aren't *any* plans to cover a breakdown on this scale.'

'And the fade-out could get worse too,' said the President.

'Don't worry about that,' said Fraser. 'The fade-out only affects the transmission and reception of radio waves. If we get hit by the cutoff zone, we won't even be able to switch on the sets.'

'Then how can we keep this whole thing together?' asked the President.

'Well, the Romans managed,' said Fraser. 'We'll find a way if we have to.'

'Do you think I ought to say something? You know – address the nation?'

503

'No, not yet. It's still small potatoes. If Allbright does his stuff, then we can relax. You can go on radio and television and tell everyone we and the Russians have saved the world.'

'Not quite. There are still the other four,' said the President.

'Yeah . . . did you know that the Defense Department helped pay for that computer up in Baltimore? I'd like to throw that bastard York in jail – and Wedderkind along with him.'

'What happens if the zone expands – before the attack?'

'According to the figures Greg Mitchell brought back, it will still only black out a circle seven hundred miles across,' said Clayson.

'Do you know how many big towns that covers?' asked Fraser. He looked back at the President. 'The short answer to that question is, call in your speechwriter.'

'Yes . . . I really don't understand why Bob went out there.'

'All the commanders down to regimental level are being issued with sealed orders,' said General Wills. 'If the cutoff zone goes to the seven hundred mark, then on your decision they'll get a radio signal to open 'em up. If there is a total radio blackout, that is also a signal to open the orders.'

'Do you think I ought to stay here or go to Camp David?'

'Camp David,' said Fraser.

USAF SPECIAL WEAPONS CENTER/KIRTLAND AFB/NEW MEXICO

At 5:30 A.M. Firebreak One and Two climbed to forty thousand feet over the New Mexico desert, lined up on the flares, and made several bombing runs over the dummy target. Before each run-in, a black card panel

504

was clipped over the normal flight instruments and all electrical systems were shut down to simulate, as far as possible, the conditions they would encounter when they flew into the cutoff zone that blanketed Crow Ridge.

The first bombs fell some two hundred yards off target, and, as anticipated, the error was mainly due to the inaccuracy of the old type of altimeter and air speed indicator. The practice bombs were retrieved by helicopter and flown to the nearby Holloman AFB to be reloaded into the B-52s. While the planes were being refuelled, the pilots and bombardiers studied the results with General Allbright and his SAC controllers.

Like cars, nuclear bombs can be 'customized' to fulfil a specific tactical requirement. For a successful attack against a 'hard' target – such as an underground missile silo, or Crusoe – the weapon has to explode at ground level. The critical factors are the CEP – Circular Error Probability – linked to the accuracy of the weapon delivery system and the energy yield. A high energy yield ground-burst produces a nice, big, satisfying hole and an explosive, pulverizing blast that reduces reinforced concrete to confetti. With Plutonium 239, the lethal radiation yield is low, reducing to a residual one per cent seven days after the blast.

Using the eloquent equations of the nuclear wargamers, it had been calculated that a weapon with a fifty-kiloton yield, delivered with a CEP of five hundred feet against a Minuteman silo hardened to withstand a pressure of three hundred psi, produced a Single Shot Kill Probability of 82 per cent. The CAMPFIRE bomb was designed to produce a shock wave ten times more powerful, a colossal three thousand explosive pounds of pressure per square inch. But Crusoe had proved to be harder than any construction the Air Force had been able to devise. For the operation

505

to have any chance of success, everyone knew the destructive effect of the bomb had to be maximized – and that meant going for a direct hit, or the nearest of near-misses.

The crews looked glumly at the diagram that plotted the fall of their bombs around the target and waited for Allbright to deliver his verdict. It wasn't long in coming.

'A CEP of six hundred feet is unacceptable, gentlemen. Go back up there and try again. I want that error cut in half by midday.'

BASE CAMP/HIGHWAY 22/MONTANA

Connors and his Crow Ridge reconnaissance party returned to the base camp to find Harris, Cameron, and the rest of the cadets still there. Larsen had brought the two diesels back from Jordan, with their twenty-foot trailers piled high with flare canisters.

'Where the hell did they come from?' asked Connors.

'General Allbright, sir,' said Larsen. 'He had them flown into Glasgow Air Force Base, and they ferried them down to us in Jordan.' Larsen produced an envelope from the cab of the diesel. 'This came in with the flares. It's addressed to you. I've given the instructions and layouts to Cameron and Harris.'

Connors read the letter. It was telegraphic and to the point. 'Dear Bob – Have learned of local problem and manner in which you have coped. Regret I must delay final evacuation still further. Air Force urgently needs flare pattern around Crow Ridge to provide aiming mark. Cameron and Harris have full instructions and will organize cadet element to place flares. On completion, I would appreciate you ensure evacuation of main party and provide ignition teams with adequate means of transport to clear fire zone, Tuesday 25th, 14:00 hours latest. Best wishes, Mitch.'

'Major Jessup sent you a message as well,' said Larsen. 'He's received an urgent signal requesting you and Mr Wedderkind to contact the White House.'

'Thanks . . .'

Connors explained the situation to Wedderkind and Rizzik. 'I think the best thing to do is to move out the rest of the research group and your base camp team, Rizz.'

'Don't you think it would be better if we stayed and helped?' asked Rizzik. 'The job would get finished a little quicker.'

'Yes,' said Wedderkind. 'I'm sure Davis and the others will want to help too.'

'Arnold, this is ridiculous. There's no need to start a mass epidemic of heroics.'

'Don't worry, I'll make sure everyone knows they have a clear choice.'

'All right . . .' Connors looked at his watch. 7:45 A.M. 'I'm going down to Miles City to see Colonel Reese, then I'll come back and pick you up. Be ready to leave for Jordan at ten.'

Connors walked over to the base camp office. As he passed the canteen, he saw Volkert outside with his face buried in a hamburger.

'What's the situation in Cohagen?'

The small township lay just beyond the evacuation area. Connors had planned to observe the explosion from the top of a tall grain silo west of the town. But now, Cohagen was marooned fifteen miles inside the expanded cutoff zone.

Volkert transferred the hamburger to his other hand and licked the ketchup off his fingers. 'It's okay. Everythin's under control. The state agency people an' the

507

Army went in an' smoothed everythin' over. Just hope this all works out okay. Some of them ain't too pleased with the Rooshians.'

'How is everybody making out?'

'They're gettin' by. Thing you city boys have to remember is that this is high plains country. Folks out here are used to roughin' it. Shit, this was one of the last parts of the West to be settled. Lot of folks don't realize that. Most people are ridin' around in pickups now but they're still cowboys at heart. Country folk draw together when there's trouble.'

'That's good to know,' said Connors. He pointed to the leaking hamburger. 'Better eat the rest of that before it gets cold.'

Connors went into the base camp office. Cameron, Harris, and Rizzik had the plans for the flare layouts spread out on the table. Connors glanced over the details. Four fifteen-hundred-yard strips bracketing the Ridge with linked clusters of flares every twenty-five yards. The run-in and run-out lines each called for an additional ten clusters set five hundred yards apart, forming a broken line, running east to west through the long axis of the Ridge. It looked like a lot of work.

'How long do you think this is going to take?' asked Connors.

'Most of the day,' said Harris. 'But don't worry. We can handle it.'

'Now that these trucks will be leaving empty, do you want to use them to move the horses out?'

'No, sir,' said Cameron. 'The diesels can't go everywhere. When we start putting down these flares, we're going to be spread out. We'll need the horses to keep in touch with the work groups.'

'Okay. I'll get out of your hair.'

It was just before nine as Larsen drove Connors down the hill past the airport. There was an Army roadblock at the northern end of the bridge across the Yellowstone.

Recognizing the yellow truck, the soldiers lifted the barrier and waved them through. Larsen paused to ask the way to the Armory, then sped across the bridge and into town, slowing to the regulation fifteen mph as they crossed over the Milwaukee Railroad tracks on to Seventh Street.

The two converted diesels loaned to Colonel Reese were parked outside the Armory. Connors was pleased to see that both of them had armed cadets sitting in the cabs. While Larsen's squad brought them up to date on the latest situation, Connors went in to see Colonel Reese. Reese had been up all night, and was in the middle of shaving.

Connors told him to go on shaving and sent for the officer in charge of the National Guard. He and Reese confirmed that their units had finally managed to move all the evacuees out of the cutoff zone, and had set up new roadblocks around the blacked-out area. Connors told them that there was a possibility that it could expand again – to a radius diameter of 691 miles.

Reese cut himself. 'Holy Moses . . .' The National Guard colonel sat down heavily. 'Do you realize the impact that could have on this town? There are nearly ten thousand people here.'

'You think that's a problem?' Connors ticked off the towns on his fingers. 'It's going to black out Helena, Butte, Billings, and Great Falls, Bismarck in North Dakota, Rapid City, South Dakota, and Sheridan and Caspar in Wyoming, and Regina, north of the border in Canada. But I must emphasize, it is *only* a possibility, and that information is top secret.'

'What the hell's causing it?' asked Reese.

'I don't have time to go into that now,' said Connors. 'But it's linked with the fade-out.'

'Do your people know when it might happen?'

'No. It could be any time between now and five A.M. on Wednesday morning.'

'Sheee-itt . . . For how long?' Reese abandoned his shave.

'We don't know,' said Connors. 'Maybe not for long. Maybe not at all.'

'But what the hell can we do?' asked the National Guard commander.

'Sit tight,' said Connors. 'You'll get immediate assistance from Washington.' There was no point in telling them that if the cutoff zone went to 691 miles, it might spread even farther. If it did, Washington wouldn't be able to help anybody. That kind of news could wait until Tuesday evening. 'How well do you know the editor of the *Miles City Star*?'

'Pretty well. Been on a couple of fishing trips together.'

'Could he get something printed in secret?'

'Yeah, I would think so. He knows how to work every machine in the place.'

'Okay, I suggest you get him to run off a few thousand leaflets setting out the situation. Maybe you could include a map. Make absolutely sure no one else sees them. Lock 'em up here. If the cutoff zone spreads and blacks you out, start distribution and use the diesels to get copies to Glendive and Billings. Ask them to reprint and pass the information on to the other cities affected. We'll take care of Glasgow. If you get the signal to stand down, burn them. Is that clear?'

'Yeah . . .'

Connors headed back up Highway 22 feeling he had one less problem on his mind. The idea of ten thousand

510

people suddenly finding themselves immobilized, deprived of all electric power – and with no means of finding out what the hell was going on – had been disturbing him. And yet their plight was piddling compared to the larger cities of Montana, Helena, Great Falls, Billings, and Butte, the big mining town. If the air pumps stopped, if the mine cages froze halfway down the mile-deep shafts . . . Connors shuddered at the thought. It was insane to go on trying to keep it secret any longer. The President would *have* to go on the radio and tell everybody what might happen . . .

Connors stopped at the base camp and picked up Wedderkind. Everyone else had disappeared. Connors looked eastward out of the cab window. 'Shouldn't there be some people working out there?'

'There are, but they're still on the run-in line about three miles away. The plan is to start at the outside and work in. That way, everyone will be close together when they get through. It'll mean a quick getaway.'

'Neat . . .'

Larsen put his foot down and drove north past the empty houses at Broken Mill.

Before leaving for Miles City, Connors had dispatched a diesel to Jordan to arrange for a plane to pick them up and fly them to Glasgow. He meant what he'd said to Arnold about not flying again, but it was a hundred and eighty miles from Jordan to Glasgow AFB by road, and in the present state of the railroads, about three days by train . . .

GLASGOW AFB/MONTANA

After calling Allbright to confirm that the flares would be positioned in time for the attack, Connors and Wedderkind both spoke to the President and gave him their

511

firsthand assessments of the situation. Connors told him about the last-minute delay over the flares, and urged him to consider making a radio address to the nation. Their conversation ended inconclusively, but Connors did manage to extract an assurance that the President would ask Press Secretary Jerry Silvermann to make immediate arrangements to relay a broadcast from Camp David. During and after the last three-week fade-out, there had been a lot of press comment about the lack of any direct pronouncement by the President on what was deemed, by many, to be a critical situation. The brunt of the questioning had been borne by Jerry, who had remained mercifully in the dark, spokesmen from the Defense Department, and NASA's Manned Flight Director Chris Matson.

Connors and Wedderkind lunched with General Golubev, Grigorienko, interpreter Dan Chaliapin, and the members of the research group who had gone to Glasgow AFB to brief them on the project, then took off for Jordan at 2:15 P.M. This time, their flight path went right over the Fort Peck reservoir. Connors, convinced that lightning never struck twice in the same place, closed his eyes, and pretended to go to sleep.

Larsen was waiting at the airstrip alongside the second backup diesel. Connors and Wedderkind climbed aboard and settled back for the fifty-mile drive to Crow Ridge.

THE WHITE HOUSE/WASHINGTON DC

By the middle of the afternoon, the President still hadn't left for Camp David. He stood at the curved window looking out on to the White House lawns, struggling to find the words that would, without creating panic, alert the nation to the dangers it faced. The President suddenly found himself wishing he'd ordered Connors to fly back

512

to Washington. He picked up the phone and asked to be put through to Major Jessup, the project link man at Glasgow AFB. As the operator went to switch the call through to the President, the line went dead. Repeated attempts over the next two minutes failed to re-establish the connection. A few seconds later, a call from SAC headquarters in Omaha, Nebraska, confirmed the breakdown. Every circuit in SAC's specially strengthened landline communication network is checked electronically every three seconds. The SAC report that zipped out of the high-speed teleprinter in the Pentagon at the rate of over six thousand characters a minute confirmed that all contact had been lost with Glasgow AFB, the Minuteman 3 missile complexes at Great Falls, and Malstrom AFB, Montana, Minot Air Force Base, North Dakota, and Ellsworth AFB, South Dakota. The cutoff zone had expanded – not in ninety hours as anticipated, but in *thirty*. The progression was now clear. In ten hours, it could expand again.

Fraser, Clayson, and Wills came across town from the Pentagon by helicopter and McKenna flew in from Virginia. They joined the President in the Situation Room, in the basement of the White House. One of Will's staff colonels projected a colour slide that had been prepared as soon as they had received news of Brecetti's predictions.

'It's bad,' said Fraser. 'If the time interval between jumps is being divided by three, the whole of the USA could be blacked out by three A.M. tomorrow morning.'

Three hours after midnight . . . The President tried hard to fix the time in his mind. Every high-speed form of transport immobilized, every communication link severed, industry crippled, cities strangled, the armed forces and law enforcement agencies paralysed, the interwoven power structure of state and federal government

513

struck blind, deaf, and dumb. How could he hold it together? How could *anyone* hold it together?

The telephone rang. Fraser picked it up. 'Good. Send it up.' He replaced the receiver and turned to the President. 'A message from the Soviet Premier just came over the hot-line teleprinter.'

The President managed to get his brain back on line. 'Oh, good.' He coughed to loosen the clamped muscles in his throat.

There was a knock on the door. An Air Force Lieutenant Colonel from the Communications section came in with the message. Fraser passed it to the President.

The President put on his glasses and scanned it quickly. 'I'll read it out. It's timed at 01:06 hours – What's that? . . . six minutes past one, Tuesday morning. Hell, is it already tomorrow over there? – and it's addressed to the President of the United States and begins "Dear John" – ' He looked up with a forced smile. 'This must be the "Dear John" letter to end them all.' He went on reading. '"We have just learned that the neutralizing field around Commissar has expanded to eleven hundred kilometres. In view of the imminent threat of a further expansion, we propose to advance the time of our attack by twenty-four hours to 06:00 hours today, Tuesday morning. We believe it is vital we synchronize attacks. Failure to act together could have incalculable consequences. I therefore urgently request you advance time over target accordingly.

'"We thank you for your recent exchange of scientific research data and look forward with renewed hope to a further period of close co-operation" – snide bastard – "Please advise me of your affirmative decision no later than 17:30 hours Washington time. Your friend, Alekseii Vasilyievich Leonovich, Premier of the Council of Ministers of the Supreme Soviet," et cetera . . .'

514

The President dropped the teleprinter message on the table and looked at the wall clock. The time was 5:13 P.M.

'That makes it thirteen minutes past three in Montana,' said Fraser. 'If we go with the Russians, that means our planes have to hit Crow Ridge at five P.M., local time.'

'But Mel, for God's sake, the place is surrounded with people putting down those flares! The Air Force cadets, Mack's people, half the research group – there're nearly two hundred and fifty people out there! Are you asking me to just wipe them out without giving them a chance to get away? Isn't there any way to get a message to them?' The President looked anxiously at the others. 'Mack? Chuck, Vernon? Surely to God you can come up with something!'

'What's more important,' asked Fraser, 'the lives of two hundred and fifty people or the future of two hundred and fifty million?'

One of the battery of telephones rang. Fraser answered. '. . . Good . . . hello, Mitch? Stand by – ' Fraser covered the phone. 'Pending your decision, do I have your permission to order the B-52s to bomb up?'

The President's hand went to grip the bridge of his nose, then dropped back on to the table. 'Yes . . . tell him to keep that line open and stay close to the phone.'

Fraser looked across at Clayson. 'Is it okay if I short-circuit the chain of command?'

Clayson nodded. 'Go right ahead.'

'Mitch? This is a CAMPFIRE takeoff alert. Bomb up and stand by for an immediate Go signal . . . No, we'll try to contact the people on Crow Ridge, but you'll have to go in without the flares. Hold this line open . . . Okay.'

USAF SPECIAL WEAPONS CENTER/KIRTLAND AFB/NEW MEXICO

Allbright hooked the phone into the amplifier and looked out of the window of the operations trailer. The hardstand on which the B-52s had been parked for the last five weeks was empty. He turned to his senior SAC controller.

'What was the last signal we received from Firebreak One and Two?'

'They just entered the approach pattern.'

Allbright and the SAC controller went outside and scanned the sky. The SAC controller pointed at the sky over the southwest corner of the airbase.

'There they are – look . . .'

The two aircraft were in loose formation, heading towards the runway, but they were still just specks with wings. Allbright cursed himself for not having kept one aircraft on the ground.

'Call them up and get them down here fast – and hit the siren.'

The SAC controller shot back into the trailer. The siren wailed. The ground crews tumbled out of the ready room and came on the double towards Allbright. He gave his voice a parade-ground boom.

'Gentlemen, your planes will be coming in over the fence in about two minutes. The White House has just called a CAMPFIRE runway alert. I want those planes bombed up, refuelled, checked out, and ready to roll in under ten minutes.'

'But sir, they haven't even landed yet. They have to come off the runway, taxi – '

'Exactly.' Allbright cut the crew chief short. 'You're going to make this the fastest turnaround time in the history of the Strategic Air Command. Get moving!'

THE WHITE HOUSE/WASHINGTON DC

Fraser looked at the wall clock. 'Five-fourteen . . . It's about eight hundred miles from New Mexico to Montana,

516

and the maximum speed of a B-52 is six hundred and sixty miles an hour. Chuck?'

'Minimum flight time, runway to target with a hot start is one hour eighteen minutes – but that's at optimum altitude. At forty thousand feet, their speed will be trimmed by fifty knots. From the latest weather reports they could have a tail wind on the last half of the trip.'

Fraser looked at the President. 'If Moscow is going to receive your message by five-thirty, you have a maximum of eight minutes to decide. Personally, I don't think there are any other options open to us. Every second we hold back reduces the time Mitch's aeroplane will have to get lined up on the target.'

'Chuck, if Mitch's plane can fly in there, can't you contact the nearest airbase and ask for a volunteer to fly in and drop a message to the people around the Ridge?'

General Clayson opened his thick data file and checked the list of active airbases outside the cutoff zone. 'The nearest is Warren AFB on the southern edge of Wyoming. It's an ADC fighter base. Nearly four hundred miles away from Crow Ridge.'

'What's that, thirty minutes' flying time?'

'Yes, plus the reaction time. They'll have to rig up a message canister and find some way to drop it. The release gear for underwing stores is electrically operated.

'So throw it out of the cockpit.'

'Sir, this is a Mach 2 aeroplane we're sending in, not an old barn-storming JN-4.'

'Chuck, I don't give a shit how it's done, just get on to it right away.'

Clayson picked up one of the phones at the far end of the room. It was five-fifteen. The President reached for the pencil and pad in front of him and wrote swiftly in sloping capitals.

*CUTOFF ZONE NOW SEVEN HUNDRED MILES. CAMP-
FIRE ATTACK WILL TAKE PLACE SEVENTEEN HUN-
DRED HOURS TODAY LOCAL TIME PRESIDENT
ORDERS YOU TO CLEAR FIRE ZONE IMMEDIATELY.*

He tore the sheet from the pad and passed it to Fraser.
'How's that?'

'Fine . . .'

'Make sure they spell out the time . . . you know – so
there's no – '

'Confusion. Right.' Fraser handed the message to
McKenna. He took it over to Clayson.

'Does that note mean we can give the Russians an
affirmative on CAMPFIRE?'

The President closed his eyes, rubbed his forehead and
nose, then looked up at Fraser. 'I'd just like to hang on
till Chuck fixes something.'

'Should be no problem. You called a full alert last
night. Warren's an ADC base so they must have a third
of their pilots strapped in on cockpit alert.' Fraser swung
round in his chair. 'Any movement on that aeroplane,
Chuck?'

Clayson was busy talking quietly in the background.
He raised his thumb.

'Make sure whoever goes in knows he'll have no
electrics,' called Fraser.

Clayson signalled he understood.

The President saw Fraser, McKenna, and General Wills
look at him expectantly. All through his term of office,
he had been dreading this moment. Under him, America's
military forces had been spared an armed conflict. No
soldier had died as a result of a Presidential decision. He
had been the Peace candidate. Now he had to face
the idea of sentencing two hundred and fifty people to
instantaneous oblivion or – depending on how far they

could run – hideous burns or a slow death from radiation sickness . . .

Fraser lifted the red telephone linking them with New Mexico. He gave General Allbright a quick rundown on the view from Washington and got a situation report on CAMPFIRE. Fraser held out the phone to the President. 'Firebreak One and Two were returning from some last-minute target practice when we called the runway alert. They're being armed and refuelled now. They'll be ready to go at 17:30. Mitch would like to talk to you.'

The President took hold of the telephone. The time was 5:17 P.M.

USAF SPECIAL WEAPONS CENTER/KIRTLAND AFB/NEW MEXICO

Allbright called the twelve crewmen into the operations trailer. The four SAC controllers stood at the back of the room.

'Gentlemen, as you know, we are now on full alert, but due to certain last-minute developments, we are going for a stripped-down operation that will give us the maximum chance of success.'

Allbright got the two captains to cut a deck of cards. Colonel William 'Smokey' Stover won the cut with a jack of clubs.

Stover handed the card back to Allbright. 'Glad to have you aboard Firebreak Two, sir.'

'Thank you.'

Allbright turned to the SAC weapons controller. 'John, get Firebreak One's bomb transferred to Smokey's aircraft.'

'Yes, sir.' The SAC officer went off at the double.

Allbright raised his voice slightly. 'I want the captains and copilots of each aircraft to remain. The rest of you can dismiss.'

As the room emptied, the SAC officers moved up to the front. Allbright turned to Colonel Westland, who'd drawn the eight of diamonds.

'Ned, your aircraft will track us to the edge of the fire zone, monitor our attack, then fly to SAC headquarters at Omaha and report the result. You can take your full crew.'

'I understand, sir.'

'Good.' Allbright picked up the telephone. 'The President wants to have a few words with the four of you.'

The President spoke briefly to Stover and his copilot first, then Westland and his copilot. Allbright had a final word with the President, then put the phone down. The four pilots looked at one another.

'There has to be another way, sir. This is crazy,' said Stover.

'We have a final approach run of three hundred and fifty miles without electrics,' said Allbright. 'The weather is starting to break twenty-four hours earlier than expected and there will be *no* marker flares. There is only one way to ensure that we hit this target, gentlemen – and that is why I propose to take Firebreak Two right down the wire.'

'Yes, but – '

'You heard what the President said. You and your copilot will arm the bombs and bail out.'

'But, sir – '

'Colonel Stover, effective 15:21 hours today, Monday, September 24, you are relieved of the command of your aircraft. That's official, Smokey. So get in line.'

Stover's lips tightened. 'Whatever happened to SAC's two-man concept?'

'Nothing,' said Allbright. 'That's still intact, but I have never been an advocate of overkill.'

At 15:22, the order from SAC headquarters in

Nebraska, confirming the cut-down CAMPFIRE mission, came up on the teleprinter. Over the line from Washington came the Presidential 'Go Code' without which no nuclear weapon could be launched. The four pilots opened their sealed envelopes and verified the authenticity of the coded mission order and the signal from the President.

Two of the four senior SAC officers assigned to the operation unlocked a blue briefcase and took out two keys, each attached to a fine chain. They gave one key to Stover and the other to his copilot. The two men signed for the keys, put them around their necks, strapped on their parachutes, and doubled out to the aircraft.

The ground and fire crews and their equipment were already in position around the two aircraft.

Stover paused by the nose access door of his B-52. 'Where do you want to sit, Captain?'

'You two go ahead,' said Allbright. 'I'll take the jump seat. We can change over when we reach the cutoff zone.'

'Crazy,' said Stover. 'We broke our asses all day trying to hit the centre of those flares, we cut the error down to three hundred feet – '

'Yes, but not by midday. Let's go, Smokey.'

The crew chief shut the access door and plugged the lead of his headset into the side of the fuselage so that he could talk to Stover.

Allbright strapped himself into the jump seat just behind Stover and his copilot while they rapidly began switching things on with precise co-ordinated movements, the product of years of training.

Firebreak One's four pairs of powerful turbojets roared into life, and a split second later Westland got Firebreak Two turning.

Stover shouted through the static on the long-wave band that linked them with the tower and got clearance for an immediate takeoff. He opened the throttles and sent Firebreak Two rolling, flaps down, towards the active runway. Firebreak One followed, trailing about fifty yards behind on the starboard side.

When the nose wheel was on the white centre line, Stover started the water pumping into the jets to augment the thrust for takeoff and put all eight engines through the gate.

Allbright looked at his watch. It was precisely 15:30 hours. Firebreak Two was airborne and climbing, trailing a thunderous cloud of black smoke and on course for Crow Ridge. He looked out of the window and saw Westland's aircraft climbing into position beyond their starboard wing.

CROW RIDGE/MONTANA

As Larsen drove through Broken Mill, Connors spotted a bright yellow blob way out on the plain to his right. He asked Larsen to back up to the junction and take the dirt road west of the highway. From there they forked left on to the track that led up to Bodell's shack. One of the diesels was parked out on the plain with about fifty people strung out in small groups behind it, and a couple of cadets on horseback. It was the work party setting the northern line of flares. Four cadets on the back of the diesel were dumping batches of flares overboard as it moved slowly towards Crow Ridge. Larsen swung off on to the grass and headed towards them, pulling up alongside the main group. Connors jumped down from the cab.

'Hi – how's it going?'

A cadet named Biggs straightened up. 'Okay. The thing that's taking the time is linking these goddam things together with this touch wire so that they ignite in series.'

Connors looked towards the Ridge. 'Doesn't look as if you have too far to go now.'

'Eight hundred and fifty yards,' said Biggs. 'That's thirty-four clusters.'

Connors looked at his watch. It was 4:15 P.M. 'Any idea when you'll get through?'

'Maybe seven – eight o'clock.'

'Where are Harris and Cameron?'

'I don't know. Ask one of the guys on horseback. I think Rizzik is over on the west line.'

'Okay, thanks.' As Connors turned to go, the sky above his head split open with a thunderous roar. He ducked instinctively along with everyone around him, then looked up. A camouflaged Phantom fighter-bomber was banking away with its wing tip about fifteen feet above the buffalo grass.

'Where the hell did *he* come from?' asked Connors.

'I think he came in over the highway,' said one of the cadets.

They watched the plane curve northward. It turned over Broken Mill and came thundering back over their heads at zero feet.

'He's waggling his wings,' said Connors. 'Do you think he's trying to give us a message?' He spun around as the aircraft roared overhead and watched it bank right again and circle around them.

Landers, the pilot of the Phantom, was the thirty-two-year-old station commander at Warren AFB, just north of Cheyenne. There'd been no time to prepare a detailed preflight plan. He'd flown at zero feet across the plains of Wyoming, into Montana, picked up the Yellowstone, and stayed with it until he'd reached the Miles City airport, where the two chrome yellow MRDC Hercules aircraft stood with their swept-up tails facing the city dump.

523

From there, Landers had followed the line of the highway to Crow Ridge. He saw about two dozen abandoned Army trucks. On the phone, General Clayson had told him to look for a black pyramid. It had all sounded incredible, but there it was, rising from the plateau rimmed with pines.

There too, south and east of the highway, were the work parties he'd come to warn. He banked left over the base camp and saw another group laying a line of flares running in from the north. This group had *two* yellow trucks. Maybe one was a command vehicle . . .

Landers headed towards them, easing down low over the grass, then banked right, heading north towards the highway. He made a low turn over some deserted buildings, then headed back towards the group with his hand on the lever that would release the empty drop tank on which the President's message had been written with a thick felt pen. He pulled the lever and banked right. The group was still standing watching him. Landers glanced backward. The drop tank was still attached to the pylon under the wing. He made another tight turn over the buildings, lined up on the group, pulled hard on the release handle and banked around for a third time. The group was watching him. There were even one or two waving. And the empty drop tank with the urgent message to clear the area was still firmly fixed under the starboard wing . . .

ABOARD FIREBREAK TWO/ABOVE WYOMING

Flying at twenty thousand feet, the two B-52s crossed over from Colorado into Wyoming. The edge of the cutoff zone lay about a hundred miles ahead of them. Allbright switched on his intercom.

'Smokey, you and Deke had better go arm the bomb while we still have lights in the bomb bay.'

Stover gave a thumbs-up signal, tapped Deke Shore, his copilot, on the shoulder, and turned an imaginary key. The two pilots switched their oxygen lines on to portable bottles. Allbright folded back the jump seat to let Stover out then took his place. Deke followed Stover down to the bomb bay.

When his copilot was ready at the tail of the first bomb with his intercom plugged in, Stover raised his key. The lock was set in the middle of a numbered dial.

'Code Insertion.'

Each of them set a secret number they had been given to memorize.

'Coded. Ready to engage.'

'Engage locks.' Stover inserted his key.

'Lock engaged. Ready to arm.'

Stover gripped the dial. 'First sequence. Set four-zero.'

'Four-zero set.'

'Lock in.' Stover turned his key.

'First sequence locked.'

When all eight sections were aligned, the bomb was primed, ready to explode as soon as it hit the ground. Stover and his copilot moved across to the nose and tail of the second. Before they had finished, the small light in the bomb bay went out.

'Fuck it.' Stover unclipped his mask. 'Can you see okay, Deke?'

'Yeah, it's okay,' shouted Shore. 'Just give me a couple of seconds . . . okay, go ahead.'

'Seventh sequence. Set nine-two.'

'Nine-two set.'

'Lock in.'

'Seventh sequence locked . . .'

* * *

525

Stover climbed back up to the cockpit and took the right-hand seat. His copilot folded down the jump seat in the doorway.

'All set?' asked Allbright.

'Yes. They're both cocked and ready to go. Any trouble when you hit the zone?'

'Not too much. I've pulled all the gen breakers and the battery circuits. I just hope we don't flame out.'

'It should be okay. The B-52 doesn't have a surge problem at twenty thousand.'

'You ready to jump?'

'Do we have a choice?'

'You can take it up personally with the President later.'

Stover looked out of the window. 'This is going to be like stepping off the moon. Are you planning to lose any altitude?'

'We're on our way down now,' said Allbright.

'Have we passed Casper?' asked Deke.

'Yes,' said Stover. 'The next bus stop's at Buffalo. Not that there's anything moving at either place – or in between. Okay, let's go. We've got the wind on our tail. If we wait any longer, it'll blow us right into the fire zone.' Stover tapped Allbright's shoulder. 'We'll go out of the rear escape hatch. Can you throttle back to two-fifty?'

Allbright nodded, throttled back, and pulled on some flap. Stover watched the air speed drop. He looked out of the window to check the position of Firebreak One. Westland was still to starboard and above their tail.

Stover turned back to Allbright and held up a gloved hand. 'Three minutes.'

Allbright nodded.

Stover paused halfway out of his seat, searching for something appropriate to say. Allbright held up three fingers, then jerked his thumb towards the cockpit door behind him.

Stover led the way to the rear of the aircraft and jettisoned the hatch. They checked each other's chutes before Stover stepped aside and let his copilot jump first.

Colonel Westland saw the two men drop away from Firebreak Two. A minute later, the flaps retracted as Allbright increased his speed.

Westland dropped his left wing and crossed over to the port side of Firebreak Two. 'Can anybody see the chutes?'

'Yep, they're both looking good,' said his radio man.

CROW RIDGE/MONTANA

Landers made several low passes over each of the groups, pulling the release handle on the drop tank. But it remained stubbornly in place. Finally, he had an idea and mentally kicked himself for not thinking of it sooner. He banked around towards the northern group, climbed up to about two hundred feet, and turned back to make a slow pass over their heads with his flaps down.

Connors, Wedderkind and the cadets on their truck had pitched in to help finish laying the flares.

'Maybe he's come to check up on how we're doing,' said Larsen.

'Or to tell us to hurry up,' said the cadet next to him. 'Can you pass me that roll of ignition wire?'

Connors straightened up and looked at the approaching aircraft. The pilot had lowered his undercarriage. As he flew over their heads he raised it, banked round, then came back towards them, and lowered his undercarriage a second time. Connors watched the Phantom sweep. The pilot lifted his wheels again.

'Why does he keep doing that?' asked Wedderkind. 'Does he want to land?'

'If he does, this is the wrong place,' said Connors. 'What the hell is he trying to tell us? Look, he's got his wheels down again . . .'

The Phantom came right down to ground level, with its wheels almost touching the grass. Then the pilot put on full power and climbed away, retracting the under-carriage.

'Takeoff . . .' Connors' brain lit up like a pinball machine as the quarter dropped. 'He's telling us to *take off*! Arnold, do you suppose – ?'

'The cutoff zone . . .'

'Jesus Christ . . . it's expanded and . . . those goons are on their way to blow up the Ridge!'

Another diesel came racing down the dirt road from Broken Mill.

'Looks as if someone else has got the message,' said Wedderkind. The diesel swung off the road and headed towards them. It was Kinner. He was driving the second diesel they'd left on the airstrip at Jordan. Volkert was in the cab. Connors ran over as it stopped.

'Jordan's blacked out!'

'When did it happen?' asked Connors.

'Three o'clock. About ten minutes after you left. We didn't know what to do at first – I thought maybe we should go to Glasgow. Then Volkert suggested we'd better tell you.'

'No point in tellin' Glasgow,' said Volkert. 'They got the news same time as we did.'

'We went down straight to the base camp, and of course nobody knew where you were.'

'Yeah, we turned off.' Connors looked at Wedderkind. 'That's it. They must have got together with the Russians and decided to advance the attack. But by how much?'

'Well, if the cutoff zone expanded at three o'clock our time, that's the middle of the night in Russia,' said

528

Wedderkind. 'That means the earliest time they could attack in reasonable light would be six A.M. – '

'Five o'clock our time,' said Connors. He looked at his watch. 'Jesus Christ, it's nearly four-thirty! How are we going to get these guys out of here?' He grabbed Biggs' arm. 'Listen, drop everything! Get everybody on that diesel, drive north, and don't stop until you're twenty-five miles away! A B-52 is going to drop a fifty-kiloton nuke on the Ridge in thirty minutes.'

Biggs dropped the flare he was holding.

'Holy shit – ' said Kinner.

Connors jumped on to the running board of Kinner's diesel. 'Head over to the west of the Ridge. Tell the party over there what's happening – then keep going west!'

Connors jumped off the running board and cupped his hands around his mouth. 'Larsen!'

'Right behind you!'

Connors spun round and grabbed Larsen's arm. 'We've got thirty minutes to warn the other two parties and get out of here before the Ridge goes up. Do you want to drive or duck out now?'

'I'll drive – hell, we don't have much chance either way.'

'Okay. The east group must be near the base camp. Arnold, come on, get in!' Connors spotted the two cadets on the horses. They were turning around indecisively. He bundled Wedderkind into the cab of the diesel and called out to them, 'If you think you can ride twenty-five miles in thirty minutes get going. If you can't, dump the horses and get on that northbound diesel!' Connors jumped in and made a grab for the door as Larsen put his foot down. He swung the truck around and headed straight across country, towards the base camp.

'Hang on,' he yelled. 'This is going to get a little rough!'

Circling low overhead, Landers saw two of the diesels go speeding off in different directions, and people clambering hurriedly aboard the third. They had finally got the message. He looked at his watch. 4:28 P.M. . . . Good luck . . . Landers pulled up his flaps, put the throttle through the gate, and headed eastward, climbing clear of the path of the approaching B-52.

ABOARD FIREBREAK TWO/OVER MONTANA

At 4:48 P.M. Allbright crossed over from Wyoming into Montana at a height of five thousand feet and a speed of six hundred miles an hour. He was now one hundred and twenty miles from Crow Ridge. Time to impact, twelve minutes. He wondered how the Russians had chosen to handle their attack. Fraser had told him they were using a one-megaton hydrogen bomb. Too big . . . He made an adjustment to the elevator trim to give him a slow, steady rate of descent. The vertical climb-and-descent indicator was one of the three instruments still working. Ahead, a horizontal smudge of green indicated the winding line of the Yellowstone.

Allbright felt strangely calm. The purposeful waste of life was something he abhorred, but death itself was something that had never frightened him. There was only one thing Allbright feared, and that was old age. In dying now, in the full flower of life, he would leave his family a strong, proud, exemplary image, instead of withering away into a toothless, witless, incontinent vegetable. It was a calculated conceit that he had carried within him since adolescence. And the two bombs in the belly of Firebreak Two would confer a kind of instant immortality. No shattered, bloody carcass to piece together, no ashes to scatter. A smooth, painless transition from life to legend.

The Yellowstone was nearer now. And, high above him, Westland would be banking away to start his wide circle around the edge of the fire zone, waiting for Crow Ridge to erupt like a supernova.

CROW RIDGE/MONTANA

One of the cadets near Connors pointed up at the sky and shouted, 'Look! He's turned off!'

Some of the other cadets paused in their scramble to get aboard the trailer of the diesel.

'Looks as if he's starting to circle!' The shout came from somebody on the trailer.

Connors and Wedderkind dropped back out of the cab and stared at the white contrail that had been approaching in a straight line from the south, and had now veered east. Connors pulled out a pair of binoculars from under the dash and rapidly focussed on the contrail. Just ahead of it, he could see the characteristic thin white arrow shape of a B-52.

Firebreak One, piloted by Colonel Westland.

'Maybe the attack isn't going to be at five,' said Connors. He looked at Wedderkind. 'They must be circling to give us a final warning.' Connors called out to Harris. 'Looks as if we've got a few more minutes! Get these people heading east. Ten miles should get you well clear of the blast, but get under cover. After the explosion, assemble everybody at Cohagen. Keep an eye on that contrail!'

'Is there time to grab those four other diesels from the base camp?'

'Have you got four drivers?'

'Yeah.'

531

'Okay, hop aboard.'

Wedderkind was already in the cab alongside Larsen.

'Did you hear all that?' asked Connors.

Larsen nodded. 'South side?'

'Yes, let's go.'

Larsen bounced the diesel back towards the highway at seventy-five, then slowed as he reached the base camp. Connors looked out of the window and waved to Harris as the four cadets jumped off and ran towards the parked trucks.

'They're clear.'

Larsen accelerated down the road and went straight through a flimsy pole and wire gate on to the range south of the Ridge. Cameron, the other senior cadet, was out with the flare party some seven miles west of the highway and, according to the last report, now quite close to the southern flank of Crow Ridge.

Allbright checked his three remaining instruments as the river swept underneath him. Altitude five hundred feet, speed ten miles a minute. Three point five minutes from impact. He brought Firebreak Two down until it was only thirty feet off the ground. Flying something this big this low was the ultimate trip. Pilot and plane fused into one. A great white falcon speeding in for the kill.

Dead ahead was the long, pine-green hump of Crow Ridge with the triangular shape of Crusoe rising above the trees like a sheepherder's rockpile, pointing the way. On the plain in front of the Ridge were yellow blobs . . . black dots . . . trucks . . . people . . .

Cameron straightened up as Connors jumped out of the truck. 'Hi – have you come to help?'

Somebody shouted. 'Jesus, look at that!'

Connors turned and found himself presented with a chilling head-on view of a second B-52 as it lifted in dreamlike slow motion to clear a fold in the ground about a half a mile away then came back down on to the deck. It was flying so low no one had seen it barrelling up the slope from Miles City. But they could all see it now. And from where he stood it seemed as if the unseen pilot was aiming the huge bomber straight at him. Connors' heart felt as if it had been slammed by a giant fist, and there was a blinding flash inside his head as his brain connected with Allbright's. He heard himself bellow at the top of his voice. 'Ruuuu-nnn! He's going to hit the Ridge!'

For a split second nobody moved. Then, suddenly, everybody except Connors started running.

Larsen's diesel roared past with people clinging on to the cab and trailer. Connors looked around desperately for somewhere to hide. There was a whispering rustle of air, then a great, rolling, thunderous wave of sound as the B-52 shot over his head.

Allbright braced both hands against the control column and aimed straight for the base of Crusoe. The black triangular shape rushed towards him, getting bigger and bigger, filling the windshield, then suddenly –

Silence . . . a deep, velvet silence . . .

Connors relaxed and let the stillness fill his mind. He seemed to be floating in the star-studded depths of space. There was a soft coolness flowing over him, through him. He felt no bodily sensations, just an intense overwhelming joy of being. Of belonging. The darkness faded. Connors felt something pressing against his chest. He opened one eye and saw his hand lying in the grass. He turned it over, felt the earth, reached out for some sage and crushed it between his fingers. He rolled over on to his back and inhaled the sweet scent. The sky above him was an incredibly deep blue.

He heard the sound of an approaching diesel and sat up. Around him, people were starting to get to their feet. Larsen stopped nearby. Wedderkind ran around the front fender of the truck.

'Are you okay?'

'Yeah, sure. What happened?'

'I don't know,' said Wedderkind. 'I didn't see.'

'He must have missed . . .' Connors got to his feet. 'Anyone see what happened?'

'Yeah,' said one of the cadets. 'But you're not going to believe it.'

'Try me,' said Connors.

'I was hanging on to the back of the trailer,' said the cadet. 'And I fell off. As I rolled over on the ground, I saw the – ' He broke off.

'Go on,' said Connors.

The cadet took a deep breath. 'Well – just as the B-52 flew into Crusoe, it – disappeared.'

Wedderkind looked quickly up at the Ridge. 'You mean Crusoe?'

'Christ, no – the B-52 . . .'

THE WHITE HOUSE/WASHINGTON DC

Clayson took the call from Colonel Westland in Nebraska. 'Okay, thank you, stay by the phone, we may want to call you back.' He put the phone down and looked at the President. Fraser, Wills, and McKenna were sitting with him at the table. The time by the wall clock was 9:18 P.M. 'The bombs didn't detonate. There was no explosion of any kind. No wreckage, and nobody's seen the aircraft.'

'Are they sure he went in?' asked Fraser.

'Yes, that's confirmed,' said Clayson. 'The people in Westland's plane had a pair of binoculars on him all the way to the Ridge. They made a low level search of the area for a whole hour. There's no sign of him.'

'Then what's the explanation?' asked the President.

'Sir, there is no explanation,' said Clayson. 'Westland says that Mitch's plane flew into Crusoe and – vanished.'

'Is that what I'm supposed to tell the nation tonight?'

Clayson didn't say anything.

Wills took the cigar from his mouth. 'Has anyone thought of getting this crew's eyes tested?'

'How much gasoline was Mitch carrying?' asked Fraser.

'Just enough for the one-way trip,' said Clayson. 'We've already considered that possibility.'

Fraser looked across at McKenna. 'Do you believe this?'

'Well . . .' McKenna put his hands together. 'Crusoe's pulled about every trick in the book. I would say anything was possible.'

'Yes, but this thing was tested. It's harder than anything we've got. I can go along with the idea of the bombs not exploding but, hell – if Mitch hit it, that B-52 should have burst into a million pieces!'

'I know,' said McKenna. 'It's there but yet it's not there. I can't explain it any better than that.'

'So how do we destroy it?' asked Fraser.

'I don't know,' said McKenna. 'But perhaps that may no longer be our most urgent problem.'

'Has anything come through from the Russians?' asked the President.

'No,' said Fraser. 'And they haven't replied to our last two messages.'

'Keep trying,' said the President. He picked up the phone by his elbow and punched a three-digit number. 'Hello – Jerry? . . . Do we still have some of the long-wave frequencies . . . Good . . . I'll make that broadcast at ten o'clock . . . No, I don't have a draft yet.' The

President hung up and looked at Fraser. 'He wanted to know if he could have an advance copy to release to the press . . .'

'What about Camp David?' asked Fraser. 'We ought to get there in case Crusoe lowers the boom on us six hours from now.'

'We'll go right after the broadcast . . . Make sure everybody's ready.'

At five minutes to ten, the President walked into the Oval Room, sat down at his desk, and shuffled through the pages of his speech. Jerry Silvermann fussed around him and made sure the technicians had got everything linked up. They did a quick mike test. Jerry gave him the thumbs up from the doorway of Marion's office.

'There'll be the announcement, then we'll cue you in with the light.' Jerry retired, closing the door.

In Marion's office, the man from NBC cleared his throat as the hands of the clock hit ten. 'Ladies and gentlemen, the President will now broadcast to you direct from the Oval Room of the White House . . . The President of the United States.'

The light by the microphone in front of the President glowed green. He moistened his lips. 'Fellow Americans – '

The room was plunged into darkness.

The President sat back in his chair and listened to the confused babble of voices coming from Marion's office. Jerry Silvermann opened the door. He was holding a butane lighter with the flame turned up. 'Stay right where you are, sir. We're trying to get hold of some lights.'

After what seemed a long time, Fraser came in carrying an acetylene lamp. He put it on the President's desk.

'Washington's blacked out.'

'Does that mean the cutoff zone has – ?'

536

'Yes,' said Fraser. 'That means it now covers the whole of America.'

Connors and Wedderkind climbed up to the crest of the Ridge and looked down at the remains of Rockville. All that was left on the Ridge were the command hut, the monitor hut stuffed full of useless TV equipment, about a dozen of the trailers, the four bulldozers shattered by Friday, the wrecked but defrosted centre section of the research lab – and Crusoe.

'That second B-52 circled around for a long time,' said Connors. 'For one awful moment, I thought they were coming in for a second try.' He looked at his watch. 'Eight o'clock . . . I guess Washington must have got the bad news.' He looked at Wedderkind. 'Who do you think was flying that first aeroplane? Allbright?'

'I'm sure it was. I had a feeling he was going to do something like that.'

'So did I,' said Connors. 'But in a way, it was more than that. It's curious. When I caught sight of the plane, I got this sudden picture of him sitting in the cockpit, yelling at us to get out of the way, then I had this weird impression of flying through deep space. There were stars all around me. I had no body. I thought, *I'm dead* . . . no pain, no fear, no regret. Just this fantastic feeling of liberation. It was incredible. Then . . . I opened my eyes and found myself lying face down in the grass.' Connors shook his head, mystified.

'There's probably a simple answer.'

'Yes,' said Connors. 'But why didn't the B-52 explode when it hit Crusoe? That really baffles me. I mean – I checked Crusoe when we came back up. He's a *solid* chunk of rock-hard crystal.'

'I think we're going to have to accept that he is more than a simple three-dimensional object,' said Wedderkind. 'It looks as if Crusoe can alter the relationship of time and space in a way we don't yet understand.'

'No . . . still, if Allbright had blown up, we wouldn't be here talking about it.'

'That was our second piece of luck today.'

'Yes,' said Connors. 'Do you realize that we landed at Jordan just fifteen minutes before the cutoff zone expanded? If we had stopped for another cup of coffee with the General in the officers' mess at Glasgow, we could have ended up at the bottom of the world's largest completed earth-fill dam.'

'Yes . . . thirty hours . . .' mused Wedderkind. 'The progression's diminishing.'

'Yes, by three. The next jump will be in ten hours.'

'Not necessarily. The divisor could also be increasing,' said Wedderkind.

'I don't get it.'

'Well, it might double each time. Ninety divided by three equals thirty, divided by *six* – '

'Equals *five*? You mean that by eight o'clock – hell, do you mean that Washington and the rest of the US is already blacked out?' asked Connors.

'It's a mathematical possibility, but no more than that.'

'Maybe . . . but you have a habit of being right.' Connors made a rapid mental calculation. 'Arnold, that means that at eight twenty-five there won't be any electricity anywhere.'

'Not any current electricity, no . . .'

'Jesus Christ . . .' Connors thought back to one of the academic conversations he'd overheard in the canteen. Some of the research group had been discussing what could happen if the world was suddenly deprived of electric power. What was it Page had said – 80 per cent

538

of the world's population might not survive the next six months? Page's morbid delight in bad news may have led him to exaggerate. There was a chance that the bulk of the well-drilled Red Chinese would – and two-thirds of India wouldn't notice the difference. Maybe he meant 80 per cent of the Western world . . .

One of the diesels climbed noisily up on to the Ridge with a load of supplies. Connors watched it cross the plateau towards Rockville. They had decided to break up the base camp and relocate everything on the Ridge. It had the virtue of being several miles off the highway, heavily fenced in, and isolated. The fence would have to be repaired, but it would be a good place to shelter if things got tough. Harris and Cameron had gone out to round up the flare parties Connors had sent racing for cover, and Wedderkind had suggested they should try to get the rest of the research group back from Glasgow AFB.

Connors didn't really have a clear idea of what he was going to do next, but he thought it would be better for everyone if he sounded decisive. They would have to make some kind of coherent plan to assist the people in the immediate area. They couldn't go scudding around forever in their converted trucks pretending that the rest of the world didn't exist. They would need more fuel, and an assured supply of starting cartridges for the diesels. They would have to start sharing the problems. And the first was how to stay alive this winter . . .

As if reading his thoughts, Wedderkind said, 'We're lucky. We have a coherent, organized unit with a high proportion of technological and scientific skills.'

And we're also armed to the teeth . . .

'I think some of them want to try and get to their families,' said Connors.

'Who doesn't?' said Wedderkind. 'But if we split up none of us will make it. The worst will be over by the end of the winter.'

'Is it going to be as bad as I think it is?' asked Connors.

'It could be,' said Wedderkind. 'Especially in and around the cities. It depends on how much people are prepared to help each other.'

Connors gazed at the rolling wheatfields west of the dry riverbed. The fallow strips had now been sown with winter wheat. When it ripened, a lot of it would have to be cut by hand. Next year, the grains would be like gold dust.

He wondered if he would ever see Washington again. And Charly. He tried to imagine what it would be like there now. Even if her parents could get their money out of the bank, it wouldn't get them very far.

'What do you think Crusoe's going to grow into, Arnold?'

'Bob, there's no way to answer that. The possibilities are enormous. Think of the acorn that grows into an oak – or the caterpillar that becomes a butterfly. Crusoe could be the seed of a city, or a whole civilization.'

'Okay, let's try another question. Is this going to be the end of the world?'

'Maybe as we know it,' said Wedderkind. 'But on the other hand, you could say it was the beginning of a *new* one. And with such possibilities! There are huge areas of technology left to us. We have steam, diesels, gas turbines, water, air, the sun. Admittedly you won't be able to turn on your quadraphonic hi-fi, but people will learn to *make* music. People don't seem to realize that most of the world's greatest music, art, literature, architecture were all completed before the age of electricity. Did they need electricity to build Versailles? St Peter's? The pyramids? Did they need a microphone to sing Handel's *Messiah*? Would Beethoven have achieved more with a hearing aid? Did Michelangelo need floodlights to paint the Sistine Chapel ceiling?'

'No,' said Connors. 'But don't try and kid me, Arnold. We're not about to enter some Golden Age. It's going to be goddamned awful.'

'For a while, perhaps. But there was nothing any of us could have done to stop this happening. You must accept it as part of the plan.'

'I'm glad to hear there is one – even if it is too big for me to understand. What is it you think we have to do?'

'Do? Why – what Man has always done. Start all over again of course!'

Behind them, the rim of the sun cut into the distant line of mountains. Tonight, there would be a new darkness over the land. Tomorrow, the sound of the human voice would only reach as far as the wind would carry it. They walked down from the Ridge in silence.

Connors considered his position. If people were prepared to recognize the letters of authority the President had given him, he would be a hot property. If they didn't, he might end his career head down in a Montana snowdrift. Connors decided it might be a good idea to learn how to skin rabbits. He began to laugh.

'What's the matter?' asked Wedderkind.

'We think we've got troubles,' said Connors. 'I just suddenly remembered that Chris Matson and Admiral Garrison are stuck in the middle of Russia.' He grinned broadly. 'I hope they like beetroot soup.'

The idea kept them both laughing all the way to the edge of the plateau. As they reached the path down to Rockville, Connors looked back at Crusoe. He was now a jet-black silhouette against the darkening sky. Perhaps by the spring, the steps he had thrust out might start to lead somewhere.

Connors walked down the path to the camp with Wedderkind. Beyond the shattered field lab he could see some of the men cutting down trees to make fires.

THE AMTRAK WARS
BOOK 1:
CLOUD WARRIOR

Patrick Tilley

The first volume of a future world epic.

Ten centuries ago the Old Time ended when Earth's
cities melted in the War of a Thousand Suns. Now the
lethal high technology of the Amtrak Federation's
underground stronghold is unleashed on Earth's other
survivors – the surface-dwelling Mutes. But the primitive
Mutes possess ancient powers greater than any
machine . . .

Other Books in the series:
THE AMTRAK WARS BOOK 2: FIRST FAMILY
THE AMTRAK WARS BOOK 3: IRON MASTER
THE AMTRAK WARS BOOK 4: BLOOD RIVER
THE AMTRAK WARS BOOK 5: DEATH-BRINGER
THE AMTRAK WARS BOOK 6: EARTH-THUNDER

The Amtrak Wars Book 1: Cloud Warrior	Patrick Tilley	£4.50
The Amtrak Wars Book 2: First Family	Patrick Tilley	£4.99
The Amtrak Wars Book 3: Iron Master	Patrick Tilley	£4.50
The Amtrak Wars Book 4: Blood River	Patrick Tilley	£4.99
The Amtrak Wars Book 5: Death-Bringer	Patrick Tilley	£4.99
The Amtrak Wars Book 6: Earth-Thunder	Patrick Tilley	£4.50
The Amtrak Wars: The Illustrated Guide	Patrick Tilley	£5.99
Mission	Patrick Tilley	£4.50

Warner Books now offers an exciting range of quality titles by both established and new authors. All of the books in this series are available from:

Little, Brown and Company (UK) Limited,
P.O. Box 11,
Falmouth,
Cornwall TR10 9EN.

Alternatively you may fax your order to the above address. Fax No. 0326 376423.

Payments can be made as follows: cheque, postal order (payable to Little, Brown and Company) or by credit cards, Visa/Access. Do not send cash or currency. UK customers and B.F.P.O. please allow £1.00 for postage and packing for the first book, plus 50p for the second book, plus 30p for each additional book up to a maximum charge of £3.00 (7 books plus).

Overseas customers including Ireland, please allow £2.00 for the first book plus £1.00 for the second book, plus 50p for each additional book.

NAME (Block Letters) ....

....

ADDRESS ....

....

....

☐ I enclose my remittance for _____

☐ I wish to pay by Access/Visa Card

Number ☐☐☐☐☐☐☐☐☐☐☐☐☐☐☐☐

Card Expiry Date ☐☐☐☐